CLÉ

SEA GEM

Sea Gem

by

Wallis Peel

GIETE

Copyright © Wallis Peel 2004
First published in 2004 by Giete
Loundshay Manor Cottage
Preston Bowyer
Milverton Somerset TA4 1QF
www.amolibros.co.uk

Distributed by Gazelle Book Services Limited
Hightown, White Cross Mills, South Rd
Lancaster, England LA1 4XS

With the exception of certain well-known historical figures, all the other
characters in this book are fictitious and any resemblance to actual people, living
or dead, is purely imaginary.

British Library Cataloguing in Publication Data
A catalogue record for this book is available from the British Library

ISBN 0-9547268-0-4

Typeset by Amolibros, Milverton, Somerset
This book production has been managed by Amolibros
Printed and bound by T J International Ltd, Padstow, Cornwall, UK

For my husband Roy –
who explored Guernsey with me

Towards the end of 1992, secret files on the German occupation of the Channel Islands were made public by the government mostly at the instigation of the Labour MP, David Winnick, who had campaigned for their disclosure.

Many names on the files were blacked out before they became available at the Public Records' Office.

The public also learned that seven files would be held back under the One Hundred Years' Rule and would not be available for public inspection until the year 2045.

By this time, one hundred years will have elapsed since World War II ended after the German occupation.

Exactly what these seven files contain can remain only a matter of conjecture but there is speculation they might contain information relating to the island of Alderney. By the time they are released, World War II will be history.

PART ONE – 1918

ONE

THE SEA WAS calm and the small steam packet, from Weymouth to Guernsey, cut through the water effortlessly, the ship's wake a narrow, straight ribbon, only deviating in the distance where the currents broke the white into separate patches. The air was fresh with a slight breeze, overhead the clouds, high and slightly broken, drifted lazily.

From where she sat, towards the packet's stern, Mary Hinton's blue eyes had an excellent view of their course. Way behind her was England and a wave of doubt rose painfully. It was incredible to think a loose boot lace was responsible for her present position. One worn lace, snapping at the wrong moment, had sent her flying on her face. A simple event which had catapulted her from dreary servitude to—to what, she asked herself? She could not yet look ahead and unexpected homesickness struck which, Mary tried to tell herself firmly, was quite ridiculous.

How could anyone be homesick for a job? But Weymouth and its nearby villages had been her home even if the word itself encompassed living in servitude. At least, her years at the house had been a vast improvement upon the orphanage and Mrs Bateson, the cook, had not been too strict while Henson, the butler, had been as friendly as a man could be in that exalted position. It had still been servitude though and not to her liking. The years had stretched ahead, dismal and monotonously the same, until the boot lace snapped so providentially. An escape route had eventually appeared but now, her conscience prodded her, should she have taken it after all? But what other course had been open for her?

A giggle left her compounded as much by hysteria as anything else. Her reputation had preceded her and Mrs Bateson had been highly dubious about accepting a kitchen maid who was prepared to outface her.

The education the orphanage had given had been basic but thorough and Mary's bright, inquisitive mind made her stand out enough to be offered a teaching post. This had lasted for two years until she felt she had had enough of the place and found a post for herself at the Oliver house. The orphanage had pointed out that domestic service was of a lower category than teaching but it had taken her to a new environment and anything fresh had to be an improvement.

Mary had not realised the cook was desperate for help. The ample staff available before the war had dwindled to nothing as ungrateful girls left domestic service for the higher wages obtainable in factories. Even Mr Henson, too old to join the army himself, had been compelled to take boys who would never have been considered years before; not that they stayed long before the army hauled them into its fighting maw.

For a while Mary even managed to enjoy life below stairs once Mrs Bateson had accepted she had a tongue in her head. At the orphanage this had got her into endless trouble because little girls should be seen and never heard—especially little girls who had been reared through charity; they should demonstrate suitable thanks and not be prepared to argue the toss with their elders and betters.

Mary learned quickly and, with the excellent food, had soon filled out and shot up until she was not far short of the butler's five feet ten inches. Then boredom struck again. The future looked bleak with a series of domestic jobs and their long hours for little money. Mary had even toyed with the idea of factory work.

It paid well but she had a shrewd suspicion that the monotony there would be no better than domestic service.

She was neither happy nor unhappy but each day seemed to be one where she moved in limbo. Sometimes she would study herself in the tiny looking glass in the room she shared with two other girls. Her features were even and of good shape but not outstanding enough to be called beautiful. Her hair, which tended to be fairer in the summer than winter, had a soft natural curl which she wore short. Mary frankly thought her eyes were her best asset. They were a deep blue, almost the colour of a spring bluebell, and she considered they topped a nice, thin nose even though her lower jaw was stiff and square.

Her bones were large and she was strong from domestic labour with a figure which could have attracted a boy if it had not been constantly hidden beneath the long white and blue aprons required for work. Not that there were many boys around now. It was true there was a military camp only a mile away but the opportunities to meet someone and walk out were few. Mrs Bateson took her moral duties seriously and followers were frowned upon without some kind of introduction.

Sometimes Mary looked at the future with a sinking heart, then she would grit her teeth, clench her strong fists and refuse to stay downhearted. She was young, healthy, and the fact she had no family to interfere was, perhaps, an asset. Technically, the orphanage was still her guardian but it was a loose arrangement. The charitable institution had been thankful to get off their hands those girls old enough to work elsewhere.

It had been a late autumn fair and Mrs Bateson had given her a precious two hours off. Eager to see fresh sights, Mary had rushed down the lane and on to the common land where tents and music beckoned. She had suddenly stumbled as the lace on her left ankle boot, clumsily tied in a hurry, caught underneath and snapped. In a second she had gone flying, sprawling inelegantly in a tumble of long, brown skirt ruffled around her knees.

Slightly winded and feeling a considerable fool, Mary had taken a deep breath, peeped forward and faced a pair of highly polished boots and neatly wound puttees.

"Well!" a voice had drawled gently. "That's not the usual way to see a fair, is it? But then, I'm not used to your English customs."

Mary had collected herself together, blushing scarlet as she hastily tugged her skirt down decently, then his hand had come out. She had hesitated but a second and let herself be lifted to her feet.

"Thank you."

He grinned at her engagingly and she eyed him quickly, smoothing her skirt down further, aware of a pair of nugget brown eyes twinkling with amusement. He wore his cap at a jaunty angle and looked down at her from an advantage of a few inches.

Words had left Mary for a minute. She was conscious of him planted before her, grinning wildly, then his hand had touched hers again.

"My name is Duret and I'm stationed nearby," he had told her, gesturing with his free hand.

"Duret?" Mary had exclaimed. "I've never heard a name like that before."

"It's a Guernsey name," he had answered with a chuckle.

Mary's forehead had puckered. "Where's that then?"

"Oh! For goodness sake! You English," he had teased. "We've been around a long time and you don't know our island. Come on, walk with me and I'll tell you."

Mary had resisted only fractionally. She was intrigued by him and acutely conscious this was the first time she had been alone with a boy.

"I cannot stop too long," she had replied, "and I'll have to get this repaired too."

He eyed the offending lace then, bending and using a pocket knife, trimmed and re-threaded it while Mary stood uncertainly. She liked his attention and had a sudden crazy urge to twine her fingers in his curly, brown hair that showed where his cap had slipped.

"There! Now you won't break your neck. Do you live near here?"

Mary found it quite natural to slip her arm into his as they strolled gently through the crowd of villagers, people from Weymouth and the many troops. She knew the locals would not miss her action but, all of a sudden, she did not care. Let Mrs Bateson disapprove. Why shouldn't she have some fun for once?

"Where do you work?" Duret had wanted to know.

"I'm in service at the Oliver house about a mile away," Mary had explained.

"Do you like it?"

Mary threw him an odd look, then shrugged without comment. "Tell me about yourself."

"I'm in the Guernsey Militia which has always had a military connection with this part of England. We are waiting to go to France."

There was nothing she could think of to say to that but she had flinched. He was young, wholesome, healthy and so different to other soldiers she had seen around.

It had seemed perfectly natural then for him to walk her back to the house and have her introduce him to Mrs Bateson. The cook had been stiff to start with but had thawed a little when she realised this quiet, young man was hardly the type to go on a drunken spree and damage Mary's morals.

From that simple beginning had developed a gentle friendship. Whenever he could, Duret called upon Mary and they walked out. Even Henson had approved of him because the young man's manners were good, he was respectful and polite but, above all, he was different.

Mary knew how lucky they had been. The soldiers were still in camp six weeks later and Duret was with her every single moment they could spare. This pleased Mary but also disconcerted her. There were a number of times when she caught Duret's eyes resting upon her like those of a trusting puppy and it was obvious what was happening. He was not openly amorous which pleased her because her feelings were confused. She liked him well enough; he was good company and there was something pleasantly delicious in walking out with a steady beau. Surely though a marriage would only be exchanging one kind of servitude for another? When she thought about it carefully, she had to admit that.

For one in her position, the only true escape route was with money. Even Mrs Bateson, with her far superior salary, was still tied and bound to her employer's house. So how did someone like an orphan girl expect to rise above her slot in life? Duret had talked a lot about his beloved island though little about his family. Mary learned he had been reared by a grandmother who, from the way Duret rolled his eyes, seemed formidable and strong. Where exactly this fascinating old lady stood financially was something Mary could not quite bring herself to ask.

She might have drifted along in this state of quiet limbo indefinitely when suddenly Duret's troop was given a short embarkation leave. They were to sail to France within a week.

"Marry me," he pleaded one evening, holding her hands in the frosty air, looking down at her with pleading eyes, eloquent and soul searching.

"I can't!" Mary gasped.

"Why not? Don't you care for me at all?"

"Oh Duret! It's not like that! I do like you. I like you very much but I don't want to tie myself down to anyone yet. I don't feel as I have lived," had been her soft cry of protest.

His hands had held hers while his lips clamped down, suddenly surprisingly possessive and not wholly unwelcome. Her instinct had been to struggle, when she realised how fit and strong he was.

"I love you," he had whispered urgently. "I can make you feel the same for me too. Please, Mary?"

"No, Duret!"

She had twisted free, backed a step and stood with one hand to her mouth when a thought crossed her mind. England offered her nothing. Guernsey could not be worse and, with luck, it might even be better. There might be potential for her there, though what this could be she had no idea. Once on Duret's precious island might not a whole new world open for her?

"I'll go to Guernsey, if you like," she extemporised, then waited with a thumping heart, aghast at what she had thought and said.

Duret considered, his head tilted a little to one side. "You could stay with my grandmother," he stated slowly. "The house is big enough and when I do come home finally—" he had let the sentence hang questioningly in the air. "I want you for my wife. I've never met anyone like you," he had murmured, one hand stoking her pink cheek.

This had made Mary give a nervous gulp. With awesome clarity she thought of past casualty lists. Were all soldiers incapable of considering they too might die? What if she did go to the island and Duret never returned? Her blood chilled and she could not meet his eyes.

"I'll write to grandmother," Duret had continued with a brisk rush as if the matter were decided. "I'll pay your fare. I've plenty of money. I've spent nothing much here and it will be wonderful for me to know you are on my island waiting for me."

Mary blushed. "Duret," she began slowly, "don't count your chickens before they hatch. You might come back from the war thinking differently. I might not like your island. Your grandmother might detest me."

"Never!" he had vowed firmly and, grabbing her quickly, had kissed her with a demand that made her cheeks flare scarlet. "At least, wear my ring."

"No, Duret!" she had repeated, feeling he was going much too quickly. She had to be honest with him. "I like you, Duret, but I don't love you."

He was not at all deflated. "That will come," he replied confidently.

Mary had bitten her lip and thought rapidly. A ring was a token but only that and also, her practical mind pointed out, it could provide the necessary excuse to leave her job even though she was still a minor at law. She took a deep breath. "All right then. I'll wear your ring but let's just try and be good friends with no firm commitment on either side," she had begged as a sudden flash of panic removed all thrill. What if she hated his island?

He went two days later and she begged time off to watch the embarkation, her fingers touching the unaccustomed ring of one diamond which Duret had slid on her left hand. It was only when the troopship had receded to a slim, dark blur that she understood what she had done. Duret did indeed love her with a quiet intensity that, suddenly, appalled her. He would write from the trenches and no doubt weave beautiful dreams of their future life together. He had certainly given her the escape she wanted but at what cost?

Mrs Bateson had talked to her long and seriously, as had the mistress. Even Henson had been sufficiently concerned to point out the unknown hazards in a strange place among foreigners.

"But they are British like us," Mary had cried, suddenly finding it necessary to defend these unknown islanders. "They're no more foreign than—Yorkshire people."

For a week they tried to make her see sense but the deep, obdurate vein in her character had stood unflinchingly against them. Go she would. What happened afterwards was in the lap of the gods.

Events had moved with an astonishing speed. Duret had given instructions, paid her passage and written to his awesome grandmother until, quite suddenly, Mary had found herself sailing on the packet for St Peter Port.

Mary turned and walked slowly towards the bows, then gasped. While she had been day-dreaming, the town had appeared, its houses climbing high, the whole place not at all what she had expected. By craning her neck, she could see great activity on the quayside in preparation for the packet's docking. Many heads bobbed around and there were carts everywhere.

Mary felt a cold, little finger touch her heart. Duret's grandmother would be there to meet her and this initial meeting was crucial to their future relationship. What if she resented this English girl foisted upon her?

She watched the docking process critically. It had not occurred to her this little capital would be such a bustling place. She stood to one side to allow other passengers to disembark first while she looked down nervously. She was suddenly aware she cut a poor figure. Her dark blue skirt hovered just above black ankle boots. It was the best she had and, she had thought, most attractive and suitable for this first, important meeting. One look around at other passengers had shown her the drab poverty of her clothing. Even her little blue coat was thin and totally unsuitable for the brisk wind that knifed across the harbour. She pulled her black shawl more tightly around her shoulders and gripped a small canvas bag. In it were her worldly possessions and, in a side pocket, her purse which contained the sum of three pounds and ten shillings. All saved painfully over the years.

Finally, she knew she could not put off the evil moment any longer. She walked carefully down the gangplank, moved aside a few paces and halted uncertainly; the only girl among a milling crowd of men moving in organised chaos to unload the packet's goods before taking aboard island produce for shipment to England.

"You girl!" a voice said sharply, breaking into her thoughts. "Are you the English girl, Mary Hinton?"

Mary spun on her heel and looked at the older woman who

stood a few paces to her left. Brown eyes regarded her steadily from an impassive face.

"Yes, mum," Mary managed to get out as her heart sank. In a clairvoyant flash she knew she faced implacable hostility from a forceful character. The old woman stood with back ramrod straight, head up, eyes narrowed, dressed in a dark, almost funereal long skirt and coat.

The brown eyes, so like those of Duret, swept her from shawl to boots and Mary felt herself flush with embarrassment but she held the other's gaze. Mary was well versed in the art of holding eye contact. When young she had been so bullied and brow-beaten she had vowed the day would come when she lowered her eyes to no one. She had quickly learned that those who stand up for themselves are the ones whom others respect.

Louise Noyen did not miss this. She was well aware that her strong personality was more than capable of dominating even the most recalcitrant of females but this one's head was held high. Duret had given few details which was typical of him. He had always been a dreamer, expecting everyone to understand even when they lacked his information. The old woman noted a firm jaw, perhaps just a little too square, unblinking, deep blue eyes and realised this Mary Hinton was no simpering faint-heart.

Louise had instantly leaped to the wrong conclusion after Duret's letter but one snap glance at the girl's abdomen hopefully put that problem to rest. This girl's stance and stare did not equate with what she knew about orphanage products. Had Duret seen in this chit something she had yet to discover? It was an interesting question and she let herself relax a fraction. She would have the girl to herself for quite a time before Duret came home to play the lovesick swain.

"I am Duret's grandmère," she announced stiffly. "You will live with me until Duret comes home. I have my trap over there," she pointed. "There is a tram but it's always full when the steamer docks. If that bag is all your luggage, follow me, girl."

Mary was taken aback when the old woman spun on her heel and strode off with the energy of someone in her thirties. She clutched her bag tightly and broke into a trot to keep up as the straightback ploughed ahead like a ship under full steam. The old woman made no allowances for others around and men hastily scattered aside as she marched forward, only stopping at a trap drawn by a bay cob whose head was tied to a lamp standard in a businesslike manner.

Louise Noyen stepped into the trap, which rocked. "Place your bag behind and untie the cob's head, girl!" she ordered briskly. "Well, come on! I don't have all day to waste."

Mary swiftly untied the cob, then scrambled up to sit beside the old woman as she drove off. Already the evening was almost upon them and it was bitterly cold. The wind blasted from the open sea and she shivered as much from its chill as rising apprehension and nerves.

"The tram runs to St Sampson but I don't live there now. I moved over to the west of the island. Did Duret tell you?"

"No, mum!" Mary replied, flashing a look at the wrinkled, proud face set in a stiff mask.

The old woman sniffed to herself. It was possible Duret had even forgotten himself. She had disapproved when he joined the Militia until the thought occurred to her that perhaps military life and training might liven her grandson up a bit. Much as she loved him, there were times when he exasperated her almost beyond endurance. She had been casting around for a suitable local girl with strength enough to push some backbone into Duret and this quiet girl at her side seemed, initially, more than capable. But who was she and from where did she come? That stiff jaw and unblinking eyes were signals only a fool ignored, so who had made the running? She or Duret? Did this chit of a girl think coming to the island was some kind of escape route or that the family had wealth? Her lips tightened into a narrow band.

She eased the cob back into a walk and turned left up the steep hill by the Candy Gardens while her mind worked briskly.

"Duret never told me your age," she said in a more gentle tone.

Mary paused only a moment. She was shrewd enough to feel the natural antagonism from her companion but also sensitive enough to understand the other's suspicion.

"I'm eighteen. I don't know my exact birth date though the orphanage thought it was somewhere around the end of February."

"I see," Louise murmured thoughtfully. A little younger than Duret. "You know nothing about your parentage?"

"Only a little," Mary replied quietly. An intuitive stab warned her that matters of breeding were important to such a matriarch. "My mother was in service in the big house and my father was the youngest son. It was the old story. My mother was dismissed when she started to show while my father was sent on a tour of Europe. He died in a boating accident. My mother never recovered from my birth, so I've been told, and that's how I was reared by charity as an orphan."

"So you went into service?" Louise prodded.

Mary flashed her a look. "I did after a while. I taught the young girls first, then I insisted upon breaking free. Actually, it wasn't too bad in service after the first two months but—"

"But what?"

"I want to make something of my life, mum. At least the orphanage gave me a good education and in my last place, the butler always let me read the papers when upstairs and himself had finished with them. He and cook even clubbed together to buy me a dictionary."

Louise was surprised at what she heard and frowned uneasily. Surely there was something odd here? From what Mary had said, she was almost too good for Duret. Louise was under no illusions that Duret's soft, almost gentle nature, would never have prodded *him* into such action. Her grandson's sole act of independence had been to join the Guernsey Militia behind her back and that had probably been done more for devilment than anything else.

Mary didn't miss her tight lips and bleak expression. The old woman was displaying the same hostility as she had shown on the quayside.

"Why don't you like me?" Mary blurted out suddenly. How awful it would be to live in a house with this hostile matriarch breathing down her neck. Better to have it all out now before they drove too far from town.

Louise pulled on the reins and the cob was quite happy to stop, bend his head and start to graze on the lane's verge.

"And what," the old woman started, " is that supposed to mean?"

Mary took a deep breath and faced her squarely. "Well, you don't, do you?" she challenged. "I felt it as soon as we met. I don't have to live with you if I don't want to."

"So where do you think you would go?" Louise asked tartly, head tilted to one side.

"I don't know yet," Mary said slowly, then her jaw stiffened, "But I'd find somewhere. I'll not live where I'm not wanted."

"Hoity-toity, miss!"

"Practical more like!" Mary retorted sharply. She knew she was being extremely rude to an older person but, suddenly, she no longer cared.

Louise was as much amused as annoyed. It was a long time since anyone had dared to stand up to her like this. Her eyebrows arched imperiously then her lips twitched as she took in the girl's pugnacious stance. She felt sudden sympathy for what the orphanage must have had to contend with in the past. At the same time, respect lifted its head an inch.

"Well, girl," she said slowly, "you've spirit! I'll hand you that but then I suppose life has taught you to stand up for yourself?"

This made Mary hesitate uncertainly as she eyed Louise dubiously. A brilliantly cutting remark died behind her lips as she saw the twinkle in the brown eyes. How like Duret's they were. She felt tension dissolve in a sharp rush as she smiled back wanly.

"Something like that," she replied carefully.

"Let's start again, shall we?" Louise offered in a softer tone. It was one of the quirky mood changes for which she had long been famous.

"If you like," Mary agreed warily. She knew this tough old woman could be a wonderful friend or an implacable enemy. She grinned impishly and nodded.

"Fine! Now let's get home and you can try your first Guernsey gauche."

Mary settled back in the trap as Louise shortened the reins and clucked at the cob.

"What's a gauche?"

"It's our famous bread, fattening but delicious," Louise explained. "We've a way to go yet now that I live at Cobo. Actually, my parents owned the house for years, then they moved into town. I hated the move when I was a young girl but I had no say in the matter. It's a good Guernsey home with the typical five windows."

The cob turned down a narrow lane with high hedges making visibility impossible.

"Who lived there after your parents?" Mary asked curiously. She sensed it was important to learn all she could about the family background.

"My brother as an adult. He inherited under the right of préciput as the firstborn but he died last year. His only children were girls who all married and moved away, so I seized the chance. My father died at sea in 1880. He was an Englishman from around the Bristol area. He was the family rebel and brought my mother, also English, to live on the island but she always hated it. He fell out with his family except for his favourite sister Joan. He always had a soft spot for Joan and she doted on him. He died hunting ormers—we think, though no one will ever know for sure. He was dead when they found him—" The old woman's voice tailed off as she looked mistily ahead.

Mary felt as if a barrier had descended sharply and she wondered at the depths of this tragedy then something struck her.

"What's an ormer?" she wanted to know.

The old woman came back to the present. "It's our highly prized sea food though some people call them sea ears. They cling to the rocks between the tide marks and are only supposed to be collected during the winter. They are a great delicacy, I can tell you."

"And your mother?" Mary asked, highly interested. Now the old woman was talking so freely she did not seem so formidable.

"She died in '85, five years after my father. Perhaps she never got over his death. Death from the sea is common here. My husband Jack was drowned when his fishing smack turned over in an unexpected storm. My son Philip—"

Louise's voice stilled.

"What happened to him?" Mary asked in a whisper.

"He died in '99. Again it was a storm at sea. There were a number of men out fishing. A squall blew up and, the next day, their bodies were washed ashore."

Mary bit her lip, remembering tiny snippets Duret had related. All this tragedy for just one person.

"Duret did mention a brother?" she asked delicately.

Louise nodded. "Charles! He was killed on the Somme two years ago. My other children died young. One from diphtheria, the other from a lung sickness. Duret is all the family left."

"I see!" Mary said thoughtfully, then she took the plunge and came out with it. "That is why you would rather have handpicked a Guernsey wife for him than have someone unknown like me turn up?"

The old woman kept her surprise hidden. The girl's perspicacity astounded her.

19

Surely this Mary was not Duret's type? So why exactly *was* she here?

"Not far now," she said, changing the subject adroitly.

Mary took the hint. Staring ahead, she fancied she saw the flash of the sea and the island's strangeness charged her blood. Come what may, she would survive, she told herself firmly.

"The house is down there on the right," Louise pointed with her light whip.

Mary was astonished. What type of home Duret came from had never entered her head. He was a private soldier so she had presumed he came from a simple, fisherman's cottage. Now she shot a peep at the old woman's clothing. It was cut with the simplicity which only comes from money. Then she turned to study the approaching house. It was large, detached and would have fitted easily into the wealthy part of her home area. Her eyes shot back to Louise's hand. She wore no jewellery, only a simple, very wide wedding band now thin from age. There were no pearls around her neck nor brooch on her coat. There was nothing to indicate financial status but Mary could sense wealth with the instinct of one who has always been poor.

"We have ten vergees and keep some cows," Louise stated, breaking into her thoughts.

Mary made herself concentrate to learn. "What's a vergee?"

"It's our land measurement," Louise explained quietly. The girl had been lost in a brown study as soon as she had pointed out her home. Why? What had that stupid boy Duret told her? She made herself reply to the question. She had a lot of thinking to do later. "A vergee makes two and a half English acres and two and a quarter on Jersey," she added with a sniff of disparagement. "They always have to be different, of course."

Mary did not miss the sarcasm and wondered again but decided to probe this another day. She was sharply conscious of her abysmal ignorance of this island.

"I know little about the islands except they belong to England," she admitted.

Louise bridled in a flash. "You know nothing at all then!" she said acidly. "These islands do *not* belong to England. They never have! If anything, England belongs to us. The Duke of Normandy, the one you call the Conqueror, came here first and *then* went to capture England so England is ours. Not the other way about. That's why the British monarch, whether King or Queen, comes here as the Duke of Normandy first and the English monarch very much second."

Mary was flabbergasted. "Oh!" was all she could manage. There was such a ring of pride in Louise's voice that she quickly realised it would pay her to tread gently.

The cob turned up a sweeping gravel drive kept free from weeds, then the trap halted gracefully at the front door. Mary let Louise alight first before she followed more slowly, looking around curiously, highly impressed and trying not to show it.

The house had been built from cream, stone blocks. The upper floor had five separate windows all of which faced west. The paintwork was in excellent condition and overall lay a discreet air of affluence. The house also exuded an aura of being a loved and cherished building. The front garden on the right and left of the drive held a variety of bulbs. To one side Mary noted stables and more outbuildings, all in a good state of repair. In the other direction were small fields that held cows, now curious spectators of their arrival.

She took a deep breath. It was a lovely, attractive house; it welcomed. This family equalled the gentry back in England. It was nearly dark and Mary's nostrils flared as they took in the tang of salt; the sea must be very near and she fancied she could hear waves ripple delicately. A cow lowed but, apart from that sound, it was quiet and tranquil. Mary felt her heart expand with fresh warmth as she fell instantly under the house's spell.

"Come and welcome," said Louise.

They entered through a fastened-back, solid, oak door and Mary followed down a long corridor that was thickly carpeted. The old woman opened a door on the left so Mary could follow.

Mary stepped into the room and halted as her eyes swivelled around. It was an enormous kitchen and pride of place was taken by a large, dark-coloured dresser which leaned against one wall. On this reposed the china which Mary's experienced eye told her was of top quality. On the far side were a climbing range of wooded shelves, the same dark colour, which held pewter plates and mugs. The third wall was where the fire nestled and overhead hung two sides of pork, smoking gently from the daily fire. Mary nodded sagely to herself. The Oliver kitchen could not better this.

"That's a funny jug, mum," she said and nodded.

Louise smiled. "It's a typical Guernsey milk can. You'll not find the like in England."

Mary nodded as her eyes roamed around again. "It *is* a nice kitchen," she remarked slowly with feeling. "One of the best I've been in."

She could not have pleased the old woman more as Louise pulled out a chair, one of six, tucked around a large, central table whose white deal top shone from daily scrubbing.

"I think so too," Louise agreed. "It has always been Duret's favourite room. I always say this is the woman's workroom so it should be comfortable and welcoming. Too many of the island women have to put up with earth floors sprinkled with sand. I don't hold with that. These flag stones were put down by my father after my mother made a fuss. I'm glad she did. I have straw scatter mats to keep the feet warm in the cold weather. That's a terpi."

Mary eyed the black arm and equally black iron kettle which nestled nearby. "We'd call that a trivet, mum," she explained, then something occurred to her. "What work will I do here?"

For a second Louise was nonplussed, then understood. This girl would never have known idleness.

"We'll discuss that another day. You've only just arrived. You'll want to explore and I'm not having Duret say I used you as a drudge. Anyhow, there is little enough to do because this is a well organised home. There is an outside male worker who has been with the family since I was a little girl and a woman comes in daily. I don't expect you've ever had a holiday in your life, so take a week now as my guest," Louise told her with an unexpected grin. "There's a cycle in the outhouse. Use it to explore the island. When you get fed up and bored come and tell me and we'll sort something out. When you go out, watch you don't trip over the iron boot scraper," she said with a nod at the back door. "I keep meaning to have it moved and never do. We're all used to it being there so don't fall and break your neck on it."

"I think I'm glad I came after all," Mary admitted slowly with her natural honesty. "I do want to make a new life for myself but when I met you on the quay—" she halted tactfully and uncertainly— "I felt your hostility and it made me cross."

"Do you always speak your mind so frankly, Mary?"

She shrugged. "I didn't dare to when younger but yes, I do now and why shouldn't I? I'm a person in my own right, not a chattel!"

Louise's eyebrows rose and her lips twitched. "Come! I'll show you to your room so you can unpack and freshen up. I can't have you calling me mum all the time. It's too antiquated. I think you'd better call me Tante, if you like. That means Aunt. We do speak our own patois here as well as English. It has a French base but not the French as spoken in France today. There's a heavy French influence here though. All around the island you'll discover old Martello towers which were built in case Napoleon decided to invade," she explained as they mounted to the top of some wide, carpeted stairs. "Now here is your room. You've a nice view of the sea from the front and countryside from the rear window.

The bathroom is down the corridor on the right, so I think you'll be comfortable. When you are ready, come down to the kitchen and we will eat in about half an hour."

"My own room!" Mary marvelled in a whisper. "I've never had a room of my own before," she said, letting her eyes slide around with awe and delight.

It seemed enormous to her with a large, double bed, chairs, a dresser complete with a huge wardrobe of deep, red wood. The carpet was thick underfoot and inviting to bare toes. It was the kind of room she had always dreamed of having but never thought she really would.

TWO

MARY WOKE SLOWLY and lay cuddled in blissful warmth for a few seconds, puzzled as to where she was, then realisation dawned gradually and she bit her lip with wonder. After a delicious tea-cum-supper, she had retired early for the night to this dream of a room. Tante had been pleasant enough while they ate, chatting gently without engaging in too many probing questions for which Mary had been grateful. She had felt bone weary from the long sea crossing and sheer nervous tension.

She turned her head and was stunned to see it was eight o'clock. It was the first time in her life she had ever stayed in bed until such a horribly late hour. This was what the gentry did. Her gaze roamed around the room with its quiet simplicity. It still seemed incredible and awesome to discover this was how Duret lived. How naïve she had been to think of him as a fisherman's son, then her face became very serious. If she wanted, all this could be hers. The eldest son was dead which made Duret the heir. It was odd though that no island girl had staked a claim on Duret Noyen before he left for England. Was he disliked and, if so, for what? Was he such a gentle dreamer that girls became impatient with him? Or was there something else she did not yet know?

She rose and went to the window which she had left open two holes. She suddenly froze as she heard Tante's voice from below. Her instinct was to back away then she paused, positioning herself so she could hear but remain unseen.

"Morning, Mistress!" a man said gruffly.

By standing on her tiptoes and stretching her neck, Mary could just make out the man below who stood facing Tante.

"Good morning to you, Sam!"

"Well, did she come then?"

"She did!" Louise said slowly and paused as if sorting out complicated thoughts.

Mary could see the man's hair was thick, grey and with a faint wave and guessed he must be the old family retainer.

"Well, what's she like then?" he demanded impatiently.

Tante shook her head as if exasperated. "Not at all what I expected I can tell you, Sam. She is independent, speaks her mind, has a very square jaw and I guess she is tough."

"Is that so?" Sam drawled slowly, "She might just be the right one to shake young Duret alive then."

"Or cause a packet of trouble!" Tante replied coldly.

"Is she pregnant? Is that it?"

"Not as far as I can tell, though it could be early days. Somehow though, I don't think she is. I get the impression her head is screwed on the right way and far too firmly for any young man to play footloose with her. It just might be fastened on too tightly for her own good."

"You mean she's after what she can get?" Sam questioned shrewdly.

There was a pause and Mary held her breath as she waited for Tante's reply. When the words came they were a measured sentence.

"It's possible. On the other hand, you know what Duret is like. He might fancy some kind of mother figure and what can I do? If I become difficult I alienate him; he can be so obstinate when the mood takes him. The weird thing is I get the impression the girl, though she wears his engagement ring, is not madly in love with Duret. She has hardly mentioned him which is surely abnormal for a girl in love."

There was a second, pregnant pause. Mary stood frozen with burning cheeks before Sam spoke methodically.

"If she is bright and has a temper to match this square jaw, she might prove a handful for you and how will Duret manage if you can't? From what you've said, she sounds more like the type of girl Charles might have picked."

Mary distinctly heard Tante's heavy sigh. "Anyhow, I'm going to let her run loose for a week. It will give me the chance to weigh her up. I've told her she can have the spare cycle but make sure she's warned about the rocks and tides in case I forget. I dare not let anything happen to her while she's in my care."

Sam grunted and Mary tensed at another pause in their conversation. She swallowed apprehensively but was surprised when the man spoke.

"I've a bit of news for you which I doubt you'll like. Young le Page is back on the island. I saw him yesterday."

"What?" Tante gasped with disbelief.

"I'd have known him without his name too," Sam continued slowly. "Blood will out all right. He looks just like—!"

"Stop!" Tante cried with agitation.

"It's no good you getting het up like that, Mistress!" Sam replied in a flat voice. "We've known each other for a long time now. Goodness me! How many years is it since I came to work here? More years than I care to remember. And it is my place to keep you in the picture, now isn't it? There are some matters which can neither be ignored nor hidden and surely, what happened long ago, becomes ancient history? Few will remember."

"I do!" Tante stated grimly.

"Oh! I'm not saying there mightn't be gossip. You know what this island is for that but it would only be a seven days' wonder, then the clacking tongues would find themselves another juicy target."

"*Stop!*" Tante shouted. "I told you long ago I *never* wanted to hear that name again. I meant it then and I mean it now!"

"Le Page is a common enough name here and you can't stop people from mentioning the matter to you if they feel so inclined," Sam pointed out quickly.

"I can!" Tante grated. "I'll snub them by walking away."

"That will only make tongues wag more," Sam retorted quickly. "Now look, Mistress, you're getting yourself all worked up over nothing and you'll end up with a heart attack. You're not a young girl any more."

"I don't need you to tell me my age!" Tante snapped back acidly and Mary almost winced at the bite of anger in her voice.

Moving very carefully on tiptoes she peeped below. The old man and woman faced each other like combatants. There was deep, genuine concern on the man's tanned face as one hand gently touched Tante's shoulders. Tante stood as if on parade but she burned with fury. Her cheeks were flushed a sharp red and her lips were two tightly compressed bands. Holding her breath, Mary moved back again and waited for this weird conversation to continue.

"Silence, Sam! I refuse to listen to any more. I am *not* interested. I do *not* want to know the first thing about him either!"

"Mistress!" Sam snorted. "You are as stubborn as your grandson when it comes down to it."

Tante gave a snort, spun on her heel and marched off, her shoes grating on the gravel.

Mary shook her head, bewildered by it all. She knew she must go downstairs so cautiously descended, opened the kitchen door and sighed with relief at the empty kitchen. There was a note propped against a mug. She was to help herself to whatever she wanted from the larder. With relief Mary hunted out a light breakfast then went outside.

She nearly tripped over the black boot scraper which stood six inches high but guessed she would soon learn to dodge it.

The air was chilly still but her clothes were warm enough. She hurried to the outhouse, found the cycle and mounted it gingerly. She wore her travelling clothes because she only had one other change which constituted her working clothes.

"You'll be Mary, I take it?"

She jumped and turned, then slipped from the saddle seat. Sam appeared unexpectedly from around the corner and Mary eyed him with interest. He was a workman from his grizzled face down to solid, brown boots. He had grey, questioning eyes and had once been a huge, powerful man but now his shoulders were rounded and stooped. He had large hands, well calloused; tough workmen's hands, and he wore a shirt with sleeves rolled up in a businesslike way. His dark grey trousers were the same shade as the shirt and their ends were tucked into boots. In one hand he carried a pitchfork.

Mary felt suddenly shy, conscious of her eavesdropping. Sam eyed her as a grin slid over his face and his eyes twinkled with amusement.

"You had your window open and heard, didn't you?" he asked softly.

Mary cringed with embarrassment. She hesitated not knowing what on earth to say as those grey eyes held hers unflinchingly. She gulped, nodded and bit her bottom lip, awaiting recrimination.

Sam chuckled. "I'd have done the same too in your position," he drawled with a rich laugh.

Mary was speechless. The old man's grin widened into frank humour at her predicament and discomfort.

"Don't worry," he reassured her quickly. "And don't take too much notice of the Mistress. She has a heart of gold really behind all that barbed wire. You see, she adores her grandson because Duret is all she has left from her family. She was devastated when Charles was killed. If anything wrong should happen to Duret too—!" Sam paused suddenly, aware of what he had said. He continued with a rush of words to hide his gaffe. "Not that anything will happen to him because they say lightning never strikes in the same place twice, does it? But perhaps you can see why the

Mistress is tetchy at times. She is worried sick. The family is so very important to her. All this—" and he gestured with his free hand, "—all this goes to Duret now…the last of the Noyen line. You are Duret's intended. She was frightened as to what kind of a girl you would turn out to be because it is you who will breed the heir and perpetuate the dynasty. Duret's girl is the most important person alive in her eyes. She was in a real state when she went to meet you yesterday. For all she knew, Duret could have picked some flighty, little miss and what can the Mistress do? Nothing! So bear with her, please?" Sam finished evenly.

Mary's heart warmed to him. With instinctive wisdom she recognised his worth. Sam was solid and reliable, loyal and utterly devoted to the family. He was a cherished retainer the likes of which the war had changed to a rare, near extinct breed. She knew nothing could ever be hidden from Sam and she itched to question him in turn. What was the real Duret like? Not the young soldier she had known so briefly. Who was the mysterious le Page and why did Tante hate him so? Questions bubbled but she stifled them. Instinct told her not to be hasty with Sam.

"Be my friend?" she pleaded in a whisper. "I think there might be times in the days to come when I'll be lonely and scared," she confessed.

He gave her a long, hard look then stepped forward and patted one shoulder. "With pleasure," he replied warmly. "My family are grown up and live in town. I've no grandchild of my own yet, so yes! Bring your worries to me and any doubts you might have. We'll talk them through and the Mistress will never know. Now you go off and explore. Go to the end of the lane, turn right and cycle up to the Grandes Rocques, then around to L'Ancresse Bay if you fancy it. The tide is coming in so if you stop off at the Rocques, do not go near the edge. It's not unknown for a freak wave to hurtle in and go right over them. We've had a few deaths from rock fishermen sitting in what they thought was lofty safety. Never trust the sea. It's bigger than you or me.

Respect it at all times, and be prepared to yield to it always. If you fancy the other direction, follow the coast road but don't park the cycle and wander on the beach with the tide coming in. There are parts around here with slippery rocks."

Mary nodded as her heart swelled with sudden happiness, her doubts and worries pushed away for the time being. With a relieved smile she straddled the black cycle and set off down the drive.

At the lane's end she reached the foreshore and stopped to watch the tide bustle in, white frothed and impatient with sudsy spume which started to cover a line of sharp, black rocks. The wind was stiff as it came from the open sea and a lacy curtain of fine spray filled the air, hurtling over the road and the handful of fishermen's cottages which huddled together nearby.

Mary turned and pedalled up the road to the right, her eyes fascinated by the incoming tide. Although she had lived near to Weymouth, the opportunities to go on the beach had been rare. This morning was sheer adventure.

Looking ahead she saw what she guessed were the Grandes Rocques, a buttress of high, grey rock which reared up to the sky. She rode up, then dismounted, parked her cycle by a stunted bush and ran forward over short, springy turf.

The wind was stronger here and, mindful of Sam's warning, she climbed up the smoother rocks but stood prudently away from the edge. The sea heaved in a convulsion of fierce activity and, as Mary stared, one enormous wave began to swell upwards. It gathered itself into a mountain of water then, white crested, tipped over seemingly slowly. The water's weight gathered momentum and impetus to thunder down on the lower rocks, sending a fountain of white froth high in the air. The grass underfoot vibrated in tune with the rocks on which she stood as the waves growled and threatened.

The sea was alive with awesome power backed by the wind, which blew straight from the north-west. The air was filled with spray and Mary's short hair was soon quite wet. Her cheeks were whipped a rich red as she stood with feet apart, bracing herself against the wind, revelling in the wonderful crisp air yet also shivering slightly. There was something mesmeric and almost terrifying about the sea in this mood. It was the first time she had ever witnessed angry water and she was both fascinated and repelled at the same time.

"You are getting soaked!" a voice cried behind her.

Mary turned sharply with shock and looked into eyes which were more violet than blue. A young man regarded her with comical amusement as he pointed to her sodden jacket and skirt.

"You'll have to wash that out when you get home otherwise the material will rot," he advised knowingly.

Mary stared at him. He had finely chiselled features the like of which she had never seen before set in a strong, well proportioned face with a high forehead. His nose was slightly bent in the middle as if it had been broken in some past fight, with lips which were full without being too thick or sensuous. His hair was straw-coloured, already damp from the spray like hers. He was much taller than Mary and she guessed he was at least six feet. His shoulders were broad and his open jacket showed narrow hips and a lean frame. His clothing was adequate but both jacket and trousers were worn indicating they had seen better days while his shoes were a little down at heel. He carried himself with a jaunty air and Mary knew instantly that he was the most handsome, attractive man she had ever met in her life.

"I thought it was supposed to be rude to stare?" he rebuked mildly.

Mary felt herself blush hotly and hastily broke eye contact while her heart pounded in a ridiculous way. There were strange tremors in her thighs and she suddenly wished she could sit down except the grass was far too wet.

"My name is Victor," he told her, smiling at her confusion, well aware of the devastating effect of his looks on girls but not conceited by it.

"Oh!" was all Mary could manage as her tongue tied itself into a knot. She looked down ruefully at her soaking skirt. What a sight she must look—like a half-drowned puppy but she knew this was but a ploy to avoid his eyes. How could a stranger produce such an uncanny response in her body? Her breathing was short and ragged but slowly, against her will, she lifted her eyes to drink in this fine-looking man before her.

He had also been examining her carefully. His first impression had been that she lacked beauty but he swiftly amended this. If beauty meant delicate looks, carefully coiffeured hair and a simpering fragility then she was plain. On the other hand, if beauty meant strength, health, wholesome vigour with red cheeks and tumbling hair and a total disregard for the sea's power, this girl had it all. She was like a strong willow tree; she did not so much resist the wind as bend with it and use it to suit her purpose.

Here was a strong character and instinctively he guessed that subtlety would never be this girl's tool. Ingenuousness would take its place and sharp interest flared through him. He held his breath, sure he could feel some awesome current pass between them.

"Who are you, girl?" he asked in a whisper as he took a step nearer. "Are you a wild mermaid from out there?" His right hand waved at the heaving sea. "Have you just come to join us mortals for a short while before you turn back into Sarnia's wild sea nymph again?"

"Sarnia?" Mary asked, fighting to break some mesmerising spell. "Where's that?"

He gave a low chuckle. "That's Guernsey's proper name."

An even larger wave thundered towards them and the wind gusted harder. A heavy shower of spray descended and he grabbed her arm, pulling her down lower and into safety, laughing and flashing strong, white teeth. The weird spell was broken.

"Oh goodness!" Mary gasped. "Now I really am soaked."

"Here!" he cried, tugging her a bit lower. "Get down below this rock and we'll also be out of the wind a bit. I take it that is

33

your cycle down there? I left mine alongside. I didn't intend to come here in such a wind but I simply had to stop and see who was crazy enough to stand and defy Neptune. Now I know. The water spirit of Sarnia, resident at Cobo Bay!" he teased, aware his heart raced as if he had been running.

"I'm no such thing!" Mary laughed back at him. She felt infected with his wild spirit. The pulse in her neck throbbed and her legs were unsteady as he held one of her hands. His were large with strong fingers; not soft but neither were they calloused from hard, manual labour. He stood two feet from her, his presence towering over her, something vital flowing from him to her which held her enthralled.

"My name is Mary Hinton," she volunteered in a nervous rush of words.

He tipped his head to one side. "That's not a Guernsey surname," he prodded.

"I'm English," Mary explained, wiping salty rivulets from her cheeks with one hand.

He released her other hand and gave a grave, courtly bow, sweeping an invisible hat from his head with a flourish.

"At your service, my fair maid from the sea!"

"You are an islander?" Mary asked, amused by his gesture.

"Correct!" he said, "Guernsey born but Jersey reared, though back in Guernsey now, for a while at least." He grinned impishly as his strange coloured eyes flashed and twinkled at her.

Victor took both of her hands into his and squeezed gently, then felt the thin band on her left hand. He extended it and looked long and hard, then slowly lifted his eyes with silent question.

"How long have you been here?"

"I came yesterday," Mary told him throatily. Was it her imagination or had his eyes changed from violet to cobalt blue? She studied them with fascination. It was as if some hidden desire triggered a colour alteration.

He was astonished. "You are new on the island then?" he exclaimed, puzzled as questions bubbled. "Where are you staying? Why have you come here?"

Mary chuckled at his bewilderment as she pointed back down the road. "I'm staying with Tante at the Noyen house."

He frowned. "Tante? So you have family here then?"

Mary hesitated, then shook her head. "She's not really my aunt, she just told me to call her that," she explained quickly.

His eyes moved away from hers and gazed thoughtfully back down the road while his forehead puckered as his mind raced. It was a most extraordinary coincidence, so where did the engagement ring fit into this puzzling picture? He had been on the island for a few days now; he had chatted, mixed and learned.

"Engaged?" he asked cautiously.

Mary knew she blushed again and furious with herself as she nodded. "To Duret Noyen," she explained simply.

"I see!" he said slowly, his words heavy with meaning. "How long have you been engaged? How long have you known Duret? Where did you meet him?" he shot at her sharply.

Mary went stiff and withdrew her hand abruptly. "I don't think that's any of your business," she replied tartly.

He realised his blunder and hastily shook his head. "I don't mean to offend!" he told her quickly, anxious to dispel the sudden frost in her eyes. "It's just that—" He hesitated unsure of himself, then he took the bull by its horns. "It's just that I think you are the most incredible girl I have ever met," he told her in a low voice. "I would like to get to know you better. An engagement is not a whole commitment, is it? It's a girl's privilege to change her mind and I *must* see you again. Please, Mary?" he begged.

"I have to go and get into some dry clothes," she told him in a flat voice, alarmed at the look in his eyes, furious with his impertinent questions and very conscious that even as they talked, Duret could well be in the trenches fighting for his life. Whether she loved him or not was not now the issue. Duret trusted her. So did Tante.

"I *must* see you again!" he cried and snatched both of her hands once more. His grasp was tight as he pulled her one step nearer. "And you want to see me again too, I know."

"Let me go!"

"Don't deny yourself, my wonderful sea witch," he crooned. "There's something magical between us. You feel it as well as me and surely there is no harm in walking and talking," he added persuasively. "Promise you will meet me again?"

"*Let-me-go!*" Mary snapped.

"Not until you promise to meet me again, please?" he chanted. "I'll meet you this afternoon, anywhere, anytime!"

Mary dithered. She knew she wanted to see him again, but then a picture of Duret rose in her mind as he appeared to stand before her with his sorrowful, brown eyes. He seemed to plead. She bit her lip, broke eye contact, tried to pull away from him but was forced to stand in his grasp.

He sensed she wavered and hastened to establish his advantage. "You came down the lane from the Noyen house," he began nodding backwards once more. "Meet me this afternoon but turn left instead of right. See, over there! That's called the Lion Rock. Cycle down there and around the corner. There is a tiny headland and path where we can walk and be alone."

"I can't!" Mary protested.

"You can!" he said urgently. "I'll be in place from two o'clock onwards and I will wait until it is dark."

"You'll wait a long time then," Mary retorted with an edge to her voice. She had the feeling she was being stampeded in the wrong direction but she knew she wanted to talk to him again.

He threw her a strange look. "I'm prepared to do that!" he replied with feeling.

He released her hands and Mary turned and ran to her cycle.

She lifted it up, futilely brushing moisture from the black saddle with a hand that trembled.

Her breath came in weird, little gasps and she felt crazily light-headed. He had run after her and she turned.

"Why?" she asked huskily.

He became serious, his eyes once more violet in colour. "We both know why," he told her in a low, throbbing tone. "It's because you have bewitched me, which I have always sworn was impossible. You have done something, touched me here—" and his right hand rested over his heart. "You've changed me in a flash of time in a way which I cannot fight. I *know* you feel the same too."

"You mustn't say silly things like that," Mary chided him hastily, embarrassed and fascinated by him. As she straddled the cycle her soaked skirt clung uncomfortably to her legs. Blinking a little, struggling to ignore the ridiculously painful lump in her throat, she moved away from him. She was furious with herself, more than a little frightened of the emotions he had aroused and downright apprehensive of the whole situation. If Tante were back, her shrewd eyes would miss little and instinct warned her to keep her meeting with Victor secret.

She regained a semblance of composure as she dismounted near the outhouses, glad to be alone for a few moments. Sam watched her from a discreet distance, a tiny frown puckering his forehead. The girl was soaked like a piece of sodden paper and this after the warning he had given her. He sniffed with annoyance. Let this soaking be a lesson to her.

Mary hastened to her room and changed into her only other skirt and blouse and carried her other jacket back down to the hall peg. Tante was back and her eyebrows lifted.

"I presume your wardrobe is scarce, Mary. We will have to remedy that when we can as well as get you some decent footwear instead of those institution boots. I cannot have you going around this island like a vagabond."

Mary flushed and had no idea what to say. Lies did not come

easily to her. She certainly wanted new clothes but did not like the thought of the Noyens buying them. At the back of her mind was a fresh wariness about Duret. What if their arrangement came to nothing? She could never stand being beholden to Tante Noyen. She stifled a sigh, conscious she might be heading into difficult waters.

Emily Ferbrache came into the kitchen and eyed her. Tante came over.

"This is Emily who comes in as our daily," she explained and Mary forced an artificial smile on her face.

The island woman gave a grunt that could have meant anything, then bustled into another room. Mary was surprised and turned to Tante.

Tante grinned and shook her head. "Emily is a proper islander," she explained. "She is highly suspicious of all things English. She will only talk patois, so if you want to break down her reserve, you will have to learn it and meet her on her terms."

Mary craned her neck to stare at the large-boned woman, big-breasted who moved around with a duster. She guessed Emily was in her forties; she moved ponderously, with purpose and seemed to be someone impossible to deflect from a given action.

"Emily has been with me a long time," Tante continued. "She runs the house and I know better than to interfere." She chuckled suddenly, "And you must not either. Emily would take dire offence and become utterly impossible. That is why there is little to do here really. Emily has this place well organised and she would resent interference which any help from you would be."

"Doesn't she speak English?"

"Of course she does! She's just knuckle-headed and considers only our patois is a fit tongue for her to speak. Duret speaks it very well," Tante added carefully.

Mary nodded her head thoughtfully. She had no intention of asking either Tante or the bossy Emily to help her learn but Sam was different. Were all these island women as strong-minded as the two in this house? There was so much to learn and she guessed her status here would improve as knowledge and skills were acquired.

Her thoughts reverted to Victor. Should she meet him again, was it prudent? If she did not turn up what was to stop him coming here? A chill went down her back as she sensed how Tante would react to that.

"I might go for another cycle ride this afternoon," Mary told Tante casually. After all, she did not have to go in his direction.

Tante eyed her, not missing her high colouring and was puzzled. Was the girl embarrassed because of her soaked clothing? The drenching would teach her to be careful, so why the stiffness in her attitude?

"The tide will be ebbing so you shouldn't get wet again but remember what you've been told about slippery rocks," she said quietly.

Later, Mary told herself she was an utter fool. She was quiet during the excellent lunch Emily prepared because Tante's eyes rested on her often. She was almost sure the old woman could see through her and it took an effort not to wriggle on the dining-room chair. It was with considerable relief that she escaped outside where the sun glowed.

There was still little warmth but Mary fancied the morning's biting wind was less keen now and had dropped as the tide turned. She collected the cycle and slowly free-wheeled down the lane to the coast road. At the bottom she halted and looked around. The handful of cottages appeared to be deserted and her heart thumped unevenly. She knew she should not turn left but could not help herself.

Pedalling slowly, not wanting to get there but afraid to stay away, Mary felt as if drawn by a magnetic force against her will. She knew she simply must talk to someone and she thought about Sam again. He had not condemned her for eavesdropping but would he be charitable if he knew she had gone to meet another man?

The slight breeze was at her back and the heavy, black cycle glided effortlessly along the deserted road. She halted at what she thought was the correct spot and stood uncertainly, her steady hands holding the wide handlebars before she walked over the road and hunted for somewhere to leave the cycle. There was a dip with two bushes leaning together and she picked that spot.

When she straightened again she saw him. A slow smile crossed her lips as she walked to where he slept. His long limbs were relaxed and she was able to study him in detail. His handsome face was reposed and he breathed lightly with the sun on the back of his head. Mary asked herself why Duret never produced in her the tangled emotions Victor had done so quickly.

He woke suddenly, as if aware he was under observation then, blinking a little, saw her and sat up abruptly, grinning his pleasure. He sprang to his feet and beamed at her.

"I nodded off," he said unnecessarily. He went to grasp her hand then thought better of it. She stood, uncertain and nervous almost on tiptoes as if ready to flee like a terrified doe. With prescience he understood. She could not deny coming to him but her conscience was in full spate.

"Let's walk a bit," he offered gently, nodding to one side. "The tide is well out now and we can go down to the sand along this track."

Mary simply nodded and let him lead. She watched the fluid movement of his powerful shoulders and the ripples from his lean waist and hips while his long legs strode strongly but without undue haste. She followed him along a meandering animal trail, dotted here and there with tiny pats of dung. The grass was stiff and wiry, blunted from wind and salt as the track sloped downwards. There were small rocks around among the sand which showed savage teeth at the sky and she quailed at any boat's peril.

"There are a number of tracks like this," he called over his shoulder. "They all head down to the sand and the views here can be lovely especially in the evening when the sun sets."

Where the track widened Mary was able to walk at his side. "You seem to know an awful lot about this island?" she probed.

He threw her a wan smile. "I listened to my father's stories for years and I came here on a few trips as a boy. Also, during the past week I've done a lot of cycling and walking about exploring though I've not seen the south coast yet. There are some magnificent views from the heights on the south, especially where one can see the Pea Stacks. They are some weird, high rocks out at sea. I intend to cycle and explore everywhere. You should come with me."

Mary ignored this blatant invitation and he did not press her but looked around, finally selecting one particular portion of shrivelled grass. He turned to her, took one hand and supported her as she sank down gracefully while he followed suit. In this place they were quite sheltered from any wind and the sun had managed to warm the grass. It was quiet and soothingly pleasant. She felt his eyes riveted upon her and looked into them. Were they violet or blue now? She could not quite decide.

"Tell me about yourself," he invited gently.

Mary gave a little shrug. "There's not much to tell," she replied slowly. "I'm an orphan, raised on charity," her face grimaced. "For a short while I taught at the orphanage before I decided to break away and go into service. I met Duret Noyen when he was stationed in England and he suggested I come here and await his return. I had nothing and no one in England, so I came," she told him simply.

It was difficult to read his expression and his features were sober while he sat silently mulling over what she had explained, then he gave a huge sigh that puzzled her.

"Duret Noyen, only living grandson of Louise Noyen, relic of Jack. Her mother was Anna Carey and her father was a rebel Englishman called Dan."

"Goodness me! You know all about the family—more than me!" Mary exclaimed.

He shook his head. "I know *of* them," he corrected slowly.

Mary frowned and wondered what he meant exactly. She turned and looked out to sea where the sun glimmered on the water in yellow ripples.

"For someone whose home was on another island, I find your knowledge about the Noyens rather strange," Mary said carefully.

His lips went tight and he regarded her frankly as his right hand stole out to imprison her left. "If I don't tell you, someone surely will."

Mary was bewildered. "Tell me what?"

"Your famous, or notorious, Tante is my grandmère too, though she will never admit to the fact and would cut me dead if she saw me."

"What!" Mary gasped. "I don't understand."

He threw her a weak grin. "My full name is Victor le Page," he said and awaited a reaction.

Mary stiffened and suddenly in a clairvoyant flash understood the conversation she had overheard.

"Go on," she encouraged in a whisper.

"Oh! It's the old story with a variation, I guess," he mused and stared out to sea as if his thoughts were so tangled he needed extra time in which to tidy them.

Mary sat silent astonished by his revelation.

"Louise Noyen had a daughter called Christine," he started, half nodding to himself. "Christine was wild, headstrong and quite unimpressed with her mother's authority. What Christine wanted, Christine took and damned the consequences. I am told she was an outstanding beauty and blessed with a charm which could make the birds fly down from the trees. Even tough, dictatorial Louise Noyen could neither tame nor control her daughter when she entered her teens and for some odd reason, she set her cap at my father who was older than she—about thirty-five. He was a Jersey man and was in Guernsey on some business trip where they met. Even though safely married, he was bewitched by her and made an utter fool of himself, which wasn't a hard thing to do with Christine, and my father was the original *roué* anyhow. How my saintly, adopted mother put up with him I'll never understand."

"Adopted?" Mary whispered.

"My father's wife was Sarah Domaille and they had no children. I have no idea how long the affair went on but my father made Christine very pregnant."

"Oh!" said Mary thoughtfully.

Victor pulled a face. "Tante Louise, as you call her, nearly went berserk. You see, apart from anything else, she detests anyone from Jersey. I don't know the ins and outs but gossip says it was something to do with her father's death."

"But she told me he died when collecting ormers!"

"That's as maybe but gossip says he had an enemy who was a Jersey man, they fought, then Dan Penford was found dead. But that's all history."

"What happened to him? Surely there was an investigation?"

He shrugged. "I honestly don't know. It's all so long ago. When Tante Noyen learned about Christine's condition and there could be no marriage, there was the most unholy row and Christine left home. She was exactly nineteen when I was produced."

"What happened to her?"

"She died giving me life," he said simply and paused. "So there I was. A bastard and with half Jersey blood to boot. I was only half a Noyen and most definitely not wanted, especially as she had two legitimate and adored grandsons already, Charles and Duret."

Mary was aghast. "But surely she could not refuse a home to an innocent baby?"

Victor shook his head. "It wasn't as simple as that. As I found out many years later, my father was a real boozer and Louise Noyen had just suffered a horrible year of three tragedies, one after the other. She was not exactly young even then, was coming up to her fifties and Duret was only a baby. My arrival was the final straw, especially with Jersey blood."

"What happened?"

"My sainted father's wife found out and she simply took me in, adopted me as her son and I've never wanted for love or affection—from her. As to my father, he broke his neck in a drunken spree in 1906. My adopted mother died only three weeks ago and that's why I'm on this island. There is a Will being dealt with, not that I expect there'll be much money after my father's drinking bouts, so I thought I'd come here and renew links with my roots."

Mary eyed him shrewdly. "Do you have financial hopes from Tante?"

He went stiff and shook his head vigorously. "No! I know better than that. Grandmère despises me. She seems to think I will be like her wild daughter. Anyhow, I'm a bastard and carry tainted blood."

Mary snorted. "I too know what it's like to carry the bastard tag around one's neck," she told him grimly. "My years at the orphanage—" Her nostrils flared with anger at memories. She turned to him. "Let no one put you down because of your birth. The only difference between me and the gentry is that their bank books are bigger than mine. I consider myself just as good as anyone else, bastardy notwithstanding," she said with spirit.

He flashed his teeth in a wide grin and squeezed her hand. "My God! That's what I think is wonderful about you. Fire and fury coupled with spirit and your own, fetching beauty. Guts enough to come to this island to strangers. Mary Hinton, you are a girl after my own heart. What a pair we would make."

Mary studied the gleam in his eye and felt uncomfortable. He held her hand more tightly than he should but her heart warmed to his words.

"So what are you going to do now that you are here?" she asked him.

"I think I'll make my life and home here now. At the moment, I'm going to go on trial as a cub reporter for the local rag. I start next week. If I'm any good, who knows? I might end up on Fleet Street!" he joked merrily.

"You didn't want to join the Services and go to France?" Mary asked curiously. Obviously conscription did not apply here.

He threw her another of his piercing looks. "What me? Why should I? Look how many have already died for England!"

"But surely the war affects here too?" Mary persisted. He couldn't possibly be a coward—could he? "Where do you live then?" she asked, thinking it better to change the subject.

"I've found myself some cheap lodgings in town. They're not much but I can't afford better. I'll have to do some smart reporting to impress my editor and get a rise. Of course, if there was some money in my mother's estate that would be splendid but it's highly unlikely, knowing my late, drunken sire." He laughed, but with a touch of bitterness.

Squeezing her hand, he wriggled nearer, making her sway as their bodies touched. Mary's heart lurched and she knew she should pull away. Once in his arms his hypnotic aura would shatter her resistance.

"You mustn't do that," she chided. "Duret is in the trenches right now and I wear his ring."

"More fool him then!" he said bluntly. "Anyhow, all is fair in love and war."

Mary was shocked at this outlook. For the past few years her country and the Empire had bled themselves white against the Kaiser. She remembered the awful days of the Somme '16 when half a million men had vanished in human hell.

She freed her hand with a sharp snatch and leaned away from him, her face cold.

"Young, strong and healthy men went to the trenches; men who were not conscripts. Those who failed to go received white feathers from women!"

He snorted with disgust. "Anyone who voluntarily fights in the murder of the trenches is a raving idiot if they go of their own free will. Politicians make wars but it is the little men who have to fight them," he retorted. "If any woman gave me a white feather I would ram it back down her throat," he said coldly.

Mary was appalled at his attitude as well as repulsed. "Are you—a coward?"

He turned to her, face bleak. "No, girl, I am not! And if you were a man you'd have lost your front teeth by now for thinking the question let alone asking it. Just because I happen to show a little good sense it does not make me any less of a man."

Mary felt ice slow in her veins and she hastened to stand. "That is a matter of opinion," she snapped at him and, turning on her heel, walked away.

"Hey!" he cried. "Where do you think you are going?" he sprang after her, grasping her shoulder and made her halt.

"Take you hands off me!" Mary spat at him, disgusted with his opinions and, at the same time, widely disappointed with them. "You may despise our boys in trenches but I don't and my Duret is there right now. He could be going through hell!"

"More fool him for volunteering!"

They stood face to face and glowered at each other. Mary's eyes were bleak and narrow while his lips and face were a compressed, rigid mask.

"You are a pacifist!" she accused hotly.

"No, I'm not!" he shouted quickly in his defence. "I'll fight as hard as the next man—when the cause is a correct one!"

"In the meantime you have a lovely, idle time leaving your taken-for-granted peace and freedom to the suffering and bravery of others. I think perhaps Tante might just be right about you, after all!" she threw back at him furious with herself. Why should tears prickle at the back of her eyes? He was nothing to her, was he?

"That's a rotten thing to say!" he grated, stung and deeply hurt. "Mary! Don't go! Surely we can agree to disagree?"

"On this subject—I doubt it!"

"But I haven't talked to you properly. I want to see you again. I must!" he told her urgently as she pulled herself free for a second time and stumbled back towards her cycle. "I want to show you the island. We can explore it together. We have so much in common, we—"

"I doubt we've anything in common, Victor le Page," Mary shouted, striding forward as he ran at her side. "Now get out of my way or does your fighting strength and precious opinions only refer to weaker females?"

"That's uncalled for!" he protested but stood and let her go.

Mary bent and pulled her cycle erect while the tears gathered momentum, ready to spill at any second. His hand grasped her handlebars.

"Mary?" he pleaded. "Don't let us part like this when we've only just met. I simply have to see you again!"

Mary sniffed, brushed the first errant tears aside and refused to look at him. She was too confused and upset to think straight and just wished he would go away and leave her alone.

"Mary! Tell me when I can see you again!"

"Never!" she snapped.

He gritted his teeth, appalled at her reaction but grimly determined this was not an ending. He knew there was only one step he could take.

"If you don't agree to see me, of your own free will, I'll call at the house," he said quietly.

Mary was appalled. "You can't do that!"

He met her hurt and angry eyes without flinching. "I can and I will!" he promised evenly. "I'll do anything to see you again because you mean so much to me. I know it sounds crazy after we only met this morning but you have done something to me, my life can never be the same again. So we have quarrelled, don't all lovers?" he asked hopefully.

"We are *not* lovers!" Mary hurled back at him. "You are simply some bumptious, odious know-all I had the misfortune to meet a few hours ago!"

"I'd like us to be lovers!" he whispered.

"Stop it! Once and for all!" she cried, nearly frantic.

"Mary! Mary!" he said, trying to gentle her temper. "I mean what I say. If you don't agree to meet me I'll defy my fierce grandmère and call at her home."

"That's blackmail!"

He thought about this for a few seconds then nodded. "True but I mean it, my wild, spirited sea witch!"

Mary had no idea what to do. The idea of his threat horrified her and she knew he meant exactly what he said.

"Know this, Victor le Page, nobody threatens me, hectors or bullies me now. I had more than enough of such antics when a child. I make my own decisions and lead my own life. No one will push me around, ever again," she snapped, hot words tumbling from her lips in wild temper. "So call at the house! And I'll tell everyone how you have tried to blackmail me into meeting you against my will."

She faced him with head high and eyes sparkling. She had no idea how beautiful she looked to him. All she did know was that she was lying in her teeth but this *he* would never know.

"My God!" he breathed softly. "You are fantastically beautiful in a rage!"

He paused, head slightly tiled to one side. "More than that, you are magnificent!" He admired her courage and defiance. She was totally unafraid of him and he knew he had lost his heart to her irrevocably. "I'll be at this spot a week today. *Please* come!"

Mary threw him one final hard look, then straddled the seat and attacked the cycle pedals. She left him with a mixture of rage and longing, but knew she was only doing the right thing.

THREE

MARY STROLLED OVER the fields with Sam and he eyed her curiously. During the last few days, the Mistress had commented upon how Mary appeared to have changed. She had sunk into a quiet apathy which alarmed Tante and disturbed Sam.

There had been a letter from Duret which should have sent Mary into raptures. Instead the girl had sunk into a deeper despondency that concerned Sam and frightened Tante. At least, Sam told himself, Tante had the good sense not to pry with questions. Sam had a shrewd idea this English girl was deep and secretive.

He had been surprised when she had come running after him, smiling a little, shy at her presumption but obviously anxious to be with him.

"Can I walk with you, Sam?" she had asked hesitantly.

"Of course, my dear!" he had agreed then, seeing her mood, offered nothing more. If she wanted to talk then he knew he was a good listener. On the other hand, if she preferred to stroll in silence that was all right with him too.

"I'm off to check the boundary hedges," he said to the fresh air in general.

Many of the leaves were already in tight, little buds, on the point of bursting into leaf. Green grass showed itself under the hedge bottoms and he thought to himself how fresh and lovely the countryside looked.

Mary's mind whirled. Duret's short letter had upset her

dreadfully. After her row with Victor le Page she had endeavoured to push him from her mind but, always before she fell asleep, she had been aghast to see his handsome face loom in her memory. Then Duret's letter had arrived saying all was quiet on the front at the moment. He had enclosed a short poem and it was this that worried Mary. Try as she might, she had been unable to make head or tail of it. It did not rhyme, it lacked sense and sudden doubts had arisen about Duret. There had been no mention of wedding plans for which she had been thankful, yet piqued. Now that she was on his island, did he presume it was all settled? Had she failed to make him understand that their engagement was simply a loose arrangement? She knew she had to talk to someone or she would burst and who else was there but Sam?

She flashed a look at him and he caught it, lifting an eyebrow in a silent question.

"Homesick?" he asked gently.

"I wish it were as simple as that," Mary sighed miserably as they reached the far hedge and a five-barred gate.

Sam stopped and leaned against the gate to face her. Mary looked towards him with misery in her eyes. Two cows in the field stared back at her with great interest and one lowed a question, thought better of it and went back to chewing her cud.

Mary took a deep breath. "I think I may have fallen in love with someone else, Sam!" she blurted out and waited with considerable trepidation.

Sam was taken aback with shock. This was something he had never expected in his wildest thoughts. He paused to sort out delicate words that would neither encourage nor condemn.

"It's someone I met the day after I arrived here and we met twice in the one day. On the last occasion we had a thundering row yet—" her voice tailed away for a moment. "I cannot get him out of my mind. There is something about him which attracts me. I am drawn to him against my will and do nothing but think of *him*—not Duret."

Sam took a deep breath and considered all this. "What about Duret and your feelings for him?"

Mary's shoulders sagged unhappily. "The trouble is, Sam, although I like Duret and wear his ring, I do not love him. I'm under some moral duress. He was so begging, so winsome and I wanted to get right away from England so I agreed to become engaged though I did make it clear that this arrangement was a loose one, capable of being broken by either party at any time. Certainly nothing would be decided until after the war. Probably I acted wrongly but it's done now. I've had a short note from Duret and, reading between the lines, it all appears to be settled by him. It's as if he's taken it—and me—for granted. He sent me a poem which I cannot understand. What kind of person is he, really?"

Sam turned away, disturbed now. He could feel her eyes riveted on him for the truth.

He turned back with a sigh and little shake of his head. "Duret? He's a dreamer. He wanders through each day in a different world to us and he's always been like that—the complete opposite to his dead brother Charles. If Duret had not been such a dreamer he could have done better at school because he is no fool. It was the same with girls here before he joined up. You'll have gathered now that young Noyen is a good, financial catch for any girl but Duret was incapable of seeing this even when a girl flung herself at him," he explained carefully.

Mary frowned with bewilderment. "As soon as he saw me, he chased me with a vengeance. I made no running!"

"Is that so?" Sam replied and looked at her anew. "Well, knowing Duret as I do, he was paying you the highest compliment. Naturally you could not appreciate this, lacking the background. You have that magical something which caught and held his eye and touched his heart," he said meaningfully.

He examined the girl. She was no beauty in his eyes, yet neither could she be called plain. Her large, blue eyes had a piercing

51

quality that plumbed to the depths of a problem. She was frankly honest, outspoken and a man would know where he stood with her. She stood strong and four-square to whatever life might throw at her and her unique spirit flared powerfully. Was it this which Duret had seen? She was so utterly different from anyone he had met before, including his grandmother.

"And the other boy?" he asked delicately.

Mary grimaced. "He is Victor le Page and I know who he is. Tante's bastard grandson!"

Sam was staggered. "Him? Good God!" he exclaimed then puffed his cheeks, turned and studied the two cows. This really did put the cat among the pigeons. Sam considered the Mistress was totally and even unreasonably stupid where young le Page was concerned. All she could remember was Christine and the disgrace brought upon the Noyen family. She had a blind spot where breeding was concerned and Sam knew it would take a better man than himself to make her change her opinions.

He turned back. "What would you do if Duret came home tomorrow and wanted an instant wedding?"

Mary threw both hands in the air. "I just don't know!"

"Well!" was all Sam could manage for a moment. "This certainly does make a pretty kettle of fish. The Mistress will throw a fit when she learns about this," he warned her. "What is le Page doing back here anyhow?"

Mary sighed. "His mother, the lady who adopted him and reared him, has recently died and he has come back to explore his roots and decide what he wants to do. His father died a number of years ago. There is a Will but he doubts he will receive much money because his father was a drinker."

Sam knew that. He shook his head with horror at the idea of le Page and Mary as his mind slipped back down the long years. Louise Penford had been eight when Sam was born and he could still remember her father. Dan Penford had been a strong, tough man; as wild and daring as they came, so was it any wonder he had bred a granddaughter as rugged as himself? What had not been anticipated was Christine's feckless nature, crude to the point of being wanton.

Sam knew that breeding was a queer, complex subject whether it be with animals or men. Certain characteristics were recessive, appearing when least expected in future generations. Victor le Page was a case in point. In looks, colouring and mannerisms, he was a replica of Dan Penford. He had the same loose-limbed build; he was tall and lean and, Sam guessed, he duplicated Dan's incredible, whipcord strength. Victor le Page was an unmistakeable Penford and once the Mistress saw him, she would have the shock of her life. She would think the young man was her father reincarnated. Danny had had a bright, swift intellect plus a fiery temper but he had never been unjust in his actions though he could be a hard man when crossed. He wondered if young le Page had also inherited these traits. Certainly, when compared to Duret Noyen, Victor le Page was far superior because Sam knew, deep down, that Duret was weak. When an obstacle reared its head, Duret would simply wander away lost in his own peculiar thoughts mentally composing his poor poetry.

Sam suspected he was totally unsuited to Mary. She was far too ingenuous to cope with someone like Duret. The Mistress knew what her grandson was like as well. Sam knew there was much about the family finances which had been divulged to the unfortunate Charles but which Louise withheld from Duret because of his flippant approach to life. So what had pushed Duret to join the Militia in the first place and chase Mary in the second? How had he managed to persuade her to come to the island? It was all very puzzling to him and now there was this added complication. His heart sank miserably.

"Well, girl," he told her at last, "the choice is yours. It has been from the start of time; the female has the prerogative to change her mind and better to do this than wear the wrong wedding band," he advised laconically, refusing to be drawn any more.

"Oh, Sam!" Mary breathed. "You don't condemn me?"

Sam gave her a smile. "Of course not!" he replied briskly. "And I'll not say a word to the Mistress or anyone but remember this, the Mistress does not miss much that happens on this island," he warned quickly. "If you do meet le Page again to sort something out, make sure you are not observed. There are few secrets anyhow on Guernsey and it never ceases to amaze me how much information the Mistress acquires without appearing to ask a single question."

"I'll remember!" Mary whispered with relief then, on an impulse, stood leaned over and kissed one leathery cheek. "Thank you, Sam! I feel much better for talking to you!"

Louise looked at the girl from across a huge, dark table in the best room. She dropped her eyes and calculated again in swift, silent checking but there was no error.

Mary studied the room. Since her talk two days ago with Sam her heart had lifted while her emotions settled down. What exactly would happen in the future she had no idea and for the time being was content to live each day as it came. She liked this room, the first time she had been in it long enough to study its detail. It was very large and filled with fine, old furniture without being cluttered. There were four large, easy chairs and dining chairs ranged themselves alongside the table. Another enormous dresser flanked one wall, filled with top quality china. A number of paintings hung from the walls, all of them seascapes and, though she knew nothing of art, Mary liked them and sensed they were well executed. Underfoot was a thick, mottled green carpet— the same shade as the long, lined curtains.

"Like it?" Tante asked suddenly. She had been examining Mary's face, puzzled by the girl but not displeased. She had brightened up recently and Louise hoped this was the end of the homesickness.

"It's lovely!" Mary replied enthusiastically. "So rich yet lived in and all those books!"

"Help yourself to whatever you wish to read," Louise replied generously. She was no great reader herself but understood the fascination print could have for others. Their vast collection had been acquired by her father who had never gone to sea without two fresh books in his cabin.

Mary nodded. "What is that?"

Louise grinned and sat back in her chair. "That is the *Jonquière*. Most good Guernsey homes have one. Even the humble fisherman's cottage. It's common name is the Green Bed. They go back a long way historically and once were nothing but fern covered couches used by the farmers for a midday rest. Now they are simply another island custom. A Guernsey home would not be that without its Green Bed."

"You have Guernsey milk cans in silver as well as two in good china." Mary pointed.

Louise eyed her thoughtfully. "For someone reared in an orphanage you have taste and knowledge but I suppose you acquired both in service. I can see too why you were given an initial teaching post. You have good handwriting and your figures are most accurate."

Mary was pleased. There had been few genuine compliments in her life to date.

Louise continued. "You said you wanted some work to do though it's not necessary," she added quickly. "As my grandson's intended you have the right to live here doing nothing until he returns and you marry. However I think such idleness might pall after a while."

Mary felt the brown eyes on her as she stared at the Green Bed. Here it came again—the ugly problem of marrying Duret plus the consequences if she did not.

"If you really want to help I'd be glad," Louise said.

"I'd like that," Mary told her honestly.

"I'm part-owner of a quarry," Louise explained receiving Mary's sharp attention. "Quarrying has always been big business on this island and it goes right back to the eighteenth century. There are many quarries here, the bulk of them in the north of this island. Ship-building is also another good business as well as growing tomatoes plus our cows with their rich milk and butter. However I suspect ship-building might decline when the war ends and perhaps too even the quarrying. In which case I'll sell out and concentrate upon the tomatoes until I think of something else worthwhile. Until that happens though I do really need someone to do the quarry accounts and books. I'm not as quick with figures as I used to be and I'm slow compared to you."

Mary nodded and waited to learn more so Tante continued.

"Our stone is exceptionally strong," Tante told her, pleased with Mary's concentrated interest. "Tests have been carried out on the mainland which prove our stone will only lose four to five pounds of wear over a given period of time while Dartmoor granite will lose twelve and a half pounds and Aberdeen stone fourteen and three-quarter pounds."

Mary sat enthralled. Acquiring information was her favourite pastime and she concentrated hard.

Louise steepled her fingers together as she explained. "In 1913 we exported nearly half a million tons of stone to the mainland. Did you know that it is our splendid stone which was used in the construction of the Bank of England and the steps to St Paul's Cathedral?"

"No, I didn't!" Mary exclaimed, then her thoughts moved to another area and she frowned. "I'm rather puzzled," she said carefully. "You own a half share of a quarry but this lovely house with its magnificent furniture and grounds must have cost a lot of money in the first place? What they call a capital investment?" and she held her breath wondering if she had been too nosy.

Louise's lips twitched. She admired the girl's perspicacity and was also annoyed by it. As yet she was not a member of the family and had no right to more information.

"There was a lot of smuggling on the island in the last century. Before England changed her tariff laws, fortunes were made here which would make you hold your breath," she explained delicately. "My father Dan was a smuggler and *that* is all I'm prepared to say," she ended flatly then added a sharp addenda. "Duret does not know and is not to be told either!"

Mary blinked. "Because he is a dreamer?"

"Mary!" Louise gasped and halted. This girl was almost too sharp for her own good.

Mary saw shutters slip down and reverted back to the quarry. "Me and the quarry books?" she prodded.

"You can soon learn to do the books for me. Check the Bills of Lading, the fob and general accounts. Then if I do sell out you could go in on the ground floor with tomatoes. By then Duret will be home and that could be a joint business venture. I had a clerk doing my books but the fool went off to war and is dead, for his pains."

Mary was surprised. "Don't you approve of men joining up then?"

Louise snorted disparagingly. "Of course I don't when they go like romantic knights after the Holy Grail!"

"But Britain has been bleeding for years and the Empire too!"

"Don't try and teach me history, girl!" Louise said coldly. "I'm perfectly well aware that someone has to go but these tiny islands carry little population and we are well tucked away from the mainland. What do you know about us? Precious little! But we are British. We give our allegiance to the Crown even if the Laws of Westminster have no authority here. Did you know the Writ of Habeas Corpus cannot run here?"

Mary shook her head realising she was suddenly out of her depth and secretly shocked by Tante's unexpected hostility.

"We have total independence from Westminster. We have a Lieutenant Governor but, when the States—which is our Parliament—sits, he has to be on a chair lower down on the platform than our Bailiff. For legal purposes we deal with the Privy Council only. What I'm saying Mary is that this is *not* our war. Oh! We'll help the mother country but this should be with professional soldiers, not giddy, starry-eyed young fools who rush off at the first note of a trumpet, dreaming of galloping into battle on a white charger. Charles was like that and look what happened to him. Duret, of course, must copy. Young men never stop to think. Sometimes they are such fools," she said bitterly.

Mary was astounded at this passionate outburst and compared it to Victor's similar views. Did this mean it was she who was out of step? Was Victor right and she wrong? Unease filled her as she remembered her cold words. She swallowed miserably and knew she would have to do something. She was far too honest to allow a lie to rest uncorrected.

"If you were against Duret enlisting, why didn't you stop him?" she asked, puzzled.

"Easier to stop the tide!" Louise snorted with anger. She thought back to her hot words and Duret's, for once, equally obdurate stance. It had been his first, independent action and she suspected it had been done deliberately, as some crazy way of proving his manhood. "Not all our young men went. Those with sense stayed and they are alive," she ended sadly.

The weather swiftly developed into the island's spring in advance of that on the mainland. As Mary wheeled her cycle out again, she felt warmth bask her shoulders from the sun. Tante had taken her into St Peter Port and bought a new, more suitable wardrobe. She wore a white, long-sleeved blouse with a dove grey skirt, shorter than normal but easier for the cycle and Mary had never been so well dressed in all her life. This bothered her conscience, particularly today, as she knew where she was going to cycle.

Sam frowned as he watched her freewheel down the lane and shook his head dubiously. He felt sorry for her and was agitated at what might happen to her. Although the girl had a strong character she had not yet met Louise on the warpath. What would happen at the inevitable showdown?

Mary turned left and pedalled easily, not really wanting to arrive in one sense but, on the other hand, why was her heart fluttering with excitement?

She was quite unaware of an observer, carefully positioned with an old-fashioned telescope.

It was a gorgeous day and Mary admired the many open spring flowers and the new leaves. The sea was placid and she guessed it was still on the ebb, then grinned at herself. Already she had started to regulate her life by the tides because she had an empathy with the island and its ways.

She had learned much from Sam who was an excellent tutor. She had fallen into the habit of strolling with him in the evening after the cows had been milked. He had started to teach her Guernsey patois and Mary was smugly pleased with the way she was picking this up. Only last evening they had walked slowly with the cows moving ahead but taking their time as only cows will. One of the animals was particularly inquisitive and kept butting Mary's skirt, trying to nibble her calves. In final exasperation Mary had swung around and, with hands on hips shouted, "Fiche le camp!"

Sam had let out a bellow of laughter and Mary was instantly disconcerted.

"Did I say it wrong?"

"Not at all!" Sam croaked holding his ribs with mirth. "You just sounded so annoyed telling the cow to 'buzz off'."

"Oh! That's all right then!" Mary told him quite delighted with herself.

Still quivering with amusement, Sam continued what he had been about to explain.

"There is another old island custom which still holds force. It goes back to the Norman times but you should know about it. It's the 'Clameur de Haro'. If anyone is wronged and they feel deeply about the matter, they simply fall on their knees where the wrong took place and, before two witnesses, cry out 'Haro! Haro! Haro!'."

"Three times?" Mary asked with interest.

Sam nodded. "Then the aggrieved person must say, 'A mon aide, mon prince! On me fait tort!' He or she must finally recite the Lord's Prayer in French."

Mary halted in astonishment. "What on earth does all that mean?" she asked practically.

"Such an action has the force of an immediate injunction!" Sam told her. "It puts a halt to the wrong until a court action can take place and it's a very powerful force, I can tell you!"

Mary was impressed. "Is that so?" she murmured thoughtfully. "I think I'd better learn the Lord's Prayer in French then. Who knows when I might need it!" she said, half in joke. It never entered her head that a day might come when this joke became deadly serious.

"Do people still actually use this ancient custom?" she wanted to know next for it still appeared far-fetched to her logic.

"Oh! My word they do!" Sam replied forcefully.

Mary smiled at the vision of herself performing some such similar act on the mainland. The local policeman would have her locked up. She thought about this as she pedalled. What a lot she had learned and what a complete ignoramus she had been with Duret. She was a different person now but was this good or bad? She was unsure.

She reached the place, dismounted and pushed her cycle to the dip near the bushes. He was already there and her heart thundered. She climbed a slope and looked around, spotting him right away. He had been at the sea's edge but, observing her, he stood, waved, then came bounding over. Two paces away, he skidded to a halt, his face alight with pleasure, his eyes sparkling a deep purple but did not speak. Eloquently, he simply held out his two hands to her.

Instinctively, Mary stepped forward two paces and placed hers in his then he drew her to him, looked deeply into her eyes for a few seconds before bending to kiss her. Mary felt his sweet taste and willingly, almost naturally, she slid into the protection of his arms to return his wholehearted affection.

Finally he pushed her back four inches and surveyed her. "I'm *so* glad you came!"

He had been terrified she wouldn't, cold at what he would then have to do but now his day blossomed into sun and light. He tucked her arm under his and they walked slowly down to the sea where they had sat before. He took off his jacket, spread it on the warm grass and they sat down, both suddenly a little shy and apprehensive.

"You do look lovely," he told her huskily.

Mary looked down and smoothed an imaginary crease away from her new skirt then, lifting her eyes, she smiled gently. Once again his close proximity affected her breathing and nerves in the strangest manner.

"I have something to say," she started in a serious voice.

He almost flinched at her tone and held his breath.

"I'm sorry about the way I spoke and behaved at our last meeting. I've had a shock because I have found out that Tante thinks just like you! It seems this island is different from the mainland in more ways than one," she said contritely.

A gentle smile lit his face as he picked up both of her hands to stroke them with his strong fingers, soothing and caressing.

"That was handsomely done," he complimented her, then gave a heavy sigh. "I've had a bad time since I last saw you," he admitted.

"Why? What has happened?" she asked anxiously.

He pulled a face. "You!" he told her simply.

For a few seconds she failed to understand, then squeezed his hands in return and gave a tiny shrug.

"I can't get you out of my mind, day or night," Victor said slowly. "I go about my work, doing it to the best of my ability but all the time I'm looking for you. At night I lie awake and see your face wreathed in the sea's spray at the Rocques. I wake in the morning and you are still with me like an eternal dream spirit. I ache for you until I suffer pure pain. Oh, my beloved sea nymph, you have bewitched me utterly for all time," his voice was grave. "I have known other girls of course on Jersey but they were—" One waving hand dismissed them impatiently. "But you, Mary Hinton? I love you! No! This is no sudden affectation. It is a true bolt of lightning. It's the tip of your sword in my heart. You are my other, natural half—" He paused and eyed her with even more feeling. "And I know, I just know, you feel the same too. We cannot fight it. All we can do is accept. Your aura even enfolds me as you sit alongside me here."

"Don't!" Mary cried, suddenly afraid. "You know I'm spoken for."

"No one is guaranteed until the gold band is on that finger!" he retorted in a soft voice.

He kissed her again and Mary had neither strength nor will to object. Duret had never touched her core like this. Her defences crumbled.

"Don't let us waste our lives like Catherine and Heathcliff. Remember *Wuthering Heights*!" he said suddenly, his voice urgent and demanding. "Marry me! Damn the Noyens! We can leave the island and go—go anywhere in the world! We have no parents, no family. We answer to no man. We are young, strong and healthy. We'll make a home elsewhere and rear our children in South Africa, or New Zealand or Australia. Anywhere you say," he beseeched.

Mary pulled herself free. He was going much, much too fast.

She felt tears prickle her eyes and shook her head helplessly. All he had said was true but the duplicity of running away secretly was not her way.

"I'll not bolt without telling Duret or Tante," she managed to get out despite the lump in her throat.

His face broke into a savage grin of triumph. "You *will* be my wife?"

"I'm mad!" Mary groaned to herself.

"You have never been more sane!" he cried and kissed her again with savage passion as if stamping his ownership on her.

Mary took a deep breath and pulled away. "Victor!" she cried, lifting her right hand. "Do not stampede me. I cannot stand that. I must think about all this first because there are other people involved. Tante has been good to me, Duret must be told the truth and to his face as well. I'll not do it through a letter's ignominy. There is Sam too, a kind, loyal friend—"

"I'll tell Noyen for you!" he growled, feeling a tinge of alarm.

"No!" she remonstrated hotly. "I'll do my own dirty work!"

He recognised the resolution in her tone and saw a strange fire in her eyes that was disconcerting. He opened his mouth to argue then thought better of it.

"I have some more news," he began moving in another direction. "I'm being sent on a commission to Sark and Alderney tomorrow. The editor likes may humble efforts and he is letting me loose around some of the other islands in the Bailiwick. I'll be gone about a month I guess, then I have to go back to Jersey for a few days. The lawyer wants to see me about my mother's estate," he told her flushed with pride. "I think there might be a little bit of money for me after all and I have to sign some papers before it is released though I don't expect it will be much even then. When I return I'm coming to see you—and my awesome grandmère."

"No!" Mary gasped. "She'll run you off the property with a shotgun!"

"We'll see!" he grinned wolfishly and played his trump card. "I met someone who knew her father and it appear I'm the spitting image of Dan Penford. When Grandmère sees me she might just be a bit more charitable."

"Not when she knows about us!" Mary pointed out quickly. "She'll hate you even more."

"I don't want any money from her," Victor said slowly, his voice cool. "Duret can have the lot because I can make my own way in life. What I do want is for Grandmère to acknowledge that I *am* her grandson and that I am *not* a black hellion. I'm respectable, decent and a better man than Noyen to boot!"

"Don't do anything foolish!" she begged him.

He sensed her worry and smiled. "I'll never do anything to hurt you. I'll only go and see her when we are committed, before we leave for abroad if you like."

He was so sure of himself and Mary's heart sank.

"I've not agreed yet," she pointed out quietly.

He was startled. "But you will be my wife, won't you?" he insisted.

Mary set her teeth together. "Don't bully me, Victor. I cannot cope with that. Let matters run their natural course. After all, you are going to be away for over a month," she pointed out shrewdly. "Anyhow, I have to tell Duret."

"But it could be months before he gets leave!" he objected.

Mary sensed something feral in him combined with the sulk of a schoolboy whose bat and ball had been taken away. With a quick move she rose, smoothed down her skirt and flicked away two blades of dried grass from the previous autumn.

"Don't say anything, Victor," she pleaded. "Don't let us rush our fences. It will all come right in the end, I'm sure it will, but I don't want you to do anything wild or foolish."

"I won't lose you!" he stated mutinously.

"I think I'd better go now, Victor," she said carefully. There was such a moody look on his face her instinct told her to depart.

He leaped to his feet. "Don't!"

"I must!"

"Why?"

"Because—!" Mary floundered. "Just because," she ended lamely.

"I'll escort you then!" he said with a quick change of mood.

"No!" she said abruptly. "I'm not your possession yet, Victor and I have some thinking to do alone," she added firmly. With a brisk wave she walked back to her cycle leaving him flat-footed and miserable.

Mary was appalled at the confusion in her heart and mind as she pedalled away without a backwards glance. She had spotted a side lane near to Cobo Bay and she turned up this and dismounted to push the cumbersome cycle, lost in deep thought. She knew her heart had been lost to Victor but the thought of telling Tante and Duret made her quail. Duret's big brown eyes would fill with water and disbelief. Tante's brown ones would narrow with scorn and contempt. Sam—? Sam would understand, surely? She must tell him first of all and take his advice and hopefully he would suggest where she could live temporarily.

"Mary! Is that you?"

She spun around and saw Sam walking quickly up the lane, waving his right hand, his face red with effort.

"I hoped I'd find you quickly," he cried, "You've to come back right away!"

"Why?" she asked puzzled and sharply uneasy. "What's the matter?"

"Come back with me now," Sam insisted. "Mistress wants you urgently!" Without another word Sam turned and strode back down the lane. Mary climbed on the saddle and pedalled after him. As she drew level he waved a hand at her.

"Get back to the house!"

Fear filled Mary as she hastened to obey. Whatever had happened, she knew it was not going to be pleasant because Sam's face was grim and hard.

She found Tante standing in the drive, dithering with agitation, her face white and drawn.

"Thank heavens Sam has found you. Quickly! Go and pack an overnight bag!"

"What has happened, Tante?"

"We've had a telegram," Tante told her, snatching the cycle from her to dump it on the gravel and bustle her inside. "Duret has been wounded and is in a hospital somewhere. I've used all my connections, plus a few extra ones and arranged for the two of us to go to him. We leave as soon as Sam gets back!"

"Oh no!" Mary groaned, as her world collapsed and guilt hit her. While she had been dallying with Victor planning a life with him, Duret had been bleeding—perhaps even dying! Duret who trusted her! Where were all her fine words now? She had been acting like a trollop and her face flamed scarlet with mortification.

Tante regarded her grimly. "It might not be as bad as the telegram indicates. Doctors like to make a drama out of a play so we'll go and see for ourselves. If Duret is capable of being moved, we will bring him back to the island," she said harshly. "My patience is exhausted with this stupid, soldiering nonsense," she finished with asperity. Although she would not admit it, she was terrified this last true grandson would be lost before he could sire an heir.

Long afterwards Mary looked back on the next two days as a nightmare period of anguish, dirt and exhausting travelling. Louise took charge with a powerful efficiency that left Mary speechless with admiration. She simply did as she was told. Her emotions were far too upset now for coherent thought.

They sailed to St Malo, then went north by a crowded, filthy train. The two of them sat together, each lost in private thought and fear. Louise sat all the time with her usual ramrod, straight back and held her head high like a guardsman and automatically Mary did likewise. Louise spoke only when spoken to or when she needed something. Porters leaped to obey her fractured French.

Drivers hurried to open car doors for her imperious manner and Mary thought how like a commanding general she was. She was utterly ruthless, tolerated no excuses, was impatient with those who were slow in understanding her French and she organised with a skill that left Mary dumb with wonder.

By the time the final taxi halted Mary felt like a dirty, limp rag and her knees creaked and wobbled with exhaustion. They arrived at a tented hospital, not all that far from the front line and in a restricted area, which had forced Tante to extend her considerable powers of persuasion before they could enter.

The hospital seethed with activity which appeared confused and haphazard but, as Mary watched, she saw methodical order. Canvas-backed lorries and ambulances arrived continually to disgorge unpleasant cargoes, then turned to depart for more. She noted many of the drivers were young girls like herself. From some ambulances came walking wounded who staggered wearily, wearing filthy uniforms, to be shepherded by brisk nurses. Now and again a white-coated doctor appeared in a running flurry to vanish equally quickly. There was a particular smell over the whole area compounded from medical odours, human sweat, dried blood, urine and excrement plus the sweet, sickly, awful smell of bodies not yet buried.

To one side, graves were being dug in a long line and men removed blankets from stretchers, checked names against clipboards then moved the sombre burdens away. Some new arrivals were also on stretchers. They groaned as they waited to be assessed. Others lay in a quiet stupor of pain while some screamed. Many wanted cigarettes while a few, so pitifully young, tried to be stoical but cried for their mothers.

"Oh, my God!" Mary cried, one hand against her mouth, horrified at the whole scene. Duret had come to this while she had been making plans with Victor and her heart shrivelled.

"This is the other side of war," Louise said grimly. "The side without the glory and the white chargers. There is no Holy Grail here. This is what young men should see before they rush off to enlist," she grated.

"Young girls too with their white feathers," Mary added heavily.

A tired, young female ambulance driver with ginger hair stood beside her now empty ambulance. She slowly lit a cigarette with hands which shook before she climbed back into her seat to start her vehicle again.

Louise looked at Mary, who had turned a queer colour. "Are you going to be sick?" she asked harshly.

"No!" Mary shook her head. "It's just the smell and all these petrol fumes which are making me queasy."

Louise pulled her to one side. There was a well worn path which led to a small tangle of wooden huts, hastily erected, still crude and unpainted.

"You wait here. I'm going to find someone in authority but don't wander away," Louise ordered firmly.

Mary felt relief wash her. She was not ready to see Duret yet. She had doubts now that she would ever be ready and she clutched the straw of this providential delay.

"I won't budge!" she promised fervently.

Louise stormed away and was lost instantly in a welter of medical personnel interspersed with khaki uniforms. Mary's stomach gave a sudden lurch and she felt her mouth water. Dear God! She was going to be sick after all. She inhaled deeply and struggled to ease the cold knot deep in her belly.

"You all right, miss?" a soldier asked appearing from somewhere.

Mary swallowed and nodded wanly. "I'm all right, thank you, Corporal."

He eyed her doubtfully. He was utterly exhausted, fed up with being on the burial detail and suddenly glad of the chance to talk to a young girl who did not stink of death.

"What are you doing here, Miss? This is a restricted area."

Mary looked at his careworn old-young face. He was plastered in soil and mud but his eyes held harrowing sights. How impossible it was for civilians to understand the reality of trench warfare.

"I'm waiting for my aunt," she told him. "We received a telegram—" and she paused miserably. "She has gone to see what she can find out."

"Here, Miss!" he said briskly. He didn't want to have to cope with a fainting female too though she looked all right at the moment. Pale around the gills and sweating a little on her forehead. This was no place for any civilian let alone a young woman.

"Have a smoke, Miss, and calm your nerves," he offered generously.

"I won't, thank you, Corporal. It might just be fatal for my stomach and I may have to go and see someone," she explained quickly.

"Cor! Look at 'er!" the soldier exclaimed and pointed with a filthy hand as Tante Louise marched back towards them. "What an old battle axe she looks! Wouldn't like to cross 'er one dark night."

An hysterical giggle hit Mary. Tante's face was set in a hard mask. She stormed across, yielding ground to no one.

"That is my aunt!"

"It is? Oh my! Poor you!" the soldier exclaimed sympathetically. "I'm off then. Can't cope with the likes of 'er as well! Good luck, Miss!" and he departed with ungallant haste.

Louise strode to a halt while Mary held her breath and waited with trepidation. There was something dreadfully bleak in the old, brown eyes and for once no words came from her thin lips.

"How is he?" Mary made herself ask while her heart pounded.

Louise did not answer. She studied the general scene and Mary knew she was hunting for the right words. Something cold formed a rock in her stomach. Her eyes lit on a small hut that stood well away from general activity.

69

"Let's go over there and talk!" Louise said purposefully and pulled Mary's left arm. "I've been told we can sit there for a bit but we must leave when the next lot of ambulances return. It's the drivers' rest hut."

Mary felt the premonition grow bigger but she made no comment and followed as quickly as she could. Louise opened the door, looked in and stepped forward, taking instant possession. The hut had bare boards with four hard, utilitarian chairs. At the far side, a stove burned sulkily on some foul-smelling fuel. On the trivet a kettle bubbled gently, a thin plume of steam wafting in the draft. To one side stood a minute table, which held a large black teapot flanked by six chipped and dirty enamel mugs.

Louise shut the door, pulled forward two of the chairs, her expression grim. Mary sat and prepared herself for the worst.

"Tell me!" Mary ordered flatly.

"His physical wounds are minor," Louise replied slowly. "A broken left arm. His mind though—that is another matter," and she hesitated.

"Go on!" Mary whispered.

"A shell came over when he and his troop were in the trenches. It exploded only a few paces from Duret. Most of the men were blown to bits but Duret lived. The trench collapsed upon him and he was buried alive for nearly twenty-four hours. They thought all the men had died and didn't start to dig until later. He was lucky because the trench was timber-shored and the baulks fell across Duret. They also made an air pocket, just enough for him to breath. By the time they did get him out—they said his mind had gone."

"He is—mad?" Mary asked appalled.

Louise hesitated, trying to be fair then slowly shook her head, "No, he is not insane as we think of the word's meaning but he is not like us now," she said slowly. Had Duret ever been normal in the first place, she asked herself?

Mary was stunned. This was something she had never expected. She closed her eyes to try and imagine what it was like to be entombed alive then shook her head at the utter impossibility.

Louise gave a deep sad sigh and looked over at her. "The trouble is, Duret has always lacked his brother's back bone. He can be mulish but he has never been tough. The doctor says there will be nightmares, terrible ones when he relives his experience and it won't be nice for whoever is with him. However, there is medication he can take and there is an outside chance, he might eventually become normal with tender, loving care once he becomes a civilian and leads a quiet life. They want to send him to some fancy hospital in England. I soon stopped that rubbish. He would never improve in a ward with others mentally ill. I've told them he is to come back home as quickly as possible."

"Did they agree?" Mary asked softly.

Louise nodded wearily. "I had to make a big issue about it all. Deep down it suits them; it releases another bed and our own doctor can treat him. With our simple island life, there is great hope."

Mary could hardly take it all in. Gentle, loving Duret with his large sorrowful brown eyes. She shook her head and looked over at Louise again upon whose face was a cruel mask with stabbing eyes which daggered back at her.

"What it now boils down to, Mary, is this. The Duret who comes home will not be the Duret you knew in England. Can you still marry him? Do you want to? Or—are you still so utterly besotted with that bastard, Victor le Page?"

FOUR

THE DOOR OPENED with a bang and two girl drivers entered, halting with surprise. Louise stood hastily.

"We are just going," she explained quickly. "Your kettle has boiled." She paused. "We had something to discuss in private."

The two girls looked wearily at each other. It was not the first time their little hut had been used by distraught civilians and the stiff-necked old woman and white-faced younger one told their own silent tale.

Mary stumbled after Louise with Tante's question ringing in her ears. She knew her cheeks must have turned bright scarlet and her wits had left her. All the stuffing had been knocked from her as Louise stopped and took her arm.

"Say nothing now," she said quietly. "We'll get back to Guernsey. I'll arrange for Sam to come for Duret. It's better a man escorts him home. I don't want you to say one word. Think about the whole situation. Think long, hard and very carefully, then we will talk on the steamer from St Malo."

Mary stared back at her, lost for words, shaking her head a little, still numb with shock.

Louise sniffed impatiently. "For goodness' sake, girl, you don't think you could keep such carryings on secret from me, do you? Guernsey is a tiny island; everyone knows me. It's impossible to have a secret there. Anyhow, I went for a walk yesterday with my father's old telescope. I saw you two from a slope," she added grimly.

Mary's head whirled with shock. She was sure the sky would descend upon her next. Tante had seen her and Victor embracing and her cheeks went redder with embarrassment. How utterly naïve she and Victor had been and she writhed with humiliation.

Louise tactfully ignored the open emotions on the girl's face though she was crippled with wrath and frightened worry. Now was not the time for recriminations.

"We'll get a taxi or car to take us back to the station and catch the first available train, no matter what. With luck, we can catch tomorrow's steamer and be back in Cobo that evening. I doubt we'll get any sleep but I don't think that matters too much now, do you?" she asked pointedly.

Long afterwards, Mary could remember no single, clear detail of the journey until they were settled on the steamer in a small private cabin, which Louise had bullied the steward into allocating them with a hefty bribe. Mary's respect for the older woman rose sky high. Neither of them had slept since leaving the island but Louise still sat straight-backed and moved on foot like a general leading his troops. Many wondered how she did it. Her head ached. There was pain in the middle of her back and a weakness in her legs as waves of lassitude threatened to engulf her.

Mary fought to copy Louise. She made herself sit straight even though muscles shrieked with fatigue. She said nothing but stared from the train window, thinking of no one but Duret now. She knew she had reached a crossroads in her life and, deep down, she was torn in two. Love and guilt; duty and wanting clashed in her heart while her mind, still far too stunned, was incapable of coherent thought.

Their cabin was minuscule with one bunk and one chair bolted to the deckhead. Louise took the tray from the steward, shut the door firmly, placing the tray on a let-down flap.

"The cabin's not much but I was lucky to get it at such short notice and it cost enough in a bribe too," she sniffed. "Now have some coffee. It will keep us awake while we sort matters out," she said briskly.

Mary thought she would scream. How could Tante display such efficiency under these circumstances? It was unnatural. But she said nothing, simply biting her bottom lip as she took the steaming coffee, thick and very black. It was welcoming, hitting her stomach with solid reassurance, settling jangling nerves and she drained the lot, then held out the cup for another.

Louise poured, then sat back on the sole chair while Mary balanced on the hard bunk bed.

"So!" Louise said slowly. "Now we can talk."

Mary looked over at her with sorrowful but wary eyes. "What happens now?" she asked more to herself than Tante.

"You make your choice, once and for all, but before you do, weigh all the pros and cons. Your decision will be final and irrevocable," Louise warned in a low voice.

"Don't you feel anything for Victor? He is also your grandson," Mary asked in a low voice.

"He is the bastard issue of a daughter whom I learned to loathe!" Louise replied evenly. "With good reason too!" she added, then sighed heavily.

"He is your flesh and blood!"

"He is no legal kith and kin of mine!" Louise retorted swiftly.

"You think he is bad just because your daughter was but he is not!" Mary cried sharply, springing to Victor's defence. "You won't even give him a chance by seeing him. He is not a blackguard. He is a very fine young man!"

Louise's lips tightened at this as her expression turned bleak. "Do you love Duret?" she asked suddenly. "Have you ever loved him?"

Mary didn't hesitate. She looked Louise straight in the eye and held her cold stare.

"No on both counts!" she replied simply, "*And* that was made very clear to Duret. He wanted to drive me into making an early commitment but I wouldn't have it. I did agree to wear his ring but only reluctantly and told him so."

"So why did you come to Guernsey then—?" Louise snapped. "You could just as easily have stayed in England!"

Again Mary was honest. "Because I was sick to death of my life there and I gambled the island offered me something fresh, a new start, better prospects and—"

"That's it then, isn't it?"

Mary frowned, then understanding dawned. Her eyes flayed angrily. "You are older than me. You've seen more of life and its tragedies than I have but you certainly do not know everything," she started coldly. "No, I did not know that Duret came from a well-off family. If I *had* known that, I doubt I would have come to the island. I know more about being poor that you'll ever know. I've forgotten details of poverty and charity unknown to you," she said hotly. "Duret never said a word to me about his background or finances and I wasn't interested enough to ask. I am *not* some little gold digger!" she snapped, her voice rising a little, her whole personality showing a side unknown to Louise. She was furious and showed it. "I was under the impression Duret and his family came from a humble fishing background. I had the shock of my life the day I arrived and the trap drew up outside that magnificent home. I can make my own way in life, willy-nilly. I don't need you nor the Noyen money, thank you very much. Indeed, Tante, if that is the way your mind has been working then I'll tell you what I intend to do." She had to pause for breath while her breasts heaved with genuine indignation.

"Which is?" Louise asked quietly. She was taken aback at this display of spirited temper and more than a little impressed.

"I'll come back to your rich, plush home and change. These—" Mary snapped, indicating some of the clothes Tante had bought, "you can have back and do with as you will. I shall collect my own bits and pieces and depart from your place and your life. You know something, old woman, even the poor have their pride

75

and dignity. It's a pity you are not sufficiently worldly-wise to realise this without making snide remarks and totally unjust accusations!"

Mary quivered. With each word she knew she was getting angrier. If she could have left Louise Noyen and the ferry she would have done so. Her blue eyes blazed and Louise nodded sagely to herself as her lips twitched.

"Fine, bold words," she replied quietly. "And Victor le Page?" she prodded.

"I love him," Mary told her simply.

Louise swore and shook her head violently. "After a few hours with him? What rubbish!" she snorted.

"Not many weeks with Duret!" Mary retorted.

"Marriage is for life. You are experiencing a brief, violent infatuation but you don't know it. Le Page gets nothing when I die!" she warned.

"He wants nothing!" Mary shot back. "The only thing he *does* want from you is your acknowledgement that he is decent and respectable!"

"I have my doubts about them too when he plays free and easy with an engaged girl!" Louise parried.

Words left Mary momentarily. She was bubbling with anger now, seething to do something but was frustrated by being trapped in the cabin.

"So Duret is tossed aside," Louise said slowly, deciding upon a new line of assault. "A simple boy, a gentle one who writes poetry—even if it is bad—who trusts you and who wants you by his side in life."

Mary cringed. This flanking attack on her conscience was hard to parry. For a few seconds, Duret's and Victor's faces swam before her eyes, merging into one gigantic vision. She felt helplessly pulled in two directions.

"Are you all right, Mary?" Louise asked suddenly. The girl had gone white and she wondered if she was seasick. The ferry was wallowing a little in the swell.

"I'm all right," Mary said slowly. "Just angry with you!" She managed a thin wan smile with her lips, though her eyes remained miserable.

"Duret needs you, Mary," Louise told her gently, her eyes boring into the blue ones. "He needs a strong wife to help and guide him. He needs a true friend to walk by his side. He is not a bad boy. If you throw him aside you'll break his heart. When I saw him—he mentioned you."

Mary looked at her sharply. "He did?"

Louise nodded. "He wanted to know where you were and if you were all right. He loves you desperately. Oh! He said nothing else but I know my grandson."

Mary's shoulders slumped. The forces lined against her were too strong, her greatest enemy her own conscience. What about Victor?

"If you marry Duret you will become a rich woman," Louise said gently. "Your past fears of poverty and charity will vanish for ever. Your children will grow up never knowing want. You will be sole mistress of a fine home, respected by the islanders, a lady of consequence. Remember—when poverty walks in the door, love flies out of the window and what exactly can le Page offer you that is as good as marriage to Duret? Do you think all marriages are based on love? Goodness me, girl, you've had a sound education. What about the gentry and aristocracy who marry to unite land and wealth—the same even with royalty? Don't tell me, child, that wealth and position are to be scorned. You've more sense in your head than that! You marry my grandson and perpetuate my line and you will be Madam Noyen, a lady of importance and respect. You marry le Page and where will you end up? God knows! I don't!"

Mary did not immediately reply. Louise's shrewd comments accurately hit the bull's eye.

"But I don't love Duret," she protested weakly.

Louise sensed she was winning. "Love grows," she said softly.

"And the variety that takes time to come is often far better than the hot flush of the all—at—once stuff!"

Mary closed her eyes miserably. Victor's wild ideas of going abroad were magnificent but—what if they did not work out? What if babies came and they did not have two halfpennies to rub together? Duret meant security; Victor offered risk. If it were herself alone she knew where the choice would lie but she must think of possible children. She could feel Louise's eyes boring into her.

"I doubt I'll ever love him," she whispered ruefully.

"But surely you must like Duret?"

Mary nodded at that. "Yes, that I do."

"Well?" Louise asked with forced gentleness. She sensed they had reached the crux of their talk but which way would the girl jump? Mary Hinton was a far more complex character than she had imagined and she had a temper to boot. She fully approved of this. Mary was the ideal mate for Duret but Louise had enough sense to know when not to press. She held her breath, feeling her nerves jangle with agitation though her expression was smoothly bland from long practice.

Mary made her decision. "I will marry Duret—on one condition!"

Louise stiffened. "Which is?"

"That it is done as quickly as possible with neither frills nor fanfare," Mary said firmly then unbent to explain. "Victor le Page is away from the island for a number of weeks. It's better for me to be a wife when he returns. I will then see him—and tell him."

Louise's breath came out with a rush of relief. She had played her cards right after all, thank God she had found out about le Page's antics with Mary in time. Praise be for gossiping island tongues! It had enabled her to formulate a plan, put it into action, then pray something tangible would happen. Duret's wounding had not been exactly what she'd had in mind but it had sufficed admirably. The editor of the newspaper, an old acquaintance of hers, had been most obliging and thought her idea of letting the cub reporter loose on his own, an excellent way to test his abilities. He had been delighted and wondered why he had failed to think of this himself. Of course, he knew who young le Page was and Louise's interest in promoting the boy's career had not been untoward. Louise Noyen was well known to have a finger stuck deep in many pies and if she wanted le Page away from Guernsey for a few weeks, that was her business. He had no intention of questioning her as to her motives.

"You'll not regret this, Mary. That is a promise!" Louise vowed.

Suddenly, Mary felt washed out. "And I'll not back down either," she said carefully, reading Tante easily. "Just make it quick."

"I will!" Louise promised grimly.

Mary shut her eyes, her heart numb but, strangely, a great weight had lifted from her shoulders now that matters had been taken out of her hands so dramatically. Thank God, she told herself, I made no direct promise to Victor but what was he going to say? She allowed herself the luxury of thinking about him for a few more moments. It would have been wonderful with him but also it might have been terrible.

Louise regarded her thoughtfully. Her conscience was quite at ease. Matters had turned out far better than she had dared to hope. The girl would mope for a bit, that was to be expected, so the urgent task was to get Duret home and the two of them married. Pray God, she added to herself, that he is still capable of his masculine duties.

She reached up, unfastened the top button of her blouse and withdrew a small deep locket suspended by a fine, golden chain worked in cable like a ship's rope. Mary watched with surprise. She had never known Tante wear jewellery.

Louise noted her stare. "It was my mother's given to her by my wild father," she smiled as she flipped the pendant off her neck, pressed a tiny catch and opened it.

"Look!"

Mary's eyes opened wider and she gasped. "That's surely not a—?"

Louise nodded. "It is a cut but unset diamond of two carets," she said slowly. "This will be made into a proper betrothal ring for you. That other you can put on your right hand."

Mary was stunned. She had seen magnificent gems before but only on the hands of gentry. She doubted whether even Lady Oliver possessed such a fine gem.

"It's beautiful," she murmured as the light in the cabin caught the facets making the stone flash white and blue.

"There are some others left too," Louise continued slowly. She had made her decision. Mary would never break her word so now was the time to explain all.

"Only Sam knows this now that Charles is dead. Duret certainly does not," she started to pick her words with care. "I was told by my parents when I was old enough to understand. I told you my father was a smuggler. Well, he did quite well from his nefarious activities and, to start with, he put his money into gold but that is heavy and cumbersome. Later he changed the gold into diamonds, which are easier to hide and transport and they are not so much subject to banking laws either. One diamond changed in the right place—at the right time—can realise much money. *These* are the source of the family wealth and now I tell you as you enter the family. One day it will be you who will end up guarding the family finances. Duret is far too vague to be allowed to deal with such important matters. Anyhow, it's been my experience that strong women are excellent at business and you are going to be another me in time," she said dryly before continuing. "When it becomes necessary to have added funds, a diamond is changed on the Continent, usually in France. I have a list of suitable names and addresses where no questions are asked. Naturally the price received is often less than on the open market but it is more convenient and still highly profitable. There are

80

not many diamonds left now and I only use one when absolutely necessary. With this stone in a ring, you will have security on your hands if the worst ever comes to the worse. When I change a diamond for money I deposit the funds in the family bank and the manager presumes these arise from Continental investments. Then, in due course, I transfer these to interest-bearing accounts, mostly on the mainland, although some go into gilt-edged shares. The remaining stones are hidden and after you are married I will show you. Secrecy is vital, of course. There is little crime on Guernsey but I take no chances. It always pays to be prudent and suspicious."

Mary could find nothing to say. The stone's fire fascinated her, making her catch her breath. She was awed to think this would be hers in the near future. Louise could not have displayed anything more provocative to indicate Mary's new situation in life.

"How many stones are left?" Mary whispered, quite unable to take her eyes off the diamond.

"Nine after this," Louise told her bluntly, "and worth a tidy heap of money too!"

Louise felt exhausted and it was a struggle to retain a stoic composure. She was still desperately afraid of Victor le Page and his emotional influence on the girl. Once she wore the gold band though, Mary was a possession of the Noyens. Le Page might cause a storm and uproar but Louise discounted this. She knew how to deal with upstart bastards, then a tiny frown puckered her forehead. She must arrange the quietest and quickest wedding ever held on the island. There would be talk of course, and constant studies of Mary's abdomen but let the gossips have their field day. Louise did not particularly care just as long as she got what she wanted.

Ten days later Mary waited with a fluttering heart. Louise had driven the trap into St Peter Port to meet the ferry which would have Sam and Duret on board. Her moment of truth was upon her and she looked down at the magnificent diamond ring on her left hand, Duret's more humble gift gracing her other hand. Only Emily was in the house and, during the past week, she had begun to thaw, perhaps because Mary tried to converse in patois. Sometimes she stumbled and became tangled but she persisted and her endeavours had won Emily over.

Sam had passed little comment when she told him about her forthcoming wedding. His wise old eyes looked at her with a long, silent question and his shoulders had twitched a fraction.

"What will be—will be!" was his brief, enigmatical comment and Mary could get nothing more from him so she let it all drop. Whether Sam approved or not she was uncertain. The one thing of which she was sure was his friendship because Sam's role had changed. Without either of them becoming aware of exactly how it had happened, Mary now turned to Sam as the grandfather she had never known.

Mary smoothed her new blue skirt because Tante had ordered a fresh wardrobe for her. She had never dreamed such clothes existed for the likes of her and she would not have been human if they had not excited her. Now she was garbed almost as the gentry had been in Weymouth and it was amazing how good clothes gave a person added confidence.

She heard the brisk rattle of the cob's hooves and retreated behind a tree to compose herself as sharp panic rose up like a ghost. She gulped, closed her eyes, took a deep breath and knew she was ready. The trap turned up the drive briskly, the cob tossing his head, sending foam flying from his bit then stopped. Tante sprang down in her usual vigorous way followed by Sam—and Duret.

Mary took another deep breath then stepped forward to show herself. Duret saw her and a great smile crossed his craggy features and he opened his arms invitingly. Suddenly, Mary needed no prodding. She ran forward, smiling sincerely because, after all, she did indeed like the Duret she had known in England. He kissed her gently, then held her at arms' length while Louise and Sam discreetly vanished, leaving them alone.

Mary examined Duret carefully. She was shocked to realise how much older he looked. There were lines on his forehead and his brown eyes were hooded, holding some secret misery. He was incredibly smart. His boots shone, his puttees were precisely spaced, his trousers held a knife-edge crease and he wore a new jacket. His cap badge gleamed, as did his jacket buttons, but when Duret removed his cap, Mary was appalled to see grey hairs visible.

"Duret," she whispered, holding out both hands to him.

"At last," he murmured and drew her nearer. "I've often thought of this moment. Sometimes it seemed it would never come but here we are at last, together on my island."

Mary's thoughts were mixed. She was conscious again of the heavy diamond on her finger and she had a fleeting vision of Victor, then she firmly pushed him away. She had committed herself, of her own free will. She would not cheat Duret but what did shellshock do to a man? There was a niggle of unease in the pit of her stomach as wild doubt rose again but wilfully she pushed that aside as well. Now she must devote herself to Duret and think only of him.

Slowly Duret looked around. His eyes took in the house, the nearby fields, then he slipped her arm into his and they strolled gently down the lane.

"I wrote many letters to you," Duret confided slowly. "I wanted to say so much but when I reread them, my letters did not seem right so I tore them up. I sent my poems instead."

Mary hesitated at this as they stopped and she leaned forward to retie the sling on one arm. She was nervously glad of something to do with her hands. Acute shyness engulfed her now.

"Is your arm painful?" she asked gently.

Duret shook his head while a warm glow filled him. When he finally met war, he had been utterly horrified. The glory image vanished with the first German shelling. Life turned into a nightmare existence. He could remember nothing of the explosion but had regained consciousness to find himself buried, almost smothered. He had panicked, making his position worse and only exhaustion had stayed his savage floundering. When realisation did dawn, the horror had been too much. His weak mind had mercifully blacked out consciousness and it was only the sound of shovelling which had brought him back to wakefulness. He had been pulled into fresh air with soil clogging his eyes and ears and he had cried like a child.

Just before his release the doctor had talked to him gently. It had taken Duret a little while to understand what the simple words meant once the medical terms had been explained to him. There was little wrong with him physically but he could expect nightmares for a long time to come.

It was this that horrified Duret. He was on the verge of matrimony. What if he had an attack in the marriage bed? Would Mary despise him? He felt an internal desperation but knew he could not yet put this fear into speech. He was critically honest with himself. Duret knew perfectly well he was a poor specimen compared to his dead brother Charles. All his grandmother's powerful ambitions would settle upon his back. It was a horrifying realisation. He loved the old woman dearly and he admired her for the way she had reared him, acting for both long-dead parents but Louise Noyen's powerful will made her far too strong a character for Duret. There were times when she terrified him.

His escape to the army had been nothing but his personal protest at her domination and the way she appeared to think she could organise his life. He never stopped thanking fate for the way in which he had been able to meet Mary Hinton. He marvelled at his daring in persuading her to come to his island. Even her acceptance of his ring with her proviso meant he was a man in his own right; no longer subject to petticoat domination.

On the battlefield though, he had suffered a hundred agonies in scenes in which Mary met someone else. A more brisk, tougher man like brother Charles. When Sam finally came to collect him, there was a note from grandmother.

"If you want the girl, don't delay," it had said with cryptic bluntness.

Duret had been horrified and questioned Sam who had, with customary island bluntness, merely grunted and echoed grandmother's comment without elaboration.

"Marry me! Marry me now!" he demanded, halting, kissing her, taking her quite by surprise.

Mary was astonished, unprepared for this display of ardour. She had not thought Duret so capable and her heart lightened, her fears receded. She had one tiny vision of Victor's face, which then dissolved as Duret claimed her complete attention.

"Of course, I will," she murmured, yielding to his arms, her spirit lifting. It was going to be all right after all. Her heart swelled for Duret. She would make him well again and, she reminded herself, after Tante's warning, she would be patient when he had nightmares. Quite suddenly, life shone bright and hopeful with not one worry on the horizon.

Exactly eight days later Mary, now a Noyen, clutched Duret's arm in happiness as Sark loomed before them sitting high in the sea, bathed in rich, spring sunshine. Their wedding had been wonderfully quiet and secret, managed discreetly by Tante and now, at last, they were alone. Mary thought of the bottle of pills in her handbag, passed over surreptitiously by Tante at the last moment.

"God bless you my dear," Louise had said, resting one hand on Mary's shoulder as relief filled her eyes. "By the time you two return, I'll have moved down the lane to my little cottage and the big house will be yours."

Duret was quiet but kept squeezing her arm and Mary felt a rare tranquillity. Tante had dragged her around the capital and bought her a simple dove-grey suit with red accessories for her marriage while Duret had worn his uniform.

There had been only two non-family witnesses present in the form of Sam and Emily. There had been a delightful wedding breakfast then it had been time to catch the ferry to Sark for the nine-mile crossing. As their boat tied up at the minute quay, she peeped at Duret who stared, wide eyed, at the steep road leading up to the top of the island. She wondered at what he was thinking.

Unknown to her, Duret had found it a disappointing day. He was proud of his Mary and had wanted nothing more than for the whole island to come to their wedding. He had been put out when his grandmother had stated it must be quiet. To start with, his bottom lip had come out and trembled in the start of a sulk which ominous sign Louise had not missed. She had taken him aside and explained that Mary was shy and that *he* must help her. This cunning ploy had worked where an argument would have failed. Duret had swelled with pride and been extra solicitous to his bride, accepting her wishes and the ceremony passed off without problems. Now he felt very manly as he helped her disembark from the small, swaying ferry and kept an eye on their baggage as it was loaded into the cart that the horses would pull up the long hill.

They had booked a tiny cottage for a week and Mary had to admit that Duret saw to everything admirably. They transferred to a trap and the driver deposited them at their honeymoon home. Inside food had been left ready and they ate a quiet meal, with Mary feeling the first tremors of apprehension. So far, Victor had been pushed firmly from her mind in the whirlpool of events and arrangements but now, for the first time, his handsome face intruded. She felt a slightly sick feeling at the meeting she must have with him in the future, then stoically banished it from her mind.

Later the gulls wheeled and screeched as she leaned from the bedroom window and looked out. Somewhere near the sea gurgled and hissed then thundered on some nearby rocks. Duret joined her and Mary smiled shyly at him. Immediately he dropped their bags, came over to her and put his arm around her shoulders. He was so proud of his wife that he bubbled to write a verse about their day soon.

"Alone at last!" Mary murmured to him, smiling gently.

Duret threw her a gentle grin. "Grandmère can be overpowering at times but she can get things done. No one dare argue with her," he replied ruefully. Mary turned back to the view, her left hand on the open window sill and she looked down at the thick, gold band which nestled against the magnificent diamond ring.

Duret stroked her hair, suddenly acutely aware of her sensitivity. He was no timid virgin himself. His mates had seen to his initiation in an appropriate brothel but this was his wife. He could not approach her like a whore. His little self-confidence had been badly shaken by his experience but much as he yearned to lean on his strong Mary, his instinct told him now was the time when he must lead.

"I'll go and lock up," he muttered and clumped down the narrow wooden stairs leaving Mary thankfully alone. For just a few seconds she could not help but make a comparison between Duret and Victor as she undressed but, by the time Duret returned, she was between the sheets, serene and composed.

Mary was pleasantly astonished. What exactly she had expected from her quiet groom she hadn't known but Duret's careful foreplay suddenly aroused her to a pitch which made her gasp with excitement. When he moved over her, she was more than ready and his drive, hard and eager, pierced her quickly. He brought her to a fine pitch and they consummated their marriage in mutual agreement and pleasure.

Afterwards they lay on their sides, simply smiling at each other in the moonlight, then they drifted into sleep. Mary awoke with a violent start. The bed writhed with movement and the howl was almost bestial in its anguish. With a lurching heart she sat up abruptly, her bemused wits struggling to understand the crescendo of awful sounds.

She leaped from the bed and stared with horror. The sheets had apexed to a cone and underneath Duret twisted and writhed while maniacal shrieks cut at her nerves. In a flash, Mary understood and her heart went out to him and his anguish. She jumped forward, pulled the sheet away and flung her arms around her husband as he lay in the foetal position, tears streaming down his face, his breath coming in great, gasping howls.

"Duret! Duret" Mary cried and hugged him savagely. He turned and burrowed his wet face between her breasts as great shudders rippled through him. Mary murmured soothing sounds, struggling to hold his paroxysms, cursing herself for forgetting to give him his tablet. She was appalled at his terrible fear.

Her heart swelled. He needed her comfort badly after his shocking experience and great tenderness rose for him. With her natural honesty she knew she could never love him as she did Victor but—Victor le Page was self-sufficient. He needed no one. Duret did.

'I did the right thing, after all,' she told herself gently. 'I love you, Victor. I probably always will but you'll find someone else. My life is worth more to Duret!'

He lay in her arms and looked up with harrowed eyes. "It comes on me suddenly," he groaned miserably. "I get no warning when everything goes black and I feel as if I am suffocating."

"Ssh!" she babied. "You are safe with me always. It's my fault. I forgot to give you your pill."

"Fine man I am to you!" he muttered between clenched teeth as tears soaked his cheeks. He wiped them away with the back of one hand.

"You're man enough for me—husband," she whispered to him,

kissing him firmly, striving to pass on her natural strength. "Together we'll beat it!" she promised.

"Oh Mary! I'm a lucky man to get you. The best thing I ever did was to enlist, come to England and meet you," he paused then his eyes went a little narrow with apprehension. "There's never been anyone else, has there?"

Mary did not hesitate. "How could there be? What a silly question. Of course not, Duret!" she lied evenly. Then she kissed him again and self-doubt died. "Come on! Now let's get to sleep. We've a lot of walking and exploring to do this week!"

FIVE

MARY SAT IN the cottage's front room. It was as comfortable as if Tante had always lived here instead of a bare week.

"Goodness me!" she exclaimed. "You have moved everything quickly!"

Louise glanced around, satisfied and smug. "Thanks to Sam and some other helpers. The house is yours now to do exactly as you wish and I have left the Green Bed for you. I'm getting a new one," she paused eyeing the young wife. "How was Duret's health?" she asked quietly.

Mary explained about their first night. "Since then I have made sure he takes those pills and there's not been any repeat but—" She hesitated. "He's not very confident. I think it is going to take time for him to return to normal."

Louise said nothing but looked thoughtfully out of the window. Would Duret ever be that, she wondered unhappily? Shell shock was something terrible and, from her investigations, not fully understood by the doctors. Thank God, Mary was strong and unflappable. Now she must take the second planned step.

Standing up, Louise nodded at Mary to come with her. She went down the short corridor leading to the kitchen door. Directly to one side Louise had hung a seascape of waves breaking viciously over a set of craggy rocks. The colours were a combination of blues and greys and it was the one picture Mary had never liked. It was too cold and cruel for her taste. Louise carefully lifted the picture down and turned the back towards Mary. There was a strip of black tape from one side of the picture to the other.

"Half of the diamonds are hidden here under this tape," she explained. "Sam is the only other person who knows apart from us two. Duret is *not* to be told. Remember, these make our nest egg. Now the other diamonds are hidden at the house. You'll find the rest in that small upstairs room in the sewing machine. They are taped underneath and are hidden except from close examination because the tape is as black as the machine's underside."

Mary nodded soberly. She felt proud to share the responsibility of their knowledge and to know Tante trusted her. She certainly agreed with this being kept from her husband. He might have an attack somewhere, and blurt everything out to a stranger.

Louise took her arm and led her back to the lounge. As Mary sat down, she sensed a wariness in Tante and wondered what was coming now.

"Le Page came back two days ago," Louise said bluntly.

"What!" Mary gasped. "I thought he was going to be away for a few more weeks!"

"So did I!" Tante said grimly. "But it seems tongues clack on other islands as well as this one. Somehow he had heard about your marriage. He came storming up to the house, demanding to see you."

"Oh no!" Mary groaned. She could see it all so plainly. Victor in a frustrated, embittered rage going bull-headed into battle. "Where were you?" she asked sharply.

"Down here, fortunately. Sam dealt with him. I don't know exactly what was said. Sam wouldn't tell me. The long and short of it is that le Page was in a very savage, totally unreasonable mood. He left uttering dire threats against Duret."

Mary closed her eyes, able to picture it all. Her heart started a wild beat and her lips compressed.

"I'll have to see him," she said flatly.

Louise eyed her. "I'm thinking of having a word with the Parish Constable."

"No!" Mary said quickly, shaking her head. "That would be the worst thing you could do. You would only make him worse. Much better for me to see him personally."

Louise was not keen on this idea. "He might be violent," she began.

"Not with me," Mary replied confidently.

"And if Duret found out—?"

"Well, I'll have to make sure he doesn't!"

Louise's lips went tight. She regretted she had sent that note to Duret with Sam. That had been a mistake but she had thought it was for the best at the time. Knowing how slow Duret was, Louise had imagined him dithering and hesitating over a proposal. Duret must never know about le Page.

"Where and when?" Louise asked anxiously.

Mary considered. "Somewhere a bit distant where Duret cannot come upon me accidentally."

Louise nodded thoughtfully, that certainly made sense and, on the day of the meeting, she would keep Duret well and truly occupied.

"Jerbourg Point!" she snapped suddenly. "I'll explain how to get there on your cycle and we'll tell Duret you have an appointment with a dressmaker in St Peter Port. Also I'll have him up here moving the furniture around. I'll say I want to try other positions as the rooms are that much smaller than up at the house."

Mary nodded slowly. "How do we let Victor know?"

"Leave that part to me. I'll make an appointment for you in about three days' time for the afternoon." She looked at Mary, deep unease touching her heart. What if the old magic between these two was still present? Louise eyed the young wife who was lost in thought, contemplating the empty fire grate. Mary had made her vows. She was honest and straight, surely she would not cheat Duret at this late stage of the game? She was well aware that Duret must cut a poor figure against le Page but she knew this proposed meeting was unavoidable. Without it, le Page would only keep coming to Cobo looking for Mary and would, one day, meet Duret. Louise's expression became grim. She knew only too well who would be the loser.

Mary looked at her suddenly. Her blue eyes were wide but her stare almost cold and calculating.

"I am no cheat," she said slowly, "so stop thinking what is in you mind, Tante. Credit me with a little decent honesty!"

Louise flinched. She had never been so addressed. Her cheeks pinked with a red spot in their centre and her nostrils flared but Mary held eye contact, cool and unblinking.

"It's quite possible when I see Victor the old magic will still be between us but—" She indicated her left hand. "I'm another man's wife now. He will be made to understand that. He will not be allowed to hector me. Neither, I might add, will anyone else!" she said firmly.

Louise bristled. "Meaning me?"

"Yes!"

"Well!" Louise snorted, almost disbelieving her ears. "I'm not used to being spoken to in such a manner!"

Mary did not blink but held the older woman's eyes in a steady stare. "I'm a wife now with status and responsibility. No one will dictate to me."

"Mary!" Louise protested, for the first time feeling deflated and hurt.

"I am not joking, Tante!" Mary emphasised. She stood up slowly, still holding Louise in an unblinking stare. "I'll have no interference in my marriage from anyone. I'll make my own mistakes and learn from them alone. I'm the mistress up at the house now," she said firmly. "I'll handle Victor in my own way!"

As she saw genuine hurt appear in Louise's eyes, Mary let herself soften a bit. She had made her point, now she could afford to be charitable.

"However, there will come days when I will wish to discuss problems and I hope I'll always be able to come here to you," she said gently.

Louise's face was cold and frigid but gradually her lips twitched, her eyebrows lifted and a gleam of admiration came into her eyes.

"It's a long time since anyone had the guts to put me in my place like that but, of course, you are quite right. I'll retire down here to be a counsellor—when required!" she added quickly. "I'll not interfere. I promise!"

Mary leaned forward and kissed one leathery cheek. "You are my friend," she reinforced firmly.

Mary arrived well before the appointed time. She didn't know the way and had decided it was prudent to explore; also she wanted time in which to compose herself. There had been a little difficulty with Duret who had wanted to drive her into town, wait while she shopped, then take her for lunch.

Thankfully Tante had handled that beautifully. "Oh no, you are not going, my lad," she told Duret with cool firmness. "I need your strong muscles this afternoon and Mary does not want you mooning around outside a dress shop. She wants to take her time selecting materials. Indeed, she might not see what she wants and will have to go back another day." Tante had flashed a sharp look at Mary who understood in a second. Here was the excuse for returning without buying anything. "And furthermore," Tante had continued with a full head of steam, "you can't drive the cob. He needs new shoes and I'm going to arrange for Sam to take him to the farrier!"

Duret had been inclined to sulk but he had not quite dared to disobey his grandmère. Mary had used her guile by winking at him and nodding at the heavy dresser.

"Help her or she'll only try and struggle on her own," she whispered and, appealed to by his adorable wife, Duret had capitulated without further fuss.

Sam took the cob to be shod and Mary slipped away on the cycle, repeating the directions given by Tante. Under other circumstances, she would have enjoyed the ride. The weather was like a summer day; the sun brilliant without a breath of wind and cycling was easy. The tide was high and the views gorgeous when she spotted the correct lane and turned inland.

Mary had dressed with care and thought. She had examined her growing wardrobe and, after much pondering, chose a gay, floral skirt which was a mixture of brightly coloured daisies, a white short-sleeved blouse with dainty ruffles at the neck and cream flat-heeled shoes. The cycle had been fitted with a small front basket pannier and in this she carried her handkerchief and purse. She felt good and knew she looked it.

She wore only the lightest touch of lipstick which complemented the tan she had acquired on breezy Sark. Her hair, kept cropped short, fluttered in the breeze of her passage and she cycled energetically as if by using up physical energy she could combat the screwing tension in her stomach.

Mary knew she was apprehensive but, at the same time, she was excited at the thought of seeing Victor again, which prodded guilt to rise in her heart. How was it possible for her to feel such anticipation when she was happily married?

She braked to a halt at Jerbourg Point which was a headland jutting into the sea. It was high and after she had parked her cycle, she walked to the edge and looked down. Way below the sea writhed as the tide began its turn with tiny frills of white on the waves. There was a thin, narrow path descending steeply, flanked on either side by scrubby bushes and she guessed it would be a real scramble to go down this.

Louise had explained the significance of this place. From it, on a clear day like today, it was possible to see all the other islands.

Mary easily picked out nearby Herm then, turning as advised, she was able to recognise Jersey. By looking in the other direction she was just able to pick out the thin shadow which marked Alderney. It was a beautiful spot and she was quite alone.

Now and again, she flashed a look backwards at the lane wondering when he would come. There was no doubt in her mind that he would. Then she saw a figure cycling purposefully up the lane. It was a man and, as he neared, she swallowed with fresh nerves.

He wore dark trousers and a similar jacket with a grey shirt and a tie that flapped loose. She saw his features were noncommittal though his eyes held hers as he dismounted, removed his cycle clips and put his vehicle against hers.

He stared at her frankly, letting admiration have its play. She looked so beautiful and serene as she waited for him. Her head was held high with dignity and though her expression was smooth he could see something burning in her blue eyes as he approached.

He stopped one pace away, gave her a long, hard look, swallowed then gritted his teeth.

"How *could* you?" he grated.

Mary was lost for words. It was still there and her heart sank. His physical presence was almost enough to overwhelm her. From him came the mystical aura that seemed to envelop her and draw her against her will. His eyes were a dark blue, cold and hard as Indian sapphires.

"Don't let's quarrel!" she begged on an impulse.

Victor compressed his mouth. His expression was austere with pinched nostrils and tight lips. Every tendon stood out on his strong neck and his breath came hard and heavy.

"I turn my back for five seconds and you—you—"

Mary's heart sank. She had never seen him like this. All her bright, prepared words of appeasement vanished in a twinkling. She stood uncertainly with dry lips and pain inside.

"I love you and you love *me*!" he stated flatly. "No!" he barked sharply. "Don't even try to deny it. What came over you? Couldn't you wait even a few weeks for me? *Why*, Mary? *Why* did you do it?" Despair filled his voice.

Mary closed her eyes, shook her head, bit her lip and half lifted her left hand. His eyes moved then, widened with shock. Suddenly he took a step nearer and snatched her hand, lifting it, his eyes hot with anger at the large diamond.

"So that's it!" he snarled down at her. "You let yourself be bought!"

Mary flinched at his contempt. "No, it wasn't that at all!" she cried in protest.

"Before I left, you had promised yourself to me, then along come the Noyens with their wealth and—!"

"No!" Mary shouted back at him striving to maintain her dignity, to defend herself and not to let him see how he could still affect her emotions. "Anyhow, it's the female's prerogative to change her mind!"

Victor refused to listen to her defence. "I never thought it of you!" he said with heavy contempt. "Bribed by wealth! You were more than willing to be mine but that odious, old woman lifts her finger, flashes a large diamond and gets you bowing and scraping to her!" he accused hotly.

Mary snatched her hand away. "That's a rotten thing to say and it's not true either!" she retorted wildly. "I'm not for sale to anyone whether it be you, Duret or Louise Noyen. If you must know, on the day I left you, there was news that Duret had been wounded. I went to France with Tante. I had no time to think or plan. It was all a whirlwind rush and nightmare."

He maintained a stony silence, more deeply hurt than he cared to show. It had not entered his head Louise Noyen would use the power of her money and to think Mary had fallen for this!

"Duret was buried alive," Mary told him with a rush of words. "I had to go to him."

"Serves him right for going in the first place," he shot back at her caustically. "But you still didn't have to marry him!"

Mary flinched again. She could feel her own temper starting to rise. He was being totally unreasonable. What was done, was done; nothing could change it.

"Tante asked me my intentions. She knew all about us, incidentally."

That shocked him. "How?" he barked at her.

Mary shrugged. "What does it matter now?" she said slowly. "Perhaps if Duret had not been hurt—it was only through him that I came here and we bumped into each other. Duret needs me. You don't, Victor. You are the most self-sufficient person I've ever met and, anyhow, upon reflection, I don't think we would have made a good team." She paused, eyeing him honestly. "We could be a little to much alike. We would both want to lead. We would only fight together. That's not much of a basis for marriage."

"Rubbish!" he snorted.

"We are fire and flint," Mary pressed on remorselessly, knowing her words were true but wondering why she had not thought along these lines before. "We are indeed who you said we were."

He was puzzled for a few seconds, still too bitter to think coherently. He frowned heavily and waited.

"We are indeed Catherine and Heathcliff," Mary whispered sorrowfully.

"They both regretted their stupid actions," he shot back at her. "Heathcliff because he worshipped his Catherine and she? Her ghost could never rest. When she was dying as Linton's wife, she knew her error all right. She had chosen the milksop instead of the man, also bewitched by money and status! I know my Bronte, too!" His voice changed to a soft, persuading tone, "Don't you see, Mary? You are Catherine. You have married a weakling. I'm Heathcliff, tossed aside for money. For God's sake, girl, look at Noyen! I've heard about him. He is useless, a dreamer, soft and weak. He'll never be a real man. All your life you will have to carry him. Duret Noyen—" He grated a harsh laugh. "Linton was a manly fellow compared to Noyen!"

"Stop it, Victor!" she cried hotly. "It won't get you anywhere. I'm married now and a Noyen. We both have to live on this island. Surely we can do it in peace?"

He snorted wildly and shook his head with anger. "You don't ask much! You think I can live here and come across you often and not have feelings? Not think what could have been between us? Good God, girl! I'm flesh and blood. Not half-baked sawdust like that fool at Cobo!"

Mary felt the waves of his anger battering at her. She gritted her teeth. "I'd better go! This is getting us nowhere!"

"Damn your eyes, Mary Hinton!" he croaked, a catch in his voice. "You have done something to me that can never be put right except by you. From that first meeting you sank your nails into my heart and I'm trapped for as long as we both live. You expect me to stand back and accept that?" He pointed to her wedding band.

Mary's shoulders slumped. She should have known better than to come. "There's nothing else to say then, is there?" she said heavily.

She half turned and he grabbed an arm, his fingers iron. A wildness filled his dark blue eyes, which burned with incredible intensity. For the first time, Mary felt a twinge of alarm. They were quite alone and he was powerfully strong, driven by sexual desire and frustration coupled with the most intense hurt.

"You will always belong to me, Mary!" he hissed down at her. "You can stay married to that effete Noyen creature until hell freezes over but he will *never* own you. *I* do!" He halted to take a deep breath. "One day, sometime, somewhere, perhaps even in the distant future, I will come to you again and this time you will *not* refuse me. That is not just a prediction, but a solemn promise. Then you'll know what it's like to go to bed with a real flesh and blood man!" He released her suddenly. "Go on then! Go back to your boy husband. The wonder poet whom no one understands. Go back to that useless Noyen object and in the weeks and months and even years to come, you think back to this day and what I have said to you." His voice sank low. "But also know this, you have broken my heart in the process and I am being neither melodramatic nor maudlin. Neither was Heathcliff when he leaned from that open window for his ghostly Catherine and froze to death. Now get away from me!" and he gave her a savage push.

Mary was white, castigated by his words, which seared her soul with their passion and intensity. There was something godly about him as he stood with upright dignity and looked straight into her eyes. He waggled the fingers of one hand and dismissed her as if she were a menial then, turning, he strode to his cycle, swung it up, mounted and pedalled savagely back down the lane.

Mary watched him disappear, one hand to her mouth as the tears welled up to flood down both her cheeks. She had never dreamed their meeting could end like this. Those hot, fiery words of his—she flinched inwardly, knowing them to be the most truthful ever hurled at her. She gulped as he vanished from sight.

She stumbled down to her cycle, hardly able to see for tears and fumbled, lifting it from the hedge, then turned and looked down the lane with a miserable expression. Sam stepped into view. The trap had been hidden around the back of a cottage whose owner he knew and Sam himself had been tucked into the hedge from which he'd had an excellent view.

"Sam!" Mary gasped.

He stepped up to her and rested one hand on her left shoulder.

"He's gone, my dear," Sam said slowly. "And you?"

Mary hastily collected her wits, her forehead puckering as her mind raced, then she scowled suddenly.

"Tante sent you!" she accused hotly. "She planned it all!"

Sam made no comment. He had approved of the mistress's

prudence and the cob had never been shod so quickly in all his life.

"Oh!" Mary cried. "As if I needed a bodyguard!"

Her cheeks flamed with anger. "I will *not* have Tante setting a watch upon me!" she protested angrily. "I can look after myself and, anyhow, Victor will never hurt me!"

"That's as maybe," Sam replied quietly.

"That interfering old woman!"

"Her intentions are only the best," Sam tried to placate.

"She thinks she owns me! Wait till I get home. I'll have a few things to say myself!"

Sam hesitated, then decided to change the subject, hoping Mary would cool down. "How did he take it?" he asked bluntly.

Mary's face fell. "He hated it!" she said slowly.

"How do you feel about him now?" Sam persisted gently.

Mary looked at him with sad eyes, then gave a deep sigh and shook her head. "I still feel the same about him but oh! don't worry, I'll be a loyal wife to my husband but I'll never have for him what's here for Victor!" and her right hand touched her heart. "If only it had all been different," she mused sadly.

Sam knew she had to know sometime and better the information came from him right now. On the cycle ride back she would have time to mull it over and, at the same time, it might cool her temper.

"He's flush now," he said quietly.

Mary looked at him sharply. "What do you mean?"

Sam shrugged. "It's fairly common knowledge so I suppose le Page himself talked but he's received more news from his advocate. His inheritance has been bigger than he ever dreamed."

"But how can that be? From what he told me—" Mary paused, thinking deeply.

"His father was a drunk, as he told you, but his adopted mother was shrewder than anyone gave her credit for. It all goes back to Sarah Martell who soon realised her son Michael, Victor's father, was a no-good wastrel. She took to her daughter-in-law who never had a baby who lived and when she legally adopted Victor as her son, the old woman's heart was touched. She also admired Lisa very much for putting up with Michael. Unknown to anyone but the two women, Sarah had money of her own. Quite a lot of money too and she settled it all upon Lisa in trust for life, the remainder to go to Victor upon Lisa's death. Old man le Page never knew a thing about it. Just as well too. He would only have bullied Lisa for drinking money."

Mary considered this. "So Victor will come into an inheritance after all? He won't be poor any more?"

Sam shook his head. "He'll end up a man of substance, you mark my words."

"But I'm surprised that Victor talked about this," Mary murmured thoughtfully.

Sam pulled a face. "After he'd received the letter he became cockahoop and told one or two people when he should have known better. He told them the money could not have come at a better time as he was getting married shortly to a wonderful girl."

"Oh no!" Mary groaned, half turning aside. Then she was hit by panic. "Did he—?"

Sam shook his head. "He had enough sense not to name names so your husband hopefully should not learn of a connection," Sam said carefully.

Mary had no words left. Now she could fully understand Victor's attitude. It wasn't simply she had gone to another man but also the fact that he now had money. Although his inheritance might not be quite the equal of the Noyen's standing, it was a drastic improvement on anything he had dared to envisage. He could give a wife security and comfort, fine clothes and a splendid home. If she had waited but a little longer; if only Duret had not been wounded. If she had not succumbed to Tante's syrupy words— Mary felt a knot of cold anger enclose her heart and squeeze viciously. Then her basic honesty returned. Tante had but presented certain facts to her. The ultimate decision, the final choice, had been left to her and she had made the wrong decision. She had taken the boy instead of the man and misery made her lower her head and bite her bottom lip.

She looked at Sam with swimming eyes. "I'll go home," she told him unhappily.

He looked at her with concern. Her expression had been so open he had followed her thoughts exactly. There was nothing he could do though but be there, as a friend, upon whose shoulders she could always lean.

Mary had regained her self-control by the time she returned home. Tante quivered with excitement, longing to know what had happened but one steady look at Mary's face stilled her questions. Later she turned to Sam.

"What did happen, Sam?"

He regarded her thoughtfully. He could understand her concern for the marriage; her need to know everything but there were limits. Further he did not exactly know himself what had been said. He did not really want to.

"I don't know," he said firmly, "And, if I did, I'd not tell you. It's not my business, Mistress, and neither is it yours!"

"Well!" Louise expostulated with anger. "I think it is my business and very much so!"

"Then go and find out from another source. You'll learn nothing from me and it's no good you coming the sergeant major with me either. I'm as ready to retire as stay on here, so now you make *your* choice!" Sam told her coldly.

Such defiance was enough to make Louise explode but she kept a curb on her temper. To lose Sam would be unthinkable. She regarded his stiff face. She read disapproval which did not unduly worry her. Whatever she had done, good or bad, had been for the benefit of the family which always came first.

"Oh!" she stuttered back at him. "Do as you like, Sam!"

"Yes, I intend to!" he told her evenly. "And I'll have no more bullying or wheedling of young Mary. She's a fine girl so just you let her alone and stop trying to manipulate everyone's lives to suit your own ends. When you make a mistake—and make them you certainly do—it's other people who have to clear up your messes. Sometimes you are the most pigheaded old woman on this island and you deserve a good slap. The trouble with you, Mistress, is that Danny spoiled you and let you have your own way too much!"

"He did no such thing!" Louise protested hotly, stung with indignation.

"I mean what I say!" Sam warned her coldly. "You put one toe nail over the line and I'm off!"

Louise glowered at him. She would love to tell him to go but did not quite dare. If Sam went so would Emily and, she thought uneasily, there would be trouble from Mary too who adored her island "grandfather".

Sam waited for a riposte, then when one did not come, knowing he had won a victory, he turned on his heels and strode away, grimly satisfied in one sense but deeply uneasy in another. It was unnatural for her to yield and Sam knew, only too well, the depth and scope of her scheming mind.

There was an uneasy lull for exactly two weeks. For Mary they were hard days. Fortunately Duret was not highly perceptive and as long as she gave him comfort, in and out of bed, her husband was calm. With the regular medication, the horrendous nightmares did not recur and Mary hoped he would eventually grow out of them.

Two weeks later Mary and Duret strolled down to the cottage to admire Tante's new garden. The weeds and rubble had been ruthlessly removed by Duret and Sam, and already the small front plot gave evidence of being capable of producing a mass of summer bedding plants. The war news was getting better, day by day, and slow hopes were rising that, this year of 1918, the appalling slaughter would end.

Between Sam and Louise there was a truce. They were perfectly civil to each other though slightly stand-offish. Mary wondered why they had quarrelled but had no intention of asking while Duret had no idea there was an atmosphere. Sometimes at night, before she fell asleep, Mary could not help but wonder about Victor. Was he still on the island? What was he going to do with his life? She suspected Sam would eventually bring news to her and she was uncertain whether she wanted to learn anything more.

Sam arrived with the trap after a trip to town. He came up the path to where the three of them stood discussing which flowers should go where. Sam handed over one lot of groceries and fish he had bought in the market. Those for the house he would take back with the trap when he stabled the cob.

"I've a couple of bits of news," he said to no one in particular.

Three heads turned to him. Sam flashed a hard look at Louise who, in turn, shot one at Duret. It really was providential Duret could be slow on the uptake because Louise's senses flared at what was coming.

"I've heard young le Page was married yesterday," Sam stated flatly, carefully not looking at Mary.

"Who's he?" Duret asked curiously.

Mary winced, took a deep breath and gazed at Sam. Louise threw her a look then asked the question for both of them.

"Who is the girl?"

"She's from Alderney. Nicole Oselton," Sam replied evenly. "Seems he met her when he was there on some working assignment."

"Bit quick, wasn't it?" Louise asked shrewdly.

Sam lifted his eyebrows, flashing a look at Mary and Louise had the grace to blush.

"The other news is that le Page was at the Greffe yesterday morning."

"What!" Louise gasped.

Mary looked at Duret not understanding. "What's that?" she hissed at him but Sam answered for her.

"It's our Land Registry Office," he explained. "The registrar himself is called the Greffier."

"For what purpose, do you know, Sam?" Louise shot at him.

"Rumour has it, he's bought himself a small hotel."

"Good God!" Louise exclaimed, genuinely astonished. "With what?" she wanted to know next.

"With a very considerable inheritance from his mother's estate. Young le Page is now a man of consequence on this island and some say he's going a long way too because he's also bought some land down in the south for tomatoes."

"Has he indeed!" Louise said, taken aback for once. She knew nothing of the Jersey side of young le Page; it had certainly never entered her head there was money there. She pursed her lips. Thank God this had not all come to light before Duret's wounding. If Mary had known, her bait of the Noyen wealth would have fallen on very stony ground. Her mind hunted for any trouble this news could make. She did not make the mistake of looking at Mary though she could feel her eyes on her, hot and challenging. Louise had been wrong. So had Mary. The only person to benefit was Duret and he stood quietly, baffled by the conversation but not particularly bothered at trying to understand it all. Somewhere two lines of poetry kept clashing in his mind and he itched to retire to the study, to put the words on paper and examine them.

"Why tomatoes as well as an hotel?" Louise asked at last.

That puzzled Mary too. Sam looked at them in turn and shrugged. It was obvious to him.

"Alderney people farm, don't they?" he asked. "I guess it's to give his wife an independent interest until the children arrive on the scene. Anyhow, tomatoes give a good income and the market will expand once the war ends."

Louise nodded sagely to herself. She too had been thinking along those lines. Not only was there a market in England but there would be a second in France. With all the land churned up by war, it would take a considerable time for the French farmers to re-establish themselves. Ever an opportunist, she had decided now was a good time to sell her quarry half share and, with the Noyen land, establish glasshouses.

Mary was quietly staggered with what Sam had related. She was also uneasy. Somewhere deep in her heart, she had hoped that Victor would leave the island and return to Jersey. Why hadn't he? She knew it was because of her. *She* was the magnet who kept him on Guernsey and suddenly the future looked worrisome.

PART TWO—1923

SIX

MARY FINISHED TURNING up the hem and stopped to run her hand lovingly over the treadle sewing machine. She was no seamstress but she enjoyed simple sewing jobs. Her fingers slid under the machine and she felt the comforting strip of tape with its indentations. The diamonds were safely hidden and she wondered if a day would come when they must be exchanged for hard cash.

She pushed her chair back and stood to look out of the window. She had two children now and should be deliriously happy but she was not. In the five years she had been on the island, she had integrated well and knew many people. England was only a memory and Mary considered herself an islander first and English very much second.

If only her life could have been with Victor because Duret had become a dreadful disappointment. Victor's prophecy had turned out accurate. Duret was not just a dreamer, he was also weak without an original thought in his head. His sole interest appeared to be the poetry he wrote which was still beyond Mary's understanding. Sometimes she wondered if Duret was two men in one. He ate the meals provided and shared her bed. He took some interest in their children but, without warning or apparent reason, he would wander off with notebook and pencil. Where he went, Mary neither knew not cared. Her initial liking for her husband had slowly changed to boredom and indifference. Even his sexual advances had declined since her last pregnancy.

That was a point on which she resolved to do something. Two children were enough especially if she added a husband as a potential third. If Tante would not advise her, Mary knew women in St Peter Port who would. She was fluent in patois now, which knowledge had opened many humble doors to her.

These days Victor was often in her thoughts with bittersweet memories. He had done well for himself displaying a business flair which, Mary knew, impressed Tante. His hotel was not large but its site was excellent and Victor was energetic and persuasive. He travelled regularly to England and she knew it was there he advertised his hotel. Certainly his clientele gave him customers nearly all year.

His wife handled their small tomato business which provided another income and Mary realised they were quite affluent. It was Sam who kept them informed as Tante, now starting to show her age, rarely went far. Sam admired Victor le Page but Tante Louise still retained her hostility though Mary was amused to note that she always listened intently when Sam returned with his gossip.

There were times when Mary guessed Tante would like to get to know this grandson better but was too proud to admit it.

The Noyen glasshouses were reasonably extensive and the cows had long gone so the fields could be utilised. Ostensibly, Duret worked there with Raoul Ozanne who, with his wife Amelia, had moved into an empty fisherman's cottage in their parish. Raoul's sister Gwen assisted Emily in the home now and again trotting down to Tante's when extra help was needed.

Mary concentrated upon domestic duties but also kept a watchful eye upon their books and accounts. Her natural flair for this work meant the purse strings had moved into her hands. She consulted Tante now and again on small matters and knew she would never take a large decision without getting Louise's shrewd opinion.

Although the years had advanced on Louise ruthlessly, there was nothing wrong with her mind. She was still bright with a sharp tongue, quite capable of being caustic when the situation warranted. True to her word though, she never interfered with the big house. Sometimes Mary guessed she itched to manipulate, order and instruct and it amused Mary to see in what check Tante had to hold her tongue.

Mary liked Tante now but her real affection was for Sam Mahy. This was reciprocated until she felt like his blood grandchild. Many a summer evening she and Sam would sit in companionable silence, contemplating the glasshouses. Mary had an affinity with Sam, impossible to have with Duret. There were days when Mary wondered uneasily if she and Duret were heading inexorably towards some dreadful showdown.

Victor le Page appeared to be happily married to his Alderney wife who had given him twins, a boy and a girl. Mary had seen her a few times in the market but they had never spoken. Nicole appeared like a timid waif who lacked a will of her own but Mary told herself this had to be impossible. Victor would want a companion who was his equal, not a doormat, so she often wondered if there were depths to Nicole unknown to her.

Mary knew she still carried a torch for Victor but equally knew that there was nothing she could do about it. Not that that stopped her heart from pounding whenever she happened to spot him in town.

She heard Margaret's voice and looked to one side. This was the credit side of marriage with Duret. This first child had come within ten months of their wedding and Mary had sailed through her pregnancy and confinement with what Tante called indecent ease for a first child. There was the same strong will without nerves or fear. Margaret had fair, curly hair and blue eyes that were as light as a summer cornflower. She was a sturdy child, sure of herself, able to wind Sam and Tante around her fingers, though more in awe of her mother.

Mary could not work out how Margaret viewed her father. It was true he only spoke kindly to her but Mary sometimes wondered if Duret really knew he had offspring. When her husband retreated into a brown study he was unreachable.

William was another matter entirely and her face stiffened because her son she did not like one jot. He had entered the world in a screaming rush of temper, red-faced with anger at being hurled from his comfortable nest in the womb. He had brown eyes and a dark mop of hair and when Mary put him to her breast that first day, she had felt a peculiar wave of something distasteful. Her instinct had been to thrust the child back at the midwife and deny him. His frantic howls of anger and writhing squeals of temper seemed aimed at her alone.

William bore no resemblance to anyone she knew. Many a time Mary stared at him and wondered at her dislike. Even Tante, despite her longing for a male great grandson, had looked long and hard at him, thrown an odd look at Mary and made no attempt to pick him up and cuddle him as she had done with Margaret.

"Mary?" a voice called and she turned as Tante entered the sewing room.

"You shouldn't have climbed all these stairs!"

Tante grunted and sat down on the nearest chair. "I know, I know, I'm getting old but I had to come and see you. I wanted some exercise," she explained.

Mary eyed her thoughtfully. She couldn't last remember when Tante had invited herself along. She looked at her dubiously. Old Louise had a set expression to her face that bordered on grimness.

Mary pulled up a chair to face her. "What is it?" she asked gently.

Louise grunted and looked deep into Mary's questioning eyes. "Can you now read me so well? I don't think I like that," she complained.

Mary sensed she was playing for time or hunting for the correct words. She sat back in her chair and waited patiently.

"It's William!" Tante said suddenly. "I don't like that child!"

Mary's eyebrows shot up. "That makes two of us then," she replied softly.

Now it was Tante's turn to be surprised. The old lady frowned heavily, bit her bottom lip, shook her head minutely and muttered.

"It's my fault, I should have spoken to you long ago but no one likes to display their dirty washing in public."

Mary had to show a tiny smile. "I'm family, not public," she chided.

Tante gave a deep sigh and reached out one age spotted hand to touch Mary's.

"It's odd really. You know about my daughter Christine. What a wild, impossible child she was but she was not evil. She was though unlike all the other Penford females. In the past, they've been the ones to hold the family together through thick or thin with no quarter asked or given. The men, though, that's been another story. Somewhere Christine became an impossible mix."

"You're talking riddles, Tante!"

"I suppose I am but you see, down through the generations, the Penford women have been the remarkable ones. Three of them lived to ninety years and they were ruthless when the need arose. From what I learned as a child from my father, they killed too for the family name—and got away with it."

"No!"

Tante nodded vigorously. "While in the men there has always been an evil strain which comes out unexpectedly in a generation. I think Christine must have been a breeding mongrel."

"What about these Penford women and men? Who were they?"

"Let me see. There was Emma who died when she was ninety. She was my great, great, great grandmother and never married. I don't know exactly why. The male Penford who tried to blight her life was Philip, who was an offshoot. Before Emma there was Anne who also lived to ninety years. From stories handed down she was a very tough character and the bad Penford blood there was her own son who murdered his father."

"What!"

"Before Anne there was Sarah who also died at ninety. There are family tales that she was some kind of spy in the civil wars. What I'm driving at is that some of the Penford females are matriarchal and live to a great age but they have to carry the honour of the family on their shoulders and quite alone. While the evil Penford men do their best to wreck this." Tante paused to catch her breath and eye Mary sharply.

She returned the look. "Are you hinting about my son?" she asked flatly.

"Yes!" was Tante's blunt reply. "I know it sounds madness but from the moment I looked down on William on the day he was born, I felt something uneasy just here," and she touched her heart.

Mary compressed her lips and averted her gaze. She gave a deep sigh before turning back to her companion.

"I didn't want to nurse him," Mary admitted slowly. "I felt as if I'd like to send him back somewhere but he's here and my son. I must admit I cannot feel for him like I do for Margaret. There is something about him which bothers me. It's ridiculous to have this feeling for a small child. Yet—" She halted uncertainly.

"It's instinct," Tante told her bluntly. "I think you've bred a bad one in William. You'll always have to watch him. You should have another child or perhaps even two more so—"

"No!" Mary said sharply.

Tante heard vehemence in her tone and she cocked her head aside slightly. "Aren't things all right with you and Duret?"

Mary's shoulders slumped miserably. "We don't row, if that's what you mean," she admitted, "but there is some void now. All Duret thinks about is that poetry of his and since he had two poems published, he's worse. He does nothing but moon about the place. I sometimes wonder just how much work he does in the glasshouses. Is Raoul carrying him? I feel at times as if I have to be both parents at once and it's not fair," she said hotly.

Tante was appalled. "What do you intend to do?" Louise asked quietly. She had not guessed matters had reached this stage.

"Do? Do? What can I do?" Mary cried with frustration. "I'd like to give Duret a kick up the arse," she said crudely. "He exasperates me beyond all patience!"

Tante was deeply shocked. This situation was far worse than she had envisaged when she had set out to have a quiet talk with Mary about the children.

"I suppose all I can do is hide my feelings and try to be extra loving to William," Mary mused heavily.

"What about Duret though?" Louise asked with worry. "Have you talked to him and told him your feelings?"

Mary threw her a look. "I can't be bothered," she explained. "Anyhow, it would be like talking to a brick wall if Duret is in one of his moods."

"Does he still have those nightmares?"

Mary shook her head. "Only occasionally now. He seems to have grown out of them with the doctor's pills but sometimes—" She paused uneasily.

"Sometimes what?"

"He looks at me queerly," Mary explained. "It's as if he wonders who I am and what I'm doing in the house," she replied then looked at the old lady sharply. "I don't think Duret is all there."

"You mean—he is mentally sick?"

Mary nodded. For a few moments the silence hung heavily and Louise's round shoulders slumped unhappily. She realised Mary had put into blunt words what she had long suspected and about which she had never allowed herself to think too much. It hit her that perhaps she had done Mary a grievous wrong all those years ago. Although she did not get out much there was little she missed on the island through contacts. What if Mary had married Victor le Page? It seemed the Penford blood ran strong and true in him, even if he had come from the wrong side of the blanket. She wondered if May knew the extent of her earlier plotting? She muttered to herself and remembered Sam's words about meddling. With a grunt, she forced herself to sit straight.

"Part of your trouble, girl, is you're spending too much time in this house instead of getting out and about. Gwen looks after the children. Emily sees to the house. You must get the book work done in the mornings. When did you last go on your cycle? It's high time you wandered again!" she stated flatly.

Mary looked out of the window. She could hear Margaret's laugh and a squeal from William. Fortunately the two of them played well together but whether this would last as William grew was a moot point. If she did have a third child, would this help the situation? The thought of letting Duret make love to her again stuck in her throat.

"You're right!" she said with sudden briskness. "And there's no time like the present. I'll walk you back to your cottage, pump up my tyres and go out for a spin."

"I'm capable of walking myself back, thank you. I'm not decrepit yet!" Louise told her tartly. "Anyhow, I want to have a chat with Emily and Sam. You get yourself out, Mary and blow some of this house's cobwebs away from your mind."

Mary pedalled briskly, breathing deeply. The air carried the salty tang from the sea and, with the sun overhead, she realised Louise had been right. She had spent too much time indoors.

The tide was coming in but there was only the gentlest of winds and the waves were barely more than a ripple. She looked at the sea. The many sharp, black rocks were already hidden and this never ceased to awe her. How many unwary ships in the past must have come to grief on this treacherous coastline? Who would think that under the sea lurked death?

She cycled on, then decided to turn inland and travel though the high-hedged country lanes. They were exceedingly narrow but gave tranquillity and Mary admitted Tante was correct. Too much time spent indoors brooding about her husband was bad for morale. As to William, she had already made up her mind about him. If he was the recipient of the notorious male Penford bad blood, it would be up to her to guide him down the straight and narrow path of respectability and common sense. Any child could be trained though she guessed this might well stretch her patience to the limit. Perhaps rubbing shoulders with Margaret would help because upon Duret she knew she could not rely.

She topped a rise, then let her legs rest as the cycle began to freewheel with gathering speed.

The lane's surface was rough and her tyres jolted but she laughed; this was great fun. Suddenly, approaching the next corner, her ears heard an ominous sound. Frantically she applied her brakes but she was going much too fast. The cycle flew around the corner, heading straight at the car. In wild panic Mary jerked her handlebars to one side, grimaced and closed her eyes in fright.

The cycle clipped the car's wing, veered right off course and Mary shot from the saddle. She flew through the air and landed heavily against the hedge bottom while the cycle crashed in a grating tangle of noise.

Mary landed with all the breath knocked from her lungs. She struggled to breathe, conscious some nettles had stung her leg where her skirt had ridden up. She lay still for a few seconds, striving to regain her wits while her eyes registered a shocked beetle two inches from her nose.

Frantically she struggled to sit up. She quickly realised nothing was broken but was acutely aware she must look an awful sight for all the world to see. Her knickers showed clearly and a man's laugh rang through the air.

"Well!" he guffawed. "At last I can see your lovely bottom!"

Mary screwed her head around, cheeks a vivid red with embarrassment. Victor le Page stood with hands on his hips, face creased in amusement as he realised she was unhurt. Her eyes took in a debonair jacket and grey trousers with shoes to match and a crisp, white shirt, open at the neck.

"Don't just stand there like an idiot!" she shouted. "Help me up!"

"Temper! Temper!" he teased. "Where is the calm maturity which comes with motherhood?"

Mary scrabbled wildly, trying to regain her feet and pull her skirt down at the same time. Tears of humiliation and rage showed.

"You have lovely legs, Catherine!"

"Don't call me that!" she raged. "I'm Madam Noyen to you!"

"Tut-tut!" he rebuked. "Show manners or I'll not help!"

"Oh! Damn your eyes, Victor le Page!"

He grinned down at her, enjoying this unexpected situation. Her face was poppy coloured from hairline to neck. Every hair bristled with fury and he let his eyes slide down her lower half. Despite all his hard work, Victor had never been able to forget her. His deep hurt and anguish at her marriage, had evaporated, yet jealousy was never far away whenever he saw Duret Noyen. Some days he itched to attack him and seize what was really his.

Never had Mary looked more desirable and he felt himself harden with natural desire. He extended his hand and unceremoniously hauled her upright, then pulled her into his arms. He knew he would never have a better chance. Certainly Nicole was incapable of arousing him like this.

"Let me go!" Mary spat at him.

He bent his head and kissed her ferociously, ramming his erection against her body then he pulled back, his eyes wild and glowing with intensity.

Mary churned with wrath and humiliation, yet his lips crammed against hers stilled immediate resistance. When she opened her

120

mouth, his tongue probed impatiently. With a sharp stab from her conscience she tried to jerk free but his arms were iron bands.

With a violent contortion, she wriggled, brought one shod foot down on his, kicked his ankle and, as he winced, jerked upwards to knee him in the groin. Another backwards leap freed her.

"You miserable, uncouth, ill bred, degenerate boor!" she spat at him.

"Why you hell cat! It's time a real man tamed you!"

"Only a madman would drive through these lanes so fast. You shouldn't bring a car along them in the first place!" she yelled. "Look what you've done to my cycle."

"There's nothing wrong with it that a bit of paint won't put right!" he bellowed back with frustration.

"Get out of my way! I'm going home!" Mary shouted at him, bending to lift the cycle erect, prop it against the hedge and examine it.

"You're going nowhere until I've made you mine!" he growled and grabbed her again.

"Let me go or I'll scream and scream!"

"Go ahead! There's no one around to hear you! It's uninhabited!"

Without further ceremony, he pulled her back to his car, fumbled for the rear door and tumbled her inside. Mary kicked and bit savagely, aware she was weak against his powerful strength. This was no compliant Duret. There was a look on Victor's face which chilled her blood.

"Victor—don't!"

He slammed the door shut and, halting momentarily in his car's large bench seat, looked down at her then, one hand holding her face steady, he kissed her again while the other commenced a deliberate exploration. Mary wriggled and struggled to bite him, her lips were imprisoned while suddenly, unexpectedly, his skilful fingers sent electric shocks through her system.

"Victor—" She tried again but his lips silenced her while a hand skilfully stripped her knickers away with a savage jerk.

Mary stilled. She had never experienced anything like the feelings which surged through her body as it responded to his foreplay. She held her breath, lay still and looked into his eyes as he paused from kissing.

"I want you, Mary. I must have you! By God! I'm only flesh and blood!"

"Victor!" she whispered, memorised by him now and her hands met behind his strong neck.

He eased his clothing aside, then turned on to her but now he played her body as if a fine instrument. His fingers caressed and stroked, lifted her up then dropped her down until he felt her quivering with anticipation. Only then did he enter, taking his time, anxious to please her, keen to demonstrate his masculine superiority.

Time stood still for Mary. She knew perfectly well she could have resisted and escaped to freedom but their coming together at long last was like something preordained. It was so good, so right and had been so delayed.

"Victor!" she murmured.

"Mary!" he crooned back.

They climaxed together and their let-down afterwards was slow and gentle. Sweat streamed from his face as he half sat, worried his weight might be too much.

"My sweet, wild sea witch of Sarnia," he whispered. "Why has it taken so long? I love you. Only you," he whispered and stroked a cheek.

"Oh Victor!" she murmured. "I should never have married Duret."

"Divorce him," he said quickly. "I'll divorce Nicole and we'll leave the island."

She was sorely tempted but slowly shook her head. "The children," she said with a catch in her voice. "They would be the sufferers. We can't do that. Anyhow, on what grounds could either of us get a divorce when we are the guilty parties?"

"Let's just run!" he tempted.

Mary sighed as tears truckled down her cheeks. "Don't!" she begged him. "You know we can't do that. Too many innocents will suffer. I made a mistake, now it must be paid for," she cried as the tears flooded.

He took her in his arms and pulled her skirt down. They had been crazy, he realised. Someone *might* have come along the lane. His blood chilled for her. Gossip would crush her spirit and he gritted his teeth with anguish. Dear God, was there no escape for them?

"What can we do?" he asked. He knew they could never get back to the status quo after this and the thought of going to bed with Nicole this evening galled him. He knew Mary was right though. He could do nothing to hurt a wife whose only crime was to be innocent and trusting. He also had his children to consider and he loved them very much. "Are we trapped then?"

Mary managed to halt her tears and look into his eyes. She nodded feebly. His lips were set and his jaw jutted pugnaciously.

"I'll not give you up now," he grated.

Mary took a deep breath. "You'll have to," she told him sadly. "Fate is simply against us."

"I'll not have it! I can't!" he told her wildly.

Mary sat up and swung her legs down, retrieving her torn knickers and pushing them into her skirt's pocket. She touched his hand, stroking his large fingers.

"You'll have to and so will I!"

He swore lustily, scowled and lowered his gaze. Mary studied him with sad eyes. She knew it was no good and that she must be the strong one for both of them.

"I must go," she said simply.

He jerked his head up. "I'll run you back. The cycle can go on the roof!"

"No!" she cried, panicking at the thought. "You mustn't!"

"Why not?" he growled unreasonably. How could he simply let her pedal away from him now they had both declared themselves? He felt like keeping her in his private prison. The idea she would go back to the house and Noyen was too much to stomach.

"It's time I went to Cobo and made my number," he grated. "It's time my grandmère looked at me as a man and not some kind of bandit. It's time—!"

"Victor! Don't make it harder for me. I live there, remember?" she said gently.

He went stiff and cold. What could she mean? "Noyen? Does he hurt you? Has he hit you? If so—"

Mary stifled an hysterical giggle. "Duret is incapable of hurting a fly because he's nearly always on cloud nine but if you do turn up, with me, you might get him thinking straight for once and that I *can* do without. Then there's Tante Louise. She's a very old lady. Don't you dare to give her a heart attack which would only put another burden on my back. To say nothing of my two children. Be patient, Victor. I'm sure one day Tante will come around. She always stops what she's doing to listen to gossip about you," she baited cunningly.

"Does she?" and he studied her, noting her large, anxious eyes and quivering lips. Did this sea witch really understand how much he loved her? Nicole had only ever had a portion of his heart and he was honest enough to know that, after today, it would be exceedingly difficult to allow her that much. Mary was correct though. How could he hurt his twins and perhaps do something to lose them. Dear God! Was there no way out of this trap? His commonsense gave him the obvious answer.

"All right, I'll not come—yet," he promised. "I have to go over to the mainland on business and possibly even make a few trips during the rest of this year. Next year is another matter though. One day I'm coming to Cobo and I'll insist upon meeting that stubborn, opinionated grandmère of mine, come hell or high water."

"Victor, thank you," Mary whispered, then, standing on tiptoes, kissed him gently. "Now I really must go. I'll have to make some excuse like I came off the cycle because of a stone but I must make it sound authentic. Tante Louise may be old but there is nothing at all wrong with her mind."

"Mary!"

"Don't!" she begged. "We've had a wild, wonderful hour. Let's treasure it," she pleaded. "Don't do anything rash to spoil such a memory. Please, Victor!"

He cursed then. Long and strong, with a rush of words she'd never heard before but, bowing his head and gritting his teeth, he let her go. It was the hardest decision he'd made in his life and he asked himself how could he possible stand life on Guernsey now? He knew he would though just because Mary was *there*.

SEVEN

MARY SAT AT her desk and ignored the account books. Her eyes were riveted on the calendar and carefully she recounted. For the third time she reached the same total and a heavy stone lodged in her stomach. It couldn't possibly be true yet her mind told her it was. Never in her life had her period been delayed and this repeated calculation showed she was over two weeks late.

Dear God, she told herself. She was pregnant with Victor's child and she and Duret had not had sex for months. Her heart quailed as her mind raced seeking an escape which would be plausible. The first frantic thought was to see Victor and tell him, then commonsense prevailed. Victor's reaction would be only too obvious. He would insist upon a divorce. With their current matrimonial laws, the only way this could be achieved would be with an open admission of their joint adultery.

She shivered slightly. It was not simply the open scandal which would be the end product of Victor's action but the knowledge she might well lose her children. Duret would have every right to fight for sole custody and, she told herself grimly, Tante would aid and abet him in this.

Tante's scorn would be too awful for words. Her contempt for Victor would descend upon Mary's shoulders. She could well be thrown out of the Noyen home and, despite Victor's grandiose schemes, both of them would end up in an awful mess. Certainly Victor's reputation as an upstanding hotelier would crash abysmally to start with. Nicole would, no doubt, obtain custody of the twins and Victor doted on his children. It was even possible they might be hounded from the island which did have strait-laced views at times.

No, she told herself firmly. Victor could not be told. Indeed it would be imprudent for him even to know. Whether he might suspect at some time in the future was a hurdle she would have to leap then.

Her mind switched to her husband. There was only one sensible escape route from her predicament but the idea revolted her. It was not simply the fact she was indifferent to Duret or was contemptuous but the idea of allowing him to make love to her stuck in her throat. There was also the additional problem of their relationship.

For weeks now the coolness between them had escalated to the point where they exchanged few words and these were but the necessary domestic ones to retain marital harmony for the children's sake. It had been at the back of Mary's mind to talk to Raoul and ascertain just how much work Duret did in the glasshouses. She could not do this now. If Duret got the idea in his head that his wife was spying on him, he would become more difficult.

Yet she must bridge the gap somehow. Was their estrangement her fault? Was it her personality which had changed her liking for Duret to indifference? She swallowed uneasily. She had to do something. Duret must make love to her but, once started did that mean his sexual floodgates would be unleashed? How could she cope—after Victor?

Mary took a deep breath and admonished herself sternly. She must find again her old liking for Duret. At least, she told herself, it would only be for two months. Once she could tell Duret she was pregnant, he would act the gentleman and move into the spare room as he had for her previous pregnancies. Even then, the baby's birth would have to be premature to fool Tante.

She sat back in her chair, lips tight, and weighed up the pros and cons of her situation. It was always the female who paid the price yet warmth flooded her heart as she remembered. How wonderful and glorious it had been.

Mary allowed herself a day-dream of life with Victor, wallowing in a heavy dose of self-pity. She sniffed as she felt tears hovering but, with a great sigh, regained self-control. All her energies had to be focused upon Duret and, biting her lip, she weighed up this need.

There were many evenings when Duret was out. She had no idea where he went or with whom. She considered another woman and rejected this idea out of hand. Gossip of that nature would have reached Tante by now. Anyway, Mary had a shrewd idea that Duret was not highly sexed. It had occurred to her that his medicine might have something to do with this so her seduction was going to be difficult.

How to go about this without arousing Duret's suspicions? Although she had been truthful when she told Tante she thought her husband was, perhaps, mentally unsound, that did not mean Duret was an absolute idiot. A fool could not write poetry, she reminded herself.

She puzzled and pondered the problem, attacking it from all angles. A tiny idea surfaced. She seized it, examined it from top to bottom, then gave a shrug. It was not brilliant but the best she could come up with at such short notice.

Immediately she stood, left the room and went upstairs to her dresser. Inside the left-hand drawer was the poetry Duret had written to her from France. It was providential she had kept this. Now she withdrew the work, written on lined notebook paper and examined it. It did not rhyme; neither did it make sense but it had to mean something to her husband.

Without pausing, she lifted down an old, small photograph, quickly unfastened it and removed the sepia picture. It was one taken years ago of the rocks at Cobo which Tante had given her. In place of this she inserted Duret's dreadful poem, fastened the back then re-hung the whole on the wall at her side of their double bed. She shook her head. It all looked rather pathetic but what else could possibly grab Duret's attention for her; enough to make him sexually aroused?

She went about her work, played with the children and watched them carefully in the bath. Margaret was a jolly child when she was not having a temper tantrum. William, although only a toddler, was totally different. He was phlegmatic in his response to his sibling's antics. It was as if he surveyed Margaret from a lofty distance and Mary felt herself chill. William did not act like a normal child. There were no tantrums from him. When he did not get his own way he relapsed into silence or turned his back and ignored Margaret. Sometimes Mary wondered uneasily what might happen when William became bigger. Already she had the ridiculous feeling he was unreachable, no matter how much she talked to him or tried to play with him.

That evening, Duret was absent for their supper so with a heavy heart Mary went to their bedroom. She wore the prettiest nightgown she owned and waited Duret's return with considerable trepidation.

It was eleven before she heard his heavy tread up the stairs and her heart started to thunder. She hastily sat up in bed and half turned as Duret opened the door. There was a smile fixed on her face as he paused to look at her with surprise.

The last thing Duret had expected was his wife still awake and obviously waiting for him. Marriage had turned into an enigma for Duret. What exactly he had expected matrimony to bring he had not been sure. For the first year of their wedding, he had adored Mary with blind love and could see no wrong in her. Then Margaret had arrived upon the scene and Duret had felt himself pushed sideways for a time.

He did not resent this because he understood a baby must come first and he had been content to observe from a discreet distance. He liked the glasshouse work and got on well with Raoul but there were many days when he felt lonely. His interest in poetry was unshared by anyone except a small handful of like-minded young men. Even then, mixing with them had initially been hard work because Duret was very shy.

Many nights he wanted to turn to his wife and make love to her but he found difficulties. First she was nursing the baby and it was not done, so Mary had told him. Then there were the times of her periods. Other nights she had headaches from working so hard so, when he had managed to catch her unaware in their bed, he had been grateful to make love quickly in case he inconvenienced his wife.

No one had been more astonished than himself when William had arrived upon the scene. A son was very nice, indeed quite delightful, and Tante had been pleased with her grandson's efforts he thought. His wife was another matter. She was always so frantically busy which would have puzzled a man less ingenuous than Duret. That his wife made excuses to avoid contact in their bed never entered his head which, anyhow, was always filled with other matters. Duret had found himself new friends—young men, rougher than Tante would have approved, but fellows who looked up to him. They praised his poetry and asked his opinions.

He had enough sense to realise these men were not the kind to be welcomed by Grandmère but, suddenly, this was of little concern. He was a man and what he did in his spare time and where he went was his affair. What made the situation worse was the knowledge his wife had changed. It was as if she copied Grandmère whose awesome character could still make Duret quake in his boots.

Mary had become strong-minded, argumentative and bossy. Duret was well aware he was no match for her. He was far too pliant to stand up to a dogmatic Mary who would always be backed by a harder grandmère. So home became the place where he slept, had some of his meals, kept his possessions and that was all. He would chuck the children under their chins, talk some prattle to them but leave them to the women because females abounded in his home. Mary, Grandmère on her visits, Emily and Gwen. His sole masculine companionship at home was with Raoul who was far too devoted to growing tomatoes and grapes for Duret's taste. His real escape was with his new friends in the evenings and gradually his need for sex declined.

Mary took a deep breath. She *must* feel something for Duret or was she about to commence Act I of her play? "Duret!" she cried. "Doesn't it look nice?"

He entered the room, quietly shut the door and peered to where she pointed. His eyes opened wide with surprise. He eyed the framed poem then glanced at his wife as his heart swelled suddenly. His nostrils caught the aroma of some flowery perfume and he noted her pretty nightgown. Then he looked back at the poem which he remembered writing from the horrific trenches. He had considered it one of his best efforts.

"You framed it!" he marvelled softly.

"Yes!" Mary said in a soft voice. "I don't know why I didn't think of it before. I'm so proud of it and—" She let a second lie lay.

"You are?" he questioned, amazed and touched as he sank down gently on her side of the bed.

Mary inched over invitingly and smiled daintily at him. "Of course I am!" she told him stoutly. What a liar she was becoming! She felt a stab of conscience as she saw the pleasure in Duret's soft, brown eyes and felt her heart ache for him. He looked like the Duret of old again. "I bet there aren't many wives on this island who have husbands who are poets—and published ones to boot! I think you are so clever, Duret," she praised lavishly and crossed her fingers under the sheet. Dear God, what if he were more obtuse than usual.

Duret preened. He unfastened his shirt buttons and enjoyed the flow of admiration in his wife's eyes. For many months now,

Mary had been unavailable for one reason or the other. Dare he hope she would be amenable to him tonight because her gesture had aroused a rare sexual passion.

Switching off the light, Duret slid into bed and lay still a moment, almost shaking with trepidation then he let one hand explore. He felt Mary stretch like a contented cat and unrebuffed, he became bolder. It was going to be all right and his chest swelled with fresh pride.

Mary blessed the darkness. For a few seconds, she felt sick at heart as he touched her. She had a flashing vision of Victor's handsome face then she forced this away. Duret was her husband. It was up to her to regain what they had known on Sark. She studied his eyes and saw a fleeting anxiety mirrored then he moved over her and suddenly, she knew it was going to work and affection rose for him.

For the next few weeks Mary waited, calculating the time. Duret turned to her only infrequently, never more than once every ten days, for which she was grateful and also sad. There were days when she felt sorry for him. Was this a latent result of his war experience compounded by the pills which she insisted he still take? Gradually her old affection for him returned but it was with relief, when two months had passed, that she told him she thought she was pregnant again.

Duret promptly removed himself from her bed as any gentleman would and he resumed his habit of coming in late again, being extra quiet so as not to disturb his wife. He was solicitous when he was home during the day, which made Mary's conscience twang and her guilt swell.

Mary found it a struggle to hide unexpected morning sickness from Emily and only managed this by staying in her room an hour longer than normal, pleading excess fatigue from all the bookwork.

Victor was rarely far from her mind. She ached to see him but never mentioned his name, even to Sam. The older man could be as prescient as Tante and Mary was acutely aware her conduct would not sit well on Sam's shoulders. He was of the same generation as Tante, whose standards and morals were rigid and old-fashioned.

When she was three and a half month's pregnant she walked down to see Tante because now she could safely say she had missed two periods. The sooner Tante knew the better.

Tante Louise was quietly worried and had been so for many weeks. She had little housework to do as the cottage ran itself with Gwen's help. Thinking back, considering and debating, had started to fill her days, which she felt were horribly empty. She yearned to be up at the big house. At the same time, she often wondered what was going on there.

Mary seemed to have turned fickle and, working it all out, Louise was able to pinpoint exactly when this had started. It had begun on the day she had made Mary get out in the fresh air. Sam had told her later that Mary had returned, rather dishevelled with a torn skirt. It appeared she had come off her cycle when the front wheel hit a stone on rounding a bend too fast.

This had surprised the old lady. Mary was an expert at whizzing around their lanes on her cycle. To come off meant she must been day-dreaming badly. She had been lucky not to break her neck. Certainly from that moment she had changed.

The girl's mood oscillated like a quick moving pendulum. Some days when she saw her, Tante Louise had almost fancied Mary hugged some secret to herself. Then on the next day she would be sunk low and too depressed to talk. This had gone on for a few weeks until it seemed as if Mary was carrying the worries of the island on her shoulders.

There was also the matter of Mary's marriage. Exactly how bad was it? Louise would never countenance divorce. It was such a sordid affair and would bring total disgrace upon the family.

It crossed her mind to wonder if Victor le Page was at the bottom of everything but no gossip had reached her. Always, when arriving at this point, her confused, frustrated thoughts would simply go back to the start again.

"Hello! Tante! It's me!"

"Mary! Come in! I was just thinking about you," Louise said, then wished she'd not. What was the matter with her to blurt out something like a child? Guile was always better than frankness.

Mary entered the room and sat down, grinning at her. "I've some news for you," she started then paused.

Louise studied her and a tiny frown creased her forehead. She knew what a blossoming female indicated from years of experience.

"You're pregnant," she said quietly.

Mary was astounded then fear shot through her. "How on earth did you know? I thought I was going to surprise you," she made herself complain. "I've missed twice," she added carefully.

Now it was Louise's turn to be puzzled. From one sharp, raking look she would have estimated Mary was more advanced than that. The glow on the young wife's cheeks gave her an ethereal shine and surely there was something hidden in her eyes? They sparkled and Mary carried herself differently. If Louise hadn't known better, she would have sworn Mary had some incredible secret.

"Have you told Duret?" she asked quietly.

Mary nodded. "He's moved into the spare room again. He is very good at times like this," she replied and meant it. Mary suddenly felt ill at ease. Tante's eyes were narrow and penetrating and it took an effort of will for Mary to appear genuinely unconcerned. Inside she bubbled at the thought of Victor's child but she could only pray the baby would resemble her. It would be catastrophic if the baby took after his father. She might fool Duret but never Tante Louise. There was still the time difference to explain when the baby came but she had already made that

134

decision. She would have a stumble on the stairs and just hope no one would realise the baby was a full-term one.

Tante was troubled. Her instinct told her something was not quite right but she was unable to put a finger on what it was. She took a deep breath. She would think it all out later.

"I'm pleased," she said in a soft voice. "Do you want a boy or a girl?"

"I don't care as long as the baby is healthy with all its bits and pieces," Mary told her truthfully.

How she would love this child. Her very own love child! Her precious secret kept from the whole world. It flashed through her mind that perhaps Victor would also do his sums but as long as she denied his questions, there was nothing he could do as long as he did not catch her alone. That, Mary knew, would be fatal. Victor was astute enough to see through the lies she could use successfully on Duret and hopefully, on Tante.

"Congratulations, my dear!" Tante told her. "I'm so glad it's all worked out again with you and Duret," she paused. "The trouble is, it's usually the woman who has to wheedle the man around. To a sharp woman, that's something easily arranged with careful planning and you, my dear girl, are clever as well as sharp."

Mary gave a tine twitch of one hand. What on earth did Tante mean by that? Surely she could not suspect anything? While she kept an even smile on her face, Mary's mind raced. Was Tante making an educated guess which she did not dare to put into words? She kept her mouth shut tight and refused to rise to any potential lure.

"Now I've told you, I'll be getting back," she said smoothly as she stood. "I've left the children with Gwen but Margaret's so mischievous I don't know how long her patience will last."

"What about William?"

Mary stilled and gave Louise a steady stare. "William is as good as gold," she replied. "He's never in any mischief even allowing for the fact he's younger than Margaret. William seems to keep himself to himself," she challenged calmly.

Tante gave a grunt that could have meant anything. "Long may it stay that way."

Louise went outside with Mary and they both studied the garden filled with summer flowers.

"What on earth is that dreadful noise?" Tante asked suddenly.

Mary turned as her heart started to thud. Oh no, she thought, surely not? The car turned the lane's corner and stopped. "Hello there, Catherine!"

Damn him, Mary told herself while her heart flipped a somersault and throbbed painfully.

"What do you want?" she called ungraciously.

"I want a word with Raoul, if you must know," Victor replied and threw a look at the old lady who stood, back ramrod straight, pretending to ignore him.

"What for?" Mary continued.

Victor strode from his car and up the path like a conqueror. "It's not really your business but to satisfy your impossible feminine curiosity, it's to let him know his mainland friend's parents can have the room. I've had a cancellation through illness. Satisfied, Mary?" he mocked.

Mary knew she had gone scarlet with mortification and wished for a quick retort but her mind had gone blank.

Victor turned his gaze and locked eyes with Louise. "So," he said slowly, "we meet at last, Grandmère. How do I compare?"

"I'm not—!" Tante began when her words dried up. "I don't believe it!" she murmured to herself. "It's uncanny! Are you flesh and blood or a ghost?"

Mary failed to understand but Victor did. He stepped forward and grasped both of Louise's hands in his large ones.

"I'm real, Grandmère! Not a ghost, simply a family extension."

Louise Noyen was so shaken that her cheeks paled. Long ago she had considered life had nothing left to throw at her that would

136

quiver her foundations. To be found wrong appalled her and she felt a shiver chase down her back.

"You are the spitting image of my father Dan. Your height, your looks, the way you walk—you even *sound* like him. I'd not have believed it possible. You wear the same cheeky expression with a don't-give-a-damn attitude. An identical chin thrust at the world. It's incredible!"

Mary stood quietly, watching the by-play, not fully aware of any implications, She simply let her eyes rest on this man whom she adored but from whom conventions barred her.

"I am—!" Louise halted, floundering for words.

"You are my grandmère,"Victor told her gently. "Words cannot deny what the flesh has produced," he said kindly. "Your daughter Christine had an affair with a Jerseyman and produced me, albeit dying in the process. I am your flesh and blood grandson!"

"You're a bastard!" Louise retorted.

"*That* is not my fault!"

Both of them ignored Mary who was taken aback at the scene. From Tante, sparks flew as, with compressed lips, the old lady glowered. Victor was quite unabashed. He stood with his hands on his hips and laughed, almost mocking the old lady.

"I've not the time to bandy words with you now," he told her quickly. "Some of us have work to do but, mark me," he said and halted. "I'm your flesh and blood and I'll match you, temper for temper, all the way down the line. When I have some time to spare, I'll be coming in your home for tea and gauche."

"You'll do no such thing!" Louise snorted. "It's my cottage and I say who comes in. Not an upstart like you!"

"You try and keep me out and I'll hammer your door down. If one grandson can enter then so can the other."

"I'll call the parish constable!"

"And make yourself the laughing stock of Guernsey!"Victor taunted with a wide grin. "It's no good, Grandmère, you've met your match in me," he challenged wolfishly. "And I'll tell you something else while I'm here," he confided, lowering his voice and leaning towards her.

"What's that?" Louise asked suspiciously, seething with him.

"You know it too!" Victor chortled then, spinning on his heels, he turned and strode back to his huge car.

"Well!" Louise grated. "The impudent nerve of him!"

Mary eyed her then threw a last, sad look at Victor as the engine bellowed into life and he drove off, cheekily waving at them.

Mary kept a prudent silence, secretly highly amused now. It was the first time she had seen Tante both angry and disconcerted. Then it hit her and she swallowed thankfully. Now Tante had something else to think about instead of her pregnancy because, with a deep, gut feeling, Mary had an awful suspicion that Tante carried a question mark in her head about the child she was expecting.

"What did he mean?" Tante asked suddenly.

Mary nearly jumped, her thoughts engrossed.

"Mean?"

"He called you Catherine?" Tante snorted. "What nonsense is that?"

Mary floundered, not ready for such a question. "Oh!" she shrugged striving to be noncommittal. "He liked the name and called me that instead of Mary all those years ago. It means nothing," she ended lamely.

Tante stared back at her uncertainly. Mary's answer was just a shade too pat and why had her cheeks gone such a fiery red? Surely to God the girl still didn't carry a torch for that wild bastard? She snorted. If there was any hanky-panky, she would soon sort it out. Nothing was ever going to happen to besmirch the honourable family name of Noyen.

EIGHT

THE CHILD WAS a boy and Mary called him Edwin. She had another of her easy confinements attended only by a nurse and Emily. Duret lingered downstairs getting under everyone's feet until shooed away by Emily back to his work.

For Mary, it was the end of a long, worrying road. A week before she calculated the child was due, she allowed herself to slip on the stairs. She was hastily put to bed, glad to be able to think in solitude because Tante's eyes, on her swelling body, the past month, had been calculating. As luck would have it, this child was not in too much fluid so she was not as gross as with her previous babies but Mary imagined Tante working through a variety of questions.

Again luck was with her because Victor spent many months travelling, advertising his hotel. She presumed he knew of her pregnancy and could only pray he thought she had succumbed to Duret again. Perhaps it was jealous pique that kept him away. She was torn in two; wanting to see him again, yet relieved he never appeared in Cobo.

Duret had been child's play to handle. He had been amazingly compliant which baffled Mary. Twice she felt inclined to walk to the glasshouses to question Raoul but each time she thought better of it. Was Duret up to something? It seemed a ridiculous thought and she could only put it down to the fact he was once again lost in composing poetry.

When the baby was put into her arms she held him tightly,

then dared to study his features; overwhelming relief filled her with gratitude because the child had blue eyes and fair hair. His features were difficult to place which did not disconcert her. She knew babies had an odd way of changing month by month and hopefully any inheritance from Victor could be put down to Duret's share of the Penford blood. It was incredible how luck seemed to come down on her side after so many months of mental anguish.

"Where's Tante?" she asked Emily in patois, surprised the old lady had not been down to see the latest family addition.

"She called in earlier but is at home now. She said she'd see you when you are up and about again," Emily told her.

Mary was alarmed. Tante was acting out of character. "Is she ill?"

"Not that I know of," Emily reassured her, "but she's not so quick on her feet as she was, Mary. She is seventy-three, remember."

Mary leaned back against the pillow and watched the baby suckle. How different he was to William. No temper, no snatching greedily at the breast. Edwin appeared to be all delicacy and gentleness and her heart throbbed with love for this son. She lay back, making a multitude of plans for him, dreamily thinking of the future then, giving a deep sigh; she regretted Victor would never know. How wonderful it would be if they were a family. Margaret would adore Victor, she knew. She was not so certain about William. She had a sneaking feeling that William only had time for one person, who was himself. She wondered if he would be jealous of the baby, then shrugged. William was only a toddler, a queer one it was true but it would be up to her to guide these three children as they grew.

With her natural good health and strength she was up in two days and five days after the birth, she walked down to the cottage, pushing Edwin in the pram. As she went up the path she saw a curtain twitch and smiled. She was surprised and even a little hurt that Tante had not come to visit her, despite Emily's warning.

She opened the door, pushed the pram inside then lifted out the baby and walked into the room.

"Here, Tante! As you couldn't come to me, I've come to you!" she cried happily and turning, held out her baby, then froze.

Tante Louise sat in her rocking chair, face white, misery in her eyes. She looked over at Mary with lips which trembled. Surely those were not tears?

Mary was horrified. "Tante! What is it?" she cried and, holding her baby, drew up a chair with one hand. "Are you ill?"

"Oh, Mary! I'm so glad you've come. I couldn't go to the house. I don't know what you must think of me—ah! The baby!"

Mary passed the child over to Tante who gave him a cursory inspection then passed him back. Mary was stunned. Where was the detailed examination that the other children had received when born? Indeed, where was the old interest? Mary felt alarmed. She bit her lip, then lifted Edwin and placed him back in the pram while her mind raced. Obviously Tante must be ill to be so disinterested when family breeding had always been of critical importance.

She went back into the room and drew her chair nearer. Reaching over she took one of Tante's hands in her own.

"Now what is it—?" she whispered with concern.

Two tears trickled down Tante's leathery cheek. With a sniff and a valiant effort, Tante fought the rest. She forced her back into its usual ramrod stiffness and fastened miserable eyes on Mary.

"The diamonds have gone," she said with a break in her voice.

Mary was stunned into momentary silence. Her mind whirled while her jaw dropped with shock. Never in her wildest nightmares had she expected to hear this.

"Gone?" she repeated uncertainly. Had she heard wrong?

"Stolen!" Tante told her miserably. "All that family wealth."

Mary struggled to find words. "Are you quite sure—?" she managed to get out at last.

Tante nodded dolefully. "I don't know what on earth made me take that picture down and look. It was the morning of your confinement. I didn't realise myself to start with. The tape is still there but there's nothing under it. I kept fingering and touching it, not able to believe my eyes, then I unfastened the tape at one end. You can see quite clearly where the diamonds have lain for years. There are indentations on the tape's underside but the diamonds are certainly not there."

Mary gasped, shook her head and struggled to come to terms with this shock. She was horrified to think they had a thief. Without a word, she stood, went over and lifted the picture down and looked for herself. What Tante had said was only too true. She noted a cobweb at the side of the picture frame so when had the theft taken place? Mary slumped down in the chair and shook her head.

"Your diamonds, are they safe?" Louise asked with worry.

"It's funny you should say that," Mary replied. "I happened to go up into the sewing room before I came here. I wanted to check some material and, from force of habit, I felt under the machine. I definitely felt hard lumps under the tape."

"Thank God, we're not quite destitute then," Tante said with relief.

"What a mercy they have always been split into two hordes. They are the family nest egg though!" Mary said, with dawning horror. "Our finances have been halved at one stroke! But who and when?" she cried.

Tante shook her head wearily. "I have no idea. I do have a horrible feeling we will never see them again."

Crime was virtually unheard of on the island. The small variety they did get was usually of the petty variety caused by youths who had drunk too much on a Saturday evening.

"We must think!" Mary said urgently. "Diamonds are not like cash," she said slowly, using her wits again. "A person cannot just walk up to someone and change a diamond into hard currency.

You told me when you wished to change one it was taken to the Continent. Surely this limits the thief's ability to exchange them without someone learning of the fact?"

Tante's mind worked slowly. The shock had devastated her. She had yearned to tell Mary, to get her help but how could she at the time of a confinement? Now though, the initial telling was over and done with, a great weight had lifted. A trouble halved was a worry shared and Mary was nobody's fool. Louise Noyen felt her age as she looked beseechingly at the younger woman.

"Has the Constable been notified?" Mary asked suddenly.

Tante shook her head. "Only three people have ever known after my father's death. You, myself and Sam. My father always impressed it upon me to keep such wealth a total secret. Even my brothers were never told. I only knew because I was his favourite. He never cared for my brothers."

"Surely your mother knew though?"

Again Tante shook her head. "My parents' marriage was not the happiest because my father brought my mother here and she hated it. I think in the end they simply rubbed along. Certainly I was told everything by my father. He treated me like a boy in many ways and I adored him, all of which turned my mother against me because she preferred her sons. My youthful days were not very happy ones—but, that's all by the by. I never told Charles or Duret about the diamonds. It was so dinned into me by my father I suppose I became ultra-secretive over them. I only told Sam because he had been with the family for such a long time and is trustworthy. Also, I felt another person should know in case anything happened to me. That's why I told you when you came into the family. It might not be prudent to let the Constable know. That makes the theft official. It would be all over the island in five minutes and I don't like the family washing out on the line, inspected by all."

Mary bit her lip. "Does Sam have any bright ideas?"

"No, he was as shocked and appalled as I was when I told him. Now you know why I've not been in the right frame of mind to come and see you and the baby. Forgive me, Mary, but this has been a hard blow to take. I'm too old for shocks like this and Sam is no young man any more either. I have been waiting for you to get over your confinement and come here. I couldn't say anything up at the house in case Emily or Gwen overheard. My instinct tells me to keep this quiet and private in the family. Oh, Mary! What shall we do?"

"We're not poor," Mary said slowly.

"That's as maybe. The day may come when we need the money those stones would fetch. One never knows what is around the corner because life is strange. I feel worried sick," she cried and tears sprang to her eyes...

Mary squeezed her hand. "Courage, Tante! We must think this out."

Mary drummed her fingers on the chair arm. She listened a few moments but Edwin was well fed and slept soundly.

"It's either someone local or an opportunistic thief. It's not, Sam. I'd trust my children's lives with him. What about Emily?"

Tante shook her head slowly. "She's been with me for years."

Mary bit her lip. "But we have to consider her though."

"Never Emily," Tante said firmly. "With all due respect to dear Emily, she is not terribly worldly wise. If she saw a diamond lying around, she'd think it nothing but a glass bead."

Mary considered and agreed. "That only leaves Raoul and Gwen," she said grimly. "Gwen has been down here to help you."

"That's true," Tante said slowly, "but she's never been alone. I've always been around. Raoul has never set foot in this cottage. There was never any reason for him to come here. I'd say he was honest. Have you ever found him fiddling the glasshouse takings?"

Mary shook her head. "Then who?"

Tante pulled a face. "It must be an outsider, perhaps at some time when I've been up at your house."

"On a Sunday when you came for lunch?" Mary said, frowning. "That has to be it."

"Often with this door unlocked too," Tante agreed miserably. "Whoever heard of doors being locked on this island and on a Sunday. Oh, Mary! This is too awful for words."

A little colour had come back into Louise's face now she had unburdened herself though there were trembles in both hands.

With a pang Mary understood how she had come to admire Tante's fortitude. Past acts that had angered her were dismissed. Tante had only acted for the best and no one was perfect.

"There is something else I've wanted to discuss with you for a while but I couldn't bother you in your pregnancy," Tante said slowly.

Mary flinched uneasily. What was coming now?

"I'm worried about what is happening in England," Tante started slowly. "I think matters are going to get worse before they get better. This means our island will be affected too. It was the war, all that fighting, those terrible casualty lists—to make a land fit for heroes they told us. Some heroes! Ex-servicemen begging on the streets, holding little trays trying to sell matches and shoe laces. Look at the poor devils incarcerated in hospitals for life. What about those who have lost arms and legs; the men who have become insane? War is bad enough but I think winning it can be worse. The payment is at too high a price. Sometimes I thank God Charles was killed outright and Duret's injury did not maim him. At least it removed him from those ghastly trenches. What I'm trying to say is that England's economy is bad and could well get worse—yet there is money around for some. It was because I was thinking so much about money that I lifted down the picture to check upon the diamonds. You see, it has been in my mind for a while that we should extend the glasshouses. Food will always be wanted when factory produce might not."

Mary's eyebrows shot up with astonishment. During the past

few months she too had been thinking about expansion. Tante awaited her reaction with interest.

"I agree with you," Mary replied. "Apart from the glasshouses we should start to buy up little cottages as and when they become available for sale."

"Do you have something specific in mind?"

Mary nodded eagerly. "People! Look at Victor. How well he has done with his hotel and it would never surprise me if he does not buy another. He is so go ahead and it's no good scowling, Tante, because I've mentioned his name. We should copy him but in another direction. Those people with money whom you mentioned could well want to spread their wings now the war is history. We can offer a lot for holidays. Although we are British we are not English. We are unique. We have a different atmosphere here but speak the same language, use the same kind of money, drive on the left and have policemen with helmets. We have the same pillar boxes even if they are a different colour. We have great beauty around our coast. There is swimming, boating and fishing; other islands to visit like Herm, Sark and Alderney. People with money will pay to come to a cottage where they can pretend they are at home. Buy their own food and look after themselves casually. No dressing up as is expected in an hotel. We buy the cottages, furnish them and let them out. Advertise in England."

"Well!" Tante gasped.

"We would have to use a good lawyer, though." Mary added.

Tante nodded thoughtfully. As long as there was correct, registered title, a property was a solid investment that might well increase in value.

"Get rid of the rest of the diamonds now," Mary told her. "Use their proceeds for this purpose."

Tante licked her bottom lip. She was struck with admiration for this idea but now they contemplated disposing of their last asset, she had to be sure in her mind.

"Sam would have to go over to France," Mary continued in full spate, ticking points off on her fingers. "Change the diamonds into hard cash, invest the money somewhere safe and we'd not be looking over our shoulders, worrying about theft."

Mary sat back, appearing to be casual but taut and on edge. She had turned this idea over in her mind during the last boring weeks of her pregnancy. Would Tante approve? Was her idea sound?

Tante weighed up the pros and cons. After this theft, the disposal would remove a major worry. If she fell in with Mary's idea, it would mean a lot of work initially: holiday-makers as well as glasshouse produce. There would have to be two sets of accounts, much running around to begin with to check upon the properties. There would have to be a system to deliver and collect keys; allowances for breakages, probably transport arrangements. A host of problems lifted quick heads and waved them.

"Well?" Mary asked softly.

"I like it!" Tante pronounced. "But it's not for me. I'm too old. It would all fall upon your shoulders and now you have three children," she pointed out shrewdly. "You don't get any help from Duret, do you? No!" She shook her head; the day was coming when she would have to have a serious talk with her grandson.

Mary pulled a face. "He's rarely in the house. I don't know where he goes and I don't think I care any more now."

Tante regarded her thoughtfully. "But you have Edwin," she hinted.

Mary gave her a long look, keeping her features impassive. "That was over nine months ago. We've had a lot of tides since then. Anyhow I like to be fully occupied. I'd love to get involved in something like holiday cottage lets," she explained firmly, changing the subject away from Duret and their marriage.

Louise realised Mary had firmly put her down in a tactful way. Where exactly *did* Duret spend his free time? She made herself think on these new business lines. "If we used someone well known and our intentions became common knowledge, prices will shoot up. Let me think about this. We need a lawyer, not long qualified who doesn't have many clients. Offer him a retainer as well as pay his fees and let him buy to preserve our anonymity." She paused: "Sam must go over to France for us, but this time no money is to be carried. Letters of Credit or Bankers' Drafts—"

"Or Credit Transfers!" Mary added.

"You have been doing a lot of thinking," Tante praised. Then she made a rare, snap decision. "We'll do it. We have nothing to lose and perhaps much to gain as well as peace of mind. My father must be spinning in his grave. He worked long and hard to acquire capital for the family."

Mary's lips twitched. She had a shrewd idea it might have all been illegal too from what she knew about the Penfords in general.

Gwen lifted baby Edwin into his pram while Margaret fidgeted nearby but William stood silently watching all that was going on.

"At least Mary had plenty of milk for this one, unlike William," she said thoughtfully. "Good job too. He has a healthy appetite."

Emily threw her a grim look but passed no comment. Margaret and William missed little that was said. Margaret would pass a childish comment but William would simply stare in silence at the commenting adult. Of course, Mary had had no milk for William. There was no rapport then or now despite the attention Mary lavished on William. They had never bonded. Luckily William liked Gwen but, Emily mused, was that because he was aware he was tiny and weak. He might become difficult as he grew and strengthened. The only person William appeared to like wholeheartedly was his father, which was strange, Emily reflected, considering how little Duret saw of his children. He was rarely in the house nowadays.

"That's another thing," Gwen muted more to herself this time. "What is wrong with the folks in this house? There's Mary walking around lost in deep thoughts, just as bad as her husband. Sam doesn't have a word to say to anyone and you'd think the pair of them carried the woes of the world upon their backs. Look! Off down to see the old girl again, walking side by side but not speaking."

Emily too had noticed the atmosphere but she was an incurious person. As long as she had work to do which she enjoyed and was left alone to do it her way, nothing troubled her. She was one of life's creatures born without curiosity, quite happy with her lot in life. Let anything trouble or attack the Noyen family though and she would change, in a flash, to a seething hell cat.

Her helper Gwen was different. She was totally unlike her bother Raoul, as dark as she was fair. As the firstborn, she had been a pushy child and had not really lost this trait, which made her ideal to discipline the children.

The Noyen children disturbed Gwen. She ached for her own and a cottage. Although neither pretty nor beautiful, she was often described as fetching. Recently a young fisherman had started to hang around the lane and Gwen was torn; delighted that someone found her attractive but sad at the thought of leaving the Noyens in the future.

Emily had taken a rooted dislike to the young man on the odd times she had met him when he called at the back door for Gwen's finishing time. She was sure Raymond Falla was not the right person for Gwen. He was a pleasant enough young man, healthy but from a poor family. He was polite to Emily and any family members he met, yet Emily did not like the thin set of his lips. She also thought his chin was on the weak side and his eyes crafty.

She sighed as Gwen went out with the children. It seemed there might be a lot to say for her single state after all. Emily had had her chances but dithered once too often. The years had flown by until one day she realised young men no longer came a-calling on her. It was then she threw herself, body and soul, into the fortunes of the Noyen family. She had never regretted this although sometimes her eyes lingered wistfully upon Sam Mahy. He was still a fine figure of a man but Sam had never viewed her as interesting even though she was a well fleshed woman. Emily was just the means to keep the house ticking over efficiently. Sometimes though, Emily could not help wistful daydreams regarding widower Sam Mahy.

Now she too peered from the window and watched Sam and Mary walk down to Louise's cottage. What on earth could they be going to discuss now? Sam and Mary had spent hours with the old lady in the past three days.

NINE

"WELL SAM," TANTE commenced, "your views on Emily and Gwen."

Sam grunted. "Forget Emily. She's not over bright enough for a well planned job like this theft and planned it certainly had to be." He paused thinking carefully. "Gwen? No. She's sharper than Emily but I don't consider her dishonest. Also, at the moment she's being courted by young Falla and all she can think of is getting married, a home and babies. Can't say I care for Falla myself. He's from around the Bay area but Gwen steal?" He shook his head. "As to young Falla. He's not from our parish and he'd never dare. Too many people have seen him hanging around this lane waiting for Gwen to finish work. If he had set one toe up your garden path, someone would have seen and spoken by now," he told Tante decidedly.

Louise nodded thoughtfully. "All of that is quite true which leaves us with no bright ideas at all as to the thief's identity."

Sam decided to change the line of conversation. The mistress looked depressed again. "You want me to go over to France?"

Mary and Louise replied with nods. Mary then explained. "The remaining diamonds must be hidden well. I could sew them into your vest," she offered.

Sam looked after himself very well and was quite adept with a needle if his socks were anything to go by but discreet, little pockets would be another matter. Tante stayed quiet. She knew everything was just about out of her hands and she was not sorry.

Mary must organise it all. What she could still do was to put her ear to the ground to locate an appropriate lawyer. It was terrible they could not get Duret's help. She took a deep breath, acknowledging how disappointed she was in him. Where had her high hopes and dreams gone? Marriage had made him worse not better.

"What do you think of the whole plan now, Sam?" Mary ended.

Sam was stunned with the details. There was a beautiful simplicity that gave indication this could only be a sound venture. It was highly unusual and cottage lets, advertised properly on the mainland, should promote good business in time.

"I like it," he said gruffly. "Ten out of ten for whoever thought of it!" he praised and looked at them in turn. Tante nodded towards Mary who blushed with pleasure.

"It will indeed take time to get off the ground and perhaps even years before any of the lets can pay for just one cottage but I think properties might increase in capital value over the years," she explained as Tante nodded vigorously. "Also a cottage is not stealable," she added grimly.

"What do you think we should do about the police, Sam?" Tante asked.

Sam shook his head. "Do nothing is my advice at the present. We have nothing for them to work on, in the first place. Also I sometimes think the police know nothing until they are told. However I'll tell you what I propose to do. As I go about the island I'll keep my ears open. I know many people and I hear more because I do not gossip. A word here, another there, can be built up into a picture—then, and only then, should we go to the police."

Tante was not quite happy with this. "But until then we end up suspecting everyone."

Sam sat back and filled his pipe, taking his time to tamp the tobacco in exactly as he liked it. He took even longer to light it with a paper spill then, sucking and inhaling, he enjoyed the nicotine's bite. He was impressed. The plan was very good and he eyed Mary surreptitiously. In this he could see her hand alone. The day had finally arrived, he mused to himself. The mistress had finally turned the family affairs over to Mary whom, he reasoned, was mature and more than ready for this responsibility. It was the end of an era, which had begun more years ago than he cared to remember.

'The Queen is dead,' he told himself. 'Long live the Queen!'

Two days later Sam presented himself for inspection. Not a diamond showed on his person because Mary had made cunning, little pockets with an overflap for safety. Each had been attached just in front of the vest seam and diamonds nestling in all of them.

"That will do nicely," Tante approved.

"Yes!" Mary agreed, hands clasped together with satisfaction. It all depended upon Sam now but he was quite unfazed by the responsibility. He was solid, reassuring and utterly dependable, yet appeared as a simple tradesman off on some minor matter.

"I'll telegraph as soon as the money is on its way to the bank," he told them, "but do not be alarmed if I am away longer than we have allowed. I am not going to sell to the first dealer. I intend to play one against the other to push the price up. Rough stones of this carat are worth plenty of money. I'll also be listening to all the gossip I can hear. There is no telling what I might not pick up in France even. News always travels quickly when it is bad."

Mary and Louise nodded in sober agreement, then kissed him farewell. Sam gave them a wink, put his pipe in his mouth and sauntered down the path as if he were going for a stroll along the front.

James le Canu was twenty-seven years of age and newly established in a small practice, which he had been able to purchase with the proceeds of an unexpected legacy.

He was of average height with dark straight hair, darker eyebrows and eyes almost black in colour. His skin was permanently tanned, the colouring due to the wind and salt not the sun because le Canu had a secret love affair. She was a small yacht, which he adored to the total exclusion of nearly anything else in his leisure hours.

As he sat in his private office, he drummed his fingers on his green leather-covered desk. It had been bought cheaply then renovated by a skilled craftsman. Now the desk gleamed with age and loving care. James le Canu realised it was a little too luxurious for his humble office because his practice was so small. He had one typist and a middle-aged woman as receptionist which number of staff were more than enough because times were hard. Business was slow in beating a path to his door.

Like any good Guernsey man, it had never entered his head to practise anywhere else but in St Peter Port. What he had not calculated was the fact that the established lawyers, with their well heeled clients, took the best business. All that came to his door were trivial bits and pieces which bored the wealthier advocates.

It was not that the young lawyer was fussy. He knew only too well a newly qualified man like himself, without family connections, would have to start off with the dross so why did Madam Noyen wish to see him?

A well established family like the Noyens always used a much larger practice and he was puzzled and perturbed why they wished to turn to him. His integrity was his pride; his honesty unimpeachable but he knew, without hesitation, he would send even the most illustrious Guernsey citizen packing if they were up to no good. This would not endear himself to the affluent but he had his principles and to these he would always stick. Why did Madam Noyen wish to consult him?

The door opened after a discreet tap and his typist entered with, behind her, a woman of his own height and generation.

154

"Madam Noyen, sir!" she intoned dutifully and withdrew.

James le Canu stood, walked around his great desk, extended his hand and placed a friendly smile on his face. He was even more intrigued. This was not the old battleaxe of tempestuous legend.

Mary returned his smile and studied him as she sat down. He picked up a pencil and pulled a large notepad before him and she sensed some odd kind of tension. She decided to speak first.

"Mr le Canu," she began carefully, "it has been decided to go into the property business. After discussion with Madam Noyen senior, we thought it would be prudent if someone were to purchase on our behalf. I will explain all the reasons. Apart from your usual fee, we would also pay you a reasonable retainer for exclusivity."

Mary proceeded to explain in detail while le Canu listened in total silence. Now and again he made a jotting on his pad while he could hardly credit this good fortune. This work, being offered to him alone, was the type he would enjoy. A retainer, plus the normal conveyancing fees, would ensure a stable income for a considerable time in the future. He understood now the reason for the visit. With a project such as this, an unknown lawyer would be far more valuable than an established one. When the details were completed he regarded the young woman carefully.

She was dressed in those simple clothes which only money and a good cut can provide. Her dress was bright red, which should have appeared garish but which, with white hat, gloves and shoes, made her extremely elegant. He was puzzled why her husband was not present. Surely this was man's work? Much as he considered himself modern, he admitted he found it disconcerting to do business of this nature with a young woman, particularly one so charming. He had not missed her square jaw, nor the way she looked him boldly eye to eye. From what he had heard of Madam Noyen senior, this young lady came from the same bolt of cloth. She looked tough and determined.

He cleared his throat. This must be settled but would she be honest? "May I ask, madam, why you have come to me?"

Mary threw him a conspiratorial grin. She had guessed his doubts. "Because no one would think you would be buying cottages for us," she said bluntly.

Le Canu flushed, then was forced to smile. He had wanted the truth and been given it. He was highly intrigued.

"So the work would be keeping an eye out for a cottage, then conveyancing?" he asked, wanting clarification in case of later doubt.

Mary crossed one leg over the other to display a sheer silk stocking. "Who knows what might not develop in the future?" she parried neatly. Her tactics had been plotted with Tante the previous evening. "Are you interested?"

Le Canu was indeed. He asked a number of questions regarding finance in general, which was, he assured, no problem and Mary discreetly kept crossed fingers out of his sight. He discussed possible mortgages, the tax situation and financial investments but Tante had primed Mary carefully. He took copious notes, one lock of hair falling across his forehead to be swept back impatiently now and again.

Mary studied him carefully. He looked so absurdly young but she realised he was about her own age after all. She wondered what he would say if he knew about the diamonds which had been lost and those about to be sold. Tante had decided though it would be more prudent to keep this information from him initially.

Le Canu finished writing, checked his facts, asked a couple more questions for verification, then saw his new client out. After she had gone he sank back in his chair, steepled his hands together and started to think deeply.

Madam was but a Noyen by marriage so who was she and from where had she come initially? He was impressed by her. Although young, he had a shrewd ability to assess character and young Madam Noyen had impressed him enormously. He was sure that, at one stage in their talk, he had seen a flash of ruthlessness in her eyes. Where was her husband?

His thoughts drifted back to a recent, long weekend on the mainland. He had spent it in an expensive country house, filled with flapper girls. They were fluffy, giggly and without a sensible thought in their heads; concerned only with personal pleasure and country house parties.

This young lady would scorn such behaviour. She would always cut through to the quick of a situation, no matter what the cost. He was deeply interested.

He went back over a particular conversation held with his uncle at that weekend's party. Whether he agreed with his uncle's opinions was neither here nor there. What was certain was that his motives were of the highest, his integrity without question and his loyalty identical to that of himself. He decided it would be of great interest to conduct a most discreet investigation into the past of young Madam Noyen. It would do no harm and there was no telling what good might not arise in the end.

Duret had decided. Enough was more than enough. For as long as he could remember, he had been subject to petticoat rule. The one time he had enjoyed sole, masculine companionship all day and night was during the war. He had hoped his marriage would change matters at home but instead they had gone from bad to worse.

Grandmère was still around behaving in her normal, dictatorial way and Duret knew he was as terrified of her now as when a boy. What made matters worse though was the fact that Mary appeared to be turning into another version of Grandmère.

Where had the pliant gentle English girl gone? He tried to pinpoint this and, frowning heavily, worked out it had happened after Edwin's conception.

He grumbled to himself with disgust when he reviewed his home life. Grandmère was in her cottage but her aura still lingered in the house. Mary ruled like a queen and Emily and Gwen were her dutiful attendants. He reviewed his children. Why did the first born also have to be female? It was not that he disliked Margaret. Far from it but because she was yet another female, he knew he had nothing in common with her.

William was different. Not only was he so obviously male in physical parts but in characteristics which Duret felt he could understand. William did not coo or shout for attention like Margaret. William could lapse into a long, thoughtful silence of which Duret thoroughly approved. When William became old enough, Duret knew he would make him an ideal companion. Perhaps he might even like poetry.

Certainly few did now. His original little circle of artistic friends had dwindled over the years as they moved from the island for work elsewhere or married and went under female thumbs. Duret was grateful for his new friends whom he had discovered quite by chance. Thank God he had his escape to them. It was true this meant being away from the home every evening and coming back late but Mary did not care, so why should he?

He liked Raoul but, here again, there was a subtle barrier. As workmates they pulled well together except that Raoul would insist upon his own planting ideas when Duret, as the sole male Noyen, knew he should be running the business. What with Raoul saying plant this and that and Mary doing the accounts, Duret had gradually realised his position was but that of a sinecure. Gradually he had started to spend less and less time in the glasshouses. He wondered if Raoul would complain to Mary or Grandmère but no sword had descended upon his neck, so he realised Raoul had covered for him.

This did make him feel guilty and he always swore he would make it up to Raoul one day. That day did not seem to appear though and now Duret had an additional heavy worry, which was enough to drive a man to distraction.

He wished he could discuss it with Mary or Grandmère but this he dared not do. They would castigate him; tear him to shreds and he quailed at the thought of their joint tempers. Duret knew he was not a very brave man. Nature had given him a girl's timidity and, taken all around, he felt miserable. Only his evenings made up for his daytime worries.

Last evening, though, he had dared to murmur his fears and his mates had spoken up. Petticoat rule? They had chortled and made ribald comments at what they would do under such circumstances. It was all very well for them to shower him with well meaning advice, Duret told himself dismally. It would be he who had to make the move.

He spent a sleepless night, fretting at the problem and awoke with unusual determination. Something must be done and—now.

Mary had gone somewhere into town. Why, no one could or would tell him which also added fuel to the little fire burning in his heart. How dare she go off out and about without informing him? He was the man; not her. He would go down to Grandmère and have it out with her too.

As he strode down the lane towards Tante's cottage a number of things happened at once. To start with, his limited courage began to evaporate rapidly the nearer he approached. Then Mary turned the corner driving the cob and the trap. At that identical moment, Grandmère appeared in her garden and waved to Mary and shouted something. While behind Mary one of those horrible modern motor cars appeared.

Duret halted, wondering whether to continue with his plan. As he did so the car drew to a stop behind the cob and trap and Mary actually turned and waved to the driver. Then she turned to Grandmère and gave a thumbs-up sign while the driver got out of his car and strode up to Mary.

Duret quickened his pace, his expression bleak. Now he knew

who the driver was. Someone with whom he had never exchanged a word but about whom he knew plenty. How dared he come here and *what* on earth were Mary and Grandmère doing talking to him?

"Mary!" he bellowed as he strode up.

Mary jumped and was shocked to see her husband one yard away with a thundercloud on his face. Tante was startled too. She had been so engrossed in listening to Mary's whispered message of affirmation. Victor le Page realised something was going on, but had sense enough not to ask questions.

"Duret!" Mary exclaimed. "I didn't know you were not at work?"

"Yes," Louise said swiftly. One raking look had seen something in Duret's eyes she did not like. "Are you and Raoul finished for the day?"

Victor said nothing but felt himself tense up. He stood next to Mary, his instinct warning him of trouble to come.

Duret jumped forward, snatched Mary's arm and hauled her away from le Page.

"Duret! What do you think you are doing?" Mary cried.

Duret turned a red face to Mary. "You are my wife," he growled, "and I'll not have you associate with a bastard like him!"

Mary was shocked, then exploded with wrath. She flung Duret aside. "Don't you ever manhandle me like that again and just remember I'm one of those too!"

Duret turned glowing eyes on her. "So—you rush to his defence," he jeered before turning back to face Victor.

All of Victor's recent frustrations rose at once. He didn't mind being denounced a bastard because facts were facts, but what had upset him was the possessive, almost cruel way, Noyen treated Mary.

"Brave man," he snarled dangerously. "Why don't you try and manhandle me?"

Duret jumped forward and lashed out with a right. It was so

unexpected and out of character that Mary and Louise froze with shock. Victor swayed his head two inches to the left and the blow whistled past. He readjusted his balance and slammed a straight right. It hit Duret in the middle, driving the air from his lungs with a whoosh. Then a left and a right to his face followed, Duret brought up his forearms defensively but far too late. The blows landed and his senses reeled, blood spurted, then he was down and sprawling ungainly. Victor stood, feet slightly apart, one knuckle grazed and looked down contemptuously.

Duret lay still and Mary gasped. "He's not—?"

"No such luck," Victor growled. He hoped Noyen would get up again to continue but Duret had more sense.

Victor turned slowly to Tante. "So," he drawled, head held high. "Who is the better grandson now? Me—or that!" he paused. "Who has been true to their bloodlines? Who is the man now?" he demanded hotly. "Me or that rubbish?" Then his voice softened. "So when am I coming into your cottage for tea and gauche? When do I experience the right of heritage? They tell me you fear nothing, old lady so show your mettle now, once and for all!" he challenged.

Louise stood still then her eyes travelled slowly to Mary who, she could see, was wild with anger. Then she regarded Duret who sprawled inelegantly, his legs twitching a little as he rubbed his jaw and looked at Mary with bleary eyes. Finally, they settled on the handsome male who faced her with a cold, set face and hard, boring eyes. She examined him in great detail. He had matured and she held her breath with awe. It was incredible and even frightening to see another Danny Penford in the flesh.

Tante quivered, acutely conscious of her age, aware also of what a resounding series of mistakes she had made in the past. She had been wearing blinkers and she had allowed herself to be swayed by the stupid prejudices of her generation.

She had two grandsons and there was no doubt who was the better. She lowered her proud head as chagrin masked her features before slowly lifting her eyes to hold those facing her. Tentatively she extended one thin arm to him.

"Take me in, grandson," she said gently.

Victor's chest swelled with pride as he stepped forward and slipped the thin arm beneath his.

"With pleasure, Grandmère but oh, what an interfering old woman you've been, now isn't that so?" he teased.

Mary watched them disappear and the front door shut firmly. She turned back to Duret who scowled up at her, trying to be hard and not succeeding. There was something implacable in his wife's eyes.

"What's he to you?" he managed to get out jealously, as he struggled to his feet. He felt light-headed and unsteady.

Mary glowered at him. This was the end. It had to be.

"I asked you a question!" Duret shouted at her. "I've heard about that bastard and the way he goes around in that rich car of his. He's nothing and never will be!"

"Careful," Mary warned. "He's just thrashed you."

"Only because he caught me unawares!"

"Oh, Duret! Don't lie any more," Mary retorted wearily. Her anger had abated to be replaced with something difficult to describe. The thought of Duret touching her now was nauseating. Her facial expression showed this and Duret flinched.

"You disgust me!" she told him. "Our marriage is over. You will never touch me again. I'm moving into the sewing room and you come near me or bother me and, I swear by God, I'll slip a knife between your ribs."

"I'm your husband!" he cried in panic, afraid of her. She had never looked at him before like that. He lifted a hand against her but all she did was stand there, proud and unafraid.

"Go on! Try it!" Mary hissed.

Duret felt sharp terror then. He turned and staggered away while Mary watched with tight lips and cold rage. She went down the lane, feeling emotionally exhausted. Who would have thought at this day's sunrise so much would have happened by sunset? Yet she felt a great relief in her heart. It was as if she had been moving slowly to this point for a long time. Now she had arrived and was glad.

She studied the sky. It would be a typical, balmy Guernsey evening. She glanced at her watch. The tide would be on the make. On a sudden impulse she started to run. Already the rocks were starting to cover and way ahead was Grandes Rocques. Taking deep breaths she increased her pace.

Her heart was feather light now. Her head was high, her spirit undaunted. She scrambled to stand on the Rocques and look out to sea. Wild, defiant and dominant.

TEN

SAM EYED THE steps ahead and made a snap decision. He wanted a drink, he needed one badly before he returned to Cobo. Part of the news was good and indeed, after sending a telegram to the mistress, he had been light-hearted, pleased that his mission had been safely accomplished. He had returned to Guernsey but something stopped him from letting the family know. Instead, he had spent a few hours with old cronies and what he had learned made him sick to the bottom of this guts. He had been so disbelieving that he had moved on elsewhere, to another part of the island to ask a few more questions. When these had only confirmed the original source, great gloom had descended upon him. It was going to be terrible going back to the family with this news and two drinks, at the very least, would be necessary to fortify him the for the trial to come.

He did not often go into this particular pub because it was off his beaten track, rather more expensive than most with its tiny, private snug room and its usual clientele were not of his kind. At least, though it was a place where a man could sit and drink alone when he carried such dreadful information.

Sam clumped up the stairs, entered, peered around the slightly darkened room and ordered two drinks. He retreated to a far corner and moodily went over his thoughts again.

At the opposite side of the room three men eyed him curiously. He was well known by nearly everyone of consequence on the island and they were curious about him. Sam Mahy was an affable fellow usually, so why had he taken himself to a corner to sit with his back to all comers?

Victor le Page's eyebrows lifted. "He looks like death warmed up," he said in a low voice.

James le Canu nodded. "Never seen him standoffish like this before," he agreed.

Constable Emil le Norman was also perplexed but because of his work he was inclined to look at a situation differently to his friends. He agreed with the others though and was puzzled.

"Woman trouble?" the policeman suggested gently. He was always eager to acquire information that could be stored away in his excellent memory.

Victor snorted with amusement. "Him? Not likely! He's a sworn widower though I heard a whisper long ago that Emily Ferbrache of Cobo wouldn't mind him popping her the question. The trouble is though he doesn't even see her."

"Why is he dressed like a fisherman?" James murmured with a frown.

Emil had also registered this fact. He mused over it for a few seconds. "Anyone would think he's been over to France and didn't want to appear well off."

The lawyer looked at him sharply, then back again to Sam. It was true. He knew for whom Mahy worked and a niggle of something touched his mind. He remembered back to Madam Noyen's appointment and her family plans. Surely there could not be any connection but, if so, was his precious integrity affected? He frowned a little, something which Emil le Norman did not miss.

Victor did miss this little by-play, too intent on studying Sam. There was something wrong somewhere and he felt uneasy. That was two double whiskies old Sam had just knocked back and everyone knew he was an ale man. Victor's eyes narrowed but he kept them turned well away from Emil, only too well aware how sharp his friend could be. It crossed his mind that another visit to his grandmère in the near future might not go amiss. Certainly if there was trouble in the family he was the only man they could turn too. That fool Noyen was useless. Now Grandmère had welcomed him back into the fold, he felt a responsibility for her and all of them, especially Mary.

Sam stood up, totally oblivious to the three interested spectators. He could not put off the evil moment any longer but even that amount of whisky had not fortified him. He must catch the bus and go straight to the mistress. Dear God, he asked himself, how strong is her heart? *What* was Mary going to say—or do?

He missed one bus, so waited nearly half an hour for the next, then, later, strode heavily up the lane to the cottage. He found Mary and the mistress sitting together, discussing domestic matters when Sam gave a rap, opened the door and entered.

"Sam!" they cried together. "So wonderful to see you back!"

Sam knew they both meant it and his heart was touched, then it went icy cold. Mary bustled around to make tea and provide food while Louise simple watched Sam, tiny puckers on her forehead. Sam knew he could not yet meet her eyes.

Louise went cold as if a ghost had walked on her grave. Now what had gone wrong? It could not be the money. That was safely on deposit, after a credit transfer, already earning interest on the mainland. Louise knew better than to badger a man before he ate. She was consumed with worried curiosity but disciplined herself to wait. Mary scurried around oblivious to anything wrong.

After Sam had eaten and finished two large mugs of tea, he sat back in his chair and eyed the womenfolk who faced him with anticipation; Louise with forebodings and Mary bubbling with excitement at the start of her plan.

Sam noticed how drawn the mistress looked. Had something happened in his absence? He took his time in filling his pipe than looked Louise straight in the eye.

"All right!" he said bluntly. "What's happened while I've been away?"

"Everything!" Louise replied for both of them after a glance at Mary and receiving her nod of agreement to speak.

"Duret, Mary and Victor le Page all turned up at the same time when Mary returned from town. Victor was standing next to Mary and Duret objected. He snatched her away. The men exchanged words and Duret threw a punch at Victor which missed."

"He did?" Sam gasped. "I didn't think he had it in him!"

"They fought," Louise continued, "and Duret received a hiding. Then I came to my stupid senses at last and brought my splendid grandson in here to have tea!"

"About time too!" Sam snorted. "It's taken you long enough, you stubborn old woman!"

Louise had the grace to blush before she intimated that Mary should continue the tale.

"I then had a set-to with Duret and it's over between us," Mary told him in a low voice. "I'm moving into the top room and there's a bolt on the door. I've told Duret if he bothers me again, in any way, I'll slide the carving knife between his ribs!"

"Have you indeed?" Sam gasped, shocked at Mary's venom though not unduly surprised. The marriage had been on the rocks from the time Mary showed with Edwin but this was an unexpected turn-up for the book. Where did that leave Mary with le Page—especially as the mistress had come to her senses about him? Sam took a deep breath.

"Where is Duret?" he asked, playing for time.

Both Mary and Louise shrugged. "We don't know, he's vanished!" Mary added.

Louise snorted. "He'll come sidling back when his belly is empty!" she said coldly.

"I've something to tell both of you about Duret too," Sam began evenly, aware he had their complete attention. "It's not nice," he warned.

"Go on!" Mary groaned. "I'm past being shocked now."

Sam doubted this but continued. "Did you know, either of you, that for weeks, perhaps even months, Raoul has been covering for Duret at work?"

"What?" Mary snapped. "Explain, Sam!"

"You can't blame Raoul. He is young, keen and inexperienced with life. He has also been in awe of Duret who, after all, is family and the heir. Raoul has been desperate to prove himself and please both of you. Also he has been highly embarrassed. Raoul simply worked harder than ever to do Duret's tasks as well as his own."

"The stupid boy!" Louise exclaimed her cheeks flaming pink. "He should have spoken to one of us!"

Sam shook his head. "How?" he asked reasonably, "You are both tough, strong characters and he is only the hired hand. He thought if he came telling tales, so to speak, you would despise him."

"How foolish!" Mary cried, every bit as angry as Tante Louise. "But where did Duret go then?"

Here we go, Sam told himself grimly. There was no way to give such news elegantly so he had decided to come straight out with it.

"He's been taking himself up to a seedy part of St Sampson."

"What!" Mary and Tante exclaimed together. "But why?"

"Gambling!" Sam told them bluntly.

Both Mary and Tante were too shocked for immediate comment. They slowly looked at each other, then back at Sam.

"Go on, Sam!" Mary said grimly.

"Duret is no gambler I'm afraid. He ran up debts. Big debts, too, I might add. He also drank the hard stuff at the same time, which all costs."

Mary could hardly believe her ears. Duret was doing—this? Had he gone stark, raving mad or was he just showing his true self? Tante shook her head with disbelief. If any one other than Sam had told her this she would have attacked them verbally. Drinking and gambling had never been family weaknesses.

An awful suspicion shot into Mary's head. Her eyes opened wide and she sat even more erect in the chair.

"It was Duret who—!"

"Took the diamonds!" Sam finished for her.

"Oh no!" Tante groaned, shaking her head, her shoulders slumping. She fell silent but they could see she was thinking when her eyes opened wide and she scowled.

"That's when he found out!" she cried. "That day I asked him to stay here and rearrange the furniture. I distinctly remember— more fool me—asking him to take that picture down and try it in another light. He must have seen the black tape at the back, perhaps felt the little lumps with his fingers, then one day when I was away, sneaked back to investigate. Oh, the disgrace of it all. Here we've been thinking it's someone else, even suspecting Gwen or Emily."

Louise's cheeks flamed with humiliation and anger.

"What did he do with them?" Mary asked in a low voice.

Sam gave it to them straight. "He settled enormous gambling debts with them."

"But they were worth thousands," Mary protested. "Didn't the fool realise?"

Sam shrugged. "I don't know," he said wearily. "But I do know he had to settle up or someone would settle up with him—the hard way."

"We must get them back quickly," Louise cried.

"Impossible!" told her bluntly. "You see, he was gambling with men off ships in the harbour. Whether they were true gambling losses or whether Duret was set up for it I don't know. The long and short of it seems to be that the cards were against him—or manipulated that way—and he ended up crushingly in debt. There were ugly threats against him and it seems he was desperate."

"The ship?" Mary asked quickly.

"It sailed the day after he handed the diamonds over *and* it was a foreign one too. It's hardly likely to put back here again under the circumstances. Personally I think Duret may have had his tongue loosened with strong drink and—" Sam shrugged. They would be able to picture the rest of it.

"I'll kill him!" Mary grated through her teeth. "He is no damned good and never has been. What I first saw in him in the first place I don't know. I must have been out of my mind!" she ranted with fury. "That was our nest egg, our inheritance, *his* children's future. Oh, just let me get my hands on him!"

Sam saw she meant it and shot a look of worry at the mistress. Louise felt as if she had been pole-axed. Her world had collapsed and her heart thumped in an ugly way. She felt unexpected tears surge up and she shook her head helplessly.

"What can we do?" Mary asked them both suddenly, looking from one face to the other.

"Nothing! They've gone for good and even if you washed this dirty linen in public, it would not bring those stones back."

"*I-want-Duret*!" Mary growled coldly.

Sam eyed her and hoped Duret had enough sense to stay vanished. Mary in that mood was capable of anything and he could not be with her all the time. He had a shrewd idea that Duret might have gone to ground near St Sampson. Should he go and find him and get him off the island? He dithered, not knowing which way to jump. He certainly could discuss nothing with Mary when she had murder in her heart and the mistress looked ill with a bad colour. Should he get Victor? Sam bowed his head. For once unable to think straight.

Tante collected herself together first. "There's nothing we can do right now," she told them slowly. "We are all worked up, so it's best to leave it all until another day. We must cool down and think carefully about what we mean to do. We must sleep on it, if we can."

Despite being furious, Mary saw Tante's distraught face and tearful eyes and nodded slowly. Sam felt the tension drop and let out a huge sigh of relief.

"Shoot all the bolts on the house tonight. No one goes in or out. I'll not sleep but if Duret tries to come back tonight, so help me God, I'll not be responsible for my actions," Mary told them in a low, icy voice. "Tomorrow is, as you say Tante, another day." With an effort she forced a grimace on her face that did not in the least resemble a smile.

That night, as anticipated, Mary did not sleep and she doubted whether Tante or Sam would either. Her mind surged backwards and forwards, going back to the day she had met Duret, which seemed a lifetime ago. What had happened to him? Had he heard stories about her and Victor which had driven him to this stupid behaviour? Was it the shell shock? Or was this the real Duret who only showed when his brown eyes became cold and his grin slid into a stranger's mask?

Mary ate a light breakfast the next morning and found it hard to be civil to Emily and Gwen, which made their eyebrows lift. What was wrong with everyone? Even Sam had nothing to say and had vanished with his hedging tools. Emily, shaking her head, decided their livers must be upset. Perhaps a good dose of salts would sort them out.

Mary harnessed the cob slowly. She had a thumping headache and felt washed out but she had to go to the market and get shopping for the weekend. She patted the cob's neck and noted how grey his muzzle had become.

"It's time you were retired to grass," she told him, "and I'll get myself a car."

Her hand touched the cob's forelock; pushing it back the correct way, she sighed. Yesterday's hot anger had been replaced by the cold variety coupled with bitterness at how her husband had duped them all. She climbed into the trap, clicked her tongue and shook the reins. The amiable cob obliged by moving into a slow trot.

She went along the coast road, intending to cut through the country lanes to King's Mill and head into town in that direction.

It made a change and the fields and hedges would be greenly soothing, a balm to her injured spirit.

Mary thought about Duret. Surely he would not know he had been found out, so how would he react? Which was the best way to get him off the island and what excuses should be made to the children? She turned once and saw a cycle in the distance but otherwise she seemed to have the island to herself. The few cottages that were around gave no indication of life as men had gone fishing and their women were inside.

One mile back, Duret glowered at the retreating trap and drove harder on his pedals. Frequent use had made his legs fit and hard and there was plenty in reserve for a burst of speed.

His tangled mind rested upon the picture of Mary and Victor standing close together like old friends. Was there something between them? Was Grandmère part and parcel of this? His warped mind considered Edwin. Why had Mary rejected him for so many months after William's birth, then enticed him back again with a framed poem? Was it possible that Edwin was le Page's brat? Had he been cuckolded?

His thrashing by le Page before the women of his family was a bitter humiliation but the final straw had been Grandmère offering her arm to the victor and taking him into her cottage.

Something black swirled in his mind that he did not understand. What he did know was he had a great headache and was obsessed with his wife. He would have all this out with her, once and for all. He had been too weak. His friends were correct. He had spent the whole night walking, mind ablaze with injustice, and now he was ready to do something about it. The evil in his wife must be burned out and, as her husband, the task was his alone.

Mary drove blithely on, worrying about the lost stones and what might have been done with them. She turned left and slowed the trap's pace, wary now of cars that might appear. Once again she wondered at the island fetish of such high hedges, which reduced nearly all visibility at bends, but the islanders guarded their land and its boundaries jealously.

Suddenly the cob began to limp on his off fore and Mary hastily pulled up, secured the reins and sprang down. She picked up the hoof and saw the shoe had moved to one side, the nails worn thin and three clenches loose. Mary stifled a groan. Sam usually checked the cob's hooves but, in his absence, she should have done this. She would have to turn around and walk home unless she could see someone but the region appeared to be deserted.

At that second, Duret shot around the corner on his rattling cycle. He had two seconds to avoid a crash and swung to the right wobbling over the grass verge while Mary stood flat-footed with astonishment.

"Duret," she growled, feeling her smouldering anger burst into flames.

Duret jerked to a halt and dismounted with a scurrying jump, then dropped the cycle and turned. He noted where the cob stood and spotted the loose shoe. He faced his wife and quickly realised she knew everything.

"I'm glad you've decided to emerge from your bolthole," Mary shouted angrily. "I want a word or two with you!"

Duret looked at the cold contempt on her face. Once such an expression would have frozen him but his jealousy was too strong. He took a step nearer, moving slowly but purposefully.

"You are a common thief!" Mary hurled at him. "You took the diamonds from behind Tante's picture to settle your miserable gambling debts and to buy drink. How dare you!"

Duret glowered at her. "They were as much mine as anyone else's. I'm the heir!"

"You're nothing but a miserable, gutless object who stoops to stealing his children's inheritance."

"If they are all my kids!"

"What!" Mary gasped. How could he know? Only she had

that knowledge. Was he making an educated guess or did he see something different in Edwin? She realised he was in a terrible mood and knew instinctively attack was the best form of defence.

"Why didn't you say you were in financial trouble?" she continued. "Why did you have to start drinking and gambling? Why didn't you do your share of the work instead of being a drone, mooning off writing that stupid poetry? You disgust me!"

Duret glared at her. She stood proud and defiant, raging at him, incredibly beautiful in her fury but all he could see was le Page standing next to her. Something was making his fingers clench and unclench as niggles of power began to surge through his muscles.

"I cannot think what I ever saw in you," Mary ranted on. "You've been no good to me since you returned to this island and don't try and plead the shell shock. Other men suffered far worse than you and recovered. No, you are simply an idle drone, not fit to associate with decent people. You expect everything to be done for you. During the last five years I've had to carry you. You are totally useless to me, the children and the Noyen family. I am more than through with you in my bed and my home. You are finished on Guernsey. You will be made to leave and what you do elsewhere is of no consequence to me now, or in the future!"

Duret took a small step nearer until he stood one foot from her. Mary glowered at him, then a tiny pucker appeared on her forehead. His brown eyes were narrow and they gleamed with an expression she had never seen before. She glanced down and saw his hands were flexing, clenching into fists then opening again. She shot a look up again and held her breath. Instead of Duret's usual dreamy face he wore an implacable mask and had become a stranger to her. In a flash it shot through Mary's head that he was no longer normal. Something had tipped him over the thin line dividing sanity from insanity. Whether it was inherited, a trick of breeding or the throwback result of the war, she had no idea. What did register was her peril.

She was memorised by his hands, which were large for his body height. The hands which had fondled her now seemed wicked and terrifying. Mary forced her mind into quick action as alarm whipped her nerves. With a sudden swerve that took him quite unawares, she spun on her heels and raced back down the lane towards the coast road in the wild hope someone might have appeared.

She was fast and agile, driven by fear and had the advantage for the moment. Behind her, she heard him below with rage.

"Stop, you slut!"

Mary's legs pounded as her chest heaved, sucking in the great gasps of air. Her ears strained to hear him behind, then she burst onto the coast road. A quick look in both directions showed it was empty; there was nowhere she could bolt to for safety. She flung a look at the rear and saw Duret pounding after her, head low, teeth bared in fury.

Running away was anathema to Mary but there was nothing else she could do. She eyed the road. It was impossible to race back to Cobo. He would catch her in no time. She flung a look at the beach where the tide was advancing briskly. It pushed forward in fairly strong waves, cream-topped, hissing and spluttering with the power of a brisk wind.

Mary hurtled over the road, leaped the tiny parapet, stumbling on the sand, down towards the waves. There were a few rocks there and surely she could at least find a stone as a weapon? The sea moaned towards her, the waves a little bigger than she had anticipated, tumbling over and over, frothy and clean.

She made for a small collection of rocks and looked around in panic for a stone then her right shoe scuffed and a piece of rock broke loose. Bending she grabbed it and turned. He was nearly on her. At the same time, the next wave was stronger than the others and advanced with a rush, surging over her knees.

"Now I've got you!" Duret snarled plunging in the water facing her, making a grab for her left hand.

"You're mad!" Mary screamed at him and raised the rock.

"You're le Page's whore!" he roared back.

His hands shot out and aimed for her long, slender neck, meeting with their finger ends at the back in a vice-like grip. Mary lifted her right hand and brought it around. She slammed the rock against Duret's forehead at the temple. At the last second he saw it, anticipated the blow and swerved aside.

"Bitch!" he snarled and tried to tighten his grip.

Mary felt his fingers had loosened a little with his swerve and jumped backwards. He followed her without thinking, his eyes wild and murderous now. Spittle flew from his mouth just as a very large wave hit them. It thundered against their legs and it was Duret who was the most off balance. He staggered while Mary fell backwards, the wave covering her. Duret was pushed the other way by the wave's power and he flung his arms out in a desperate attempt to regain his equilibrium. Then his feet went from under him and he disappeared in the wave.

Gasping and spitting Mary struggled to stand. Her sodden clothing was heavy and there was a pain in her side. The wave went back a few feet then another came, even larger and stronger. She felt its power and tried to push forward, out of the sea's reach. With a mighty effort she waded clear and stood bent over, gasping for breath which rasped in her throat. The red mist in her eyes began to retreat and slowly turning her head, she look for Duret.

Her eyes widened as she saw him floating face down, going backwards and forwards in the waves' tugs. She stood frozen. His body was limp, his head and neck moving aimlessly to the sea's surges. Her shoulders slumped as she closed her eyes. Duret was dead but from her hand or by the sea? Violent trembles rolled through her nerves as she started to shake uncontrollably.

"Lady! Lady! Are you in trouble?"

Mary turned quickly, one hand going to her hair, feeling its sodden cap clinging to her skull. A man appeared, jumped the parapet and ran towards her with huge strides. She saw he was young, dressed in a rough fisherman's guernsey which had seen better days. He wore light shoes which were sandy and which, oddly, matched his ginger hair and freckled face.

"Here!" Mary called and pointed.

He took one look then waded into the water, grasped Duret's arms and dragged him back on the sand. The body flopped inelegantly, the head and neck lying at a crazy angle.

"He's dead, lady!" The young man looked at her with a question in his eyes.

Mary struggled to collect her wits, appalled at what had happened. She was trembling all over and hastily plonked herself down on the sand, oblivious to her wet state. She bowed her head and fought for control. Finally, gritting her teeth, she looked at the young man who stood in uneasy silence regarding her carefully.

"Do you know Cobo?" Mary asked.

He nodded and waited, catching his breath. He certainly did know it and well too even though it wasn't his parish.

"Go to the Noyens," Mary said wearily, waving one hand northwards. "Get Sam Mahy. The cob and trap are in the lane up there. The cob's shoe has moved. Sam will have to borrow something else."

Mary paused. It was difficult to think straight and she had gone bitterly cold. She shivered and bit her lip.

"Drag the body against the wall and I'll sit there until you bring help," she said, then looked up into his serious eyes. "What's your name?"

"Raymond Falla, Madam, and I'm courting Gwen Ozanne so I do know where to go."

Mary blinked and examined him a little more closely. Emily had given her a brief résumé of the young man who was hanging around showing an interest in Raoul's sister.

"I see," she said thoughtfully, then took a deep breath. "Well, off you go then and please hurry. I'm cold."

"There's my cottage half a mile away," Falla said.

Mary shook her head quickly. "No! I'll stay with the body."

Raymond Falla waited no longer. His mind buzzed with questions. What on earth was the young Madam Noyen doing in the sea in the first place and fully dressed? He scented an exciting story and was anxious to relate what he had seen to Gwen.

The Fallas were an old island family who had always been poor; poverty was a way of life with them. He and his parents lived in a bleak two-roomed cottage, set well back from the coast road and hidden, so it was unknown to most people. The floor was only hard packed earth. The furniture was skimpy and sparse except for a cherished Green Bed. The three of them often lived a hand-to-mouth existence relying upon the sea whose moods could be fickle. When they caught fish they ate well. When they didn't, they existed on root soup or went hungry. Their cottage had neither sanitation nor good well water so Raymond was the only one of a bunch of children who had not succumbed to disease.

For a long time, Raymond Falla had not given all that much thought to how other people lived on the island. They had no pony and trap, no cycle and even his young, tough legs rarely did the walk to the capital. What was the point when he never had money to spend? It had been chance that had taken him to Cobo one day when he had seen Gwen Ozanne hanging out washing. There had been something about her that had attracted his attention. She was well made with elfish features and eyes that twinkled.

He had ventured to strike up a conversation and gradually, in what spare time he had from gardening, growing food and fishing, he had commenced a gentle courtship. He was the type who would have little interest in the town girls whose first thoughts were for make-up and pretty clothes combined with trips to the pictures.

Somehow, without either of them knowing exactly how it had happened, they knew they were pledged to marry but Raymond's great problem was upon what. Fishing was a precarious way in which to earn a living and he had often been awed at what he had seen inside the Noyen house when the door was left open. It was possibly the first time he had become envious of those with money, wanting some of it for himself. No children of his were going to be reared in an unhealthy cottage with an earth floor.

As he trotted easily up the coast road towards Cobo, his mind revolved with plans and possibilities. What exactly had happened puzzled him but, more important than that, was the fact that if he helped the Noyens, perhaps they too would help him. With young Noyen well and truly dead, wouldn't they want an extra hand in their glasshouses? With a regular wage, guaranteed as long as he did the work properly, he and Gwen could get married sooner rather than later. Perhaps this day's mysterious happenings would turn out to be beneficial for both of them. With hope in his heart he jogged on.

Mary's mind had ceased to function. She could not think straight so she simply stared at the approaching waves and refused to look at Duret's body. Eventually though, she could not help it. How ugly he looked in death—but had *she* killed him? It was an appalling thought and she forced herself to go back over it all, step by step. The memory was terrible but as she thought it through with care she knew she was no killer. Her rock had missed Duret's head though her intentions at the time had been lethal. He had avoided her blow, the wave had come, larger than its predecessors, Duret had lost his balance, fallen and it was the sea which had smashed him against the hidden rocks and killed him.

She was a widow! She was free of him but she could find no exultation in her heart for his end. They had started off so well and happily. It was tragic their marriage had died, that Duret had turned into a gambling thief but, worst of all, was the realisation that he had set out to kill from jealousy. Suddenly tears flowed from shock and nervous exhaustion. Bowing her head, she cried like a child, her head on her knees, with arms around herself. She felt incredibly lonely and vulnerable. She wanted Tante and Sam and Victor and anyone who would be a friend and on her side.

Gradually there were no tears left and she lifted her red face to stare with tight lips at the sea, now at high water. As a widow she would have to start again. She had three children to rear and Tante was an old lady now. Thank God at least she had taken the first steps for a new career through James le Canu. He would be a rock at her side. Sam would be another. So would Tante but she must think and plan now as never before. But Victor! She caught her breath. How would he react? She knew, without a shadow of a doubt, that in due course he would be around and the mutual attraction was still just as strong between them. Perhaps it would never go but on this island, where it seemed impossible to keep anything secret, Mary knew a hole-in-the-corner affair with Victor would damn her in all eyes.

If she wished to establish herself as a successful business lady, her morals must be impeccable. She was shrewd enough to know how gossip flew before the wind and there were always those around ready to twist statements and actions to suit their warped minds. There was a dull weight in her stomach acute enough to be a real pain. Whatever Victor and she might feel for each other, they were doomed to be apart. Her children and their financial security came first. Biting her bottom lip, her resolution became firmer. When Victor turned up she would have to make all these thoughts quite clear. Any plans which flew into Victor's head now that she was single would have to be thrown out of it. If there had not been young children—and for a few moments she allowed herself the luxury of fanciful plans. One thing was for sure though, she told herself firmly, no more sexual encounters with Victor. Another child would be catastrophic.

A horse's hooves, clopping at a fast pace, pushed her dreams away as she craned her neck, then stood slowly. She recognised one of the local farmer's brown mares and she could spot Sam's stance on the driving seat from a distance. Beside him sat the young man, both of them staring anxiously at her.

Mary stood still, aware she was a dreadful sight. The trap stopped and the young man leaped from it energetically while Sam, moving slowly, hurried as quickly as his age allowed.

"Mary?" he rasped with worry.

"I'm all right," she told him quickly and nodded. "Duret is here. He's dead."

Sam threw her a look which held a dozen questions, then turned his attention to Raymond Falla.

"Come on! Help me lift him in the trap, then you drive him back home and return here. I'll stay with Madam."

Raymond hastened to obey, anxious to ingratiate himself in every possible way; it was vital he impress these well-off islanders.

As Raymond drove off more slowly with his burden Sam turned to Mary: "What happened?"

Mary felt the tears well up again and spill down her cheeks. "He just seemed to go mad," she said and told her tale. "You see, he came for me. I rushed down here but that young man wasn't around just then. Duret meant to kill me. He had his hands around my throat when he caught me but I'd been able to snatch a rock—"

"You hit him with it?" Sam asked quickly.

Mary shook her head violently. "I tried to but he dodged. Then a big wave came. We were both knocked down and I think that's when Duret was thrown against a small reef down there. It's quite covered now. He must have landed badly and it broke his neck. Oh Sam! He tried to kill me!" She flung herself on his chest.

Sam was horrified. He closed his eyes as his arms went around her. Dear God! He had never imagined anything like this. When young Falla had burst into the kitchen like a madman while he was having a cup of Emily's tea, he had been ready to blast him out of the parish, but one look at Falla's face and the words he had shouted had stirred Sam into fast action. He had not realised how quickly he could still move, and he knew his old body would demand recompense later. Yes, he mused, I'm not surprised. Perhaps he was always unbalanced in a way and no one recognised this.

"Young Falla did a good job," he growled more to himself than her.

Mary lifted her head with swimming eyes. She sniffed and nodded. "He did," she agreed. "We must do something for him in return. Can you see to it, Sam? I don't think I can cope with anything else today and there is still Tante to be told."

"Leave it all to me!" he said as he hugged her tightly. What a state she was in. "We must get you back and straight into a hot bath with a brandy. I'll let the authorities know too and I'll see Emily keeps the children away. I expect it'll all be a seven days' wonder. Deaths from the sea are not rare on the island."

James le Canu moodily eyed his beer and decided it had been a mistake to come for his usual evening drink with Emil. The past few days had been unusual ones, which disturbed him greatly and he eyed Emil dubiously. The police officer was also too quiet for his peace of mind. He sat brooding upon some weighty problem, chewing his lip as if he wanted to question his friend but realised, if he did so, their friendship could turn into thin ice.

"Spit it out!" James snapped.

Emil blinked. James was usually the soul of tact and discretion and such a blunt question was rare enough to warrant attention. Emil eyed him, eyebrows raised a little sardonically. How far could he go? Even young lawyers could turn difficult but Emil sensed he had not been told everything on a subject that intrigued him. The whole affair had a funny ring to it but his superior was satisfied as well as the coroner, so why did something niggle him?

"Madam Noyen's your client, isn't she?" Emil asked suddenly.

Before James could reply, the door opened and Victor le Page strode over to them, waving at the barman for his usual to be poured.

"I'm back," he grinned happily, pleased to find his pals in their usual place. "And I had a good trip too. I warrant my second hotel will soon be as full as my first. People in England are really keen on Channel Island holidays and the right publicity, in the correct places, is worth its weight in gold."

Victor took a gulp from the offered drink, sucking greedily, for he was always delighted to get back to the island.

"So what's been happening while I've been away?" he asked cheerily.

James and Emil exchanged wary glances, then turned to Victor with serious looks. They both knew of the gossip that his eye had been on the young Madam Noyen for many years. Emil also knew about the diamonds. He had his informers but as the theft had not been reported, there could hardly be a criminal investigation.

"You've not answered my question!" Emil said suddenly as Victor sat down.

"I'm not prepared to discuss persons who may or may not be my clients!" James replied frostily, ignoring Victor's raised eyebrows.

"There's no harm in such a question," Emil said mildly. He knew he had been snubbed and though this did not particularly bother him, it did tell him what he wanted to know.

"Then the same goes for my reply!" James shot back rapidly.

"Hey! What's up with you two?" Victor asked with a grin. "You look like two dogs ready to scrap over a bone!"

James and Emil turned to face him, expressions grave, eyes sombre, lips pinched. Victor felt the first flicker of alarm. He saw that Emil wore a dark scarf loosely at his throat and a mac, though he still wore his uniform trousers. Under other circumstances this attempt at denying his occupation would have amused Victor. Everyone knew he was a police officer.

James, he saw, was dressed in a smartly cut black suit and wore a black tie. He always dressed in sober colours as befitted his calling but this sombreness was enough to make him appear funereal.

"In that case, why go to the funeral?" Emil barked suddenly

The question was unexpected and, for once, James was caught flat-footed. "Respect!" was the best he could do.

"Hold it, you two! Who has died? Don't forget I've been away for just over a week. And for heaven's sake, stop glowering at each other as if you hate the other's guts when everyone knows you're big mates," Victor said mildly.

The two men paused as if reluctant to give the information, then Emil shook his head and spoke: "Duret Noyen was buried today," he said flatly.

Victor, who had been in the act of taking a large gulp, froze, spluttered, downed the pot on the table with a bang and stared at them, speechless, unable to trust his ears.

"Did you say—?" he managed to get out hoarsely.

"That's right," James confirmed. "I went to the funeral and indeed I only left the family a short while ago."

"Good God!" Victor blurted out. "What the hell happened?"

Emil told him what he knew. "It appears young Noyen had some kind of brain storm. Perhaps something had upset him the day before," he said smoothly and waited.

"Upset him?" Victor repeated like a parrot.

184

"Yes," James said. "He vanished from his home and the next day attacked his wife and tried to kill her."

Victor went white. This was getting worse by the minute. He looked from one to the other, then, shaking his head with his ears ringing at their words, he could only wait helplessly for one of them to continue.

"It seems he followed her when she was driving the trap. The cob loosened a shoe and Madam Noyen stopped to check it. Just then her husband came around the bend. There were hot words between them!"

"About what?" Victor grated.

Emil chimed in then, taking time to pick his words with care. "This did not all come out at the public inquest for the sake of the widow. But Sam Mahy did tell me that Noyen accused her of having a lover."

"Hell!" Victor swore.

Emil carried on. "The long and short of it is that she became afraid of him and bolted to the coast road—this all took place at Vazon Bay incidentally. The tide was nearly full and Madam Noyen found no one around. She went down on the sand to pick up a stone with which to defend herself. Noyen went for her then, intending to throttle her. She threw the rock she'd picked up, which missed and the post mortem confirms this. Madam did not kill her husband. The sea did. A very large wave came, which caught both of them. Madam went under but managed to get out again. Noyen went down and broke his neck on submerged rocks."

"Bloody hell!" Victor gasped, sat back and closed his eyes, then shook his head as if to clear it. He was more appalled by this story than anything he had heard in his life. His blood went icy cold as he visualised the scene. It was the thrashing he'd given Duret which must have turned his mind, tipping the scales to insanity. Then he reminded himself, to rub salt into this wound, his grandmère had taken him into her cosy home like a prodigal

185

son. How savage Noyen must have been; he had automatically taken it out on Mary. Dear heavens! She could so easily have been killed. A shiver shot down his back as he opened his eyes slowly to find the other two watching him calculatingly.

"I can hardly take this in," Victor murmured. His beer had gone flat and he had lost interest in it. "Noyen dead after trying to kill Mary?"

Slowly he stood, snapping a look at his watch. With a nod to the other two, he turned to go, wits bemused. With a sharp flash of instinct James stood as well.

"Back in a moment!" he told Emil whose eyes opened wide. Now what did foxy James find he had to say in private? He would give a lot to know but made no attempt to follow.

"Victor!" James called urgently.

"What?"

"If you're thinking of going out there right now to see your—Grandmère—don't! Let them alone for today. It's been rough on both of the Noyen ladies, so don't intrude," he advised firmly.

Victor turned to him frowning heavily. "With all due respect James, what business is it of yours?" he asked coolly.

"Madam Noyen, the younger, happens to be my client and I'll not have her badgered today by you or anyone else," James told him stiffly.

Victor was staggered. James was—Mary's lawyer? But what did Mary need a lawyer for in the first place? Grandmère was head of the family, wasn't she? He frowned heavily. Was something happening about which he knew nothing? His lips went tight and he returned James' cold stare.

"All right," he agreed slowly, "but I'm going there tomorrow. The old lady is my grandmère and I've the moral right to see how the family is."

James could think of no suitable objection to this and he nodded slowly. "Go easy though," he advised. "They've had a terrible shock."

As Victor departed, it crossed James' mind to wonder if the rumours had reached Madam le Page. He knew very little about Nicole le Page except that she hailed from Alderney, was reputed to be a gentle, quiet, almost docile girl but, he thought, that's often the type in which still waters can run very deep indeed.

Thank God the Noyens had recently installed a telephone. At least they were only a few rings away from him in case of need. He took a deep breath. Known only to himself, Madam Noyen senior had telephoned for an appointment only yesterday and he had arranged to see her tomorrow afternoon. He was not sure what this involved but he had a shrewd idea that it might concern Noyen's death. Something had certainly shaken the old lady to make her turn to him instead of one of the older lawyers whom she had favoured in the past. Did she feel the time had come for him to know all? This could pose a problem. If she had some plans which ran counter to those of Madam Noyen junior, then he would be ethically bound to send the old lady packing. Mary Noyen had come to him first and he had accepted her instructions, which made her the senior client. He shook his head, composed his features and returned to his drink and Emil. He had to have his wits about him with Emil. The policeman was sharp, intelligent, ambitious to get on and there was precious little happening on the island which did not come to his ears sooner if not later. Sometimes he wondered about the probity of having a policeman as a friend, but Emil's cousin Jane was a most attractive young lady who had caught his eye a few weeks ago. To his utmost surprise, the lawyer had found himself thinking more and more of Jane and less and less of his yacht.

ELEVEN

SAM SAT WITH the mistress. The past week's shocks and distress had put ten years on her. Seemingly overnight, the skin of both face and neck had sagged into heavy wrinkles and her hair had turned from light grey to white.

"But for the grace of God and a big wave, Mary would be dead now," she said heavily. "I can hardly bear to think about what might have been."

"Life has to go on," Sam reminded her practically, "no matter what."

"At what cost though for all of us? Especially Mary!"

Sam drew on his pipe. "Mary's tough!" he stated flatly. "She'll survive once she's recovered from the whole shocking affair and she'll be better off without Duret. He never was much good when you think back."

Louise agreed. "Let Mary do what she wants for the time being. We must run the place."

Sam nodded but knew now was the time to bring up something. "She won't find it easy rearing three children alone," he started carefully, "and there's that big house to run. I'm not getting any younger and neither are you."

Louise gave him a questioning look. She knew that when Sam started going all around a subject it was because he had some proposition he thought she might reject.

"I think Raoul should work on the house property. He's clever with his hands and could gradually take over from me. Mary has been talking of buying a car and Raoul wants to learn to drive. It wouldn't surprise me if he doesn't have a mechanical flair. I'm too old to learn about engines so I suggest Raoul is asked to leave the glasshouses. He could, if he wanted to, always go back and help if they were short-handed. As to the tomatoes, why not engage that young Raymond Falla? He's courting Raoul's sister so would want to settle in this parish and have local work. Another point: once Mary gets the holiday cottages going, wouldn't it be better to turn the whole thing into a small private company and the tomatoes into another? If you did that, Raoul could perhaps help check on the properties, see to repairs and jobs like that which means if he were given a small percentage cut, he would have an incentive?"

Louise was impressed. She could not last remember when Sam had come forward with ideas. Was it because Mary's dynamic nature had recharged all of them? How good she had been for the family, a fresh gale which was long overdue.

"I like it," she agreed, a little colour coming back to her cheeks with something else to think about. "It makes sense."

"Good!" Sam grunted with pleasure. The ideas were his own and he felt wanted now he too could contribute. "Hello! There's a car drawn up outside."

Louise stilled. She did not have to look to know who it was. She compressed her lips and looked over at Sam.

"Go and tell Mary Victor is here. He'll want to see her. It's not good me trying to send him away until he has. He'll only get difficult. Pop back to the house and warn her. Let me see, I know!" she said brightly. "Tell her to take a walk up to the Rocques and I'll send him up there in thirty minutes."

Sam nodded to her and clumped from the cottage around the back as Victor came to the front. Sam found Mary grooming the cob for want of some physical activity. Emily and Gwen had closed ranks around her protectively and she felt there was little for her to do. She had become an empty shell, drifting with the tidal currents, rudderless and useless.

"Mary!" Sam said, approaching her. She'd brush the animal away if she kept on like that. "The mistress wants you to walk up the Rocques in thirty minutes' time."

Mary stilled, then turned to regard him uneasily. "Victor?"

Sam nodded. "He's been in England, didn't get back until yesterday. He'll want to talk to you and it's no good trying to dodge him. Better to have it out with him, once and for all. You both have to live on this island," he advised.

Mary knew he was right but was she ready to talk to Victor and make him realise how matters must now be between them? Her earlier decision had not changed. He was a married man and divorce was something she would not countenance.

"I'll go," she said reluctantly, "but there's something else, Sam." She paused before continuing. "After this experience, when I have never felt so helpless, I've made myself a promise. I will never be so defenceless again, come what may. I want to be able to protect myself at all times."

Sam was puzzled. "What do you have in mind?"

Mary told him quietly and Sam's eyebrows shot up. He had not contemplated anything quite so drastic and felt inclined to argue but one look at Mary's obstinate expression made him change his mind. After a quick think, he reluctantly came down on her side of logic.

"It would just be for insurance purposes," Mary ended, "and no one would have to know, not even Tante."

Sam chewed his lip. "I think I can manage it though it might take a little while," he warned her. "It's possible to get hold of nearly anything from certain ships which come into St Sampson if one has the money." He added quickly, "It might be expensive."

"Hang the cost!" Mary replied swiftly. "It's what I want and must have for my own peace of mind."

"You'd have to keep your mouth shut!"

Mary threw him a wolfish grin. "I will until—" She let the

190

sentence hang in the air. Sam understood and could not find it in himself to blame after her experience.

"Leave it to me then," he promised quietly. This was one piece of information which simply must not reach the ears of either James le Canu or Emil le Norman. "And then I'll help you learn. It's no good having one without being skilled, is it?"

Mary hugged him. "God bless you, dear Sam. I don't know what I'd do without you. My marriage was worth it because it meant coming here and meeting you," she told him sincerely.

Sam sniffed and averted his gaze. "Get off with you then," he told her gruffly and, seeing through his emotion, Mary turned to walk to the Rocques.

Victor left his car outside the cottage. He had decided to walk to give himself time in which to think. Grandmère had told him so much that had staggered him, shocking him into utter silence. Diamonds! Who would have thought it of the family? And he could not help but grin with admiration at his unknown English ancestor. What a wild, rip-roaring hellion, Danny Penford must have been but what a wonderful chap to know. A man after his own heart and, he mused, in many ways Grandmère was like him. She was ruthless, intelligent, domineering and, when it suited her own ends, downright devious. A vision of Mary shot into his head. He started to think deeply as he walked without hurrying. Mary was like Grandmère without the blood tie. The similarity was startling and he wondered why he had failed to see this before. Was it because he had been so besotted with love for her as Heathcliff's Catherine?

His mind moved to Nicole. She was a good wife and mother. He could not fault her in any way but Nicole had no spark. She was utterly predictable and he suspected that, over the years, he might even find her boring. Why had he married her then? He knew why and the fault was of his own making. He had tried to be clever with youth's impetuosity. When he had learned of Mary's marriage he had thrown himself at the first available girl. That this happened to be Nicole, whom he had met on Alderney, was pure chance; it could just as soon have been anyone. Who was to blame? Duret Noyen was for one and now he was dead. Grandmère had been a big culprit in despising him unjustly and for her action in pushing Mary towards Noyen. Mary had been weak for just once in her life, yielding to emotional pressure and financial dazzlements but—now she was free!

His mind was spun with implications. She was a widow and he had been admitted back into the family fold but—there was Nicole and his children. He ground his teeth together. It went against his nature to hurt the innocent under normal circumstances but Victor knew his feelings for Mary had never been normal.

He looked ahead and with his keen eyes could see a female silhouette against the skyline, muffled in a loose jacket. His heart thudded and he wondered why his steps slowed. He should be running towards her. Something dragged his feet and he had a gnawing feeling that today was not going to be one of his best.

Mary saw him coming and realised the bitter moment of truth was approaching. She turned to face him as he left the road and walked over the short grass. He was dressed in discreet dark clothes to suit the family's solemnity.

She felt a stiffness inside her as well as the old magic that sight of him could produce. For a few seconds she writhed at the injustice of it all, then her common sense reared its head. She remembered what she had decided and there was no going back.

Victor eyed her, suddenly lost for words. She seemed remote, waiting for him to speak. He gave a little shake of his head, moved both hands with an eloquent gesture and said, "Let's walk, shall we?"

Mary nodded and fell into step as they strolled gently over the turf. There was a brisk wind and it had turned cool. The sky in the west held dark grey clouds which loomed low and threatening. They reached the top of the rock and looked down to where the sea boiled as the tide prepared to turn. In between the lower rocks were cracks and crevices into which small stones had been deposited over the years. The greedy waves now teased these, sucking and pulling them in the start of anger. There was constant motion and the sea was as grey as the sky near to them but, further back, it turned to a dull black. Mary shivered and closed her eyes. "There's going to be a storm. I'm not stopping here long."

Victor nodded and looked at her carefully. She was dressed in a deep grey skirt with a black blouse but she wore no hat and her hands were unrestrained by gloves.

Mary sensed his thoughts. "Why wear full mourning?" she asked quietly. "It would be hypocritical. I have enough on to conform with custom and suit the gossips."

"I'd be a canting humbug if I said I was sorry at his death," Victor told her slowly.

He wanted to reach out and grasp her hand but something stopped him. She stood rigidly aloof and he felt as if a mile separated them instead of a pace. He knew that if he attempted any physical contact she would recoil from him because, somehow, she had altered. It was difficult for him to put a finger on the change but he felt as if she had erected an enormous barrier between them, strong and unclimbable, and she stood well back inside its ramparts. His heart ached with sadness and also joy at her presence in a way which confused him.

"So where does that leave us?" he asked quietly.

Mary gave him her full attention. She stared deep into violet-coloured eyes only inches above hers. She knew he wanted to hold her, take her into his protection, lay her head on his chest. Once, oh! How she would have thrilled to this but now, though Duret was dead and buried, in his going he had done what was impossible while he lived. Mary felt him around her as something not evil but unpleasant; as if his spirit spied upon them to confirm he *had* been right after all.

"Nowhere, Victor," she replied gently. "It was simply never meant to be."

"That's crazy," he protested quickly. "Nothing has changed between us. I know it. I still want you and only you."

"You are married with children," Mary told him and was astonished at how calm she felt. "I will not be a party to shattering a marriage. My life now is here on this island and I wish to be respected, not held in contempt. It's no good, Victor. There are no words to make me change my mind. I have three children to raise and I intend to be a business woman in the process. I must therefore be whiter than white."

"Oh, Mary!" he groaned in anguish. "Don't reject me out of hand again."

"I must!" she told him simply.

Victor took a slow, deep breath while his mind worked rapidly. He must try another ploy because the look on her face was implacable. How *could* she deny what he knew *had* to be in her heart? So dirt might fly but surely two people had the right to live the lives they chose?

"Grandmère told me about your land deals," he started carefully. "I think holiday lets are a good idea. I know there are people who come here and who might well prefer a cottage to themselves," he said forcing a grin on his face that did not quite reach his eyes. "I've had a couple in the hotel only a month ago. They were cluttered up with fishing rods and gear. Now in a cottage they wouldn't be any bother; they'd be able to do as they liked but in an hotel they were a nuisance to other guests. So how about us joining forces in business? No one can object to that—surely?"

Mary gave him a long, hard look. It flashed through her mind this could be Tante's idea. During the last appalling week she had sensed something brewing in her head and that it concerned her. As Tante had ruthlessly pushed her towards Duret, surely to God she did not now intend to push her and Victor together? Her lips set tight. Tante had manipulated her for the last time.

"Whose idea is this?" she asked coldly.

Victor was surprised at her tone. "Well, actually it's mine but I did mention it to Grandmère and she thought it made sense. We would both benefit. I could push in your direction the visitors I don't really want without giving great offence. We could advertise ourselves as an hotel plus self-catering accommodation." He paused, puzzled by her reaction which was openly hostile. "It's a sound thought, Mary. Why don't you think about it?"

"I don't have to," she told him flatly. "I'm not working with you, Victor in any capacity, come what may. My business is mine and will stay that way. Yours belongs to you and your family." She looked at him with exasperation. "It's no good, Victor. It wouldn't work for us to see each other on a day-to-day basis. Nicole isn't that much of a fool, surely to God?"

He scowled pugnaciously. "My business doesn't concern Nicole!"

"It should do," Mary retorted tartly.

"As long as I keep her supplied with adequate money, that's all she needs to care about," he hurled back angrily. He supposed he should have known better. Mary was so fiercely independent but he had allowed himself to hope they could be with each other on a daily, legitimate basis. He opened his mouth to argue more forcefully.

"No!" Mary forestalled him. "It's finished, Victor."

He snorted. "I wasn't aware it had ever begun," he grumbled almost petulantly.

"Victor, this is getting us nowhere. I'm going because rain will be here shortly. You can walk back down the road with me then we'll shake hands, and that—will be that!"

He couldn't believe it. Surely she could not mean it. An abrupt severing of all that lay between them was impossible for him and he considered it to be the same for her, so who was this proud, stiff jawed girl? Where had his wild Mary gone?

"Mary! *I love you!*" he affirmed holding her gaze, trying to pour his adoration into her.

Mary broke eye contact first, feeling an awful sadness well up and a lump to start to stick in the middle of her throat. She knew he spoke the truth. She guessed he knew her pose was a charade but she was also aware that if she yielded but a fraction it would be fatal for both of them. Now was the time when she must be the stronger, no matter what it might cost.

She tipped her head slightly, as if saluting him, then walked by. He went to grab her hand but she anticipated this and swung it briskly as she lengthened her stride. The clouds were coming nearer and already she fancied there was a fine spray coming from the sea. Suddenly the first raindrops hit them with a vengeance and she broke into a run.

He loped at her side. "Put some speed on," he encouraged, "or we're going to get soaked!"

By the time they reached the cottage the rain was coming down steadily, slanting with the wind as the clouds boiled up ready for a storm.

"I'm going home," Mary called, her soaking hair stuck to her head, her clothes clinging to her figure, outlining it, making it look even more wonderful. "Goodbye, Victor!"

"No!" he shouted, springing before her to block her path. "Please see me again!" he cried frantically, then grabbed her hands. "Mary, I've never begged a man for anything in my life and certainly not a woman. I beg you, I beseech you, see me again?"

Mary's shoulders sagged wearily and she went to shake her head. He was making it all so agonising.

"Not next week or next month," he told her in a panic now. "Look!" he shouted above the torrential rain. "Let some time go by and think about it all. I'll meet you exactly two months today at—" His mind worked frantically. It had to be somewhere very private. Inspiration hit him. "At Torteval, Pleinmont Point. The hill there, up the track and I'll be waiting halfway for you. Please come."

Mary felt the rain lashing her face, making her eyes narrow. They must look a pair of idiots standing out in such weather with him holding her hands. She must, simply must, get away from him. She looked again into his begging eyes and softened. A lot could happen in two months.

"Oh, very well," she agreed reluctantly.

He released her hands, triumphant with victory. "I'll be there," he promised.

Mary turned and started to hurry towards her home as the rain pounded down. She was sodden yet also strangely exhilarated. Was he sending her mad? She knew she would see him again if only to emphasise her decision because in two months' time her resolution would surely have grown harder and more set. He had to accept her judgement so they could both live in peace on Guernsey.

A week later Sam spoke to her. "I have one," he said quietly aware that Emily was in the kitchen.

Mary looked at him sharply. The kitchen door was wide open and though she stood outside near the back patio she had long ago learned that Emily had keen hearing. She felt a flutter of excitement and Sam looked smugly pleased with himself.

"Slip out in the next hour," Sam hissed, "and I'll show you."

"But where can we go?" Mary asked, aware that in daytime people were around in the nearby glasshouses.

Sam thought a moment. "We'll take the trap and I'm showing you a cottage," he grinned roguishly.

Her spirits were slowly rising. Sometimes she felt dreadful because she did not miss Duret at all; indeed there was a lighter atmosphere in the house. The children seemed more agreeable and Raoul, busy training Raymond to take over in the glasshouses, with a boy to help him, was spending as much time as he could with Sam. She liked Raoul. He did not speak in a hurry but what he did say held sense. In many ways, he was not unlike Sam and, give him a few more years, he would be Sam's double in thought and action. Raoul's wife Amelia was quite happy with the new arrangements because Mary had taken the chance and confided in Raoul with Sam at her side. He had been very impressed with her plans and flattered when she had indicated that, once the business was on a good footing, it would become a small private company and he would be cut in.

Raymond too was highly satisfied with the way matters had turned out. He was on hand to court Gwen who was also delighted and they had their eye on a small cottage up the lane. It was in a bad state of repair but Mary had bought it and told Raymond that if he did it up, he could live there rent-free for as long as he worked for the family. Raymond never ceased to count his blessings that he had peeped through his father's hedge that day and seen the odd sight of two fully dressed adults having a row while standing in the sea. It was only later he had learned more details and even then, unknown to either him or Gwen, they had been told only what Mary and Tante thought they should know. James le Canu had been with them and the lawyer's presence had impressed both Raymond and Gwen with the seriousness of it all.

"They seem decent enough, Madam," James had said after the young couple left, "but I've found it a good policy in life not to let the left hand know all the right hand does!" he had finished, giving Louise a straight look.

Mary had missed the byplay which was just as well because, very quickly, Louise had given a slow secretive wink to the young lawyer and it had taken him all his time to keep a suitably straight face. James le Canu wondered what the senior lady would have thought at the other matter which had been in his mind for a while and which had been carefully discussed with someone as deep and secretive as himself. Their conversation would have appeared odd if there had been an eavesdropper, which was impossible because they were both too sharp and wary. In this year of 1923, surely life was settling down after the terrible war despite the worries of unemployment and trade recession.

In a short while, Mary sat beside Sam as he drove gently up the lane and headed into the countryside. There had been a heavy dew and globules of moisture still stuck to the grasses and hedges' lower leaves but the sun had come out. Though a little watery Sam knew it would turn into a nice early summer's day. He drew the cob back to a walk at a gate, jumped down, opened it, then lead the cob and trap through.

Mary looked ahead to a small spinney and an ancient cottage, then she gazed around. They were quite alone and seemingly miles from the sea though she guessed they were barely over one from the coast as the crow flew.

"Come on!" Sam grunted stepping into the lead. "We'll go around the back of the cottage but I'll just check there are no children playing in it. It's a holiday for them today," he reminded her.

Mary did not need to be told this. Margaret was racing around, full of energy, into all sorts of mischief and dragging William with her. She hoped that Gwen would soon take them down to the beach to build sandcastles or hunt for shells.

After a few moments, Sam came back. "We're alone all right," he grunted and dived into the front of his shirt to withdraw the pistol.

Mary took it gingerly and studied it carefully. It was small which made it perfect and she flashed her delight at Sam. She had already started to insert pockets into all of her skirts and whatever she acquired from now on would have the same. This tiny pistol could fit snug and hidden, unsuspected by any attacker.

"Now I'll show you how to load and use it. It's an American Derringer," Sam told her. "They have always been popular with ladies because they can slide into a small handbag. Gamblers use them a lot too. They can be dressed up wearing a smart evening jacket which looks innocent but one of these tiny pistols is easily concealed. There are two barrels which means you'll only ever have two shots. It's not like a revolver with six or more," he warned her seriously.

"If I can't get out of trouble with two shots, then I doubt I'd manage it with six!" Mary said bleakly.

"Pay attention!" Sam told her sternly. "This is only a small weapon. I doubt you'd get a tinier one so you are limited in both range and accuracy. It's best to consider this a pistol to use on someone close to. Not yards away because though it has an explosive charge, it's small; the power soon wears off and the bullet starts to fall." Mary listened attentively, nodding at the points he made.

"It's best to aim for the body which is a larger target than the head," Sam touched his middle. "There's a big artery here. You put a bullet in the middle of that and no one is going to recover," he added grimly. "It's not a toy, Mary. Don't think that because it *is* small. This can kill just as efficiently as a large service revolver, given the right range and accuracy."

Under Sam's guidance Mary practised loading and unloading, the operation of the safety catch, then firing the weapon. To Sam's surprise she had a good eye and steady hand. It took very little practice for her to hit the target he had erected near an oak tree.

"The secret of shooting," Sam continued," is constant practice. It's just like anything else. Practice does indeed make perfect."

"I'll do that," Mary told him in a hard voice. She doubted whether even Sam fully understood the terror Duret had instilled in her with his big hands locked around her neck. From now on, she would be able to defend herself and if anything happened in which the law heard of the derringer and confiscated it, she would simply get another.

"Good," Sam grunted after a while. "That's enough for today. Little and often is better than two hours at a stretch and, Mary, this must remain our secret. I'm now an accomplice," he reminded her.

Mary wondered from whom he had obtained the pistol but she knew better than to ask. She knew Sam was discreet enough not to have left a trail for any inquisitive policeman to follow like that nosy Emil le Norman.

As the weeks slipped past Mary resumed her new life, throwing herself into a careful study of any old cottages that came on the market. Some she instructed the lawyer to buy while others she rejected outright and gradually she came to know him well enough to use his first name like Tante. The cottages near the sea were the ones she favoured though she had bought two useful small houses near Sous l'Eglise almost in the island's centre, reckoning there might be holiday-makers not interested in the sea—artists perhaps or people who might prefer simple country walks. She always discussed everything with Sam and Tante; if one did not know the area, the other did and finally they decided upon the name of Noyen Enterprises for their little company. They gave the lawyer instructions to see about forming this for the following year.

She never mentioned Victor and neither did Tante, although Mary was sure she saw her grandson on a regular basis.

On the eve before she had promised to meet him, she stood talking to Tante examining her front garden, which was now a picture of bedding plants and shrubs against the boundary wall. The heavy jobs of cutting the grass had been taken over by Raoul who had turned into a fine right-hand man. Even Sam could find no fault with him and Amelia was a good wife, rearing their two young sons.

"I'm seeing Victor tomorrow afternoon," Mary said casually. Tante went stiff and flashed a sharp look at her. "I'm glad you're friends," she said carefully.

"I don't know about that," Mary replied with equal precision. "We are rather alike which makes fighting material, doesn't it?"

"So what are you seeing him for then?"

Mary faced her. "To reaffirm what I said two months ago. That it's best we keep apart if we are both to live and work here. I shall not be joining him in any business venture either. Seeing him daily would be most unwise."

"For whom?"

Mary paused then shrugged. "For both of us, I think, Tante," she admitted and knew, with those words, she had said it all.

"But you are going to see him though?"

Mary pulled a face. "I gave my word."

Old Tante put one brown age-spotted hand on Mary's shoulder. "Don't quarrel with him," she asked. "I'd hate him to stop coming here."

Mary laughed then. "I can assure you nothing will stop Victor doing what he wants when he wants."

So the next afternoon May quietly drove the trap around the coast road to their meeting. She was astonished to find she was wildly excited and chastised herself severely. She wore a skirt which was old but which she liked. It came to just below her knees, daringly exposing a lot of leg. It was white with green dots and her blouse was the same shade of pale green. She wore sandals and had brought a white cardigan with her. She knew she looked fresh and wholesome. Wearing her favourite perfume made her feel extra good and, under other circumstances, it would have been a gorgeous afternoon.

He saw the trap coming and knew it was her, recognising the way she sat as he admired how she handled the reins. That cob was getting old though and he wondered when the family would buy another. As she halted and tied the horse's head to a post he stood up, in two minds whether to stride down to her, then made himself wait. His heart was like a machine gun with its rapid rate of beat. The past two months had been a time of agony for him; a period in which he had been so quiet at home even Nicole had given him some strange looks. Victor knew he was powerless though. He was not just besotted with Mary; his feelings went much deeper and were strong enough to keep him awake, night after agitated night.

Mary toiled up the path to him then stopped a pace away, smiling gently. How beautiful she was, he thought.

"Thank you for coming," he said softly, then pointed behind him. "Let's climb to the top and walk around the point," he invited.

Mary was glad to put off the evil moment and scrambled after him until they could stand together looking out over the sea that was two shades of green-blue depending upon the water's depth.

Mary threw a quick look around. They were certainly alone and for a second she felt a tiny pang of alarm but dismissed it, turning back to where he pointed out to sea in one particular direction.

"It's a treacherous coastline we have on the west side," he told her. "Did you know that most shipping charts carry a 'Caution' warning not to approach the island nearer than three miles on this side?"

Mary became interested as always in anything to do with the island. "No, I did not."

"Way over there is the Hanois Bank which has always been a nightmare for mariners. A lot of good men have met their Maker on that reef. Further down is Lithou Island which can be reached by a causeway at low tide but caution is needed. If someone's halfway across and the tide has turned, they can die. The sea rips through in a fierce current. There used to be a priory there to our Lady of Lithou but it's a ruin now."

Mary had heard of the island but not realised its exact position. "Doesn't anyone go there now?"

He nodded. "Oh yes! Many people go over to collect the *vraic*. Gathering the seaweed from the foreshore used to be a very important industry. Then it was dried in the open air before being burned in a brick-line pit. Iodine can be made from the ashes."

Mary was grateful to him for his casual conversation; it helped to settle her nerves, which had started their usual jangle the moment she saw him. Victor looked around and pointed.

"Let's sit there," he suggested, leading the way back from the path to some short, dry grass, making a tiny dell between some furze bushes. Mary noted he had brought a rug, which he placed on the ground and helped her to sit, before flopping down with his back to the sea so he could face her.

"I still love you," he said simply and waited hopefully. Surely over these past weeks she had recovered from Duret's death and would see sense? He had thought long and hard about what they could do and though he had talked none of this over with Grandmère, he knew instinctively she would agree.

Mary simply looked blankly at him, almost hooding her eyes, hiding her feelings though a dull ache had entered her heart. He had not changed. He still thought he could wear her down with persistence and charm. She suddenly realised this was going to be more difficult than she had anticipated.

"Well, say something," he protested at her silence," even if it's only to tell me you don't like me!"

Mary smiled miserably. "You know that's not true," she said, pausing a little uncertainly.

He reached over and grabbed one hand. "You are free now and—!"

"But you are not," Mary said quickly.

"I've decided to divorce Nicole!"

Mary caught her breath, then shook her head violently. "You can't do that to her for having the bad fortune to marry you. That's no remedy!"

"I don't really care for her. I never did," he said in a low voice, breaking off a piece of grass and twiddling with it before looking up at her again. "I only married her in a fit of pique," he admitted.

"She is the mother of your twins," Mary told him sternly. "I won't be a party to anything like that!"

He leaned over and took her other hand. Instantly Mary knew what was going to happen. There was a look in his eyes that flashed fire for her, which she could not hold.

"Mary! Oh my wonderful, spirited Mary!" he crooned, pulling her nearer until she felt she was tumbling. "Don't deny facts. I've told you before we're made only for each other. Look how the sun beams on us. Feel how soft the grass is. I want you, Mary. Let's love each other again!"

Mary felt a surge of panic. She knew how strong he was but still struggled to free her hands. She must get away from him. She had been mad to agree to this meeting. Suddenly he was half over her, his mouth seizing hers. She fought wildly, jerking and trying to knee him, anything to make him release her hands. Then with an effort she twisted and both hands shot from his grasp as he grabbed her shoulders, pushing her down on her back, one hand plunging into the open neck of her blouse, fondling her breast.

Mary twisted her head aside and screeched at him, wriggling to get away but only making her skirt ride up more to expose long legs that inflamed him further. He shot one hand downwards while hunting for her lips as all finesse left him. Once they had made love again she could not deny him and he knew he could then persuade her to follow his wishes.

Mary went berserk, twisting and writhing, visualising getting pregnant again through him. Hot anger exploded in a sheet of flame at his arrogance presumption that she would yield a second time. Thrusting with her feet, her shoes found a hidden rock. Using it as a brace she pushed, twisted violently to the left and, with springy ankles, regained her feet. She stood panting down at him, incoherent with fury. She gasped, sucking air into her lungs and turned to get back on the path and down to the safety of the trap, and home to Cobo.

He regained his feet with a bound, eyes narrow, nostrils pinched and eyes ablaze with desire. He prepared to grab her again when she jumped back another pace, one hand shot into a deep pocket in her skirt and the tiny pistol appeared.

"Stop!" she hissed warningly.

Victor froze with astonishment, his jaw dropping with shock. He noted how firmly the pistol was held with a finger on the trigger. He recognised the make and realised he was well within range.

"You come one step nearer and I'll shoot!" Mary panted. "Don't push me! I mean it, Victor!"

A slow, confident smile touched his lips. He shook his head. "Not me!"

This display of self-assurance infuriated Mary even more.

"Give me that pistol," he said coolly, holding out his hand. The pulse pounded in his throat as he realised he had gone about this like a bull in a china shop. He should have aroused her with love play and he groaned inwardly. It was the old story. She did something to him that pushed reason and sense aside.

"I will shoot!"

She sensed he was going to leap at her and remembered Sam's words. She could not hit his middle. He would die! Had he gone crazy? Had he planned this? But her heart hardened. She was not a bitch on heat to be taken with force. He leaped. Mary's fast reflexes warned her one heartbeat before his feet moved. She swung the pistol's barrel slightly to her right and fired coolly. The derringer gave a tiny bark and the bullet hit his left upper arm with surprising power. He stopped dead in his tracks, looked down at the wound already showing blood, then over at her with shocked disbelief.

"You've just shot me!"

"I've another bullet, Victor!"

"Why you cold-blooded little bitch!" he shouted as his right hand tried to stem the blood flow.

"Get out of my life then, once and for all!" Mary cried at him.

"I'll have you up in court for this!" he shot back, wild-eyed with humiliation.

"I'll counter charge with intended rape!" she retorted still keeping the pistol on him, steady and unwavering.

"That's illegal. I'll have it taken away from you!" he cried with frustration.

"Then I'll simply get another to deal with the likes of you!" she spat at him.

"Mary!"

She turned on her heel. Sweat poured from her forehead; her legs dithered and she knew she must get away from him and go home. Later, she would be in tears with shock. She had known she must end their relationship but had never dreamed it would come to this. "Men!" she stormed to herself as she began to slither back down the path. "I hate them all! All except Sam!" she added as a rider.

She regained the road, ran to the cob, unfastened his head, leapt in the trap and, snapping the reins, hurried the old animal into a sharp trot to his surprise. She threw one look behind her. He stood halfway down the path, one hand clasped to the left arm, bewilderment etched on every feature.

She drove back at a pace that made the cob sweat and that would annoy Sam but she knew she must hurry. Reaction had started to set in. She wanted a stiff brandy or whisky. She had to tell someone but not just anyone. She knew she was going to have a fearsome headache later and she swore lustily to herself. Oh damn him, damn, damn, *DAMN*! Why couldn't he just accept the situation as she did?

She turned up her home lane and brought the cob to a sharp halt, jumped from the trap and ran up Tante's path, bursting in without even a knock. The old woman was startled and so was Sam who, smoking his pipe, was allowing himself the luxury of some idleness now that Raoul was around.

Mary halted abruptly, white-faced, tense and angry. "I've just left your grandson," she told the old woman. She felt far too angry to be diplomatic. "He tried to rape me so I've shot him!"

"You've what!" Tante gasped, eyes opening wide with disbelief.

"Oh no!" Sam groaned, closing his eyes.

"Yes I did!" Mary stormed. "I'm not someone to be pushed on my back just because he has an infatuation. I've told him and told him until I'm blue in the face but he thinks because he is bigger and stronger, he can do just as he likes. Well, he can't! It's over! Finished! I never want to see or speak to him again. In future, Tante, I'll be obliged if you'd inform me when he's coming to visit you so I can make sure I'm elsewhere and Sam, if he attempts to set foot on the house property, you are to get the constable!"

Sam collected his wits "Is he badly hurt?" he asked practically, standing ready to get a doctor.

"I've winged his left arm. It's only a flesh wound," Mary said without sympathy.

"Where is the pistol?" Sam wanted to know next.

"With me and that's where it stays!"

Tante gulped and flashed a look at Sam. She had known nothing about a pistol but commonsense told her how and why Mary had acquired one.

"I'll drive round and see how he is," Sam grunted, tamping out his pipe. "I'll try and keep this quiet but it all depends upon le Page," he pointed out.

"One word in public from him and I'll scream rape!" Mary promised hotly.

Both Sam and Tante could see she meant it. Tante smothered a groan. Where were all the delicious plans she had dared to make? Let enough time elapse and perhaps something might be tactfully arranged regarding Nicole. Louise knew more about Nicole's family than was realised and also she knew that money was capable of opening many doors seemingly shut. Her scheming mind had toyed with the idea of persuading Nicole to divorce on the mainland with money as the bait. Victor could have gone there too for an arranged adultery then, in due course, Mary and Victor could have married. The family would have ended up with the best of both worlds. True Penford blood and a very strong man as family head.

Now she swore to herself. Mary's temper was aroused. Despite any latent suspicions she harboured regarding Edwin, Louise knew the family now had a real schism that made the Duret affair elementary. Both Mary and Victor were knuckle-headed; neither would ever give way; one from righteous indignation and the other from masculine pride.

"Go on, Sam," she said in a low voice. "Sort something out and let me know."

Mary felt her rage evaporating. Later she would talk to Tante about it all but right now was not the time. She was going home and would talk to no one. She would climb the stairs to her sewing room, shut the door and have a long, bitter, private cry.

PART THREE—1933

TWELVE

MARY FLASHED HER teeth in a wide grin and pressed down a little harder on the accelerator. She adored her car and, with the hood down on this warm day, she felt wildly happy and carefree. She wore her new tan-coloured linen slacks with a tan and white shirt to match. Around her neck she had casually fastened a white chiffon scarf which flowed behind like a triumphant pennant. She was bareheaded as always, her hair shaped short and in a cheeky cut while her skin was tanned from the weather. She was out of doors as much as possible and at thirty-three felt better than at any time in her life. She flung a mischievous glance at her companion.

Tante sat nervously poised, one hand restraining a large-brimmed white hat which threatened to depart in a rush. The old lady, now an incredible eighty-three years, was not so sure about this method of transport. She had felt much safer in an old-fashioned pony and trap.

"How fast are we going?" Tante gasped.

"Nearly thirty miles an hour. Isn't it fun?"

"Don't you dare go any faster, my girl!" Tante told her sternly. "My nervous system won't stand it!"

"Rubbish! You're as tough as old boots!"

Old Tante sniffed in her famous way, then allowed herself a twinge of pride. It was true, at her age, she was quite remarkable. She still had all her mental faculties and, apart from the more frequent bouts of rheumatism, was active for her years. Her sight had let her down though and she was forced to peer owlishly through black-rimmed glasses. Lately, she had fancied her hearing might also be deteriorating but this did not bother her. It could be useful at times not to hear what was said. It made a perfect excuse to go her own way in blithe indifference to other's opinions. Her hair had thinned a little but was still an attractive crown of white to her wise old face. She considered she had aged with dignity, which was more than could be said for some she reminded herself.

"You'll live to be a hundred!" Mary shouted back at her, turning to take the bend at Grand Havre. She had taken to driving easily and was proud of her skill. Retiring the cob, selling the trap and buying the car had been one of her better moves.

Tante wasn't at all sure she wished to live for a century but she passed no comment. When Mary was in one of these jolly moods she was inclined to let her hair down and become childishly young and refreshing with it.

The old woman thought back wistfully. Did the good times really outweigh the bad ones? The last really bad memory had been when Mary shot Victor. His wound had been slight and easily attended to with discretion. His pride though had been mauled and for days he breathed fire and thunder concerning Mary who had not turned a hair. Louise often wondered what Nicole le Page thought when her husband returned with his wound. Victor had never said and Louise had always been aware that any mention of Nicole put their relationship on thin ice, though he had calmed down about the actual shooting.

Victor visited his grandmère weekly and Mary, as promised, kept well away on these occasions and Victor had sense enough not to try and force an issue by walking up to the house.

Tante was always amused to notice though that, after Victor's visit, Mary would casually appear and listen attentively to what they had discussed. If it had not been so deadly serious between the pair of them, old Tante would have found it hilariously funny.

Deep down though, when in a more sober mood, she reflected upon how incredibly sad it all was.

Mary brought the car to a slow halt where the lane ended at the edge of Ladies Bay. The land was flat, broken only here and there by old Martello towers. She dived into her handbag for a cigarette, which caused Tante to frown though she said nothing. Mary quietly handed over a bag of toffees instead, her eyes twinkling, daring her companion to pass a comment.

"Well," Mary said leaning back, exhaling smoke. "What is the news?"

Louise's eyes twinkling maliciously. "If you would unbend enough to talk to him yourself, you'd find out!" she teased coldly.

"Tante!"

"Oh very well," Tante said with another sniff.

"The le Pages seem well and thriving. The twins are nice children. Victor brought them to see me two weeks ago but I've not yet met James, he's only three. It was a shame they lost Anna from the whooping cough in '27. She was the spitting image of her father."

"And Madam le Page?" Mary asked carefully.

Tante threw her a sideways look and did not reply. Victor had told her where his heart truly lay but after the shooting she had fancied his relationship with Nicole had entered a better phase. She could only deduce he had given up his wild ideas for the time being.

Knowing how gossip flew around the island, Louise often asked herself uneasily exactly what Nicole did know. Surely she did not live in blind ignorance? Would she ever dare make trouble for the family? As each year sped by and when nothing happened, Louise's fears gradually evaporated, almost allowing Nicole le Page to vanish from her mind.

Nor did Mary think about Victor often now. She considered she had conquered that ghost at last and though it was true they bumped into each other occasionally, both behaved with the utmost civility and manners. She admired Victor for the way he had gone ahead. His two hotels were now three, all in different parts of the island, which enabled him to cope with visitors of differing tastes and requirements. He kept one open all year round and acquired three first-class managers, which left him free to concentrate upon administration and supervision. Mary knew he was well thought of with a respected name just as she was aware of his regular visits to his grandmère.

The terrible heartache she had known for so long when thinking of him had gradually died down to be replaced with a warm glow. Whether this was maturity or the fact she worked so hard and was exhausted each night, she was uncertain. She slept and ate well, enjoying tremendous health and fitness. Now she could think about Victor without churning nerves or pounding heart.

The number of properties they acquired was numerous, though some stood vacant needing considerable repair. James advised her to advance cautiously and Mary did this. Gradually, a cottage here or a bungalow there were refurbished and joined those available to let on monthly or weekly terms.

She had two properties on the south coast with its magnificent walks; four on the west, two on the north and two inland. The east coast she ignored because of St Peter Port and St Sampson. These properties, when occupied, provided a steady income, which grew because their business was becoming well known.

Raoul proved a godsend with his various skills. He learned to drive and a second vehicle was obtained for his exclusive use. The little cream van could be seen in various parts of the island transporting Raoul and his tools on a repair or renovation work. Mary was vastly encouraged and had also toyed with the idea of a town house if she could find one, though premises of this nature were difficult and expensive to obtain. All in all, during the years since Duret's death, she had gone steadily forward and was well satisfied.

Her thoughts switched to her children. She smiled gently as she considered Margaret who was now fourteen years old and well on the way to considering herself a young lady. There had been a few boisterous years when Margaret had lived as a tomboy but abruptly these had ceased so Mary guessed there was a boy at school. Margaret was bright with a great capacity to learn and she was a pleasant child though had a will of her own and was difficult to turn aside when she had set her heart upon anything. From the start, Mary had learned that she was easy to discipline if a reason was given for her not to do anything. Blind obedience would never be Margaret's forte but a logical explanation was always accepted though detail had to be correct to the nth degree. Sometimes Mary worried about her daughter. She was gifted enough to go to university which might mean the mainland and once there, would she lose her love for Guernsey? On the other hand, she had never asked the girl what her future plans were. Sometimes Margaret could fall into a deep reserve where even Mary hesitated to trespass. She had learned it was better to wait because, in time, Margaret would come to her and ask advice.

Edwin was a docile little boy. At ten years he was so reserved he was almost solemn but his face would light up whenever he saw her. Mary knew she loved him to distraction and it was a struggle to keep this hidden from the other children. He was a lean child without much strength, mostly long arms and thin legs and it seemed as if a puff of wind would blow him away.

He adored big sister Margaret but was wary of elder brother William, which worried Mary. Edwin liked collecting things especially seashells. Margaret was not greatly interested but went along with her young brother. William though looked down upon such juvenile interests, as beneath him.

Mary's mind then turned to William and her lips went tight. William! At twelve years he had nothing in common with the other two children. He was a tall, very solid boy and Mary suspected he would make a huge, powerful man. She had once asked old Tante whom he took after. The old woman hesitated a long time before replying that she did not quite know. Although Danny had been a tall man he had not been hugely muscled whereas William already had protruding biceps muscles and William was secretive. Mary doubted whether any of them really knew what went on in his head. It was not that he was impolite or downright disobedient. Mary suspected he was cunning and liked his creature comforts far too much to jeopardise himself, but always at the back of Mary's head was the thought she could not like this child. She hoped she never showed it. Indeed she went out of her way to talk to William and to show an interest in him. He was a great reader, far in advance even of Margaret and he had an excellent ear for mimicry. Mary suspected languages would come easily to him and that might be where his future path would lay.

Mary knew that Margaret detested her younger brother and she wondered if William tried to bully Edwin. Certainly her love child had such a gentle nature he could never hope to stand up to someone so sure of himself as William. Apart from his mother and great grandmère, there was only one person of whom William was afraid and that was his sister, whom he knew did not like him. Margaret was a big girl and, as she had always been active, she could hit hard and true as William had learned to his cost. She, on her part, ignored him to the best of her ability and was almost distasteful in her tone when forced to speak of him.

Mary was bothered about this. She hated a situation where family children were at loggerheads though she knew there was little she could do except keep a watchful eye on the three of them. At the moment, William might be able to bully Edwin except that Margaret was always around as his watchdog and, for the time being, she was too strong for William to dominate. What would happen in a few years' time though when William entered his teens and acquired a man's body?

"Penny for them?" old Tante said softly.

Mary turned to her. "I was thinking of the children and how different they all are."

Tante threw her a quizzing look. "Including William?"

Mary nodded. "At least he's caused me no trouble yet, thank God, but I still can't find it in my heart to like him—yet I can't give you a reason to dislike him."

"As I said years ago, it's instinct," Louise replied gently. "So far so good with him but Mary, never trust that boy!"

"Come on, I'll run you over to Sam's while I pop into town and I'll pick you up later," she said starting the engine.

Sam was long retired and lived happily with his pipe and foul-smelling tobacco in a small flat adjacent to where one of his married daughters had a home. He was perfectly happy in the evening of his life because he had a small balcony, complete with cane chair and table, which was sheltered so he could sit outdoors and stare at the sea. By twisting his head to one side he was able to make out St Peter Port and Castle Cornet. Once a week Mary drove Louise over to see Sam for an afternoon of happy reminiscence.

Emily too had retired, slightly put out that Sam had never spoken for her and she lived on the fringes of the town with another old friend. Raymond and Gwen worked together in the glasshouses now that the Noyen children had grown. The Falla children were also at school so, gradually, Raymond had taken over the complete running of the tomato side of the business. Mary just checked the books once a month because there was no doubt that Raymond had green fingers and their profit margin was constantly healthy, particularly since they had branched into flowers.

As she drove at a more sensible speed Mary was slightly puzzled. She had told no one but James had made an appointment to see her and not in his offices either. This was strange because it indicated he wished to discuss something not connected with Noyen Enterprises.

James had married his Jane and produced one girl who was the apple of his eye and who went to an exclusive school on the mainland. Why this should be, Mary did not understand because Guernsey had its own excellent schools. Miss le Canu boarded five days a week and spent the weekends with an uncle of James only coming back to the island for holidays—although Mary had heard that James and Jane often went over to the mainland for weekend breaks with their daughter. Really, Mary thought with some irritation, I never thought James was such a snob.

James' friend, Emil, the police sergeant, was far more down to earth. His son Derek and daughter Denise were educated on the island. Even Victor, despite his many English contacts and trips, was educating his children in St Peter Port where they went to the same school as her own children. Once or twice it had crossed Mary's mind to wonder exactly who was the boy who had succeeded in converting Margaret from her tomboy habits. What if it should be young Michael le Page? She was not sure she liked this thought because it would inevitably draw her and Victor together again. On the other hand, there was nothing she could do about it.

Her mind came back to James and his request to see her. He had suggested they meet at the bottom of Havelet Bay and so it was that half an hour after seeing Tante into a chair alongside that of Sam, she had driven away, parked the car and now she stood looking out at the castle, eyes narrowed in thought. She could not help worry in case something traumatic had gone wrong with Noyen Enterprises.

James spotted her waiting and increased his pace. He had been delayed at the last moment by a telephone call with a client who would go on and on over nothing of importance. He was wearing a light grey suit with black shoes and the inevitable discreetly coloured tie. Indeed, it was only two days ago that Emil had teased him, saying a lawyer's dress was just as much a uniform as that any policeman wore. James had known this was true, so on this important day he had ransacked his wardrobe for something just a little bit different. Even his secretary had been astonished enough to raise an eyebrow which had risen even higher when her employer had calmly informed her that he would not be available for three hours. He was busy seeing a client which was, James told himself with satisfaction, the absolute truth.

Mary spotted his long, swinging stride and studied him carefully as he came along the pavement. He had matured beautifully with the elegant manners and bearing of a distinguished gentleman and he lived in some style.

Once Mary had taken the trouble to work out what he had received from them in legal fees and retainer payments and even she had been astounded at her total. It was not that she begrudged one penny because James was good indeed. He was foxy, extremely well versed in law, with a razor-sharp mind which instantly spotted a problem and which could, just as rapidly, come up with an answer. She had learned to lean heavily upon him in the last ten years.

She knew that James, Emil and Victor were all of an age and old drinking companions but James was elegant compared to the other two. Emil had become dignified but a little ponderous with his promotion though James had once hinted to her that Emil was not a man who should be underestimated. As he gave her this warning, Mary sensed a silent something else that put her on her guard. Did James or Emil guess she kept a pistol? If Emil wanted to find out, an appropriate search warrant would have to be obtained by which time the little derringer would be long hidden. Since that oblique warning Mary had watched her tongue when near Emil.

When she attempted to make a comparison between the three men, one thing did stand out. James was a handsome, polite, well mannered gentleman. Emil was a suspicious, inquisitive police officer. And Victor? Victor, despite his fine clothes and impeccable manners, was a wild, rakish pirate compared to his friends. Victor had a silent presence that could dominate a room without a word spoken. He was known as a clever business man whom none tried to fool because he was very capable with his fists to settle a dispute if necessary. Mary never ceased to think he was indeed exactly like Heathcliff.

"James!" she said as the lawyer reached her, offering her hand.

"I'm glad to see you, Madam," he replied meaning it. She was his favourite client and in the past ten years he had studied her carefully. She was sound, reliable, though, a bit dogmatic if in the wrong mood and seemingly unafraid of no one. Surely this made her into the perfect person for him? The trouble was though, how would she react? Now he would find out.

"Shall we stroll up the hill?" he suggested. "There's a seat at the top and it's highly unlikely it will be occupied this early in the spring."

Mary was thoroughly mystified but had no intention of asking premature questions. He would speak when he was ready but she doubted now there could be a problem with the business. Sitting on a form with grass underfoot, overlooking the bay, was not where a good lawyer gave his client shocks.

They climbed the hill in silence then took the vacant seat. For a few minutes Mary stared out to sea, first at dainty Herm Island, then further into the distance where a haze drew sky and water together in a lacy mist. James took time to admire her well cut slacks. Madam always dressed in the latest fashions, then added her own personal touches. The scarf loosely knotted about her throat fluttered in the gentle breeze and, much as he disliked women in trousers, he had to admit they suited her. What a splendid figure she had despite three children and he wondered to himself whether Victor had indeed got over his crazy infatuation. Anyone who could coolly wing another showed control and determination, ideal material indeed. No wonder Emil had sniffed around for weeks after the shooting.

"You love this island, don't you, Madam?" James started gently.

Mary turned to him smiling happily. "I do!" she agreed. "I sometimes forget I wasn't born here. England and Weymouth are a long time ago."

James' eyes held hers. "Yet I would guess you are fiercely loyal to the Union Flag as well?"

Mary was astonished. "Of course I am? Who isn't?"

If she had been given a dozen guesses she would never have thought his conversation would lead off like this. Where was it going to go?

James took a deep breath, turned to face her, changing his position on the seat.

"You are as tough as Madam Noyen senior," he said slowly, working up to the crux of the matter in careful stages. "You have a cool head in emergencies as you proved when you shot Victor le Page." He paused.

Mary's nostrils tightened a fraction though she did not bat an eyelid even if her features went stiff. Automatically one hand slid into her right hand slack's pocket where the derringer rested without causing even the tiniest bulge.

James spotted the movement from the corner of his eye and his lips twitched. "Just as you would be ready to shoot me if I put a toenail wrong?" he guessed and waited but still Mary stared back at him, blank and unfathomable. Suddenly he felt a funny little chill creep down his back. Despite the years of knowing her, James acknowledged that Madam Noyen might indeed be exceedingly dangerous if provoked too far. "I applaud!" he added hastily.

One of Mary's eyebrows lifted a fraction but she still said nothing and neither did her hand budge. A pulse pounded in her neck and Mary tested her natural instinct. She did not feel in danger yet she had never met James in this cold, calculating mood and they were very alone indeed. Every sense was alert and she was poised to act as the situation might dictate.

"I am your friend, Madam," James said quickly, aware the

atmosphere had become decidedly prickly. "I was only stating facts which I knew and have known for a long time. It is because of who you are and what I know about you that you have become of great interest."

Mary spoke then. "To whom?" she asked in a low voice.

"Names I cannot give," James said slowly, "and when I explain you'll understand. Before I do though, would I be right in thinking you read the newspaper and listen to the wireless. You are familiar with current political affairs?"

Now Mary was taken completely aback. This was the most weird conversation she'd had with anyone, let alone her lawyer. She took a deep breath but still kept her hand on her little protector.

"I think I am," she told him carefully. "Mr MacDonald leads the British National Government and was the Prime Minister of the first two Labour Governments."

James nodded, pleased with her reply. "That is it," he told her sitting back against he seat's iron rest. "A National Government because of all the economic unrest and we are not alone. It's worse in Germany, far worse with a mark which is just about valueless. I predict that soon Germany will have the leader of their National Socialist Party, Adolf Hitler, as Reich Chancellor. I will foretell something else too," he said grimly, leaning forward to emphasise his point. "When Hindenburg dies, Hitler will become the Fuhrer. Do you understand what that means, Madam?"

Mary did not and shook her head blankly, slowly removing her right hand and placing it in open view. She sensed this was something dreadfully important. She had never seen James so solemn.

"You tell me."

James sat back a moment to marshall his thoughts and facts to make a coherent, understandable picture. "Germany has never recovered from the humiliation of being forced to sign the Peace Treaty of Versailles. She has never ceased to resent the fact she had to cede Alsace-Lorraine to France as well as Posen and the Corridor to Poland. She also resents the fact she was forced to disarm, to abolish military service and was allowed to keep only an army of one hundred thousand men with a tiny navy. She resents the fact her colonies were shared out to the victorious allies under League of Nation Mandates. She resents the war reparations that she has had to pay. It is all of this that collapsed the German economy. Germans do not take kindly to defeat any more than the British would. The National Socialists in Germany are nothing but arrogant, dangerous, power-hungry Nazis. If Hitler does become Fuhrer—as I'm afraid he will—then God help all of us. Another war will be inevitable because Germans, and particularly the Nazis, want revenge for their last defeat."

Mary let out her breath slowly unable to take her eyes off his serious face as her mind whirled with what he had said. Surely he had to be in error? Another ghastly war, she shuddered miserably. She remembered that awful time when she and Tante went to find Duret! The carnage, the sights and smells, the dead and dying. Not again, she thought.

"Surely not?" she protested, in a whisper of horror.

James shook his head vigorously. "Europe stands in terrible danger again and this time it will be worse because of technical advances," he told her in a low, hard voice. "In a new war, no one will be exempted. Look how planes have improved out of all recognition." He paused, taking a deep breath. Now he had reached the important bit. "There are some shrewd men," he continued, holding her blue eyes in a stern stare, "who don't like this picture of the future. They have started to look ahead and make plans ready for the worst."

Mary had a sudden sharp instinct that what he had said before was merely a preamble. Now he was slowly leading her towards something of vital importance and she had a feeling she was not going to like it one bit. She waited uneasily.

"What plans?" she whispered.

"Here and there, very carefully picked people are being asked to prepare themselves to help if the situation deteriorates into war. Just now, they have nothing to do at all. They are simply in place, ready and waiting. They might never be used but, on the other hand, a day or night might come when what they see and hear becomes of great value to Britain. Sometimes they are called sleepers because they lie low for years until officially activated."

Mary was stunned with the implication. "You mean—spies?"

"They're not called that," he replied smoothly.

"You are connected with espionage!"

He held her gaze unblinking. "I admit to nothing."

"But I live on tiny Guernsey. What can I do here?"

She was stunned by what he had said. Never in a thousand days had any such activity entered her mind and, indeed, she told herself, although well read and up to date with current affairs, she had not considered them as of a concern to herself. She turned away from him and looked out to sea.

He studied her carefully, understanding her shock and controlled a soft sigh of exasperation. How many more were there like Madam? Were people so complacent? Couldn't they see the implications of wrong political moves? To him, it was so clear as to be frightening.

"You could do a lot," he told her. "You have excellent business connections not only with your holiday properties, which incidentally could be publicised on the continent too, but also with the tomatoes. You could develop first-class business links in a number of places."

Mary heard his words but was thinking of something else at the same time. Was *this* why his daughter went to that exclusive English school? Now she thought she understood why the girl's parents made so many trips to England. Innocuous weekends to see their daughter but what else did the girl's father do when he was over there? She had been completely fooled which meant others had too.

"But doing what when I get there?" she asked slowly.

"You have the brains to assimilate information and tabulate observations. You have the wits to sift out the chaff from the corn and, should the day ever arise, pass on the nucleus when requested. You have proved you are cold and ruthless. You would make a most valuable sleeping agent."

Mary gave an impatient shake of her head. "I cannot for the life of me see how little Guernsey can be of interest to anyone and, even if I did what you suggested, surely there would be limitations? Wouldn't it be better to have someone in France and—oh!" She gasped. "You already have!"

She frowned, then began to work it all out while he waited with patient interest. He saw her face brighten and her eyes grow wide with expectation.

"You want insurance," she told him in a little rush of words. "You want more than one observer so that, should the worst happen, you would have two strings to a spying bow."

"I knew you were sharp," he praised her quietly, filled with exultation. He had not underestimated her and the gamble appeared to have paid off.

"But if war came," Mary asked, "I surely would have to be told what information to collect and how it would be passed on?"

He threw her a sad smile. "If the inevitable comes," knowing in his heart it would, "what will the men do? Exactly the same as the last time. They will rush off to fight but women will stay at home. And, further, women are usually accepted at face value. Women can be extremely valuable just because they are female and non-combatants. Of course, women bleed and die the same as men. Look at Nurse Cavell in the last war. She was shot for helping soldiers escape to Holland. Throughout history there have been some very brave women observers, shall I call them? Look at the British Civil Wars and Hannah Rhodes who was caught and executed by the Royalists. Although women do not normally lift a rifle and pull a trigger they can be most effective in their own right. It's no job for the faint-hearted though but you have passed all the necessary tests." He gave her an encouraging grin.

Mary eyed him warily, not quite able to take it all in or believe him except that his eyes were coldly serious.

"What I want you to do is think about everything I've said. You realise of course no one—and I do mean no one—must know this conversation took place for obvious reasons. It will not be held against you if your answer is negative but, because of the gravity of what has been related to you, you would have to sign the Official Secrets Act. And the penalty for breaking your oath would not be pleasant."

Mary shook her head. "I wondered what on earth you wanted to see me for out of your office, James. I never thought it would be for anything like this." Who would have thought this of James? It did cross her mind to wonder who else might be involved but his two friends she had to dismiss. Wild, pirate Victor—never! Dour, stickler-for-details Emil, surely not?

"I don't suppose I'm allowed to ask questions?"

He shook his head. "You accept it all at face value."

He indicated he had plenty of time with another headshake and Mary stood up.

"Give me ten minutes," she said. "Stay here while I stroll. It doesn't take me long to reach a decision, especially one like this."

"Go ahead," he encouraged. It would suit him admirably to learn her decision right away before his next weekend trip to see his daughter.

Mary strolled off to one side until she was well away from him. She bent down, pulled a blade of grass and idly started bending it while her mind raced. What he had said was all so encompassing she still found it difficult to assimilate his statements. Only for the fact she had known him for all these long years and found him worthy and true was she able to believe his opinions. The thought of another war chilled her blood.

She knew she was flattered by his proposal but also filled with apprehension. If astute people could see war clouds looming again, surely everyone must help. But why had he approached her? She argued with herself that a man in this position knew a great many people. He must have considered them all before alighting on herself, which does not, she thought gloomily, speak much for the rest of the islanders. Or did it? He was a very clever man. Could he see something in her that she was not even aware of? It was a rather disconcerting thought.

Mary stood with her back towards him, eyes staring at the sea but not seeing it. She could feel something growing inside and knew her decision had been reached. She turned on her heel and strolled back, dropping the twisted grass blade. Stopping a couple of paces from him, she looked him full in the eye.

"I'll do what I can willingly but I don't think you've made a brilliant choice with me. I cannot see I have the necessary skills," she said, then slowly sat at the far side of the form and waited.

A slow smile broke on his face and he nodded but more to himself than her. It was always so very satisfactory to be proved right in the end.

"You are quite sure?"

Mary nodded firmly. "Positive!" she reassured him, then threw him a lopsided grin. "I've done some odd jobs in my time but this one looks like taking the biscuit with a vengeance."

"Right!" he said, going serious. "Lesson number one. Know your territory as well as the back of your hand. Know it in such detail you could find your way around it at night. Stroll the beaches and coves. You have three children. I'm sure they'll be delighted to help you explore. Rule number two, never stand out like a sore thumb if you can help it. Sometimes a situation develops which makes this difficult though. Rule number three, teach yourself to observe. Train your mind. When you go out memorise how many specific types of trees, shrubs, flowers and birds you see. How many trees on some crossroads, for example. It doesn't matter what exercise you use except that it should involve abilities to develop the brain and store information. Teach your eyes, ears and other senses to function together and finally, rule number four, if you should ever be activated, trust no one. Naturally, you talk to no one either," he added dryly. "You might never be needed but if you are called upon, Britain will want what your brain can collect, collate and pass on. Naturally should this ever arise you will be paid, that goes without saying."

Mary nodded, not taking much notice of the latter point about which she did not particularly care anyhow. She still thought that perhaps greater seriousness was being given to the current political situation than it warranted until she remembered the assassination that had started the First World War.

She spoke slowly, concentrating carefully. "It's obvious that I'll not be the only person here, or on the other islands or even in France and naturally I don't want to know who they are but there is one point. I had been toying with the idea of looking for a town flat for holiday lets in case some people want to be nearer restaurants and night life. I think now it might be more useful if I found a flat which I could keep for myself. A town base if you like."

"That could be expensive," he pointed out. "A lot more expensive than doing up a cottage."

Mary shook her head. "Not if I can find one over a shop and buy both together. A shop which could be run by a young girl and later on perhaps by my daughter. I don't think she knows exactly what she wants to do when she leaves school. She might, of course, pick university because her exam marks are high but, on the other hand, she could well not chose higher education. In which case, a shop could be something for her to get her teeth into while she decides what to do. Also with three children at home plus Amelia, Raoul's wife, coming in daily, there is often little privacy if anyone wished to call on me. My home can be as busy as The Pollet on a Saturday at times."

"What would you sell?" he asked shrewdly.

Mary did not hesitate. "Produce from the glasshouses instead of shipping all of it to England and what all holiday makers seem to want—newspapers."

James could see the advantage of such a place. It was true she could always call at his practice on official legal business but it was always prudent to have a second venue. Although he had his telephone, he also had his addresses in England about which his family knew nothing.

"Good!" he grunted. "When you find a place let me have the details. In the meanwhile learn all about this island and the others," he told her firmly.

"If this awful day does come, as you seem to fear, I take it I would report to you?"

"You would receive the appropriate instructions beforehand. For the time being, apart from the mental training I want you to give yourself, we will not discuss this again. If something should crop up, I will raise the subject, with you, is that clear?"

Mary studied him, realising she had been given her first order. Her eyebrows lifted but she nodded. Somehow he seemed so much older than his years.

"It's understood," she replied evenly.

He stood slowly and looked at his watch. "Come, I'll walk you back down the hill. I have a client due shortly."

Mary had nothing to say as they headed back down the road though her mind buzzed with speculation. Surely it was all too pessimistic—or was it? She resolved to pay even more attention to current affairs on the wireless.

He stopped on the road. "I'll get on my way to my car, Madam," he told her gripping her hand. "Thank you—for a conversation which has never taken place."

THIRTEEN

SAM AND HIS old friend had talked themselves dry and sat watching the sea, both of them basking in the sun. It was not what could be called warm but up here, sheltered even from a breeze, Sam's balcony was comfortable.

Louise eyed him carefully as he started the rigmarole with his pipe. She was quietly shocked. Sam seemed older than herself although he was in fact several years younger. There was also something about him that she did not like but she knew better than to mention her worry. She had noticed how stiffly he moved as if all his joints were gripped by rheumatism but it was his face which gave the game away. He lacked the healthy red colour and she fancied she could detect a slight blue pallor. She also saw how he favoured his arm as if it pained him. She had lived too long and seen too much not to recognise the signs of a slowly weakening heart. Sometime in the near future, dear old Sam would leave her.

When Mary came running up the stairs to join them Louise's face was smooth. "Business done then?" she asked quietly. Mary seemed tense, more than a little on edge. Surely she had not bumped into Victor?

"Not quite," Mary said sitting down on a nearby cane stool. "I'm going to buy a shop."

The old people looked at her blankly. This was utterly out of character and they stared at each other. Had she gone mad? As if she didn't have enough to do.

Mary read their thoughts and hastened to explain herself, censoring her conversation as she now realised she must always do.

It was Louise who first saw the advantage. "You might be on to something. Margaret could run it if she doesn't want to go for higher education. I think she'd have a flair for commerce but what's put all this in your head?"

Mary shrugged noncommittally. "It's been there a while actually but I wanted to consider it in depth before I spoke to both of you. But where though? Do you know somewhere suitable, Sam, in town?"

Sam still knew as much about island activities as ever. He had a succession of old cronies who came to visit with their smelly pipes and Mary swore their tongues wagged far worse than women's ever could.

"I might," he said slowly, "it's not big though," Sam added hastily.

"I don't want anything too large," Mary explained. "A shop with a good backroom for storage and perhaps a couple of rooms overhead."

"I've heard of a place down south of St Martins," Sam told her, "not far from Jerbourg Road and Sausmarez Manor. It might suit you but I don't have any idea what the asking price will be," Sam warned her. "The owner is old and wishes to retire because she was widowed a few weeks ago. It's a small general stores but it might have potential for you."

Mary stood up quickly. She felt it imperative to go and look right away.

"I'll come back for you, Tante!" she told Louise briskly, then was gone before Louise could ask to come with her. Suddenly Mary wanted to do this quite alone. Although Tante was shrewd, there were times when Mary yearned to make her own decisions without discussing them with anyone else. Ruefully the old lady understood but made no comment. This was one of the penalties of age but sometimes the young had to learn from their own mistakes. She hoped Mary was not about to put her foot in it.

As soon as Mary had parked her car she walked the area, observing the layout of the roads and the few houses, studying the bus routes and working out where the nearest beaches were. It was also near to the centre of St Peter Port, so the location could hardly be bettered. She guessed it was a tiny lock-up shop at the moment because there was a shabby air about the upper windows which had not been cleaned in a long time. When she entered, a bell gave a tinny clang and as she stood, her eye ran over a general air of dilapidation.

A rear door opened and a small woman appeared to eye her hopefully. Mary placed her in her early sixties, noting the white hair, a face starting to wrinkle and two dainty hands that already wore brown age spots. A pair of very sharp, keen brown eyes fixed her questioningly.

"I'm Madam Noyen junior," Mary began, knowing this was not a good start because their well-known name could put the price up but too many people knew her personally. "I understand these premises are for sale?"

The brown eyes narrowed a fraction. "I'm Madam Martell," came back to Mary who suddenly realised she was being sized up like an opponent. Her heart sank. She recognised the breed immediately. This was a typical islander who would be stubborn, obdurate and who knew the value of every penny. She took a deep breath knowing she must have her wits about her with this little dot of a woman.

Madam Martell's heart thumped with excitement. She was astute enough to know her shop did have some potential left but not for her to run it. Without living premises it could also prove difficult to sell but she knew of the Noyens. She was not interested as to why a member of that well-off family should want a small lock-up shop but she was keen enough to scent the prospect of good money. Well-off people often did things which made little sense to lesser mortals. The more cash she received from the sale then the more comfortable she could make the retirement cottage she had spotted on the outskirts of St Sampson. She licked her lips but stood quietly as Mary walked around, testing the floorboards for soundness, eyeing the skirting boards, studying the ceiling then opening the back door to examine a large, dusty storeroom.

She took her time. The property was dirty but appeared to be sound though a private survey would have to be arranged. There were two double doors at the rear of the storeroom, ideal for offloading. Mary stepped outside and saw they gave way to a winding but short grass and dirt lane which led to the main road. There were a few tired weeds and bushes against the shop wall which all added to its run-down condition. It was easy for her to visualise the little old woman and an old husband struggling to keep going but unable to maintain a decent standard.

She was delighted with the upstairs with its one large room extending the length of the downstairs. She stood eyeing it, planning carefully. A plasterboard wall could be erected two-thirds of the way along and electricity and drainage could be brought up from below. This could make a small washroom with a geyser, a connection from which could come into the main part of the room for simple cooking. There were windows back and front. Those at the rear overlooked the dirt lane while the front ones gave a good view of the busy junction of roads nearby. She stood a moment, placing imaginary carpets and furniture into positions and saw how it could be transformed into a very comfortable little sitting room with a wall bed on the left-hand wall. Her heart thumped with eagerness. It was the perfect place for her; she must have it but as she went back down the uncarpeted, dirty stairs, she schooled her face into a poker expression.

"It's been very neglected," she started quietly.

Bright eyes looked at her carefully. "But it's sound and there's only surface dirt."

Mary thought how like a cheeky sparrow the little woman was with her head tilted slightly to one side calculatingly, her little eyes shining and alert.

"What is your price for it all, lock stock and barrel?" Mary asked waving with her right hand.

The sparrow did not hesitate. "Two hundred plus the stock at valuation."

Mary's lips tightened with annoyance. The stock should be thrown in for that price and she wondered how much she dared to haggle.

"Two hundred plus half the stock at valuation?" she countered smoothly.

Little sparrow sensed she was going to win if she kept her nerve. The two hundred pounds was a good price so if she could squeeze more out for a ridiculous valuation it only went to show how much Madam wanted her premises.

"No!" she said slowly. "My first price stands," and the tiny head bobbed sideways once more. "I do have another interested purchaser."

Mary only just managed to keep her face calm as she wondered whether this was true.

"Are the premises freehold and what about taxes?" she asked, stalling for time, wondering how to attack next. She must have this place. She knew now she should have let James negotiate for her but it was too late now.

"You are a tough haggler," she said finally, unable to hold back a grudging smile.

"I'm just a little old widow lady," sparrow replied evenly, eyes gleaming as victory moved a step nearer.

"Oh very well," Mary told her, extending her hand. "Two hundred pounds plus stock at valuation."

Sparrow shook the proffered hand and her eyes twinkled as Mary fumbled in her handbag.

"And here's five pounds as a deposit which you can pass to

your lawyer," she said. From what she had learned, she doubted this did hold a price but surely it could be made to constitute part of the contract? She was worried in case there was indeed someone else sniffing around.

"Done!" sparrow agreed. "It's freehold too and all taxes are paid up to date."

They shook hands again but as Mary left the shop she knew she had not got the best part of the bargain. Not that it worried her. She had the money and already the thought of owning something private was as exciting as a toy to a child.

After she had taken Tante back, giving her a detailed account of the shop, she went into a huddle with Raoul. She would let him find a girl to serve in the shop once she had changed from groceries to what she had in mind. Raoul would also clean and decorate the premises to her standard and she bubbled inwardly. During that week she thought it odd that only a few short days ago her life had seemed set on quiet tracks. Since meeting James, everything had turned upside down. She admitted to herself she had fallen into a placid rut and it was pleasurable to have a new venture because she was determined the shop would pay its way.

"It will do for excess greenhouse produce," she explained to Raoul carefully, "and it will also be a place where I can keep my private accounts and if ever, I want a night in town, I can stay there," she told him tongue in cheek.

Raoul did not have a curious nature and accepted her statements at face value. It had long been agreed that Amelia would stay at the house on the rare occasions when Mary should be late home now that Emily had retired. With their own two sons, often joining the Noyen children, they made a boisterous herd and he could understand the mistress wanting a quiet retreat.

Exactly a week later, Mary drove over to the shop again, having left a message she wished to call to measure up for curtains to the upstairs windows. When she entered, listening to the old-fashioned bell ting, she did not realise someone else was there.

A man stood at the counter to one side and it was only when he turned and moved that she gasped.

"Victor!" and her lips parted. How long was it since they had last talked? Her heart gave a ridiculous thump-thump and she knew her face broke into a sincere smile though her eyes were wary. He was dressed casually in grey flannel slacks with a short-sleeved shirt of fawn. A sports jacket was slung over one shoulder held by the little finger from the left hand. My God, she thought, he gets more handsome as each year passes. He held his head high and jaunty, feet slightly apart, a wide grin on his face while his eyes lit with pleasure at seeing her and she relaxed a fraction.

Damn her, Victor thought. She gets more attractive with each year and he knew his feelings for her were as strong as ever. He let his eyes dwell for a few seconds on her swelling breasts beneath a soft green shirt-blouse and green trousers. It crossed his mind to wonder whether the slacks' pocket was empty; he could not detect any slight bulge but he had a shrewd idea she never went anywhere without her protector. Emil would lay eggs if he knew of her pistol but Victor knew he would never talk.

It was true there had been the most almighty uproar when he had returned home. Nicole had, for once shown sharp fangs of concern. It had taken all his considerable charm to calm her down, dodge her questions and maintain a casual indifference, which he had certainly not felt at the time. He carried a small scar and often let his fingers slide around this when he bathed, wondering, imagining, shaking his head and muttering soft curses coupled with downright admiration. His resolve had not weakened. One day, somewhere, somehow, she would be his. He respected Nicole now and had done so for years, which allowed a decent relationship to grow between them.

They shook hands and Mary knew her smile was wide and delighted, then she became aware of sparrow watching, head inevitably tipped to one side.

"We have known each other a long time," Mary explained,

quickly moving a pace away from him but highly aware of his powerful masculinity.

Madam Martell's expression changed to relief. "Oh! I'm so glad!" she cried brightly. "So you'll understand."

Mary looked at the widow and wondered why she should feel a prickle of warning touch her spine. She turned to Victor, a frown puckering her forehead.

"Understand what?" she asked both of them.

Victor grinned at her. "I've just bought this shop," he explained casually. "Nicole has been wanted one for a long time. She wants her own little business and fancies a haberdashery."

Mary's eyes opened wide with horror then she glowered at sparrow. "You can't!" she snapped decisively. "We shook hands on a deal and you took a deposit which can make part of the contract!" She was not at all sure this was true but she was desperate for these premises.

Sparrow almost twittered as words tumbled out. "That kind of deposit has no force in law, not where property is concerned and this gentleman has made me a much better offer. Here! I'll give you your money back!" she said opening the till, removing a large note.

Mary backed a pace, glowering angrily. "I'm shocked you go back on your word!" she cried hotly. She flung a furious look at Victor who stood silently, a grin on his face. It was if he was watching some theatre play. "This shop is mine!" she snapped.

Victor shook his head slowly. "No, it's *mine*!" he said with a chuckle. "Just what Nicole wants too. I'm buying it for three hundred pounds."

"What!" Mary shouted. "That's daylight robbery!"

He knew she was right but that did not change the facts. "Nicole has a friend who lives down the road a piece," he explained reasonably.

Mary knew she was on the verge of losing her temper. It would have to be him of course. He looked so smug and sure of himself and it flashed through her mind he was enjoying the situation, taking his revenge.

"I don't care if the king lives down the road!" she shot back at him.

"Now, now, Catherine," he whispered, face crinkling with amusement, "don't show yourself a bad loser!" he mocked.

"A deal is a deal!" Mary flung at him hotly, and little sparrow became uneasy for the first time. She had been thrilled with the highest offer but Madam Noyen's temper was awesome and well known. Then her jaw hardened. She owned the shop; it was hers to sell for whatever price she chose to accept, not for one of the wealthy Noyens to take because it suited them.

"I've accepted Mr Le Page's offer and that is all there is to it!" she said coldly.

"Be reasonable," Victor told her in a low voice. "There are other shops around."

Mary knew there were no others so well suited as this one. Also she could not stand being beaten by him when he wore that smug expression. She went to argue when the door opened abruptly and two men entered in working clothes. They looked at the odd scene before them, then moved to the counter.

"Twenty Goldflakes please," one said.

"I'll have twenty Players."

Mary felt a surge of panic and for a second lost the ability to think straight. She quivered with mortification and knew she had gone scarlet with anger. Then her mind started to work again. Something said to her long ago resurfaced in her mind and she knew what she had to do.

The two men picked up their cigarette packets, took their change, turned and prepared to stroll to the door.

Mary sprang forward, blocking their path. "Stop!" she screeched making everyone jump. With all eyes now on her, Mary fell to her knees, lifting her hands high in supplication. She took a deep breath and prayed her memory would not let her down.

"*Haro! Haro! Haro!*" she cried slowly while the four spectators went stiff with shock. "*A mon aide, mon prince! On me fait tort!*"

Mary concentrated upon the two workmen as witnesses. They gazed back goggle-eyed, their mouths agape. Sparrow had stopped twittering and leaned against the counter, not believing her ears while Victor stood thunderstruck and frozen to the spot.

Mary started to speak slowly and distinctly as she recited the Lord's Prayer in French. She need not have worried. Her good brain and superb memory did not let her down and when she had finished there was silence as Mary blessed Sam's lessons all those years ago. Slowly she stood and, with uplifted eyebrows, waited for the witnesses to speak.

"Well!" drawled the Goldflakes man. "I don't know what all this is about but there's a halt to it whatever it is until the court sits!"

"That's right!" Players agreed. "My! That's the first time I've ever head the *Clameur de Haro* used and I'm island-born and fifty years old," he marvelled.

"Damn your eyes!" Victor swore at her. She had outfoxed him very cleverly; it had never entered his head she even knew about the *Haro*. Sparrow slowly sat on her stool and looked from one face to the other with shock.

"The sale of this shop and premises is frozen," Mary stated firmly.

"I only wanted the best price for my old age," Sparrow said miserably.

Mary turned to her adversary, her lips tight, her eyes flashing a challenge. Victor felt a wild urge to grab her and shake her until her teeth fell out but he stood frozen. What she had done was perfectly legal as the two witnesses could confirm. Now it mean bringing in the lawyers and he knew to whom she would go. James would be a devil to beat on this one and his anger swelled. First the shooting and then this. What came over her whenever she saw him, he asked unreasonably?

Mary saw his eyes had changed from violent to blue. They always did when he went into a passion, then something flashed through her mind; what James had said. "Do nothing to draw attention to yourself!" he had ordered and already she had disobeyed. She knew she must go and see him straight away and he must also represent her in court about this. Her heart sank a little as she studied Victor's face. Why was it that whenever they met something awful happened leaving them at each other's throats?

She turned to the smokers. "May I have your names and addresses please for my lawyer who is James le Canu?"

The Goldflakes man grinned. He was thoroughly enjoying the situation which would enliven a few pub evenings yet to come. "I'm Jack le Marquand!"

"And I'm Bob Ogier!" Players introduced himself, shaking her hand.

Mary jotted their names down, then handed the pocket diary over for them to add their addresses.

Victor scowled moodily, looking over at the widow and shrugged his shoulders eloquently.

"Thank you," Mary said as they finished, carefully replacing her diary. "You'll be hearing from Mr le Canu, no doubt," she smiled generously at them, ducking her head the tiniest fraction.

"You really are a—!"

"Don't say it, Victor!" Mary turned on him. "I might just have to repeat it in court," she pointed out acidly.

She threw a piercing look at Madam Martell, glanced at Victor then, with great dignity, opened the door and left, taking pains to shut it very quietly. She was thoughtful as she drove home but decided not to tell Tante yet. She was quite sure Victor would do this on his next visit. Suddenly she felt smugly pleased with herself; the last vestiges of English rearing had vanished. The only qualm she felt was in James' reaction. Then she copied Tante with a colourful sniff. All was grist to the mill.

James was both annoyed and amused but long ago he had trained his features not to register emotion. He kept Mary waiting deliberately for the first time. When she did enter his room and sat facing him she was not able to hold eye contact at first.

Mary felt embarrassed. How was it James could show annoyance without saying a word? She wriggled on the chair feeling like a naughty, little girl.

"I know what you're thinking, James and I'm sorry but the circumstances did indeed get out of hand. You see James, this particular shop and flat are perfect and I do dislike being cheated. A bargain is a bargain when there's a handshake to boot," she said, in a hurry to get her defence in first.

"That cuts no ice in law," James stated frostily. He knew it was unnecessary to say any more. He was conscious she had agreed to work for them of her own free will and hammering a point too much removed its accuracy. She would not do it again. On the other hand, he silently applauded her quick reaction to the situation and his amusement arose from information he had, as yet unknown to her.

"I've had the widow's lawyer on the phone and he states his client is very upset with your *Haro*," he began smoothly.

"Well, that's her fault for breaking her word!"

"This can go to court, but I would not be very pleased if it did. The *Haro* is not used all that often so when a case does arise, there is mass publicity," he told her icily. "Also a buyer is entitled to get the best price for a sale."

Mary weighed up his words, not missing the sharp barb and hesitated. Indeed such a case would be the talk of the island and what if somehow she lost? She knew enough about the law now to know very few cases were cut and dried. If Madam Martell's lawyer was also clever, James might be hard put to swing the decision for her. Deep down she felt a guilty, little niggling feeling that Sparrow was right. She could ask for what she thought she could get from another party because the deposit was not enough in conveyancing. If only it were someone else involved and not Victor. It was not that she minded too much about yielding except she had a sneaking feeling he might become a trifle unbearable. Mary also had a suspicion the whole story would provide a good laugh for Tante for weeks to come. Was she really being a bad loser, she asked herself honestly? Then lifted her head to become aware James' eyes held a barely suppressed twinkle. It flashed through her mind he knew something she did not and she was not going to like this either.

"Go on," she groaned. "Now what is it?"

"Let me point out something else first," James said slowly. "You are a well known family and so is your financial stability. Can't you imagine what an extra field day the press would have if it became a straight fight between a rich Noyen and a poor, little widow lady? Goodness me! You could all end up being pilloried and I am sure Madam Noyen senior would not take kindly to that. From what I know about her, she sets great store in upholding the family name."

Mary nodded slowly. He was right, as usual. It was her own fault for charging off like a demented bull to try and buy the place herself. She had made a complete fiasco of it all.

"You're right," she agreed in a low voice then saw a smile twitch his lips. She was puzzled. What *was* so amusing?

"If you really want those premises you will have to better the other offer even if it is outrageous."

"That poor, little widow, as you call her, is as dangerous as an uncaged tiger and her acting ability could take her to Hollywood!" she said, then shrugged her shoulders, her lips twitching a little. She had been caught in her own trap and Tante would never let her live it down.

"So do you want me to make an offer on your behalf of just over three hundred pounds?" James asked, struggling to control his mirth.

"Oh very well!" Mary said with exasperation. "But it's daylight robbery. Damn Victor le Page!"

James broke into a bellow of laughter unable to hold it back any longer. Mary looked at him in bewilderment.

"All right," she said slowly. "What have I done that I shouldn't have done which is making me the joke of the day?"

"Fallen into the beginner's trap," he grinned, then broke into another open chuckle which transformed his features from the severe lawyer to one of almost a young man.

Mary knew she was going pink. Very slowly, a tiny suspicion had started to send a shoot in her mind. She frowned and narrowed her eyes thoughtfully. Surely he did not mean—? "It was a put-up job!"

James nodded, laughing at her again. "I'm afraid so," he agreed, sitting back in his chair.

"Victor le Page!" Mary accused hotly. "It's him again!"

James nodded, his merriment at the trick, sending him into another gale of laughter that reverberated through the room.

"I found out two days ago when I began to investigate after you had given me the facts," he told her, trying to control himself from such undignified behaviour. "Madam Martell is a close relation of Mrs le Page. Her maiden name was Oselton and, yes, that's right, she came from Alderney originally. She told her niece, who informed Victor and heads were then put together very quickly. I have a shrewd suspicion, which I hasten to add I cannot prove enough for a law court, that the extra hundred pounds will be split evenly between Mrs Martell and Mrs le Page—all nicely done at your expense." Then his face became serious as he leaned forward towards her. "I know that you and Victor le Page have had your differences. I'm afraid you will have to accept this as a subtle revenge; his need to take you down a peg or two to even the score."

Mary was furious, then her honesty arose and she saw the financial joke was upon herself with a vengeance. She examined it for a moment or two and ruefully shook her head with admiration. Never again would she attempt to buy a property herself. It had been a painful lesson but Mary never required two. Slowly, her good humour returned and she grinned back at him.

"I'd like to wring his neck," she said softly. "How clever though and I fell for it."

"Well, if you have that urge bad enough why don't you go and take a short drive down to the Point?" he asked creamily.

Mary became extra alert. She could see it all now. Victor knew exactly what was going to happen. He had also made sure she knew exactly where he would be if she choose to see him; cocky in his victory. Confound him, she told herself. Of course she would see him and to her surprise her heart gave a few extra strong flips as her blood quickened. How many years ago was it since they had talked privately together; not since she had been forced to shoot him. The years had flown past and they were both into their thirties with, she suddenly hoped, more sense and control. She stood up, her eyebrows arched looking at James.

"Madam!" James said, with tongue in his cheek. "Please leave my drinking friend sound of wind and limb!"

Mary gave him a long dignified look. "I haven't the faintest idea what you mean," she replied blandly.

Not much, James thought as he saw her from his office and watched her walk to her car. When the meeting had been arranged the previous evening James had spoken strongly and pointedly to his friend.

"Don't press your luck!" he warned him coldly.

Mary drove slowly to Jerbourg Point with her natural sense of humour bubbling. What an idiot she had made of herself. As she parked her car, her eyes roved around looking for him while her heart was at its usual disgraceful thundering. He was not in sight so Mary stepped out, crossing the grass and looked down the steps to the waves far below. The sea gurgled, then threatened as it tried to strangle the rocks but she still could not see him. She walked back past the car in the other direction, then spotted him in the distance. He lifted one arm and waved casually.

Her heart increased its tempo and blood pounded in her temples. She noted he made no move to come to her. Why should he? By the time she reached him she was puffing slightly.

"Hello!" he cried, then taking her arm quite casually, he pointed down and out. "Look! Don't the Pea Stacks Rocks look fine with the sea pounding them?"

Quite naturally they held hands and watched as the incoming tide assaulted the columns of rocks, famous for their weird shapes and the way they dared defy the waves. The sky held a gentle sun whose golden rays turned the water to a subtle mixture of dark and light greens and where these surged around the Pea Stacks, these colours vanished to white. The whole made a pleasing combination to the eye.

"Goodness!" Mary gasped. "It's breezy here!"

"It usually is," he agreed. "In winter the winds howl in and blow all the cobwebs away. Let's sit in that hollow. We can be sheltered but still watch the sea and I promise to behave myself if you'll not act like a Hollywood cowboy," he joked gently.

Mary chuckled at him and allowed him to guide her down. It was true, down here, although still in some wind, it was not so unpleasant as standing to face the main assault of the weather. Quite naturally, he slipped his left arm around her and she leaned against him. He smelt of pure maleness. She had noticed this before; it was as if his aura could also produce scent. He was fresh, clean and virile while the arm around her was rock hard with developed, fit muscles. She peeped at his eyes and saw they were violet.

"Please ma'am, can I have a kiss without being shot?" he quipped.

Mary turned and let her lips feel his and he responded in a flash. There was a faint tinge of tobacco on his but it was not unpleasant, it seemed to blend in with him. With both his arms around her his kiss went on and on and now he was gentle though still firm and dominant.

"Oh Victor!" she murmured and buried her head in his chest letting his arms protect her from life, allowing herself a rare few minutes of utter relaxation.

"Ssh!" he soothed, stroking and kissing her ears and neck, feeling his heart swell so much it became an ache. From her came a scent of perfume as light as if made from spring flowers. He could feel the swell of her breasts against him which, in turn, made his groin harden enough for him to have to stifle a groan of anguish. She always aroused him even when they did not touch but this close sweetness was agonising though he had learned his lesson too. He would never go farther or faster than she wanted. Indeed, he had sworn to himself that though she would be his one day she must come to him; there must be a reversal of the natural roles. Only by doing that would he know for sure she came of her own volition.

Slowly Mary sat up, looking at him wistfully, a sad smile on her face with her eyes gentle and caring.

"Oh! You stubborn little madam!" he chided in a low voice, kissing her again. "All these wasted years!"

"What's done is done," Mary told him in a low voice tinged with sadness. "Anyhow I'll not come directly between husband and wife especially now you and Nicole get on so well. It would be grossly unfair of me and think how your children would hate me—and you!"

Victor nodded in slow agreement. She was right in many ways because he had developed a queer stilted affection for Nicole and adored his children. It would break his heart if they turned against him and he was well aware that the mother's place in the hearts of children was usually before that of the father. Nicole trusted him, he thought, and for a few seconds a heavy gloom descended.

Mary wriggled back a few inches and grinned. "Do you know something? We are not fighting for once!" she teased as her eyes danced with mischief.

He fell in with her mood. "I'll be astonished if it stays like that," he shot back, "but—" He allowed the rest of the sentence to hang unsaid in the air between them.

Mary knew what he meant. "I'm having that shop and paying that outrageous price too," she informed him. "Goodness me, you certainly came out of that smelling of roses. It was cleverly done, Heathcliff," she praised.

He chuckled. "Damn it all, Catherine. You simply cannot be allowed to win all the time. It's bad for you."

"So that innocent, little widow lady will receive one pound over the price you offered for the shop and stock with all taxes paid up to date. I'll drop the *Haro* and won't mention any fraud," she finished sweetly.

"Fraud? What are you on about?" he blurted with alarm.

"Well, didn't you and the widow conspire together to raise the price after I had made an offer *and* paid a deposit *and* shaken hands on the deal? she asked in a voice of syrup.

"Well," he halted, floundering a little now. Then he read the mischief in her eyes and shook his head. "You sea witch! This is your idea!" he accused.

"Of course!" she agreed daintily. "I can't let you think you have had a complete victory, now can I? It would only go to your head, wouldn't it?"

"You are impertinent, Madam!"

"Yes!" she agreed blithely, enjoying the shock she had just given him. He gave her a gentle shake, then settled her back down in the crook of his arm again and they watched the sea in companionable silence.

"There's something else you should know," he said softly.

Mary pulled away from him in alarm. Now what was wrong?

"Michael is in love!" he said softly.

Mary blinked, having to collect her thoughts. "He's only a child."

"I'm not so sure of that," he told her slowly. "In many ways Mike is a serious boy, very advanced for his age. When I talk to him I often forget he's only thirteen. Sometimes he could be in his late teens the way he thinks."

Mary understood. William too had a precocious, adult manner which often shocked her and which she neither liked nor considered healthy. Boys of his age should be mischievous rascals so it was peculiar that Michael and William had something in common.

"Mike can come out with statements that rock me at times," he said quietly.

"Who is the light of his young life?" Mary jested.

He gave her a firm look. "Your Margaret!"

"What!"

"I have a feeling he means it too," Victor added carefully. "Don't underestimate the feelings of the young. They grow up more quickly than we did."

"It's just a childish infatuation."

He shook his head. "I don't think it is!" he replied gently. "Michael can be very obstinate in his quiet manner," he explained, "and if he says he is in love with Margaret and is going to marry her when adult, he will do exactly that."

Mary felt miffed. "Margaret might have something to say about that!" she pointed out.

"What if she happened to agree?" he asked steadily. "How do you feel about our families being joined through our children?"

"I still think you are running ahead of this," she protested.

"What I'm leading up to is this," he told her. "In the summer holidays those two will want to spend time together. I hope you won't be antagonistic. Don't pour scorn on young love. It is

250

innocent and very beautiful. Your daughter is going to grow into a lovely woman and Michael is a handsome lad," he said, managing not to make any joke about taking after his father. Her expression was a trifle too bleak for that. "It means of course, you could end up with a tribe at your home because, don't forget, Mike is a twin!"

"I don't mind that," Mary told him quickly, "it's just that children should be children and not develop crushes at such a young age!"

"What about Romeo and Juliet and then there's Heloise and Abelard—!"

"Stop!" she cried. "It's bad enough with you always on about Catherine and Heathcliff. Don't drag in more literary figures!"

"You'll be gentle with them though?"

Mary nodded, recognising his anxiety, her heart going out to him afresh, though what Nicole le Page would chose to say was something she didn't care to think about. On the few occasions when she had bumped into Madam le Page in the market, the other woman had often paused in whatever she was doing, to throw Mary an odd, keen look which was neither friendly nor hostile but which left Mary feeling peculiar. Madam le Page had picked up gossip and, Mary knew that no matter what she might say or protest, Nicole obviously did not like the Noyens and herself in particular. So if Victor's crazy thoughts moved to fruition in due course, how would Michael's mother like the idea of a Noyen daughter-in-law? The thought made Mary a little uneasy, then she gave herself a brisk shake. She would cross that bridge when she reached it.

"I promise!" she told him. "But I still think your imagination is overworked and that of your son too!"

With that he was content. She never broke her word. Then he shivered. "By God, it's getting chilly."

It was true. The wind had freshened, blowing hard and there was no protection from it. He pulled her up and, arm in arm, they strolled to her car.

"Mine's over there," he nodded and Mary wondered why she had not spotted this before. She castigated herself. She simply must do better and be more observant, otherwise James would be displeased again and she would be failing his trust.

He took a quick look around but they were alone so he took her in his arms for a kiss, not hurrying about it and Mary wondered whether he was storing up something. It was true they could go months before they bumped into each other again because she still would not have him at her home and neither would she go down to Tante's cottage when he was due to visit his grandmère. Tante and Victor made far too powerful a combination.

She decided it was time to withdraw from him. "It's time I was going," she whispered, "and this is pretty public here. If anyone came down and saw us, I'd never be able to look Nicole in the face again."

"Go on then," he said with a sigh; suddenly he didn't really care who saw them, including Nicole.

FOURTEEN

THE WHOLE FAMILY agreed it turned into a fantastic summer, Margaret particularly, because they had so many days out with their mother. She knew it would be a time to remember. Mary took them on innumerable trips around the island discovering and exploring tiny bays and coves. There were long walks on the south cliffs and more strolls inland when Mary parked the car, took a picnic basket, and entertained the children as she trained her eyes.

It did not stop there either because they visited Herm and Sark as well as Jersey and France. The only island still unexplored was Alderney and the promise of a trip there was about to be fulfilled and Michael would be with them. Margaret was excited.

After Victor's words, Mary surreptitiously watched Margaret and Michael. He was a tall, well spoken boy who gave promise of turning into the same powerful man as his father. It was obvious to Mary that Mike thought the world of Margaret who seemed to reciprocate this feeling though it was, as yet, something so charmingly innocent that it touched Mary's heart. Mike was fun to be with. He was merry, open faced with an equable temperament which could certainly keep Margaret in check. If the two of them continued to develop like this into their late teens, they could make a splendid match. Mary had been forced to stifle a deep mirth upon one of Margaret's outbursts. Mike simply gave her a peculiar look, shook his head almost with pity, collected his cycle and rode away. Margaret had been stunned at this performance, unable to take it in. Since that day, she became a lot more circumspect in her behaviour so Mary acknowledged Mike was a splendid influence on her daughter. Victor was correct; Mike was remarkably mature for his age.

Jenny and Edwin made a nice twosome though Jenny was a proper cry-baby and not Mary's kind of child at all. Sometimes Mary suspected that Jenny cried before anything happened and she was amazed at this. How could twins be so different? Still, she made a good playmate for Edwin.

Then there was—William! William the loner who Mary suspected was an inveterate bully. She had seen his actions twice but before she could intervene Margaret had done what was necessary for which Mary was thankful. It was not that she dodged the issue of disciplining a child whom she disliked, it was just that she was always conscious of her personal feelings.

As they sat in the launch, Mary's mind twisted and turned on many matters. It was a long sea crossing to Alderney because Aurigny, called by its correct name, was the farthest island from Guernsey and very near to the French coast. She debated whether it was necessary to come to the island, thinking of the Oselton family, but Margaret and Michael had both pleaded for a day exploring somewhere new.

She studied the children though the pack was incomplete today. Both Jenny and little James had stayed at home because Nicole, fearing the trip might be rather too far for them, had objected.

She saw that Margaret and Michael sat close, heads almost touching as they discussed something of great interest. William was by himself looking out to sea while Edwin sat at her side doing nothing in particular. Mary itched to ruffle his hair affectionately but restrained herself with William so near.

Tante was initially astonished with her behaviour that summer and she was thankful for the children's company. As James had so wisely pointed out, they gave her a perfect excuse for gadding about.

"I've never spent a whole summer with the children, Tante," Mary pointed out, "so for once I'm going to let my hair down and have a bit of fun with them. I'm sure Raoul can cope with the properties and Raymond seems capable working alone."

Tante considered this novel idea, then slowly nodded her head. It made sense because Margaret was already blossoming into a young lady and Mary had rarely spent time with her daughter. She was curious about Michael but pronounced herself satisfied when she had met him. Her grandson had bred true; the only aggravating point was Michael's surname had to be le Page and not Noyen but there was nothing she could do about that.

Tante often felt sorry for Edwin. He lacked confidence and Jenny's appearance was a godsend though Tante considered her a weakling. Michael's twin was an Oselton, not a Noyen. It didn't matter though because she made up for this by being a companion for Edwin.

William needed no one. Let a few more years pass and Tante sensed William might move out to live his own secretive life, which would be best for all concerned. Whenever she met this grandchild he worried her. There was nothing of Duret in him and not much of Christine either, she decided. William was an individual not to be trusted. It was eerie how no one could read his mind. She never mentioned these feelings though because Mary was far too busy racing here and there, checking, supervising, suggesting improvements as well as paying attention to all their accounts. The way Mary rushed about might have been considered abnormal by many but the wise old lady guessed the real reason; she preferred the night sleep of exhaustion to that of lying awake in a lonely bed. Mary was a healthy girl and obviously still sexually capable, yet her true love was denied.

James never once asked Mary how she progressed but she guessed he had a shrewd idea where she went. It was impossible for someone like her, accompanied with an exuberant gaggle of children, to avoid notice.

For herself, she was greatly pleased with her efforts. James' comments proved true. It was possible to train the senses and gradually her mind developed as her memory expanded. Sometimes she thought she had only been using a section of her brain in the past. Now a bird could not fly over the garden without her noting the breed, where it had gone, whether alone and for what purpose.

At the same time, she had thrown herself into a detailed study of the general political situation. It had taken a little while to sort out the wheat from the chaff but the more she read or heard on the wireless the more apprehensive she became. She could look at her children and worry what might happen in the next few years. She discussed this with no one, hugging her apprehension to herself like a black cloak.

They disembarked and, after Mary had checked the time of the return ferry, she hired a horse and trap for their use. The children all piled around and behind her as she drove off gently. She was half aware of the chatter from Margaret and Michael, conscious of Edwin and William's silence while, at the same time, her eyes travelled around as she observed and assimilated anything which could be grist to her particular mill.

The island's capital, St Annes, seemed ludicrously tiny, hardly more than a village. While preparing for this outing she had done her homework and was secretly amused to find out that the people of Alderney held those from Guernsey in as low an opinion as Guernsey islanders regarded their fellows in Jersey.

It was a small island, barely three and a half miles by one and a half. As yet it had no telephone system; electric lighting was a little known luxury and all water still came from wells. It seemed primitive yet the people looked healthy and rugged.

"Where are we going now?" Margaret asked, breaking into her thoughts.

"We'll go down the High Street and along Longis Road to the Bay. I studied the map yesterday and we'll find ourselves a nice beach for a picnic. Later we'll drive around the island."

Margaret was satisfied and beamed at Michael, then became aware of William's dark eyes fixed on her. She turned her head and poked her tongue at him. He continued to stare stonily at her and Margaret tossed her head. She wished they did not have to trail William along with them all the time. She peeped at Edwin and it crossed her mind she must keep an eye on him as Jenny wasn't with them. The trouble with Edwin was that he did not complain. He suffered in silence, which Margaret considered dreadful. It was true she had attacked William before and driven him away but she sometimes wondered uneasily what went on between the two of them when she was not around. Edwin would never tell which was stupid as well as exasperating. She grinned at Mike. What fun he was, though she knew she had to treat him with respect.

"We'll go and explore, shall we?" she whispered to him.

"What about Edwin?" Mike rejoined, having a good idea of where William stood in the family hierarchy, a boy whom he disliked intently.

"He'll probably stay with mother," Margaret told him hopefully.

Mary studied the sky. It was almost hot, with the sky a delicate duck egg blue and only a light breeze when she drove down to the promising beach.

"Here we are!" she cried. "This will do. Now, you boys, unload the basket and take care. Don't spill the lemonade."

They ate their lunch with the two older children chattering away briskly, Edwin munching while eyeing the beach and William chewing stolidly, saying nothing and missing nothing either. As Mary repacked the remains and made sure the beach was tidy, she sighed with satisfaction. The sun beamed down and she felt warm in her thin cotton slacks and blouse. She almost wished she had brought a bathing costume.

"Can we go and explore?" Margaret asked, fidgeting for permission.

Mary nodded. "All right but don't wander too far," she warned. Instantly they were off, racing like young gazelles. Mary grinned at their youth and energy.

"And what are you two going to do?" she asked, turning to Edwin and William.

"Look for shells," Edwin replied promptly. He had become an avid collector over the past year, forever scouring the beaches for shells of different colours, shapes and sizes, which he would then try and identify from a book Mary had bought him. It was a harmless, gentle hobby for a quiet little boy and Mary encouraged her youngest child. He asked for so little; was so quiet and well behaved, that it gave her great pleasure to fulfil his few wishes.

"And you, William?" she said, turning to the tall, stocky boy on her other side. Dear heavens, she thought, he gets bigger every week. He would soon reach her own height and he was still so young. She studied his face, becoming aware how strongly formed were his features but how cold they were too. As always, William's face was set in its usual mask which gave no indication of his thoughts.

"I'll look for some too," he told her.

Mary's eyebrows shot up. She wondered if this was to copy Edwin or to rival him; most likely the latter, she mused.

"All right, but don't wander far away either," she warned them sternly. "I'll be here sunbathing."

Once the children had departed, Mary felt her eyes become heavy. I'll just close my eyes against the sun, she told herself, lying down on a soft portion of sand. She had no intention of sleeping with four children off exploring but the food and the sun, the long sea crossing plus the period of hard work, all combined and gradually she drifted into a light doze.

William followed Edwin morosely, now and again throwing a glance at the sea. It was amazing how quickly they wandered away from their picnic area. He watched Edwin wading in the shallow water, bending to peer down at shells, selecting and picking avidly.

William started to look through the gentle waves. It was true there were some shells he had not seen before and, in a desultory manner, he began to copy his brother. Deep down, William thought collecting shells was kid's stuff; something that only Edwin would do but he could not help competing against his brother. Why he felt the need to do this he did not know but to beat his siblings at anything gave him tremendous satisfaction. A feeling he kept hidden and buried deep in his heart. Nothing pleased him more than to outdo Margaret academically, which happened quite often despite the years between them. William knew he was the cleverest of the children but this again was something he kept a devious secret. Some latent instinct told him that brains coupled with an enigmatic exterior puzzled people and made them wary of him. It was a tactic he used to good effect at school to make him the envy of his peers.

"Another!" Edwin shouted with glee and bounded forward into water which surged over his knees.

William's eyes narrowed as Edwin held his treasure on the palm of one hand. It was a periwinkle, bright yellow with wetness which, William knew, would turn to pale lemon when dry. His eyes scanned the water where Edwin stood, near to some tiny, half submerged rocks. "There's another!"

Edwin turned as William waded in to pick up a brilliant, shining orange shell that really was a beauty. He was aware that Edwin was regarding him wistfully but although he did not particularly want the shell, he had no intention of handing it over.

Edwin looked around ruefully. If only he could find one of that colour. Both boys spotted the shell at the identical moment. It was black and white striped, glistening under the water, inviting itself to be collected.

"That's mine!" Edwin shouted with excitement and pushed against the water to collect the striped shell.

Suddenly William saw red. He wanted that shell. He sprang forward and with his greater weight and strength shouldered Edwin aside, bent and snatched the shell from under his nose.

"I saw it first!" Edwin protested with a hurt cry.

"I grabbed it first!" William crowed. "If you want it, come and get it, I dare you!" he jeered.

Edwin hesitated a second, only too well aware how strong William was. There was a look of malice on William's face which mocked and challenged. Then months of resentment reached ignition point inside Edwin. He forgot William's muscles and moods. All he could think of was the striped shell that should be his. He sprang, taking William quite by surprise; it was the first time Edwin had dared to oppose him outright.

Edwin reached over to grab William's tightly closed knuckles and force him to yield the shell while his face went red with anger. William hesitated only long enough for the shock to wear off, then reacted in the only way he knew how and with a force he had always wanted to use but had never dared before.

His fist opened, the shell dropped and he struck out at Edwin's face. More by luck than judgement his fist connected with Edwin's jaw. His brother stopped in his tracks, his eyes opened wide with shock and he swayed as another wave licked around their bare legs. William seized the advantage. He sprang through the water, sending it sheeting high, and pummelled Edwin's face and body, making the other wince and lower his guard to protect pained ribs.

William jabbed again so Edwin kicked out but his sandaled foot did not connect. What it did do was infuriate William, who had never dreamed Edwin would dare attack. William lashed out with both fists, suddenly all over Edwin who felt sharp fear. There was a horrible look in William's dark eyes and his teeth snarled as he jumped forward again.

Edwin desperately tried to back away but the water was a little too deep. He stumbled and went flying backwards. William sprang landing on top of him, his fighting blood at top pitch. His hands shot out and grabbed Edwin's head and he flung him back further, pushing him under the water.

There were only a few rocks and they were smooth from the tides but William's force was enough to ram Edwin's skull against them. At the same moment, in an instinctive reflex action to live, Edwin jerked himself half around. There was an ugly crack and Edwin went limp in William's hands. His neck broken; he died instantly as his spinal cord was severed.

William suddenly grasped something was very wrong. He froze. "Edwin?" he cried nervously. "Eddie!" he quavered, then, half bent, he stared with horror as Edwin's body floated on the water with the head bent at a queer angle. Gingerly he reached out and touched the body, tugging at it as it moved listlessly towards him. William felt his skin cringe as his eyes opened wide with panic and terrible fear. He stood up sharply, backing away from the body, one hand at his mouth while his eyes rolled with sheer terror. He had killed Edwin.

He splashed from the water and fell on his bare knees, panting heavily with shock and terror, then his sharp wits lurched into action. He flung a wild look all around but he was quite alone. The tide was gently coming in and swiftly he pushed Edwin's body out a little further to where the waves were stronger then he sank down and made himself wait. His heart pounded as he forced himself to count for over three minutes during which time two larger waves had washed out the tracks on the sand.

With large eyes flaring their whites, his nostrils pinched and forehead dappled with beads of sweat, William made himself wait a little longer, all the time checking he was unobserved. Finally he judged the time was right. Swiftly he stood and bolted back the way they had both come, shouting and waving to attract attention.

Mary woke with a violent start and a thumping heart. She sat up, looked around quickly then scrambled to her feet as William

261

raced madly towards her, waving and shouting like a mad thing. Her heart lurched as she turned to run towards him."

"What is it?" she cried as he reached her, sweating madly, lungs labouring for breath, his eyes filled with distress.

"It's Edwin!" He gabbled frantically. "A wave came when he was collecting shells. He fell backwards and is lying all queer. I can't get him out!" William screamed at her, half believing it himself now.

"Dear God! Where?"

William pointed with a shaking hand then Mary was gone, speeding over the sand. "Get your sister!" she screamed at him before she moved off and William, bent double to catch his breath, did nothing at all. She'd find out soon enough and he had to compose himself and double-check his quickly thought-out story.

Mary saw Edwin's body moving almost lazily and her face twisted with anguish. One glimpse was enough to tell her but she plunged into the sea, grabbed the arms and dragged Edwin on the sand. Then falling to her knees she looked at the queerly angled head and neck while a wild sob rose in her throat. Edwin was—dead! She bent her head and felt the first hot flood of wild tears as she cradled his head against her breasts.

The child she and Victor had made so long ago. He who was her favourite even above Margaret. She stared down at his wet face and ran gentle fingers down one cheek. She felt that her heart would burst. Never before had she felt such terrible anguish. Dear, quiet little Edwin who was not like either of his parents but who was so loveable.

She peered through the flood of tears. There were marks on his cheeks and around his jaw. Slowly she lifted her head and looked at the innocent sea. It was true hidden rocks could be anywhere at high water but how could they make such marks on the childish skin?

Something horribly sinister rose in Mary's mind. She shivered, frozen to the marrow of her bones despite the blazing sun. She knew Edwin's neck was broken but surely the rock which did that would not lacerate the skin? Those marks on his face could not have been caused by rocks because there was not even the tiniest graze. Again evil flashed through her mind, impossible to accept.

She cradled Edwin's body and broke into a fresh paroxysm of grief. She could not think straight; not while her son's body was still wet and warm in her arms.

Michael and Margaret raced up followed by William. The children ground to a halt and stared aghast at Mary's wild grief and Edwin's stillness. Great sobs broke from Mary's lips and it was Michael who knelt down by her side and slipped an arm around her shoulders.

Margaret could not move. She was frozen in time, her eyes riveted upon Edwin's body, watching as very gently, with an adult gesture, Michael leaned forward and closed Edwin's staring eyes. Mary turned to him, seeing him through a curtain of liquid misery, unable to frame one word as she shuddered and quivered with shock.

"Margaret, stay with your mother!" Michael said firmly, getting to his feet. "I'm going to take the trap and get help from town!"

Michael flashed a warning look at his friend and Margaret took his place, one arm around her mother as her own tears poured. William stood one pace back, nervously going from one foot to another. Then Mary opened her mouth and let out a keening wail of human misery. The sound was the most awful William had ever heard. It hit him straight and deep in the guts and his skin cringed, then crawled. He had never thought the human voice was capable of expressing such depth of misery and sorrow. Fear, terror and guilt smothered him and suddenly he became aware of a lump in his own throat. At the same time, he felt something else.

William flashed a look to his left and Margaret's salty, narrowed eyes bored into his. There was a white, bleak look on her face.

Her nostrils were pinched and her teeth showed, barred with lips drawn back in a silent snarl. It tore through William's mind that his sister suspected; she even *knew* this was no accident. He gulped, tried to avert his eyes but found he could not. Margaret glowered at him with twitching nostrils and lips which moved and uttered some silent words. William backed a step, desperately afraid of his sister. There was something savagely barbaric emanating from her which sent ice down the length of his backbone. Her cold stare went deeper and deeper, making William avert his gaze, lower his head and, finally cry, not for his dead brother, but in abject terror for himself.

Very gradually Mary regained control of herself as she hugged Edwin's thin, lanky body, feeling the warmth and companionship of Margaret's arms hugging her tightly. Mary knew. There was not the slightest doubt in her mind. She knew with the mother's instinct that it was Cain and Abel all over again. William had killed his brother Edwin and she had not a shred of proof.

She tried to say something but the words stuck in her throat so slowly she turned and looked at William. He returned her stare gravely with a coolness almost more than Mary could bear. How could one brother kill another? Was this what William had been leading up to since birth? Was it this which had made her dislike him from the first sight?

Margaret was different. She wiped her eyes and turned them, red-rimmed and icy, upon her brother.

"What happened?" she asked in a low but firm tone.

William related the tale of shell hunting and the large wave, then Edwin being thrown by it into the rocks.

"Why are your knuckles skinned then?" Margaret snapped with hostility.

William thought quickly but did not make the mistake of trying to hide his hands. With a calmness which, afterwards, he admired in himself, he extended his hands before him and looked at them before replying.

"I must have skinned them when I was trying to help Edwin," he replied evenly.

Margaret opened her mouth to scream an accusation, then thought better of it with her distressed mother in hearing. There would be a time to reckon with William later. She stared at his face, then at the marks on Edwin's. Mary caught her eyes and they exchanged a long look. Mary knew it was possible Edwin's bruises had been caused by the sea and William's answer for his skinned knuckles was plausible. Nonetheless she knew, without any doubt, he was lying. Dear God, the asked herself, what kind of monster have I bred?

Then everything misted before Mary's eyes and she was only conscious of Margaret's strong, young arms and later Michael, returning with some men.

There were questions and answers and it was young Michael who acted with the astounding maturity Victor had mentioned. Mary's heart went out to him in gratitude though she could find no words. She had become encased in frozen hunks of ice in which she was led here and there, sat on chairs, given copious cups of tea with a double brandy until she did not know whether she was coming or going.

It was Michael who arranged for their return to Guernsey. It was he who collected the car, put Mary behind the wheel and encouraged her to drive back to Cobo with himself sitting alongside. It was Michael who slipped off somewhere and told them at the house and hurried back to help her. It was Michael who took his father aside when he drove up unawares to collect his son from the day's outing.

Victor was in a quandary. His instinct was to stay and help his Catherine and his grandmère yet he had to get Michael home to his mother. He had sufficient sense to understand that perhaps the two women were best left alone. He could give the practical help required by the law starting with James and Emil.

When they were alone, Mary could only sit slumped in the

265

chair. She was cried out with not a tear left. Louise was stunned into immobility and sat white-faced with shoulders which sagged.

"Oh, Tante," Mary moaned in a low voice as she lit a cigarette with a trembling hand, "this has been the worst day of my life. When I woke this morning I was gay and light-hearted. The sun shone, the children were excited and now the day has ended in black. My son is dead. I have lost my gentle Edwin and Tante, oh Tante, that's not the worst of it."

Louise regarded her with hooded eyes. She was over the initial shock but what made her feel even more haggard and sick was the news she had but which, she told herself, must be kept awhile. So now what could Mary mean? What could be more horrific?

"Go on," she said, hardly daring to breath.

Mary spoke in a whisper, her face wretched. "I cannot prove it but I'm convinced William killed Edwin!"

Louise took a deep breath, closed her eyes and counted slowly to ten. This time her discipline faltered and her shoulders slumped heavily while she thought about what she had heard. She licked dry lips, shook her head and finally spoke.

"Tell me all," she said slowly, "I have to know."

Mary's sorrowful eyes started to swim as fresh tears arose. "It's not just me but Margaret too. Nothing has actually been said. William has given a logical explanation but there's more to it than that and I'm scared."

"Take a deep breath, speak slowly and explain," Louise encouraged.

Mary obeyed, then slowly related the tragic story. Tante listened in silence while her mind raced. It was possible that William had told the truth but it was also highly unlikely. She could so easily picture some scene in which the two boys clashed and William, with this superior strength, had simply attacked his brother. He had either killed him wilfully or created some situation that had caused Edwin's death. Murder or manslaughter, it mattered not what they called it. The boy was under the age of criminal responsibility. He could not be touched by the law and anyhow, where was the evidence? It was possible a clever-tongued adult could wheedle, browbeat or trick William into confessing the truth but for what? What good would it do? He was only twelve. Tante shuddered suddenly. Child's body he might have but what went on in that head of his?

"It's the bad blood in the Penfords," she muttered. "Duret had it. Christine did to a minor extent and now—William."

"What do I do?" Mary asked between fresh sobs.

"Victor will get help for the legal side of it, which means William will be questioned." Not that that would do much good, she told herself. "Then there is Margaret to think about," she pointed out slowly.

Mary blinked. "Margaret?" she asked uncertainly.

"If, as you say, Margaret suspects, it will be most imprudent to leave those two alone. Where is she?"

Mary shook her head. "Back at the house but Raoul and Amelia will be with the two of them."

Tante shook her head. "Get William out of the house somewhere," she advised quickly and thought deeply. "Can Amelia or Gwen take him in for the moment? Yes, that's it, I'm sure one of them would and you can make arrangements then for Margaret without him around. Margaret is going to be in shock and be filled with cold rage too. It would be wise to send the child away somewhere fresh."

"She's done nothing wrong!" Mary protested, springing to her daughter's defence.

"Not yet she hasn't because she's lacked the opportunity," Tante said sharply, her wits working quickly now. "But let her and William be alone—no, Mary! You'll have to separate them for the time being. Let me see—James has a girl at school in England. He has family there—why don't you see if Margaret can spend a few terms completing her education there? Then you'll only have William at home. Margaret might welcome a change of scenery too and it wouldn't be a bad thing to separate her and Michael as well. If they are both on this island all the while they could well spend too much time together when they are too young. A little absence will harm neither of them."

"I'll not force Margaret to go," Mary said slowly, "and what happens when she comes home for holidays? William will still be at home."

"Then you send William away somewhere. Find a Continental family who would take him in. You say he's keen on languages. Let him go and learn them."

Mary pondered these suggestions which held wisdom. It was just that the thought of Margaret leaving was hurtful and she dreaded the idea of living at home with just William. Somewhere she had read that the Jesuits said if they had a child until he was seven years they had made the man. At twelve William's character was certainly formed and she had reservations as to whether she could do anything more with him. There would always be a barrier between them, yet she could not throw him from his home. He was only a child and she had no real proof of her suspicions.

Slowly she nodded in dull agreement and the old lady regarded her carefully. Should she tell her now instead of in the morning? She certainly had to know. Wasn't it better after all to have all the shocks at once than one per day? She made up her mind.

"You are a brave, strong girl, Mary. You have proved this time and again without today. I'm afraid I have another bit of news for you, which has upset me, too. You have to know, so here it is. Sam is dead. He died sitting in his chair smoking his pipe. It was so peaceful no one knew he had gone until his pipe tumbled on the floor."

Mary sprang to her feet, her eyes flaring horror. "No!" she wailed, one hand to her mouth. "No! Not Sam too!" Shudders rippled through her body then she opened her mouth and let out a screeching scream of protesting agony.

Tante struggled from her chair, stepped forward and let fly with her right hand. Then she whipped her hand backwards across Mary's other cheek.

"Stop that!" she grated harshly. "Control yourself, girl! Don't you think I don't know what it's like? Look what I went through in '99. My son died. Christine died. My daughter-in-law also died and I was left to rear two grandchildren when all alone and one new baby. But life has to go on. You still have a fine daughter and even if you loathe William at this moment, he is still your flesh and blood. Pull yourself together, Mary! This is no time for screaming hysterics."

The harsh words rang in Mary's ears, echoing and reverberating back and forth as she stared aghast at the wrinkled old face only a foot from hers. Tante's eyes blazed and her face was a cold mask of iron will. She stood upright with her back straight, just as if she were on parade, exactly as Mary remembered her that first day on St Peter Port quay all those years ago.

As her words penetrated Mary's mind, she closed her eyes a moment while her jaw went stiff. When she opened her eyes again they were clear and blue, still salty with tears sliding down her cheeks but their flow was abating as self-control returned. She nodded wanly as Tante's hand touched a shoulder with reassurance and comradeship. Mary took a number of a slow, deep breaths and visibly relaxed.

"Thank you, Tante," she whispered heavily and looked ruefully at her dear friend. "I don't know what I'd do without you."

Louise's' lips went tight. One day Mary would have to manage without her and cope she would. Louise knew she was living on borrowed time.

Aloud she said, "It was a shock but you had to know, didn't you?" she said cleverly, hitting the ball back into Mary's court.

The young woman nodded miserably and wiped her eyes with the back of one hand.

"Everything always happens at once, doesn't it?" she questioned sadly. "First Edwin and now Sam. Dear God, I'll miss both of them so much, far more than words can ever say."

"But you are a fighter and will go on—Sam would expect this of you," Tante pointed out quickly. "He had no time for a quitter, had he?"

Mary could only shake her head. A great weariness filled her but she knew she would never sleep. She must go home though.

"Send William down to me for the night if no one else can take him," Louise offered, "and give a lot of attention to your daughter. The best thing you can do is to take a large brandy and you might let Margaret have a drop too. It won't hurt her just this once."

Mary knew she was right again. She must get William out of the house away from Margaret. She knew how her daughter could react and William would have no chance against her. Dear God, she asked silently, do other families have such problems?

FIFTEEN

THE NEXT DAY, after an uneasy, brandy-induced sleep Mary woke as the sun streamed through her window. She knew something dreadful had happened but her bemused mind took time to slip into gear again. When it did and memory returned, so too did the tears, flowing unchecked as she sobbed her heart out for her beloved Edwin.

It was Margaret who slipped into her room. The girl had white cheeks and was quiet, lacking all her normal bounce and noise. She sat on the side her mother's bed as gradually Mary's tears slowed and their hands met and held firmly.

"Oh Margaret!" Mary moaned, shaking her head. "The words just won't come today."

Margaret felt she was a new person. Her girlhood had ended on Alderney. All of a sudden she had been shot into premature adulthood and she knew she was different even if she looked the same. To her surprise she had slept well, not realising it was emotional shock that had driven an exhausted mind into the oblivion of sleep. She woke early, lay thinking, then slipped from her room to find her mother.

"Where's William?" Margaret asked carefully.

Mary half sat up, pulling the girl nearer, slipping an arm around her shoulders.

"He stayed the night elsewhere," she explained slowly. "I don't actually know whether it was with Granny, Gwen or Amelia."

Margaret sensed she did not really care as long as her son was out of the house.

"William killed Edwin," Margaret stated flatly.

Mary eyed her carefully. Was it possible her features had matured overnight? Mary knew this was nonsense yet there was a change in her daughter. It was not easy to pinpoint the alteration but the young eyes which held hers were clear and steady, even if hard. She waited for her mother's reply.

"We have no proof," Mary said, stalling. To agree with Margaret wholeheartedly would simply turn a difficult situation into an impossible one.

"I just *know* he did," Margaret repeated flatly. "William is a nasty bully and always has been. Edwin was afraid of him. I tried to protect him and it's partly my fault he's dead," and Margaret's voice broke.

"Margaret! Margaret! What do you mean?"

Margaret's tears started to flow. "I always try to watch him when he is alone with William but I forgot yesterday. I went off with Michael and never thought," she wailed.

Mary's lips tightened. They had all forgotten that Edwin was without his usual companion. William wouldn't have tried anything with Margaret present. They were all guilty in their own little ways.

"Hush!" she soothed. "What's done is done."

Margaret sniffed and looked at her mother. "I hate William. I have never liked him but now I loathe him," she said fiercely. "I could beat the truth out of him. I'm bigger and stronger than he is."

Mary sighed and shook her head. "I don't think you could," she said patiently, "because even if we are both right, no matter what we do to William he is never going to admit such a thing, now is he?"

Margaret started. "You think the same as me, Mother!" she exclaimed.

Mary nodded miserably. "I do," she admitted, turning to her daughter as another adult, "but we cannot prove it."

"And without proof—?" Margaret began, frowning, trying hard to understand an adult's world.

"We can do nothing. William is only twelve. He is too young to have to account for his actions in law," she explained heavily.

"I hate him. I don't want to live with him," Margaret blurted out hotly.

Mary snatched her opportunity. "My dear," she began nervously, not having had time to sort out her words, "would you like to go away to finish your education so that you wouldn't have to see William?"

Margaret went stiff and quiet, then turned solemn eyes to her mother. "What do you mean?"

"Dear daughter, this is a terrible time for both of us with Edwin gone and the way we think but, as I say, our hands are tied. William is still my flesh and blood and is my responsibility to rear and train. Do you want to live in this house with him?"

"No!" Margaret said vehemently. "But I don't want to leave you!"

Mary hugged her passionately. "You are very precious to me and I don't want you to go but perhaps it might be better all round. It would be a new experience for you. You could stretch your wings and think how wonderful it would be when you came home on holidays. What fun we could have together and—" Mary paused. "I promise William would not be here during those times. You see, William could then go away to the Continent to concentrate upon his languages. Much as I hate to say it, William is clever. Indeed, Margaret, although he is younger than you, in many ways he is your academic equal. Now if you went away to a fine school you could end up better qualified than him," she ended cunningly.

Margaret considered this, well aware it was the truth. She felt an intense love for her mother as they sat talking as adults.

"Where?" she asked nervously.

"Well, Mr le Canu's daughter goes to a splendid school in England and I expect arrangements could be made for you to start in the autumn term but only if you want to do this. No one is forcing you. You are not being driven away. The choice is yours entirely," Mary added hastily.

"What would happen until then?" Margaret asked quietly.

"William can stay elsewhere for the time being," Mary replied with a smoothness she did not feel.

"I'd miss Michael," Margaret said a little plaintively.

"But think what fun you'd have in your holidays getting together again," Mary pointed out quickly.

Margaret let this new idea roll about in her mind. It would indeed be fun to go to England, particularly as it meant she never had to mix with William again.

"But what about you, Mother, with William I mean?" she whispered apprehensively.

Mary's face went hard. "I can handle William," she said shortly. "Don't you get any fears about him and me," she added grimly.

"I think I'd like to go," Margaret said suddenly. "But William is going to pay. I don't know how or when but something awful is going to happen to William for what he did to Edwin. I only hope I am there to see it," she said soberly, looking at her mother, her young face rigid and hard.

Mary gathered her in her arms. Dear heaven, she thought. What a way for a child to grow up. This one child, this precious daughter was so like herself in many ways.

"Go and see Gran," she whispered. "I think I'll lie back and doze again," she said in a low voice. It was an excuse to try and compose her harrowed thoughts and let Tante talk to Margaret. There was rapport between them despite the generation gap and Margaret must now be kept occupied until the necessary arrangements could be made.

Mary was not aware she had fallen asleep again until her senses, always highly tuned, warned her she was not alone. She lay still, a second or two, awake but unmoving, then her sixth sense warned her. His aroma was powerful.

"Victor!" she gasped.

"So!" he drawled gently. "You have come back to us and I have you in bed at last," he said with a feeble joke.

He was uncertain how to behave, for the first time in his life he felt nervous. The news had appalled him and after taking Michael home he had been compelled to return to his grandmère and it was she who had spoken frankly. The tale she related had chilled his blood. Brother killing brother! He had been torn in two. Should he keep away because of the Noyen family grief or be with his darling Catherine? It was Grandmère who pointed the way and he had driven over this morning. Amelia had shown him upstairs and he had sat patiently on the bedside, studying her face, seeing the lines left by tears. His heart ached as he wanted to pick her up and cradle her against his strength but he had sat quietly and patiently.

"What on earth are you doing here?" Mary gasped.

"You look beautiful," he said gently; once again she did something to his heart Nicole never managed. "Oh! My sweet girl, what a terrible event. Grandmère has told me all," he said quietly, "and you have been wise to get that boy away from your home for the time being."

He paused, looked down at this hands then up at her again. "I wish I could do something to help you."

Mary sat up and pulled a shawl around her shoulders. She took a deep breath. It was wonderful to see him, but even now, he did not know the whole truth and she wondered whether today was the moment to tell him. Commonsense warned her not to. Victor accepted Edwin as Duret's son. What good could come from raking up the past again, especially now? Yet she knew one day she would tell him. She looked over and saw his eyes.

"There is one thing though," Mary began firmly. "I agree with everything you said about Michael. Your son was wonderful yesterday. He took complete charge and acted like an adult. Quite frankly, I don't know what I would have done without him. He is a very wonderful boy."

Victor nodded. "I think so too. I have been lucky with my children. Jenny is the only weak one which is strange when you realise she is Mike's twin but she might change as she gets older. She's an Oselton. Mike is a Noyen," he told her firmly.

"Does Nicole know you are here?" Mary asked with sharp nervousness.

"I neither know nor care," he replied coolly. "Yesterday's circumstances warrant unusual situations today as far as I am concerned," he told her firmly. "Grandmère is Grandmère and you are her family which makes you mine in turn."

Mary's head spun. It was complicated logic but she would not argue with him, she was too pleased to see him.

"Do you know everything?" she whispered miserably.

His face went grim. "I do!"

"If I thought about it long enough I'd go crazy," she said in a low voice. "For some reason I never liked William from the first moment I saw him but it never entered my mind something horrible like this could happen. I'm sending Margaret away to a school in England," she began then went on to explain the plan in detail.

Victor listened carefully without interruption. It all made sense to him. James would be of invaluable help and he resolved to talk to him about this later.

"I'm thinking of sending Mike to school over there too," he said almost casually. "I think it does youngsters good to go away when they reach a certain age. It certainly makes them appreciate home when they come back for their holidays. Look at the British middle and upper classes. They think nothing of sending their sons off to boarding school as young as seven. I might be able to arrange a place near Margaret so that, under supervision, those two could meet now and again," he offered.

Mary brightened. Such an arrangement would be almost perfect and they could travel to and from the island together. After yesterday, Mary knew she could always trust Michael le Page. Tante might not approve though, she thought, but surely she would accept the sense of it?

"What does your wife say to that?" she asked uncertainly.

Victor gave a wolfish grin. "She doesn't know yet because I've not told her and when she does learn, it won't be much good objecting either. I expect you can see the feeling between Mike and Margaret. Do you think he'd want to stay here with Margaret in England? Wild horses wouldn't hold him and I'll not stand in his way. Nicole will have to live with it," he replied a little harshly. His wife would still have children at home to fulfil her maternal instincts but Michael was his child and Mike came first. He had the right to act as he thought fit for his elder son. If Nicole was foolish enough to place a wrong interpretation upon his actions Victor knew he no longer cared. Edwin's horrific death had affected them all in different ways.

William was petrified. There had been so many adults asking a barrage of questions that even his stoicism nearly broke. Only the desperate knowledge of what a revelation would mean had kept him to his story without deviation.

A police sergeant had bombarded him with questions in a quiet but insistent voice that had gone on and on. It had been the same with his mother's lawyer. Both these men's eyes had been narrow and cold as William stood and faced them, hands at his sides.

He had gone over it again and again, polishing a phrase here, slightly changing a word there but never the gist of the details. He returned the two men's looks openly without flinching and he knew they accepted his story finally. There was nothing else they could do and this filled him with surging triumph and wild elation at his superiority over adult authority.

Uncle Victor also questioned him but now he was word perfect with gestures and mannerisms polished. The one person whose questioning he did fear was that of the old lady. William knew she was hostile to him and he had always been wary of her. Her brown eyes could be so piercing and hard but again he managed to hold her stare firmly without flinching as he went through his act yet again.

At night, in the attic of Raoul's cottage, he felt a flood of elation. He had never dreamed it was possible to fool and defy adults and William realised he had left his childhood behind forever.

He was glad to get away from home. Margaret's reactions worried him because though he would divulge nothing to her, no matter what she might do to him, William knew he would writhe in impotent fury and that might make him lose his temper. And that he could not afford to do. It had suddenly dawned upon him that loss of temper weakened a person. The superior always had himself under rigid control—like the old lady in her cottage.

He had been delighted to live in the Ozanne cottage even though the children there were not his type. He sensed this was but a delaying tactic while other matters were arranged but he would never lower himself to question. Long ago, William had learned that information overheard and stored away was usually more valuable than direct conversation.

When he learned Margaret would be going to school in England, he was thrilled. That would get her out of the way for most of the year and he would then rule the home roost. With his father dead, there would be no more children and he swelled with delight. Gradually he also learned of the plans for Margaret's holidays, again with approval. He had no wish to be in the house when she came home, especially if the le Page boy would be hanging around.

The thought he would go to stay with continental families to improve his languages delighted him. This was something in which he had tremendous interest and in which he knew he could excel. Although Margaret was that much older, William had long known he had the better brain. He was also sharp enough to understand the Noyen's financial standing in the community and one day he intended to have a major share of this. With a grasp of European languages, he would be in a much stronger position than Margaret, and his mother would have to give him a majority shareholding.

His mother! William's heart always quailed when he reached this point in his thinking.

If there was one human being who genuinely frightened him it was his mother. Whether this was because he had recognised her antipathy to him since birth, despite the attention she had always given him, he was never wholly certain. All he did know was that his mother was someone with whom it was decidedly unwise to cross swords.

She could be loving but implacable, gentle yet rough. She was a mixture of human emotions and attributes which he found totally unpredictable. In many ways she fascinated him. There was so much about her that he admired enormously, yet there was that in her which frightened him.

As he strolled morosely along the beach near the old lady's cottage, he yearned to go and see her and talk to her. He felt an urge to tell his story to her, yet he dared not approach her uninvited. Deep down, he suspected his mother knew the whole truth. How this could be he had no idea, not being adult enough to understand the depths of feminine and maternal instinct. Even if he had, he might have scorned them both as being too intangible to be practical.

What had started to terrify him was the knowledge that once his sister left for her new school in England, he would return home to live with his mother. He had seen her, of course, before

Edwin's funeral, which he had not been allowed to attend, which suited him. Then he had been whisked away by Raoul on a walking expedition which he knew was but an excuse to get him out of the way for the rest of the funeral day.

Raoul was all right. He said little. He passed no judgements and William was inclined to look down his nose at him as being just an employee of low intellect. Amelia he dismissed as being of little consequence. Raymond and his wife Gwen were a couple about whom he had not yet made a decision. Their paths rarely crossed due to greenhouse work.

On the day after Margaret and Michael had sailed to England with Victor as escort, plus James, William returned home ready for starting school the next day. He had not seen his mother. Amelia had given him his meal and he had retired to bed alone but happy in his odd way. The next morning at breakfast though his mother was there. It was the first time they had been alone since the day of Edwin's death and William steeled himself as he walked into the kitchen. Now came the ultimate trial. What would she say? How would she start upon him?

Mary did nothing. "Get your meal," she told him briskly, "then get yourself off to school."

William was flabbergasted, so shocked he obeyed without thinking, not even daring to lift his head from his food to peep at her. For her part, Mary studied him carefully. He wore his school shirt and tie, grey short trousers and he was clean and fresh looking. His cheeks were pink and healthy and his dark eyes held no emotion whatsoever as he chewed through his meal.

She tried to examine how she felt about him sitting at the opposite side of the table but there was only numbness when she could not see Edwin alongside him. This was the son with whom she was left. This was the one she had to control and guide. Her senses told her the task was too late. Whatever went on in William's mind was unreachable by her or anyone. All she could do was learn to live with him until something should happen.

What that might be or when it would occur she had no idea and indeed did not wish to know. It was bad enough to live each day as it came because already the house was only half a home without Margaret.

For his part, William sat quietly, anxious not to draw attention to himself. He knew his mother's iron will and flaring temper just as he was aware he was still too young to contend with either. He waited and waited for her to mention Edwin until it dawned upon him she was not going to. Her calm and coldness bothered him. He would much rather she came out with an accusation that he could refute with his polished story. When she did not, William became internally agitated. Was this how it was going to be? Would his mother maintain her aloofness for days and weeks, then suddenly, out of the blue, strike? It frightened him. She was so strong and implacable. In many ways, unknown to either of them, he was emotionally more of his mother's child than Margaret or Edwin. A prognosis would have shown they were utterly different yet exactly the same and one day one of them would have to yield to the other with lethal consequences.

PART FOUR—*1940*

SIXTEEN

IT WAS A quiet May night, balmy and pleasant and the only sound was the light breathing. Mary gave a silent sigh as she sat on the chair by the open window not far from the bed, now and again looking at the frail old lady. It was her turn to sit through the night with Tante who was, as the doctor had told them, slowly starting to die. The clock was running down after ninety years. An age was slowly coming to its close and she could hardly take it all in. Tante had been with her for so many years that it did not seem possible she was preparing to go.

Mary felt incredibly sad, yet there were no tears. The old lady spent much of her time sleeping in her bed at the cottage, having refused point-blank to return to the house for her last days. Mary knew her going would leave the most terrible void in her heart but perhaps, if Tante had to go, now was the time, when Britain had been at war for over a year and the situation was looking increasingly frightening.

Not long after Edwin's death, Margaret had left for her new school and Mary had missed her more than she had thought possible. Without her daughter's gay laughter and noisy ways, the house had echoed dismally. The holidays though had been a wonderful time when mother and daughter continually rediscovered each other with Mike always around at Cobo. Margaret constantly said that when she returned, she felt as if she did not start to live again until the steamer came down through The Russel at St Peter Port.

Margaret returned home finally in 1936, well educated but without any desire to go to university. Mary did not mind; it was too wonderful to have her daughter back. Perhaps Margaret had realised the grind of university was not for her. Also she had been astute enough to take note of the way Europe appeared to be changing for the worse.

To Mary's surprise, Margaret had taken over control of the small shop and displayed a sound commercial flair, making changes which Mary approved and the shop had rapidly doubled its takings. Within another year, a second shop had been bought which Margaret managed and there were plans for a third.

She was formally engaged to Michael who stayed on in England where he had, to everyone's surprise, joined the army as a regular soldier. Michael never wavered as to where his heart lay and Margaret seemed equally sure of her own. Mary knew it was a good match and now the couple talked of wedding plans but would these be possible?

When Margaret came home on holidays, William was always away and when her daughter was home for good, Mary tactfully made her flat over to Margaret as a private home. That way brother and sister were kept relatively apart although they did bump into each other now and again. They were like two stiff-legged dogs facing a juicy bone. Margaret would go all cold and awkward while William clammed up and said nothing but never relaxed either.

To Mary's astonishment and great relief, William settled down and was now fluent in French and German. To her surprise he had caused no more trouble yet between them, an atmosphere was ever present; but at least he did as he was told. Mary suspected she still had the stronger character but William had to be watched. He was a powerful young man and kept himself fit with running and swimming. Where he went in his spare time Mary did not know though she often wondered with unease. He seemed to get on well with Raymond and Gwen, was diffident with Raoul, sullen with Victor and James and what he thought of Emil Mary did not know.

When Britain declared war on the 3rd September 1939, Mary's spirits had sunk although, as yet, few of the islanders took the matter seriously. Although their men folk had fought well in the last war, the Channel Islands themselves had been totally unaffected and few could see things might be different a second time around. Indeed, there had been the usual influx of holiday visitors and Mary had been as busy as ever with many people saying they considered the islands a safe place to come, to avoid air raids.

She saw James on a weekly basis, sometimes to discuss the business matters but always to converse in low voices on the dangerous situation. Mary could not help marvelling how prescient some Britons had been so many years ago.

"It's bad, isn't it?" Mary had asked with worry.

James gave her a long, hard look. "Yes and it will get worse. The public won't be told this either because of the danger of morale collapsing."

They sat in silence until he spoke again. "Are you ready to work as planned?"

Mary nodded, though her face was white. "Surely these islands won't be affected?"

James turned aside and looked through the window thoughtfully before turning back to her with a grave face.

"If Germany overruns France, as she will, Hitler will invade here I'm afraid. Anyhow that is the policy on which we plan to work."

"Germans—here?" Mary cried, aghast.

James had nodded grimly. "With France, Belgium, Holland and Norway gone what is there to stop them? Britain is stretched to the limit and is standing quite alone. I can tell you if the worst happens, all of the Channel Islands will have to be demilitarised. Do you understand what that means? There will be too few troops to fight and the RAF will be withdrawn back to the mainland. The islands will be alone."

"But how can we defend ourselves?" Mary had protested.

"You can't," James told her bluntly, "and there is also another aspect to this as well. If a military stand were made here, think about the appalling civilian casualties. There are no shelters. There is nowhere for the public to flee to for safety. The blood loss would be too enormous to contemplate so the Channel Islands will have to be left for Hitler."

"What will happen to us?" Mary asked, an icy finger creeping up her spine.

"I'm afraid you are going to be invaded and occupied by Germany!"

"We rely on Britain! We cannot grow enough food for everyone here. We get our coal and goods from Britain. What will we do?"

"Suffer and bear it, I'm afraid," he said firmly. "There is nothing else *to* do and you know all this is now classified. Can you now see why we planted people here long ago to be Britain's ears and eyes? I can tell you the Bailiffs of both Guernsey and Jersey will be ordered to stay at their posts while efforts will be made to get those off the island who wish to go."

Mary sat stunned and appalled. "I can hardly take it in."

"So now I tell you officially we wish to activate you the moment the Germans land here. I take it you will stay?"

Mary's temper flared. "Of course I shall stay. I'll not run from Germans!" she had snorted. "No one drives me from my island home!"

"Good!"

Mary studied him. He had changed. There was a worried look in his eyes and he seemed older. It was his gravity that stabbed another knife deep in her guts. If James was worried, then she should get really alarmed but she kept her face straight.

"Your daughter lives in the flat," James said suddenly, chewing his lip. "That will have to change. That flat must be where you can be found," he had told her steadily.

Mary nodded. She had been half expecting this. "I doubt Margaret will stay here much longer. Her fiancé is on active service. Any day I expect her to tell me she is going back to the mainland to join one of the women's services."

James stood up and went to the window, looking through it but seeing nothing then he turned back and slowly sat down facing her.

"My wife and daughter have already gone," he had said slowly. "They flew out two days ago. I'm off at the end of this week as well—on active service, shall I say—and don't ask me any questions please."

Mary sat frozen. "You too!" she whispered. "But your practice, your home?"

He shrugged. "If a lawyer is any good, he can rebuild a practice. As to my home, certain precautions have been taken and Emil has the keys."

Precautions? Mary's mind had buzzed then she understood. Personal valuables had been hidden but his lovely expensive home…?

"Our world is collapsing," she murmured.

"It's already collapsed!"

"What should I do?" was Mary's next question.

He leaned forward, his eyes narrow and sharply hard. "You must let yourself fall into a pattern whereby you spend a certain amount of time in the flat doing—your accounts, shall I say? That way, whoever comes will be able to contact you. Remember there are always brave people who act as couriers to get information out. Your job will be to collect and assess it. You must write it down using small handwriting, condensing the material and naturally you must have some foolproof hiding place which I leave to your sense. Remember, if the Germans come, as they will, do not underestimate them. They are not fools and they can be extremely harsh."

"*What* kind of information?"

"Everything and anything which gives a complete, current picture of enemy troops here on this island. The calibre of the troops. The way they are armed, their morale—all and everything is grist to the mill of general information which, when slotted together, gives those who make military decisions the complete picture of the enemy's strength. You will have the code name of Lihou and your contact will be Jethou. Each word is to be used in a natural sentence."

"Man or woman?"

He shook his head wearily. "I don't know and if I did, I wouldn't tell you."

Mary gnawed her bottom lip. "What happens if—?"

"This would be known which is why you will have a second contact name of Burhou and your opposite number will be Brecqhou. We have tried to keep matters simple by using local island names. You will divulge nothing to a person who fails to identify himself with either of these names. Remember, every country and every race has its share of informers so trust only those whom you really know because your neck will be on the block. If anything happens to you, there will be no chance of rescue," he warned her gravely.

"I'll know only the courier who comes—and you?"

He paused, looking bleak. "I doubt you'll see me again until it's all over."

"When you first talked to me years ago I never really took it all in," she told him in a low voice. "I simply could not believe it would happen a second time in half a century."

"Your contact will make himself known to you in the shop just about at closing time so it will be natural for you to invite him up to your flat for a cup of tea," he had told her. "Always see your shop girl off, then delay locking up yourself for ten minutes or more and do this twice a week to a regular pattern. That way any islanders will accept your being there," he had advised her.

Mary nodded; she experienced a sharp flash of panic. Despite the way she had trained her memory and senses, now they were to be needed seriously, she felt a great load of responsibility descend upon her back, then her resolve hardened. She could do it and she would.

"There is one more point," James told her thoughtfully. "If the Germans do have a fault, it is their Prussian regularity. Sometimes this can be used against them but be careful of them. Very careful!"

Slowly he stood and took her hand, he kissed it in the continental manner and as she left, Mary wondered when she would ever see him again.

For a number of days now she had not seen Victor, which puzzled her because he was meticulous in visiting his grandmère. She had sent a message warning him of the old lady's imminent end but still he had not come and Mary's shoulders slumped.

"Mary?" a light whisper rose from the bed.

Mary whipped round and shot from the chair kneeling by the bed side. "Tante?" she said taking a thin, frail hand into hers.

The old woman managed a wan smile before speaking again with an effort. "This dying is a tedious business," she murmured.

Mary felt tears hover and struggled to hold them back. Tante would scorn their appearance now.

"If you say so," she managed to choke out.

"I'm glad you are here, girl," Tante said slowly. "It's been a long time since you landed at the quay. My will is with James and everything is divided equally between you and Victor and all liquid holdings are in England and have been for a while. The house though is yours and so is my cottage. One day when this ghastly war is over, you might want to live there so that Margaret and Michael can raise their family in the house. It is in the natural order of events, isn't it?"

Words stuck in Mary's throat. James could well have gone by the time Tante died so she guessed another lawyer would have to deal with it though, knowing the wily old lady, everything would be in apple-pie order. As if she cared. All she wanted was Tante yet such a wish was selfish. The old lady had been slowly failing for a year and the quality of her life had deteriorated. It was kinder for her to go; certainly before there were German jackboots on Guernsey.

"Mary!" Tante said heavily. "This war is going to be bad. I feel it in my bones. The Germans will come and I have a presentiment it might be for a long time. Take no chances. Get Raoul to help you bury everything of value that won't rot in the soil but do not let William know," she warned anxiously. "Get in as much food as you can. Make sure you carry your pistol and ammunition with you at all times and Mary, do what you can to help Britain as James wants!"

Mary's eyes opened wide with shock. She was astounded James had confided in the old lady.

Tante read her mind. "He did not tell me. I slowly put two and two together in the many months in which I have been able to think. Your business is not so vast that you need to see a lawyer every week and neither is it quite necessary to go flying all around the island as if you were going to map it!" she managed to get out dryly.

"Well!" was all Mary could manage to get out, equally dryly.

"Raoul and Amelia are sound and trustworthy like Victor but don't trust Nicole le Page. I suspect she's known the feeling between you two for a long time but she's been too deep and cunning to come out with it. Be wary of her. Never trust William of course and don't turn your back on him either. I still think he's not finished giving you trouble because the older he gets the more difficult he will become. He is seventeen but could easily pass as a man in his twenties," she sighed. "Promise me you will never trust him."

"I won't!" Mary vowed. How could she, after Edwin?

"I can't make up my mind about Raymond and Gwen. They are good workers, that I grant, yet I've never cared much for Raymond and he leads Gwen. Reserve judgement with those two. James, as you know, is trustworthy and Emil, but always remember he is a policeman first and islander second."

"I will," Mary whispered with breaking heart.

"Victor has always loved you and always will. What a stupid old fool I was but you must live your own life now. If chance lets you find happiness with Victor, take it. Watch out for Nicole though. Those Oseltons are a queer lot, too inbred for my liking." She paused to catch her breath. "Tell me though, Mary, who was Edwin's father?"

"How on earth—?" Mary began, then bit her lip. "Victor was his father. That day I came back and said I'd come off the cycle because of a stone," she explained softly.

Tante nodded half to herself. "So I was right there at least," she stated triumphantly, "though it took me a long, long time to work it out. Does Victor know?"

Mary shook her head. "There was no point after Edwin's death, it would have made a terrible situation even worse."

"You must tell him before he goes off to fight," Tante said urgently. "In wartime, don't have secrets from those you love in case—" and she let the sentence hang.

Mary could see her chest was barely moving and she realised Louise was going. She leaned forward and kissed each cheek gently then stood, looked down and knew Tante had gone. At that moment the door opened and Victor tiptoed in.

"She's not—?" he asked swiftly.

Mary faced him, white, with tears threatening. "Just now."

Victor groaned. "I couldn't get here before because—well never mind that now."

"It's the end of an era," Mary said sadly.

Victor touched the old cheeks and gently closed Tante's eyes.

"We'll not see her like again for a long time, if ever. I just wished I'd known her when I was a boy," he said with bowed head.

They held hands like children, united in their absolute grief. Mary turned to him.

"Will you be going to war?" she asked quietly.

He nodded gravely. "There's a chance able-bodied men who stay here may be interned and even someone of my age has a part to play in war but from the mainland."

Mary's shoulders slumped. "In that case, there's something you should know before you go," she paused. "Edwin was your son."

He stilled, eyes opening wide with shock. "Oh my God, why didn't you tell me before, Mary?"

"How could I? Think back to those times with Duret still alive. When Edwin died I was too distraught. Tante knew though. She had guessed but I don't know how. She said I should tell you before you left for war."

"Edwin my boy!" he murmured and shook his head, passing a hand over his forehead. He turned back to her. "I did wonder. I did some counting myself but when you never said—I presumed Duret had used you."

They were quiet. "If I had known," Victor said grimly, "I'd have—done something."

Mary nodded. "And the whole island would have known, the family name would have been ruined and dear old Tante would have suffered cruelly. Do you see now why I could *not* tell you?"

He was forced to nod reluctantly. "It rankles though," he had to admit. "Especially thinking of how he died. Perhaps it's as well you've only told me now," he ended grimly. "Come, let us leave Tante. There are arrangements to be made and we will have a precious hour in which to talk. God knows when there'll be another opportunity and to hell with what your workers think either."

294

On the 8th June, the islanders saw a pall of smoke on the horizon which seemed to block out the sun and Mary guessed the French were burning their oil storage tanks before the Germans came.

Victor came to her that evening and together they strolled up the coast to the Rocques, saying little, content to be with each other, both weighed down by worry. They ambled along for a while in silence both immersed in their own thoughts.

Mary's heart was heavy but from force of habit she looked around. There were more cottages here than when she had first come and the little village had spread. It was not often the coast road was empty nowadays and she knew this was a step forward but somehow, when shared by others, this cherished spot lost its magic.

Victor led her up the grass, past the hotel to the high point where he had first seen her. He studied a woman of forty. She had worn extremely well and still had a remarkable effect upon him. As she stood solemnly looking out to sea a tiny breeze pressed her blouse against her breasts, outlining them to show their beauty. Her slacks, not quite as neatly pressed as usual, were dark green, a colour she favoured and her tan sandals were the same shade as her blouse. Her short hair stirred gently and he wanted to run his fingers through it. Her lips were richly full and inviting though there were shadows under her eyes from grief and lack of sleep.

Mary felt his eyes and, turning to him, smiled wanly giving a tiny shrug to her shoulders. She saw his face was grave though his eyes, violet today, were warm for her. His charisma reached her heart as always and she marvelled at his looks. There were a few early grey hairs dotted here and there and yet these framed his head in a distinguished way. His well-shaped face had a few maturity lines around the eye corners yet the crinkle marks around his mouth showed his humour. He wore grey flannels, open necked shirt and unbuttoned jacket with careless nonchalance but carried his clothes as if they were expensively tailored. His erect, almost military, carriage, often reminded her of old Tante. His back was every bit as straight as hers had been.

He held out his right hand and Mary slipped her left into it. Turning he led the way back. Mary thought how natural it was to have contact with him and when he squeezed she reciprocated.

"What's going to happen to all of us?"

He stopped, turned to her and his face became serious. "I don't know," he replied honestly, "but I do know you will weather whatever is thrown at you."

"And you, Victor?"

Again he hesitated as if turning over in his mind news which he was reluctant to impart but which he knew he must despite its effect on her.

"I'm leaving, very soon," he said.

"You scorned the last war," she reminded him gently.

He nodded grimly. "This is different and worse. Kaiser Bill was bad enough but Hitler and his gang of thugs are madmen. Last time it was just Belgium and France—look how far Hitler has spread himself already."

Mary said nothing. His sombre words only added to her gloom and worry. Her shoulders sagged for a moment, then she straightened resolutely.

"At least they can't take our memories away from us," she murmured.

He chuckled at that. "I wish the memories could be better though," he said pointedly.

He took both of her hands in his and slowly shook his head ruefully. "It's no good," he told her firmly. "My feelings for you have never, never changed. Your heart is meshed with mine for all time. Ours is a great love even if unfulfilled and there is nothing that will change how I feel. Time, war, Nicole— nothing matters except that I know you are alive and well, my sweet Catherine."

"Oh Victor," she cried softly. "Please don't!"

He kissed her, then pushed her away six inches. "In all the years we have known each other I've told you often what you mean to me but you have never once said you loved me," he complained.

Mary kissed him back. "Oh, you big, silly thing. I adore you and always have; more is the tragedy of it all because there is nothing we can do about it."

When he started to kiss her again, Mary knew she must distract him or things would get out of hand. He was doing something to her which made her thighs weak with desire.

"Come on, let's walk back," she told him, holding his arm tightly, urging them into action. "What are you going to do about your hotels?"

He grimaced. "What everyone else will have to do if they leave for Britain. Abandon them and pick up the pieces again when it's all over. I've decent managers who are in their fifties. They'll stay and hold the fort as best they can but I expect all hotels—indeed many homes—will be requisitioned when the Germans come for billets. You'll lose your holiday cottages," he warned her.

"When will you go?" she asked him, anxious to know how much time they had left.

He thought a moment. "Very shortly. Jenny is coming to join up."

"Nicole?"

"She is in a quandary and I feel sorry for her," he admitted. "She wants to go to Britain with me, Michael and Jenny and also see James in school there, but she cannot bear to leave her family who are still on Alderney, without knowing what's going to happen to that island." He threw her a glance. "You are staying, of course?"

Mary did not bother to reply, merely looked at him. They reached the little cottage and, as if knowing the old lady had gone, it seemed to have changed; to have lost its character. She saw Margaret up the road and waved, turning to him.

"Take care," she whispered. "Try and let me know when you go."

"I will and you take care, sweet Catherine. Don't go shooting Germans with that little pistol of yours either," he ended, trying to make a jest for both of their sakes.

Then he was gone, striding off to where he had parked his car and Mary walked up to her home, lost in miserable, apprehensive thoughts.

On the 19th June an official letter came from Whitehall ordering the Bailiff to stay at his post with all Crown Officers and this news spread in a flash throughout the island, starting fresh panic.

Margaret came downstairs and hunted for her mother, then ran back up to the sewing room. She found her sitting pensively looking out of the window.

"Come to Britain with me, to safety," she pleaded suddenly.

Mary looked at her daughter who was now her own height and who had a wonderful fresh vitality and loveliness. No wonder Michael adored her.

"Here I am and here I stay!" Mary told her firmly.

Margaret set her lip, opened her mouth to argue, then changed her mind. She squatted down so their eyes were level.

"I don't like the thought of you being here during an occupation, especially with brother William," she said slowly.

Mary eyed her and saw worry. Margaret rarely mentioned William but Mary knew her daughter had not forgotten any more than she had. That dreadful day was as clear as if it had been yesterday.

"Don't you worry your head about me and a seventeen year old."

"Some seventeen year old," Margaret shot back. "He's as big as any man."

"I can handle William," Mary reassured her. "To start with, I never trust him. You see, daughter dear, William gets frustrated and cannot stand his views or attitudes being dismissed or ignored. He hasn't worked out why I never said a word to him about Edwin. That got through to him more than a dozen hidings. He waited and waited on thorns and—still does. So you see, whatever William says or does, if it annoys or conflicts with my wishes, I just dismiss him as an unimportant little boy, which he hates. He then hangs around underfoot, being a nuisance but—" Mary grinned wickedly: "I know where he is and what he is doing. Sometimes he goes off but I doubt he can cause trouble."

"*Yet!*" Margaret pointed out sharply.

Mary saw her daughter's worry and leaning forward, hugged her. "William is still a minor and if he ever overstepped the line, I would go to the law about him and William would *hate* that," she said with a malicious grin.

Margaret knew her mother's will was as unbendable as her own. She did not like the situation and resolved to have a quiet, private word with Raoul before she left. William had killed once; Margaret would put nothing past him in the future.

"When do you go, have you decided?" Mary asked.

Margaret took a deep breath. "It's tomorrow," she whispered.

Mary flinched. "So soon?"

"I've just come in from town and it's hell there," Margaret told her slowly. "There's a run on the banks and each person can only have twenty-five pounds. I saw something else upsetting too," she halted, shaking her head. "There was a long queue of people taking their pet cats and dogs to the vets to be destroyed. There are parents milling around crying about their children. They don't know whether to keep them or let them go to where there might be the danger of air raids. Ambrose Sherwell is staying with his wife and children and so is Victor Carey and he's not a young man at all."

Mary stiffened. "What about ships?"

"Britain is sending all she can spare to take off those who want to leave," Margaret told her quickly.

Mary stood up. "I think you'd better get down to the quay today," she said quickly. "And only take hand baggage. If there is a crush of panicky parents, there will be restrictions. Pack your hand baggage while I get the car out. Draw on your British account for what you need when over there."

Margaret was alarmed. Although mentally prepared to go, her mother's abruptness almost unnerved her but she saw the logic. How long would ships be able to get in and out of the harbour? She nodded and went quickly to repack a bag while Mary went for her car. Margaret then flew outside to see Raoul.

"I'm going to Britain, Raoul. Please stay and look after Mother and, most of all, watch William. I have an awful feeling here."

She touched her heart. "Never trust him, please," she begged and her eyes shone mistily.

"Trust me, Margaret!" Raoul promised. "Nothing will happen to your mother if I can help it!"

Within far too short a space of time, Mary had the car at the door and Margaret found herself bundled into it with no time for farewells to others. Raoul watched with large grave eyes and lifted his right hand as Mary drove down the drive. Then he turned and saw Amelia watching him sadly. Their own two sons had already gone to join up as had so many other young men. Now they were just two alone as it had been in the beginning.

Mary was appalled. Even on the outskirts of St Peter Port there was a crowd and progress was almost impossible.

"I'll park here. We'll have to walk!" she said, suddenly in a stew of worry at the thought that Margaret might not get a passage.

They walked one behind the other with Mary trying to emulate old Tante and cleave a passage through the crowds but these became thicker and more distraught with every step down the quay. Parents were weeping hysterically as they said farewell to their children while others dithered, not knowing what to do for the best. Down at the harbour the crowd was enormous and Mary and Margaret found themselves jammed against a wall. Crush barriers had been erected but by standing on tiptoes, Mary was able to see that embarkation had started on the *Antwerp* and other ships awaited nearby.

Mary was appalled. The multiple distress around her harrowed her nerves and suddenly she knew she could not stay. She would break down and bawl like a child. It was of desperate importance that Margaret saw her mother as defiant and clear eyed.

In a clairvoyant flash, Margaret understood. She grasped Mary's hand. "This is as far as you go," she said firmly. "You go down in that crowd and you'll be caught and wedged, taken to Britain whether you want it or not!"

Relief flashed on Mary's face then it sagged a little. "Oh Margaret!" was all she could whisper, biting her lip savagely.

"Go!" Margaret shouted, kissing her fiercely. "Go—now!"

Mary felt herself spun around by Margaret's hands and pushed back up the steps they had struggled down. She moaned as the tears slid down her cheeks, then savagely berated herself as she took in the human distress around her; the anguish on parents' faces, the shocked cries of children terrified at what was happening.

Mary saw an opening and shoved in an unladylike manner to get up against a short wall, where she wedged herself. She turned to watch the scene below where somewhere her darling daughter was inching along to a ship and Britain. She saw batches of children herded together, shepherded on board as priority. There were weeping men and women as their children were hauled back from the steps of gangways as parents changed their minds. The air was filled with cries, screams, shouts and a great ululating weeping of undiluted distress.

Later Mary knew it was one of the most traumatic days of her life. Ships came, were filled with their human cargo and left while others moved to vacant berths. Mary watched the boys from Elizabeth College march down to the harbour in an orderly line and embark en bloc. The heat was stifling and many distraught adults fainted, to be dragged to one side where they would not be trampled on.

She saw Major Sherwell still had some troops with rifles and bayonets fixed in case the crowd got out of control through fear and grief. Finally, unable to stand any more of these distressing scenes, Mary pushed and jostled her way back to her car. She could not go home yet; the house would be too empty so she drove slowly towards her shop, inching her way along and parked around the back. It was quiet here but uneasily so. Mary stood for a moment frowning a little. What was different? Then it hit her. There were no children's voices; only the small, sick and downright stubborn remained on Guernsey.

She unlocked the door, pushed it open as a step came from behind her. She turned and her face brightened a second.

"Victor!" she cried, then noted his grim jaw. "Inside and tell me!"

He slammed the door and locked it. "I can't stay more than a few moments and I took a wild chance you would be here. All hell has broken loose on Alderney. Judge French held a vote and every man, woman and child has decided to go to Britain except a couple of men who are either brave or stupid."

Mary gasped. "But how can they get everyone off in time? Alderney is too near to occupied France."

Victor shook his head. "That's the military's problem. It's crazy over there. I've had a devil's own job to get back. Animals are being let loose wherever possible and the butcher is killing people's pet cats and dogs. People can only take two suitcases with them and can't you imagine what it's like? Your home and life reduced to two suitcases in a few, short hours. What to take; what to leave?"

Mary sank down on the shop counter. "It must be pandemonium." She had a flashing vision of moving the sick, the old and babies. "What is happening on Sark, do you know?"

Victor grimaced, though his eyes flashed with respect. "Dame Sybil refuses to budge one inch. She and her American husband are staying, come hell or high water."

Mary thought about that for a moment. "Do you know something?" she said very slowly. "I think the Germans who do go over to Sark had better watch their manners. What about Jersey?"

"They've just about cleared the island of children and all the non-combatants who wish to leave. I've heard that about one-fifth of the Jersey population have left all they possess to sail to Britain. They calculate it will be about half of Guernsey," he said, then leaned on the counter next to her, his expression bleak.

"Your family?"

"They are embarking from Alderney right now—I hope. I said I had to come here to sort out last minute business." He fell quiet as he relived the violent scene Nicole had thrown in the back garden of her parents' home.

"It's that woman!" she had screeched turning from the quiet, placid girl he had married to a harridan. "You're running back to Guernsey to see her!" she accused. "You've always run after her even though she shot you, more fool you! You'll get nowhere with stuck up, high and mighty Madam Noyen! That's it, isn't it? You are going to see *her*!"

Nicole's words had initially left him thunderstruck, then his own temper had flared. Perhaps it was realisation he had lived with her for years and never realised how much she knew and how it was eating away at her.

"Yes, I am!" he hurled back at her. "At least, I'm going to say my farewell to a woman who doesn't go into screaming hysterics!"

He had stormed off, quite unable to say another word without lifting a hand to her. In a flash, he knew they had both been living a lie from the start. Neither of them would find it possible to forget, let alone forgive, and deep down, Victor knew he did not want to. For the first time in many a long year, he felt a great weight lift from his back. He might still be tied to Nicole in law but he was finally free of her.

"What has happened?" Mary asked him quietly, sensing something had.

He shrugged, pulled a face, then told her. Mary caught her breath as she listened.

"So Tante was right yet again!"

Victor nodded, then seized her arms at the shoulders. "I have to go or I'll be stuck here and that won't do at all," he said grimly. "I don't know what will happen to me in the future but I want you to know this. I love you, my sweet Catherine. Hold that in your heart during the bad times that are coming, promise?"

Mary nodded. "I promise and I love you too, Victor le Page!"

Then he was gone, leaving the shop like a rocket, running down the street and Mary heard his footsteps echoing away into silence. Her heart slumped and she knew she would have to weep to relieve her tension. She would cry for Victor. For Margaret. For her island people and, most of all, for herself.

When she had no more tears left she washed her face and knew she would have to go home. She must see what William had been up to. He had been conspicuously absent for the past two days and it was time she tracked him down. She locked up her shop but not without throwing a glance upstairs. Soon, very soon, she must start to develop the habit of working late in the evenings. She thought about her lovely car. That would either be commandeered by the occupiers or there would be no petrol. Thank God she had kept her rattling old cycle and, she remembered with a sudden flash of inspiration, surely she had bought two new tyres before she purchased her car? She thought they must be in the loft and, if the rubber had not perished, she had a shrewd idea that cycle tyres would soon be worth their weight in gold.

SEVENTEEN

WILLIAM GRINNED TO himself as he straightened his tie and eyed his appearance. He might only be seventeen but William knew perfectly well he was a man physically. He was six feet tall, weighed twelve stone and could handle himself in a fight as he had proved on the continent. He was no longer a schoolboy. From today he was a man. After all, he told himself with a leer, how many others of his age group had travelled as he had—thanks to his mother—had his language abilities and had—killed? His chest swelled with pride. *He* was someone.

Then he gave a nervous gulp. What would his mother say when he went down not dressed in school clothes but in a man's? It occurred to him there could be no school today anyhow; not with the islanders in their state of unbridled panic. He took a deep breath. He was *not* afraid of his mother he told himself sternly. She was merely a woman and it was man who ruled. He was also her sole heir with an absolute right to know what went on, how and when.

He turned and marched purposefully down the carpeted stairs but his steps became slower as he approached the open kitchen door. He heard movement and wondered if it was just his mother or whether Amelia was there. He peeped into the door and saw his mother alone.

"Morning," he grunted as he stepped into the room and walked over to where a place was laid for him at the table.

Mary threw him one startled look, weighed up his mood in

a flash and turned back to the boiling kettle to make fresh tea and hide her anger. She knew how she must act. Cool and unconcerned, William could not stand that; it was the perfect weapon against him but, she marvelled to herself, dressed in men's clothes, he was a huge man. He was as tall as Victor and she guessed he must weight half a stone more and none of it fat either.

"Your meal is there, I'm going out," she said brusquely.

William took the plunge. "I'm not going to school any more. I know all I need to know." He waited, holding his breath.

"Suit yourself," Mary said equally short.

"I'm going to work for the Germans when they come."

"Bully for you!"

Mary walked out and made a point of shutting the door quietly, then she raced up to the sewing room. With gritted teeth she reached under the machine to where the diamonds had once nestled. Her fingers carefully stripped away the retaining tape and the derringer slid neatly into her hand. She eyed it and locked the door while her hand felt for the ammunition that Sam had obtained all those years ago. Taking a drawcloth from another hiding place, she carefully cleaned the barrel. She added two drops of sewing-machine oil to the mechanism and finally loaded it. For a few seconds she hefted it thoughtfully in her hand before slipping it into her slacks' pocket. From now on she would never be without it. She replaced the spare ammunition and only then unlocked the door.

Slowly, she went back downstairs and was surprised to see William still at the table, a petulant look to his face. Her eyebrows rose but she said nothing as she poured herself a cup of tea, sat down opposite William and looked evenly at him.

William seethed. He had expected his mother to argue hotly with him and her casual dismissal was infuriating. It was always like this. Was it because she did not take him seriously? He looked over at her and knew she was totally unimpressed with his height, weight and strength or ability. Was it even possible that there was a wicked gleam in her eyes? He was uncertain. What he did know was that not once since that day on Alderney had his mother mentioned Edwin or levelled a single accusation at him and this rankled.

"This is my home and it belongs to me," Mary started coolly. "I make the rules and when you don't like them, you go," she told him out of the blue.

William blinked. Now what had got into her? His mouth opened a little to show Mary she had him flat footed.

"You can do what you like, go where you like and I don't care a hoot," she continued, "but in this house you will obey me. Germans or no Germans!" She paused, eyeing him. "We both know what we think of each other. You do not like me and it is reciprocated in full."

There, that was something out in the open at last, Mary told herself. She waited with interest to see what he had to say. A surprisingly cynical look crossed his face and he held her eyes boldly.

"We know why, don't we?" William shot back in a low voice, determined to make her bring up Edwin's name at last.

Mary smiled scornfully though it made her face muscles ache. She longed to lash out and wipe the leer from his face.

"Do we?" she asked acidly, seeing through his game. William might be far more academically clever than her but Mary was worldly wise and incredibly sharp. "You tell me!" she challenged, knocking the ball right back into his court with a hard volley. "Come on, son of mine, or are you all mouth too?" she asked with sweet acidity.

William's nostrils pinched tight. He itched to slam his fist into her face but dared not. It flashed through his mind that he must never underestimate her. He also realised he could never match her in a game of words like this.

"You never had time for me," he scowled sulkily.

Mary knew this was true. "That was not for lack of trying. You were never the most lovable of children and the older you became the more you retreated into yourself and away from people—except when you were bullying them. The hands of love and friendship were often offered to you but you scorned them, so you only have yourself to blame. People only give back what they receive. All you want to do is take to suit yourself. And, William, there is something you should know," Mary told him, dropping her voice, low and cutting. "My Will was made out quite a while ago. It's lodged in a very safe place so if anything happens to me, don't think you would walk into everything, lock, stock and barrel. There is something else you'd better digest too, my son. The Germans are great believers in law and order. If I die while they are here, my Will would be proved meticulously— by them. Don't get any fancy ideas of being my sole heir either. I happen to have a daughter too. There is provision made for a Trust of Supervision over my stipulated wishes. Never count chickens before they leave their shells, you will only get egg on your face," she told him, mixing metaphors to make her point. "I trust I have made myself *very* clear?"

William said nothing. He had never envisaged such an icy tirade and he was stung and hurt.

"There is one more point you might like to think about," Mary added carefully. "Don't bank too much on the Germans. They are not crass idiots. They will see through anyone foolish enough to fawn on them and they will use such people for their own ends. In their eyes, you are British and the enemy. If you think the great master race is preparing to lay down the red carpet for you, my son, you are in for an almighty shock and serve you right too!" she finished, then left him.

She had to get outside because her anger was bubbling like a hot cauldron. The self-control she had exercised had sapped her strength and her lips were dry while her heart fluttered like a trapped butterfly. She took a few deep breaths, then decided to go and see Raymond and Gwen and make plans for growing food. She had a strong suspicion that one day food would be in short supply and they must all plan ahead. With the Ozanne children gone to Britain, as well as the Falla offspring, they must all buckle down and help with the mundane chores. With no holiday cottages to let, Mary's thoughts turned to the glasshouses and the shops which were going to be their only source of income until it was all over. Thank God she had Raymond's wonderful green fingers in the glasshouses because Mary knew that, although she could plan and organise, she was nowhere near Raymond's equal when it came to crops.

She found Raymond tending to the tomatoes and, paying close attention to him for once, realised he had not changed a great deal since the day Duret had died. Indeed she fancied he was even more ginger-coloured than ever; certainly his face was a mass of tiny freckles. There was little fat on him, which she guessed was because he worked physically. Certainly Gwen had once mentioned that Raymond ate like the proverbial horse.

Mary examined the glasshouses thoroughly. While she was so busy with the holiday lets, Raymond had been allowed free rein but now, with the changes which were due to come, her eyes hunted around carefully. "That piece of land between the houses, Raymond, could such be cultivated for root crops?" she asked.

He eyed where she pointed and nodded slowly. The ground was impacted from years of being trodden on but the earth would be virgin and he could see where her thoughts lay.

"Labour is going to be scarce, Madam," he pointed out. "That land will take some hard work."

Mary took a deep breath. "Then I'll have to help and Raoul too," she told him and wondered why Raymond's eyes had changed direction. How strange; was it a trick of the sunlight or had she simply imagined Raymond did not want her and Raoul? Her resolve stiffened.

"William will help also," she stated firmly.

Raymond could not argue. She was the boss but he liked to feel he was in sole charge of the glasshouses. Wouldn't life acquire problems with the boss breathing down his neck and, anyhow, he didn't care for his wife's brother. Raoul was too deep and silent for his tastes. William was another matter. Raymond liked the son and heir and knew he could get on with him.

"As you say, Madam," he muttered, then deliberately turned away from her to carry on working.

Later that night she spoke to William again as they ate their supper in a stiff silence. Mary had been prepared to find him in a mood but William had turned over her comments during a long walk that day and had reached a conclusion. Much as it galled him, he had to admit his mother was still the boss but, he had told himself, that had to change when the Germans came. So in the meanwhile he would play along with her and be agreeable.

"You'll have to work with Raymond in the glasshouses. We all will, come to that," she told him and waited for him to become difficult.

"That's all right with me. I want something to do," he replied and meant it. Long walks were all very well now and again and if he showed the Germans hard work did not frighten him, that had to impress them.

Mary was startled, eyed her son dubiously but decided not to reveal her caution. Her sole weapon against William was her enigmatic exterior.

"You go along then tomorrow and start at whatever Raymond says."

"Fine," he agreed pleasantly.

Mary left him, frowning a little. Now what was he up to and, more to the point, why? She spent some time on the telephone trying to find out what might be going to happen and learned the Rev John Leale had declared there could be no resistance against an occupying force. There was nowhere for guerrillas to hide and retribution would be simple to administer to the remaining population. As Leale was a senior and well trusted member of the States of Deliberation, as well as on the Controlling Committee of the eight men who would handle Guernsey, she had to believe him.

There came an uneasy lull on the island as it tried to shake itself back into normality with so many of its inhabitants gone. Mary shut one shop but reopened the first one, which had the living accommodation overhead. She engaged Alice Cantan as the shop girl in place of the previous employee who had left for Britain for the women's services. She was only sixteen but Alice was already proving useful and handled customers well. Mary had high hopes for her.

On Friday the 28th June, Mary locked up the shop ready to see Alice away. It was a pleasant, sunny day and on an impulse she decided to drive into town to gather the latest news. She parked slightly back from the harbour, then strolled around in an aimless manner. She missed Margaret so badly it was like a physical hurt. She had never felt like this when she was at school because an ending had always been in sight. Now the future was impossible to assess. She missed Victor too and Tante and her heart ached with anguish for the three of them as her feet led her down towards the harbour. It appeared to be back to normality with lorries lined up in an orderly fashion, all loaded with boxes of packed tomatoes ready for the mainland. Shipping would now be scarce although there was a vessel tied up which had just brought men and cattle over from deserted Alderney.

Mary stood and watched, listening to the lowing of the cattle when, from out of the clear sky, German planes screamed in from nowhere. She flung herself flat against a low wall as bombs fell with appalling noise. Machine guns roared and, in seconds, there was pandemonium. From her prone position Mary stared in horror.

Some of the drivers had dived under their vehicles but some lorries were hit. Petrol tanks exploded with men incinerated in agony. Tomato boxes were spilled, smashed on the cobbles and, in seconds, tomato juice flooded everywhere mixing with human blood. It made a macabre picture.

The cattle from Alderney went into a wild panic, breaking loose, kicking and bellowing their fear, plunging through the squashed tomatoes. She could hear firing from elsewhere and it flashed through her mind that Guernsey was under attack prior to an invasion.

As swiftly as they had arrived, the planes vanished and, slowly, Mary scrambled erect only to stand frozen at the carnage around the harbour, her legs trembling as she gazed wide eyed at the dead and dying, lying amid tomato juice. She made herself move, as people rushed to help. Had Whitehall thought of this when they demilitarised Guernsey? All Guernsey had was one machine gun and one Lewis gun against the Luftwaffe. Then it hit her. From which part of the island had the other firing come? Was it Cobo?

She turned and bolted for her car, flung herself in and savagely started the engine. She drove quickly, crashing her gears, then pulled herself together

Seeing a group of people shouting and gesticulating, she stopped, lowered her window and leaned out.

"What is it?"

One old man turned to her, eyes wild with rage. "The German bastards have machine gunned people making hay in the fields!"

Another younger man hurried over, shaking one first impotently into the air. "They say the lifeboat has been machine gunned while at sea too!"

"I've just come from the harbour!" Mary told the growing crowd what she had seen.

The old man growled again. "The Boche don't change!" he spat venomously. "Swine like they were in the last war!"

"What shall we all do, Missus?" a woman asked, fear making her voice sound like a saw.

Mary turned to her quickly. "Go back to your homes where you're under cover from anything but a direct hit. Keep near your radios so the Committee can tell us what to do," she paused. "If any of you had family down at the harbour—it might be wise to make—enquiries," she said tactfully.

"My Bert!" one middle-aged woman suddenly shrieked.

"And my George!"

"Here!" Mary snapped. "Get in my car and, you people, give me room to turn around. I'll drive you down there."

She drove back to the harbour, grim faced while the two distraught women sat trembling in the rear seats. As they neared people milled around in general confusion and shock. Many had brilliant red arms but whether this was blood or tomato juice, Mary did not care to think.

"I doubt I'll get any nearer," she told the two women as she braked. "Shall I come with you both?"

"No, Missus!" they cried as one. "But God bless you for helping!"

Mary watched them struggling through the horde then turned around, her mind in a turmoil; glad that Margaret and Victor were safely off the island and that Tante had not lived to see this day.

She drove back to Cobo safely and Raoul came running as she halted outside her home. Quickly she gave her story. He listened white-faced then shook his head.

"News flies quickly. The coxswain's son was killed in the lifeboat and the Germans also machine gunned a clearly marked ambulance. A patient's been killed and an attendant wounded."

They looked at each other, lost for words at the devastation which had come from the blue sky. Raoul let fly a stream of oaths and Mary's ears tingled. There was one word there she had never heard before and she considered herself a woman of the world. Raoul turned back to her, wild eyed with savagery.

"We must make German lives hell," he snarled.

Mary hesitated doubtfully. "That might be unwise," she reminded him slowly. "Think of the reprisals occupiers can take on us. Don't think I'm ready to knuckle down to Germans but we are so helpless here. We can do little against them—yet," she finished in a low voice.

Raoul's eyes were hot opals. "I can't stand by and do nothing," he barked back at her, showing an unusual ferocity that shook Mary. So Raoul had hidden depths too. Where had the quiet man vanished who had worked for the family for years?

Mary touched his arm. "Be careful at all times, Raoul," she said quietly, "and do not trust my son. Also—" she paused uneasily, not knowing why she felt a sudden disquiet, "be wary of Raymond."

Raoul's eyes went narrow and hard. William—he could understand the need to watch but Raymond? His eyes reflected questions.

Mary picked her words with care. "I may be doing Raymond an injustice," she started slowly, "but something tells me that Raymond might be the kind to do business with the devil for money. I've told William he's to work out there too and I'm not so sure that was one of my better ideas but I don't want William hanging around underfoot. He thinks he'll get translation work when the enemy come," she shrugged. "Perhaps he will but I want him to work in the glasshouses too where he is under my nose for at least part of the time."

Mary bit her lip with apprehension. Raymond and Raoul were brothers-in-law. Had she offended him? She waited nervously, watching various emotions cross Raoul's rugged face.

"You may be right," he said at last, nodding his head slowly. "You may just be right," he repeated more to himself than her. "I'll watch the pair of them." Then he glared at the empty sky. "At least my boys have gone over there to fight back."

The next morning news flew around the island that twenty-nine people had died in the air attacks on Guernsey and nine on Jersey and the islanders' resentment was compounded by their inability to retaliate.

On Sunday morning, Mary mooned aimlessly around her empty house. William had gone off walking and both Raoul and Amelia were in their cottage. It was not as if she had chores to attend to but her restlessness arose from the ominous waiting for the next move by the Germans. Margaret and Victor were constantly in her thoughts and tears hovered near the surface as worry grew and enlarged with each hour. Suddenly at midday she heard a plane and flinched. Was this the preliminary to another air raid? She waited with growing apprehension for the sound of bombs then, unable to restrain herself, hastily telephoned a contact in town.

When she had taken in the news she ran to where Raoul stood in his front garden. Amelia was with him, looking pale.

"Raoul!" she cried. "A German plane has landed at the airfield."

He turned and grunted. "It's the start then. They are on their way."

"I'm going to find out what I can!" Mary gasped. Now was the time for her to start work. She eyed the car, then shook her head. She had little petrol left and she turned to her cycle. She felt Raoul's eyes on her as she pedalled down briskly, feeling the pull of muscles not used for a long time.

Then she was in the swing of it, moving with familiarity through the lanes she now knew so well, cutting through St Saviours. She appeared to be the only person in the world. The sun beamed down and the countryside was calm and beautiful. She even felt hot in her sleeveless top and slacks with her old sandals on her feet, so she slowed to conserve energy. As she neared the airfield, she parked her cycle around the back of a thin hedge then, snapping around to check she was unobserved, she padded forward. There was an ideal place between two thick bushes at the rear of which was a young oak sapling. She squatted down, made herself comfortable and waited. There was soft hum of insects, two early butterflies and a rabbit who never caught her scent.

They came in the evening with deep, bellying growls. Four large German transport planes approached the airfield, terrifying the grazing cows and Mary watched them land to disgorge troops, wishing she had small binoculars. Details were impossible at her distance but she was able to make a careful account of the men, then watch them drive away.

So, she thought, they have come. Our lives will alter and it won't be for the better either. It was odd to see some drive away in taxis; obviously officers she told herself as she stood, brushing some twigs from her trousers.

She was thoughtful as she pedalled back to Cobo and it was after tea by the time she had arrived. When she went into the kitchen she found William there. Amelia had left their tea and, as she made a drink, she found William in a rare affable mood.

"Do you have any money?" she asked him.

Surprised, he dived into his trousers, pulling out a few coins. Mary opened her hip wallet and gave him five pounds.

"Make it last," she warned. "There is no more from the banks. I expect the Germans will organise the money but, until they do, we will have to be careful."

William was astonished but pleased. It made the perfect finale to a good day. He had spent a number of hours working with Raymond to his directions and learning at the same time. The man was no fool and, William thought, hugging this titbit to himself, he might not be averse to his idea. Raymond had shown that, although he was the glasshouse expert, he was, at the same time, conscious his assistant was the son of the boss and heir apparent. He had been deferential, and respectful which fed William's ego beautifully.

Directly after this the Germans flooded the island. The local papers went under occupation supervision and one evening, with a grim face, Mary read the strong proclamation which had been signed by Victor Carey, the Bailiff. It was obviously a direct order and poor Mr Carey had been given no option but to append his signature.

From now on they were under curfew from eleven o'clock at night until six in the morning. There were dire threats about any possible acts of sabotage or civilian resistance; all firearms of any kind and other weapons must be delivered to the Royal Hotel by noon of the next day. Mary sniffed at that in Tante's best fashion. No boat could leave the harbour without permission and no cars could be used. Blackout curtains had to go up forthwith and all the food was to be requisitioned, especially meat.

Her thoughts reverted to Margaret and Victor. Where were they? When could she hope to hear from them and how could a letter reach her? Suddenly terrible loneliness swept through her. If only she could lean her head on Victor's chest and feel him run his fingers through her hair before they slid down her cheeks and neck to fondle her breasts. She gave herself a hard shake.

Later that day she took all her accounts and business papers to the shop and prepared to take up late lodgings in the flat although allowing herself time to get home before curfew. It crossed · her mind to wonder about Alice. She was such a quiet, almost mousy girl but any girl's head could be turned by the sight of soldiers in uniform and she knew these island occupiers would, initially at least, be the cream of German manhood.

One evening, just before locking up, she took the bull by the horns. "What do you think about all this, Alice?" she asked quietly.

Alice was a lot more mature than her age indicated. She thought a lot and, though not bright, she was no fool. She had been heartily glad to leave school and get this job. When Madam was away, she ran the shop to suit herself and she enjoyed the work. She was a short girl with a figure which would get dumpy with the years but she was clean, fresh faced and if she had shortened her hair, she could have made herself look more attractive than she did.

"I don't mind," Alice replied slowly.

"What don't you mind?" Mary asked puzzled.

"I mean I don't mind whom I serve, Madam, as long as their money is all right!" she said with a flash of shrewdness.

"Well," Mary replied uneasily. It was not up to her to take a parent's place but Alice was so quiet and gentle. "Just be careful. Don't get too friendly with these Germans. They won't be here forever and girls who go with them might have a bad time when it's all over!"

Alice considered, then gave her employer a rueful smile. "I don't expect they'd want to bother with me, would they? I mean, my pa says I'm nothing to look at for a man."

Mary bristled in a flash. What a thing for a father to say.

"Handsome is as handsome does, my dear!"

Alice flushed, then dimpled. She liked Madam very much but was a little in awe of her. She was so efficient and nearly always in a hurry, rushing in, then departing in a flurry.

"I don't want anyone going upstairs to my flat," Mary said casually. "I'm going to keep all my accounts there because it is quieter to work here than at home especially if troops are billeted upon me. It would be such a nuisance if they were disturbed or I was bothered, wouldn't it?" she asked hopefully.

"I'll tell no one, Madam, and neither will you be bothered when I'm here," she promised, pleased to be appealed to.

With that Mary was content as she settled into her routine of travelling around the island, ostensibly on business but carefully noting all which she saw that was easy to memorise.

The Germans fixed an exchange rate of five marks to the pound which was outrageous and caused massive protests as they grossly over-valued their currency at the expense of sterling. Already prices for goods had begun to climb swiftly as they descended like a plague of locusts upon the town shops.

With the troops came others including the German secret police who Mary learned were called the Geheime Feldpolizei and who were a back-up to the ordinary military police. Although the secret police wore civilian clothes, they stuck out like sore thumbs and an islander could spot one at a distance.

Mary drove her legs to a peak of fitness as well as establishing her presence on the roads and lanes. She absorbed everything and later wrote it down in the flat using tiny script on fine paper though there were many times when she asked herself whether what she was doing was of any value.

At least, she told herself, the occupation has passed off without the rape and plunder feared by the islanders. The Germans were exceedingly well disciplined and, by and large, polite with the islanders, wanting to make friends with their British "cousins". They paraded in St Peter Port with their band and were stared at by cool-faced islanders who were totally unimpressed.

Like all newcomers to Guernsey, the Germans were baffled and confused by the maze of winding lanes with their high hedges. The islanders had carefully removed every signpost before the occupation and the new arrivals were left with an unmapped, bewildering new land. One amusing story reached Mary's ears, which she carefully noted down. A patrol was sent out and simply vanished. A second was sent to find it and this too seemingly went off the face of the earth. Eventually, in worried desperation, the occupiers sent out a third patrol to find the first two. After much marching, twisting and turning plus peering over high hedges, all the Germans did meet up to their intense relief. They had not been killed but simply lost in Guernsey's lanes and when they had questioned the few locals they met, each had turned out to be a halfwit; an act at which an islander was an expert when it suited him. The next thing Mary learned was that the occupiers had decided to map the island themselves.

Mary mulled over this information carefully. She went up to the glasshouses where Raymond and William were working together amicably. Mary pulled on an old coat and started to help them clear some spare ground for root crops.

"What's going to happen to all the tomatoes?" she wanted to know.

Raymond stopped hoeing. "We can sell to the Germans."

Mary considered. Would that be collaborating? She hesitated and decided it would not—yet.

"That's true and what we don't sell can go to the islanders to be made into jam—if they have any sugar. The trouble is, it's going to take us ages to get anywhere with horses or bullocks. I get so lost in the lanes," she lied easily. "It is a shame no one ever mapped this place."

Raymond regarded her innocent face, then had to agree with her. He had already made a few delicate contacts, which William had encouraged.

"I'll see what I can do in that line," he told her and Mary was content. A detailed island map would be of great value to her and a copy could go to her contact when he called.

Emboldened, Raymond spoke again. "Some German officers want flowers as well as tomatoes. Two came here. William spoke to them," he added.

Mary turned quickly to her son who flushed a little uncertain as to how she would react.

"It's just business," he stammered, furious at himself. Why did she continue to make him apprehensive and in front of the hired man too.

"Of course!" Mary agreed quickly, weighing him up in a flash. "This is our only source of income now so, by all means, develop it," she told both of them. "Just as long as no one can say afterwards that *we* were collaborators," she warned them coldly.

William grinned at her departure then turned to Raymond, eyed him and chuckled. The officer who had approached them had been haughty to start with until William talked to him in his language. The German had been startled not only because of William's fluent German but also because of his polite attitude.

Mary kept a discreet eye on the airfield without getting too dangerously close. More and more planes came in to help in the Battle for Britain. These joined others based in occupied France and Mary could not but feel the distress of islanders who had let their children go to Britain. As the skies filled with droning planes, all heavily loaded with bombs, Mary's heart would sink low.

There were nights when she could not sleep. There were days when she worried anew especially after a couple of exploratory raids were made by soldiers from Britain which infuriated the Germans and horrified the Controlling Committee. What if reprisals were taken?

Mary fretted about her lack of money, worried about the position of food supplies and viewed the coming winter with apprehension. At home William was quietly smug but had sense enough not to upset his mother. It was true the occupiers were bending over backwards to appease the locals. They were not too dictatorial and their censorship was strictly correct but none of this could alleviate the general atmosphere and worry about loved ones far away with no postal links.

The Jerrybags appeared. It did not take long for some women to realise that fit and healthy soldiers with plenty of money were there for the taking, at a time when young Guernsey men were absent. So, very slowly, some of the islanders started to side with the occupiers and Mary even heard of two foolish girls who wished to marry German soldiers. This was strictly forbidden by the Germans themselves but it all began to leave a nasty taste. Soon the Jerrybags, shortened to plain Bags, provided the services needed which, as Raoul pointed out to her solemnly, at least kept rape in check even if there should be a harsh day of reckoning.

Then Mary received official notification that all her holiday cottages were to be requisitioned for troops and in addition a billeting officer turned up at her home.

She had been half expecting this but made no attempt to welcome the stiff officer. Mary showed him around her home, watching while he made notations on his clipboard, then suddenly realised she was going to be lucky.

"You will have officers, Frau Noyen," she was told.

Mary knew that attack was always the best form of defence. "In that case, your young officers had better realise there will be house rules in my home," she started coldly.

"Frau!"

"Don't you Frau me!" Mary shot back at him, ignoring his stern expression. "This is my home. There are many fine objects in it. Your officers will treat my home as they would respect their own. They will wipe their feet before they enter. They will not bother my kitchen help. They will cause no damage whatsoever because—" she paused for effect "—I will not hesitate to lay a complaint in the correct direction."

The billeting officer's face had gone cold, so Mary fixed him with a piercing stare.

"But of course," she said then with sudden sweetness, "German offizieren will know their manners, won't they?"

The German blinked, totally thrown by this flanking attack. He nodded slowly, aware he had been trounced without quite knowing how. Frau Noyen looked at him with a charming smile on her face.

"Good!" Mary told him, nodded her head and walked away leaving him flat-footed and too astounded to be furious.

The next day four young, very uncertain Germans appeared with the billeting officer. Mary took a deep breath and kept them waiting for exactly five minutes before going down to the front lounge where Amelia had placed them. At her entrance the young men sprang to their feet clicking heels then stood at ramrod attention.

"Ha!" Mary exclaimed, acting her part. "The young offizieren! Gentlemen! My house rules. No damage to my property in any way. No loud noise at night and no women either. My top floor is where my room is and that is 'Out of Bounds' to you. Is that clear?"

"Ja, meine Frau!" they chorused together.

Mary had to stifle a grin. They looked almost terrified of her. Good God, they seemed to be as young as William. Then she turned back to attack the billeting officer once more, pressing home her advantage.

"I employ a husband and wife here as well as at my glasshouses. I was going to dismiss them," she lied casually, "but with four extra men in the house I'll need help but who is going to pay for their time here?"

"We will pay," she was told.

"What about rations?" Mary asked sweetly.

"They will bring their own food and perhaps a little extra?" the Hauptmann countered, starting to enjoy the game.

Mary pretended to think about this in an infuriatingly casual way. "Yes, that might mean better meals for them," she finished tongue in cheek. She and the German eyed each other, both acknowledging they had scored some points and the Hauptmann's eyes twinkled a little. This Frau Noyen was interesting and he had heard she was a widow too. Well, well, he thought to himself. Will the non-fraternisation rules be changed for officers?

Mary stifled an internal chortle. From the corner of her eye she could see the young officers still standing straight as if made of wood. She felt she had won some small victory and her morale had improved. The Germans might be difficult but they were most certainly not invincible.

When they had gone she met Raoul and Amelia down at their

cottage and told them the story. To her surprise, Raoul became hostile.

"I don't fancy working for the Boche," he growled.

Mary was thunderstruck at the mulish expression on his face. "But we all must!" she cried sharply. "Look, if it is going to be a long occupation what about the food stocks? While we billet Germans they have to provide for us too. We can then sneak some away to those less lucky than ourselves."

Raoul was good and loyal but sometimes slow to assess a situation. Mary bit her lip with anxiety. She would be lost without these faithful workers and friends.

"You must!" she repeated anxiously. "There's no telling what we might learn with Germans here and there is also William. You know what he's like."

Raoul gave her a long, probing look. "I understand, but don't expect me to like it," he agreed reluctantly.

Mary felt exasperated with him. "Well, how do you think *I* feel with them in my home?" She turned to Amelia. "Steal whatever food you can from them without being found out, especially things which will keep like sugar and flour, tea, coffee, anything like that, then hoard it for the bad days."

Amelia was also a bit slow, like her husband. "The bad days?"

Mary nodded grimly. "I cannot see relief for us for a while yet," she told them slowly, "so let's look on the black side for our own protection and that of others."

Raoul and Amelia exchanged looks before Raoul turned back to her. "I didn't think," he said lamely.

"Forget it!" Mary smiled with relief.

Raoul turned, nodded at his wife who, understanding some secret message, left them alone. Raoul took Mary's hands in his and looked her firmly in the eyes.

"Don't you take any risks either. Your daughter charged me with your safety when she left. I want to be able to look her in the face when she returns."

Mary was stunned. "She did?"

"You are a brave, bold woman with a bad son," Raoul continued, pausing to frown and chew his lip. "You lost a son in weird circumstances. We have both often wondered about it because you've never liked William. Did he quarrel with Edwin?"

Mary lowered her head. Was this the time to tell him the truth? Surely she could trust him implicitly but she remembered James' warning. On the other hand though, old Tante had thought the world of him. Perhaps it would be prudent to warn Raoul so he was always on his guard too.

She lifted her head to hold his eyes again. "William murdered Edwin but I could never prove it."

"Good God!"

Raoul was shocked. Words failed him. This was something he had never imagined in his wildest prognostications. "He was only a child himself!"

"Exactly!" Mary agreed grimly. "Under the age of liability without one single shred of evidence too!"

Slowly Mary told him the whole story along with the suspicions of herself, Margaret and old Tante. Raoul listened, his face masked with horror as his handgrip tightened. When Mary stopped he could only stare at her for a few minutes.

"You've carried this burden all these years!" he breathed with respect, more shocked than he had thought possible. He gave a deep sigh, releasing her hands with another squeeze.

"I'll watch him now," he muttered grimly, and I'll watch Madam's back too, he told himself. William had killed once—what was there to stop him doing the same again? His blood chilled. "Yes!" he muttered, now nodding his head vigorously. "After what you've told me, it's just as well to put up with Germans here. They are not stupid. They are disciplined. If William puts one toenail wrong, the Germans will jump on him. They are an insurance."

"Exactly!" Mary breathed with relief.

"Who else knows of this?"

"Old Tante did and Victor. Margaret guessed. Actually," she thought quickly, "there's only me and you on this island now who knows but," Mary halted, grinning wolfishly, "it's all down in a letter lodged at James' office and, even though he's gone, if anything did happen to me, I'm sure my letter would get to Emil."

Raoul nodded with relief. He remembered back to an odd rumour or two he had heard long ago which he had dismissed as trivial gossip. Someone had once shot Victor in his arm. Had she shot him? Did she still have the weapon? He itched to ask but restrained himself. He hoped his guess was right. William was dangerous.

It was at that point that his mind moved in another direction. It did not hurry, that was never Raoul's way, but its ponderous progress was difficult to halt once started. He stood frowning heavily, then his eyes opened wide suddenly.

"Hah!" he grunted.

Mary waited apprehensively. "What is it?" she whispered.

"I wondered why you wanted all that furniture taking to the flat above your first shop," Raoul said slowly, working it all out at last. "That's your retreat! Your private bolt hole against William— and the world. James!" Raoul gasped. "He's tied up in this somehow but he's gone and yet—" Raoul hesitated once more as he laboriously went through various permutations of possibilities. Then his eyes widened once more. "Mary!"

"Yes?"

Each gazed at the other. Raoul with awe, having arrived at a conclusion that amazed him. Mary sat with baited breath, ready to lie black was white.

"Don't you think I should have a key to your flat in case—?" Raoul shrugged nonchalantly. "In case of some kind of emergency or if I wanted to find you in a hurry for any reason?" he asked softly, his eyes gleaming. Who would have thought it of her? She was working for Britain on something, arranged by James before he vanished so quickly and quietly.

Mary narrowed her eyes. It was a valid point. "I'll get another cut but only use it in dire emergencies," she said with quiet firmness. "And no one is to know including Amelia!"

Raoul nodded soberly. He too had heard about Gestapo methods of interrogation by torture. He yearned to tell her to take care but could not. That would be an insult to her bravery and integrity. What Raoul did know was that from now on he would be living in a constant state of apprehension regarding her safety.

"If ever you want help," he began in a very low voice, "come to me, no matter what the circumstances. Promise, Mary?"

Her heart swelled. It would be incredible to know she was not totally alone but she prayed to God such a situation would never arise. Insurance of any kind though was always valuable.

"I will!" she promised in a whisper.

"Give you a few more years Mary, and you'll be a bigger legend than even the Mistress was!" he prophesied.

"What? Rubbish!" Mary snorted but thrilled with the implied compliment. "You'd better go in. Amelia will wonder what we've been discussing. You'd better make it the glasshouses or the Germans!" she suggested.

Raoul knew she was right. Patting her shoulder he turned and walked away, hastily constructing a tale for his wife.

EIGHTEEN

NEWS FLEW AROUND the island at the speed of light despite all the occupiers trying to halt rumour. When Major Sherwell was arrested, for trying to assist two officers to escape, there were rumbles. When Sherwell was taken to France a heavy gloom fell upon Guernsey because what chance was there for anyone to return?

Mary compiled her notes with meticulous care but there were times when doubt assailed her. When would someone come to collect it? The sheath of papers, thin and capable of being folded very flat, were secreted under a loose floorboard which Mary hoped would escape any prying eyes.

In early November it became raw-cold and she let Alice leave early as a fog misted the island. Mary shivered. It was going to be a miserable ride home and she was tempted to leave too. She had waited so many evenings, all alone, a prey to miserable thoughts, and no one had appeared. Had something gone wrong with James' arrangements? Had Guernsey perhaps been forgotten?

Guernsey seemed weighed down with German troops, all of which she had observed. Which troops, from where, their numbers and vehicles, the state of their morale, the numbers of officers, the secret police, her dossier gave a complete picture of the occupation. Sometimes she ran her fingers over the tidy notes, musing idly to herself. What was the point of it all really? Britain had no chance at the moment of freeing them.

She watched Alice trot down the road then shut the door, ready to lock up. She had just turned to the till to check the day's takings when the door opened and the bell gave its tinny warning. She swore to herself. She felt in no mood to deal with a last-minute shopper.

"I've closed for the night!" she said briskly.

The man who entered stood in the gloom because the lights had been switched off as Mary erected the blackout. He was tall and she could just make out he wore a dirty guernsey sweater over crumpled, corduroy trousers whose ends were tucked into rubber boots. Obviously a late fisherman wanting something.

"The fog comes straight from Jethou tonight," he said quietly.

Mary's heart flipped a beat as she recognised the code word. She swallowed, bit her lip and moved from behind the counter. She knew that voice! The figure and its stance were familiar.

Then she remembered. "But it hasn't reached Lihou yet!" she replied as James had instructed.

The man whipped around, slammed the door's bolts to, then strode across to the rear doors at the store room and checked they were secured. He looked upwards and nodded at the stairs to her flat.

Mary gulped with excitement and flew up them with him following, taking them two at a time. She raced around upstairs, drawing the blackout then switched on a small lamp that gave muted light. Then she turned and faced him.

"Victor!" she gasped, one hand flying to her throat, then he was across the room, holding her shoulders, kissing her savagely. Mary responded, her heart thudding with joy. They kissed again and again, then he stepped back, studying her.

"My sweet Catherine. I *never* thought it would be you! I had it in my head the contact was the shop girl!"

Mary shook her head with equal amazement. "To think it's you who are Jethou! My heart stopped when you used the code and I knew your voice but I simply couldn't take it all in!"

He pulled her into his arms again, letting his hands tangle

329

then smooth her hair before they slid down her cheeks, turning her lips to his once more.

"You!" he murmured, between kisses. "You! That old fox James!"

Mary stiffened and pulled back. "James?" she whispered stunned. "James recruited you as well? But I thought you—I mean—" She shook her head bewildered as they sank down together on her settee.

He grinned happily at her and chuckled. "He fooled us both!"

"When were you recruited?" Mary had to know.

He frowned. "Years ago!"

"Me too!"

"I thought I'd make the contact, then try to slip over to Cobo to have five minutes with you because my time is short," he told her softly.

Mary flinched. "Good job you didn't! I've German officers billeted on me, and William lives there too, don't forget!"

He pulled a face and shook his head, then smiled again, half to himself. "James would have worked that one out too, I bet!"

Mary broke into a fit of giggles like a young girl. The idea of quiet little mousy Alice doing secret work was a huge joke to her.

"What is it?"

Mary laughed softly. "If you knew my shop girl, nice though she is, you'd laugh yourself. But you said you don't have long?"

He shook his head sadly. "I have to—move on and make a rendezvous," he told her tactfully. She looked at his watch, which she saw was not his own. It was large and encased in rubber and she guessed it was a special service's one. The rubber gave her a clue. Had he swum ashore somewhere, hidden protective clothing, removed these clothes from some waterproof container then come to her? She studied him. He appeared little changed, perhaps a shade leaner as if he had been trained razor sharp. His face was weatherbeaten and when she leaned against him she

330

felt something hard. She pulled back, lifted the guernsey and her lips tightened as she saw a pistol and a long sheath knife.

"Tools of the trade, I call 'em," he joked lightly, knowing he did not fool her for an instant. "Got any gauche?"

Mary sprang to her feet. "Of course. Let me get you something to eat."

She was glad to bustle about, taking quick peeps at him as she did so. He leaned back against the settee as if weary but she saw he was alert, listening all the time.

Victor watched her, glad to relax his muscles and recover his strength. The swim had been hard and exceedingly cold, then there had been the screwing up of his nerves as he had slipped through the town streets, mingling like other locals in the gloom, ignoring walking Germans. She had changed in some subtle manner. Her clothes were not as smart as they had once been, yet she moved with her old brisk efficiency.

He cursed himself. His time was so short. He knew instinctively that if it had been longer and he made a move towards her, she would not rebuff him. He felt himself erect and the ache came as he saw the movement of her breasts against her cardigan as she leaned forward with the teapot. Dear God, she affected him more each time he saw her. It crossed his mind to debate as to whether he was the proper person to be her contact after all— yet he was Guernsey through and through. His fluency with patois plus his good French and local knowledge made him the obvious man to come but his heart pained him.

Mary brought him his food. "Eat!" she said briskly and slowly sat to watch him wolf the gauche. She had kept just one light glowing, enough to throw a small pool on the carpet which gave the room a snug appearance and which was impossible to see from outside. Once again, as so often in the past, she felt his aura spread around her like a safe, comforting cloak while his sheer masculine presence dominated her flat.

When he had finished he licked his fingers. "That was good," he said. Then he lifted his arms and slipped off the guernsey to reveal a British army battledress jacket underneath with a captain's three pips. Mary wondered if he wore officer's trousers under the corduroys but doubted it.

His hand went into his jacket pocket and he gave her a sealed envelope. "From Margaret," he told her, "and don't ask questions!"

Mary gasped, snatched the letter and held it in both hands cuddled against her breasts.

"Tell me quickly, is she all right?"

He grinned. "She was fine when I saw her last week."

"Last week!" Mary exclaimed. Only seven days ago. "Tell me what you can," she begged.

"She's joined the ATS and is a lorry driver and already has a stripe up. She's stationed in the Midlands not far from Leicester. She's in the pink of health and condition, as happy as possible with her work, thriving in service life but misses you, Michael and Guernsey, though I'm not sure in which order," he chuckled.

"Michael?"

"In the army somewhere. I can't tell you any more because I just don't know myself. I saw him a month ago. He looks well too, but has fined down and there's a toughness about him. I don't think I'd care to cross him one dark night."

Mary paused but she felt she had to ask. "Your family? Are they well?"

Victor paused. "Jenny is in the WAAF. James is chomping at the bit at a good school in Bristol, cursing because he's too young to join up, and Nicole? I suppose she's all right," he said casually.

Mary's eyebrows lifted for a second. There was indeed something amiss there. She wondered if she could question him, and thought better of it but Victor read her mind. If there had been more time he would have confirmed that the Alderney row had finished whatever relationship he and Nicole had had. They were married in name only, living separate lives, kept in loose contact by their children. It was really only for the sake of young James that he bothered to see her. James required roots and Nicole at least provided a home base for him. Once the war finished he intended to divorce her, come what may, and make a fresh start with Mary.

"What do you have for me?" he asked suddenly.

Mary nodded and retrieved her hidden papers, passing them to him. He rolled them in a thin sheet of waterproof then slipped them next to his skin under his military battle jacket before putting his guernsey back on.

"Sherwell is in trouble," Mary told him, not sure how much he knew.

He was more up to date than her. "He's in Paris but you don't know that!" he warned her quickly.

"Will he be shot?"

"We hope not. It was all most unfortunate. The two men who came to the island couldn't get off again. Something went wrong and you know it's virtually impossible to find a safe hiding place here. They had to surrender to the Germans but no one had time to brief them. Different stories were told and the Germans pounced."

"Victor," Mary began a little hesitantly, "please don't think I'm complaining or backing away but all this writing—" She pointed at where her notes were hidden. "It seems so useless to me. The Germans are entrenched here and I cannot see any chance of them leaving for a long time. Neither do I see any opportunity of Britain invading to release us for many reasons, so aren't I wasting my efforts?" she asked bluntly.

"No!" he replied with quick firmness. "Every tiny scrap of information about an enemy is always of vital importance. You might never see the end result but, take it from me, there is one. The men the Germans have poured onto these Channel Islands are men tied down—not fighting elsewhere. They are men wasted. It's reached my ears that Hitler's grand Master Plan"—Victor said the latter words with a sneer—"is to turn the islands into land battleships. How crazy! Who does he think is going to sail up and fight?"

"I see!" Mary murmured thoughtfully. "Well, I feel a bit better about it all now!" she admitted with a smile.

"Have you heard anything not in these notes?"

Mary considered, then nodded. "The Germans are going to bring a lot of horses here as well as to the other islands. I heard that this morning because they've been round the farms requisitioning hay and oats."

"Interesting," he drawled, narrowing his eyes. "They could be for the officers to ride but who knows the workings of the Germanic mind. Anything else?"

"Yes!" Mary said briskly. "At home this morning I noticed two of the officers talking briskly together and later I asked William what it was all about. He was very pleased because it seems the Germans are bringing over surveyors and engineers. I do know that all around the coast there are huge dumps of concrete-making materials and there's talk of the Germans getting a railway going at some time."

"So they intend to build fortifications. Excellent! While they are spending money on materials for that, they can't use them elsewhere. You see, look at the value of your work. Not just in these notes but in what you've just told me. Don't belittle what you do, you are only one person observing in one place but take all of you as a whole, it's as if there was a radio broadcast of Hitler's intentions!" Then he became grave: "But be very, very careful, my love. Don't fall into a pattern with your observation trips and always try to have an excuse for being where you are, should you ever be stopped and questioned. Do *not* underestimate the enemy!"

"I won't," Mary replied grimly. There was not chance of that when she had the daily reminder of their presence in her home. "When will you come again?"

"I don't know and if I did, I'd not tell you. It might be weeks or even months but carry on with the good work."

Mary had deduced she was not the only operative and she presumed he was going on to see someone else or perhaps even to another island.

"You are beautifully placed to keep us informed. Never forget that," he emphasised again. "If other sources, shall I say, dried up—!"

She nodded soberly. "Well I have four officers with me but I just wish I spoke better German. I only have a few words. William, of course, is in his element with it all, idolising the master race," she said scornfully. "Raoul is reliable and completely trustworthy. I think he has guessed something. Certainly he knows this flat is not what it seems but Tante said he was all right. I'm not so certain about Raymond. He and William work together in the glasshouses and I think Raymond is more keen on making money than on anything else. Raymond is, how shall I put it—Raymond is very concerned about Raymond!" she told him acidly.

He nodded seriously. "There'll be informers and collaborators here as well as many who favour the Germans for one reason or the other. I repeat my warning because if anything happened to you, heart of my hearts—" His voice stopped; clipped short as he took her in his arms again.

Mary saw his eyes were violet, soft and glowing in the dim light. She laid her head on his chest. Oh! How many times had she wanted to be able to do this in the past half year. He smelt so strong with the slightest tang of tobacco and dried sweat.

He ran his hands down to her breasts and fondled them, murmuring more to himself than her.

"I wish I had more time," he groaned. "I don't think I'd be shot this time!" he sighed. "What a waste this all is."

"You need a shave," she whispered, feeling his stubble.

"I'd like to grow a beard but regulations won't allow!"

"I should hope not!" she protested. "A beard indeed. You'd look just like a pirate!"

"But a lovely one, you must admit," he told her as he thrust his head between her breasts then, reluctantly, straightened to look at his watch.

Mary felt gorgeously light-headed. She knew her nipples were erect and her thighs were nearly jelly.

"I have to make tracks," he sighed heavily. "And surely it's time you were on the way home? What about the curfew and patrols?"

Mary chuckled. "The Germans are so methodical and regular that I can set my watch to the patrol's arrival!"

She looked at the clock. "Another fifteen minutes before the local patrol comes. Time for you to slip away and me to cycle home. It doesn't take me long normally, though I might have to walk part of the way in this fog."

Very slowly, still holding hands, they went down to the darkened shop, moving quietly towards the back entrance.

"You carry your pistol, I hope?" he hissed.

Mary nodded as she quietly slid the bolts, opened the door casually and peered out, straining her ears.

"All clear," she whispered.

Victor turned for one last kiss. "If ever you have to use that pistol, get rid of it straightaway. Don't keep in on your person or anywhere at home or the shop."

Mary nodded, suddenly terribly anxious for him, biting her lip but trying to show a brave face.

His right hand touched her left cheek. "My sweet Catherine." Then he was gone. She craned her neck and watched him pad down the rough track, peer up the road in both directions and vanish, melting into the night as quietly as a cat.

Slowly Mary locked the back door and went back to the flat to check nothing was out of place. Her heart was thumping and she realised she strained to hear shots but the night was dark.

For a few seconds she was reluctant to go. She could still feel his presence and she wanted to stay treasuring it but the time was moving on. With a heavy heart, she fetched her cycle from the back, opened the front door and slipped out, locking up quietly with the well oiled locks.

The fog had thinned, so switching on the hooded lights to comply with the German blackout regulations she started pedalling. The fog lingered in patches and darted fingers at her. The night was silent and ghostly, almost macabre but she pedalled steadily, Margaret's letter tucked between her breasts.

When only a few hundred yards from her home she halted silently to listen. There was no sound anywhere. It was as if she was the only person left alive on earth and a shudder ran through her. She looked at her watch again. She was late so she unfastened the valve cap and let the air out of her front tyre before retightening the valve head.

With the feeble headlight she started to walk, not briskly but as if very weary. She crunched up the drive to the house and saw a figure loom at her then another. It was a worried Raoul with William at his heels.

"I was getting worried," Raoul told her in a gross understatement. He had been nearly out of his mind, made worse by William hovering around.

Mary panted with feigned exhaustion. "It's been a long walk with a flat tyre," she complained bitterly thrusting the cycle into Raoul's hands. "Can you see to it for me?"

Raoul caught a look in her eyes and nodded quickly. His instinct warned him the flat was deliberate. He would "mend" the tyre that very night before the Germans could show any interest in it.

"Your son was getting worried like me," he told her trying to appear casual.

"And so were we, Frau!" one of the German officers said. "It's a raw night!"

Mary wondered if there was a question in the words and decided to attack at once.

"That's true," she agreed coolly. "That's why only a fool or someone with a flat tyre would be out in it!"

She turned to William. There was something bubbling inside him. She went to tighten her lips but restrained herself. She must act naturally.

"You look pleased with yourself, son?" she prodded.

"I've been engaged to do translation work," William boasted eagerly. It was rare for him to display emotion but he was highly thrilled at having been approached and the pay was generous too.

Mary pursed her lips thoughtfully, aware all four Germans were now interested spectators.

"Have you?" she replied casually. "Well, that's all right just as long as you do not neglect your glasshouse work. Food production is of vital importance, isn't it?" she asked turning to the officers.

They broke into a chorus of agreements which William could not miss as his mother's barb also registered. She would not fuss just as long as he did not rock her particular boat.

"I'm tired. I want a hot drink, my supper and then I'm going to bed," she announced and walked up the stairs in her occupied home. At least, nothing had been damaged. The officers were meticulously careful with faultless manners. Indeed, in other circumstances, it would have been pleasant having them as guests.

She itched for the privacy of her room to read the precious letter. Once in it, she locked the door carefully and rammed two bolts home, which Raoul had installed for her. First she skimmed through the lines which were so dreadfully short then she went back to luxuriate in very word.

"My dear Mother,

This letter has to be done at top speed because, only an hour ago, Uncle Victor turned up and told me he would see it reached you but questions were forbidden. I am well and incredibly happy though I miss my lovely island so much it hurts. I miss you too. There is so much I'd like to tell you especially about darling Michael. We managed to sneak a day together only last week but I don't know when I'll be able to see him again, damn this war. As soon as it ends, we are going to marry, come back to Guernsey and hurry to make you a grandmère. I love driving though I had some problems to start with. I nearly stripped the gears from the first lorry until I got the hang of double declutching. Why didn't you teach me that? I thought I'd end up on a fizzer! Now I have the hang of it all and love it, though the blackout can get dicey at times. However, I've not dented a lorry yet, though that is more by good luck than judgement. I must close this short note now. Do give my love to all those close to me—if you think this wise. Don't forget what I said about William. Watch that odious brother of mine. With luck he might even break his neck on the boot scraper if he comes in drunk. Much love, Mother, until we meet again on our dear little island.

MARGARET
XXXXXXXXXXXX

She read the letter three times then hugged it to her breasts, feeling her heart swell with love while tears hovered. Where could she hide it? Every place on which her eyes landed had to be rejected because any Germans who searched would be thorough. Finally, in desperation, she slipped it right at the bottom of the rubber bag where she kept her very personal toilet articles. Let them look there and get embarrassed.

Mary slid between the sheets that night with heart soaring

then plummeting in turns as she thought about Margaret's letter. Then her mind switched to Victor who was somewhere out in the night defying the Germans. When she did fall asleep she had a rare dream that changed into a violent nightmare, so realistic it awoke her, sweating and trembling with horrified fear.

To start with, the dream was shapeless, as something nebulous ghosted in and out of her mind until a dark form showed. This began to expand and approach ever nearer until it reached a size of grotesque proportion. It hammered at her subconscious mind as something unspeakably deadly which concerned only her and which was of the most vital importance. She opened her mouth in her sleep and screaming soundlessly, thrusting out her hands against the strangling evil but its advance was inexorable. From the centre of its black shape emerged two equally spaced red holes that threatened to engulf her and she felt the most appalling peril. Suddenly there were two bangs and she woke with a jerk, covered in sweat, her heart hammering a tattoo.

One hand shot to her mouth as she gazed around, wild eyed with fright, but she was alone. The door was firmly bolted. Only one inch of window was open and, without a drainpipe, there was no way anyone could climb to the third floor to molest her. Mary slumped back on the pillows but her heart continued its erratic thunder, only very slowly quietening down. The evil had been so vividly intense, so realistic that she was more frightened that at any time before in her life.

What did it mean? From where would this danger come? She was rarely conscious of dreams, her sleep was usually unbroken, but this had been so genuine, such a nightmare that she rose, opened the window and sat on a chair looking out at the night. She forced herself to go back over every ghastly image because if dreams were sent to warn, then dear God, she must recognise the peril.

She saw the dawn touch the sky with fingers of gold and felt washed out, fit for nothing. With luck there might be a little tepid water and a bath would wash away the horror. Certainly she did not wish to face sharp-eyed William looking anything other than normal.

Life fell into a dull period in which they all lived quiet lives geared to the occupiers. William thrived, indeed blossomed, because the Germans had found his linguistic skills excellent. Very gradually he did less and less work at the glasshouses and Mary and Raoul did more and more under Raymond's supervision.

Mary thought a lot about Margaret and her heart ached for her girl because she too must be fretting about Michael. She worried about Victor, wondering where he was and what he was doing. When the bad days came she spent hours working with the plants, glad of the mind-numbing labour. She also had a good reason to visit the shop at least twice a week for her accounts needed regular attention. At other times she talked a lot with Amelia, concerned about food.

It was true the Germans brought quite a lot of their own rations but they had commandeered so much that the islanders were already starting to feel the pinch. She and Amelia poured over the various ad hoc recipes and advice in the censored papers. They studied the adverts carefully as a system of barter began to take place.

"It says here that rice pudding can be made from potatoes and toothpaste from ground-up cuttlefish," Amelia told her one morning as they stood in the Ozanne cottage, trying to learn about improvisation.

Mary snorted. "With all the beaches mined and the Germans grabbing the fish that are caught, we've little chance of getting hold of cuttlefish!"

"Soap can be made from ivy leaves and wood ash," Amelia continued reading aloud unabashed.

Mary considered. "Well, we can try that at least," she agreed. "There's all that ivy at the back here."

"I don't fancy this though," Amelia told her pulling a face. "Coffee can be made from lupins and chips fried in white vaseline! Ugh!"

Amelia was now a rotund body with bright, twinkling dark eyes and still adored Raoul. She never mentioned the sons who had gone off to war but Mary knew her heart must ache for them. Having no news was one way to deflate public morale and lower resistance.

"Now that's helpful," Amelia cried, referring once again to two lists which had been passed on. "We can dry cabbage stalks for the fire because one day we are going to have no proper fuel—and conkers as well."

"Right," Mary agreed briskly. "We'll save anything which can be burned and Raoul can see to drying it. Then we'll bring it indoors and lock it up. How are you with food rations from—them?" she asked nodding her head up the lane.

Amelia shrugged. "I can't steal so much now," she replied, eyes twinkling. "I think they have become suspicious of the food that was going."

"Don't run risks!" Mary told her with alarm.

"Look!" Amelia cried with excitement turning to the one sheet newspaper. "Someone wants a pair of men's wellingtons size 9 in exchange for soap powder. I'm sure there's a pair in the loft."

"Try and get flour or sugar instead but, if not, settle for the soap powder," Mary advised.

They had fallen into the habit of storing everything in the loft of the Ozanne cottage and making sure someone was always there in case of theft. Mary had a gut feeling that food and fuel were soon going to become top priority.

"Let me know if you see any more items wanted and I'll go through my goods. God!" she cried. "What a state we are in! We are bartering like tribal savages instead of civilised people, thanks to be the damned Germans!"

Mary walked home in a thoughtful mood. Her four officers

had gone and been replaced by others who were slightly older. So had the fine young men who had initially come to the island. This was significant, she knew. Now that America was in the war and Hitler had to fight on two fronts, the crack troops were too good to leave on tiny islands in the Channel. Not that the number of the occupiers decreased. Mary had calculated they had, if anything, increased significantly. The 319 Infantry Division arrived under Major-General Muller plus even more horses. Some were splendid animals for the officers to ride but, Mary knew, horses ate a lot of food. What would happen to them when the hay and oats had all gone?

Her walking was restricted now as the coves and sands had been laid with mines and patrols were regular. Enormous concrete fortifications were slowly being erected, great grey blots which fouled the landscape.

The island's occupation was peaceful because the islanders could do nothing but obey, though they did this in typical Guernsey fashion. Which meant being, awkward, slow, deaf or simply feeble minded, depending upon the German order in question. A few commando raids took place, which caused fury from the occupiers and apprehension to the islanders. The Controlling Committee worked hard ensuring that no islander jeopardised his neighbours with acts of sabotage.

William came and went. His glasshouse work was almost non-existent though Mary did see him occasionally discussing matters with Raymond. He had found his niche at last, working with relish as a translator. Sometimes he was in St Peter Port and, at other times, Mary had no idea where he went. She had always felt it prudent to keep a wary eye on him. With the German work this was difficult.

It was a time of limbo when German propaganda could have undermined the islanders' morale except for their sneak listening to the truth of the BBC. Mary wondered when Victor might return. It was many months now and her collection of papers had become substantial requiring a number of hiding places in the flat.

He came out of the blue the following autumn, again picking a time when Alice had left to go home and Mary was on the verge of locking up. Her heart missed a beat, then resumed with increased pounding as he pretended to buy something from her. Luckily the autumn evenings were starting to draw in, which meant the blackout was required. While she closed it he went upstairs and Mary felt a niggle of worry, despite her pleasure at seeing him. Where was his usual bounce, saucy look and exploring hands? He had not even kissed her. She checked both doors were locked, then flew up the stairs after him.

In the flat she rushed to him and he opened his arms to her but, even as they kissed, Mary sensed something was different. He was again dressed as a fisherman with crumpled smelly clothes, worn and patched trousers and an old beret on his head.

"Victor!" she whispered. "What is it?"

He pulled her down to the settee with him, half turning to her, holding one hand.

"Later," he said. "Any food? I'm ravenous and here's another letter for you and, yes, Margaret is thriving and now has two stripes on her arm!"

"Oh Victor," she breathed, then hastened to make a meal from the emergency rations she kept in the flat for the purpose. "The food isn't what it used to be," she told him nervously. "No gauche I'm afraid!"

He eyed her. "Like that, is it? Anything will do to fill a hole," he joked, though this fact registered and would be reported back.

While he ate some very coarse dry bread with a thin, runny jam made from surplus tomatoes, she hastily read Margaret's letter. It rang full of hope and happiness, though she noted it was a number of weeks old. She came and sat with him again, taking one of his hands in both of hers, looking at him tenderly.

His face was harsher with tiny crow lines around his eyes. His hair had more frost, yet he was only a little older than herself. He held himself differently and seemed very tense.

"Tell me," she asked in a gentle voice.

"Jenny is dead!" he said harshly.

"Oh no!" Mary cried, aghast. "What happened?"

"She was on leave and went to Bristol. James had arranged to have a day off school. There was a sneak raid—it was after the Bristol blitz—and she took shelter in a building. It had a direct hit. We had nothing left to bury!"

"James?"

He took a deep breath. "Somehow they became separated and went into different shelters. James survived in his. Nicole has taken it badly. She's had a nervous breakdown." He paused. The doctor had held a lengthy discussion with him. In his opinion, the girl's death had precipitated something in Nicole's mind which had its roots elsewhere. Victor knew what that was with a guilty lurch but he kept a neutral expression on his face and the doctor was too harassed to probe too deeply. There could be a cure but it would take time and patience and anything untoward could inflict a further breakdown. Victor had wondered whether the doctor was telling him, in an oblique way, that Nicole's mind was now unstable and would remain so. However, he had no intention of discussing this with his love right now. As usual, his time was limited.

"That's not all though," he said slowly. This she had to know. "Michael is missing in action!"

"Oh God!" Mary groaned. "Margaret must be going through hell and I cannot help her!"

She was but he had no intention of telling her that either. His heart ached for his wonderful son and this, plus Jenny's death, made him act decisively.

"I'll not be coming again," he began slowly. "I'm not a young man but neither am I senile. Others can do this courier work in my place. I have more value elsewhere. I don't know when I'll be seeing you again, Catherine."

Mary's heart went cold and she closed her eyes, suppressing a sob of fear. Was *this* that dreadful nightmare? She looked at him, her forehead crinkling, her eyes narrow with anguish but she set her lips firmly. He was going to war the hard way. Her mind worked rapidly. He was going to some theatre of war or to something dangerously clandestine where his skills would be of more value. More to the point, he was going to some place where he could kill Germans to avenge his twins.

She groaned, lowered her head and battled not to cry. He reached over, reading her so well as always, pulling her against him and she hid herself in the grey folds of the grubby guernsey sweater. He had been a little uncertain as to her reaction and he was proud of her now. She was so like Grandmère. She did not complain or whine. She faced facts and life, trying to take what was dished out to her with a bravery of her own.

"My sweet love," he crooned in her ear. He was content simply to hold her. He felt no urge for sex. The fact that she leaned against him for comfort and reassurance was more than enough to make his heart swell with his own desperate pain.

"Just keep on with your work," he whispered. "Someone else will come and use your second code words but take care. I don't know who it will be or when but we must continue to know German strength and intentions here."

Mary sniffed hard and pulled back to look ruefully at him. Now she could understand his change and she shivered. She had a flashing vision of him stalking and killing Germans with a knife in his hand. He would be extremely dangerous to cross.

"Just carry on with your excellent work. Remember a woman's observations can provide a different interpretation to those from a man. Your comments about food improvisations for example. There have been a number of compliments concerning your work."

"Really?" and she was pleased.

"Remember Germany now fights on two fronts which is a classic move of military stupidity. One day the Allies will invade. It might not be this year or even next but come they will. Therefore the more men and machinery tied up here the better for us. Remember only pass your papers on to the person who gives you the correct code word. No one else, no matter what they might say. You are still being careful?" he asked anxiously.

Mary nodded. "So careful it almost hurts."

"Your son?"

"Working for the Germans just about full-time as a translator!"

"I see," he murmured thoughtfully. "Pity he's out from under your nose but there's nothing you can do about that. I hate to say this, Catherine, but I will have to go."

"So soon!"

He nodded, checking his watch, his face once again heavy and grave. "Give me ten minutes to get clear before you leave!" and he took her hands, drawing her to him for a final kiss. "I'll survive!" he grinned knowing he was being over-optimistic. He doubted whether he would but he knew he'd take plenty of Germans with him if his number came up.

Reluctantly they broke apart as Mary repeated the caution of his first visit.

"All's clear!" she hissed, then tiptoed down the track after him, to watch him vanish in the night.

Knowing this might be her last glimpse of him, she was completely unaware of the figure in a doorway higher up the road. A man had stood motionless for a long time and now his patience and curiosity were being rewarded. His eyebrows rose with interest. Well, he told himself. Is that so! Interesting! Interesting indeed!

Mary counted ten minutes, on tenterhooks for rifle shots or a challenge, but the night was quiet. She was reluctant to move; there was too much on her mind but she had to get home. If she delayed too long, Raoul would get into a panic and he might break the curfew to come and find her.

Carefully she rechecked there was no traces of his presence then, collecting her cycle, she went on the road, locked up and began to ride back to Cobo. Mary thought carefully. Once again she was going to be late and a number of ideas were tried then thrown away. Certainly she could not use the flat tyre stunt a second time. Pulling a face she knew she had no alternative though the idea made her skin crawl with apprehension.

God go with you, Victor, she kept thinking, over and over again, her heart writhing with his news. Poor Margaret. Poor Michael and poor her—but this was what war did. So Jenny had gone. She had been an empty-headed but harmless girl and how young James must fret to grow and join up. Dear God, don't let that happen. For Nicole, she had little thought. She carried too much weight in her own mind now to feel concern for someone she barely knew and who no doubt loathed her guts.

Mary waited until she reached a slope in the lane, which she had been subconsciously noting for days now. The road surface here was in a dreadful state from all the German traffic. She suddenly caught her breath, closed her eyes and let herself fall from the cycle. She landed awkwardly, slithering on her knees, ripping the skin from them. They started to bleed heavily with little chips under the skin. She sat up, gritting her teeth but still alert enough to take particular notice of the position. Knowing the methodical Germans they would check back and indeed find a rough road surface, treacherous for a cyclist not allowed to have proper headlights.

Her knees smarted but a quick glance showed her that although she would be lame for a few days, the damage was only superficial; it looked far worse than it was. Muttering a few choice oaths she slowly picked up her cycle. The front wheel was bent and she doubted even Raoul's clever fingers could work a miracle. Mary patted the black saddle, which was twisted askew. The cycle had given her yeoman service but the tyres were worn and it was impossible to get new ones. Although some people managed to get around on rope tyres, she did not fancy this. From now on, she would walk and take short cuts over the fields and through the countryside she knew so well.

She limped home with blood streaming down her legs, ruining her slacks. They flapped from two large tears and she knew they too had reached the end of a long line. By the time she stumbled up the drive she was sweating and muttering to herself. She hurt, she was upset for Margaret. She was worried about Michael and she was in a funk of fear for Victor. So it was unfortunate that the first person she met was William.

William liked to show alertness to the Germans, so jumped forward as Mary wearily halted by the front door. Raoul came from around the back and two middle-aged officers also appeared behind William.

"Where have you been, Mother?" William demanded.

Mary turned hot eyes upon him. "Swimming of course!" she snapped.

She turned upon the Germans. Attack, she reminded herself, still remains the best form of defence. "While you are on this island, you might at least keep the lanes in good repair. When we were wholly British, people did not fall off cycles and ruin them to boot!" she said caustically. Then she turned her wrath upon her son. "Why aren't you in bed?" she barked.

William went red. "I'm a man, not a boy. I work!" he retorted.

"You are still a minor living in my house and responsible to me!" Mary shot back at him. She glared at the astounded lieutenants. "Is this what goes on behind a mother's back? I think I shall be making a strong complaint to the Hauptmann in the morning. My injuries have been caused by you people and my son, employed by Germans, shows disrespect to his mother. I thought you people believed in discipline in the home?" she ranted, temper and shock all combined with worry and fear. "Until my son is of age he does as I tell him. After that, he can go and live elsewhere!"

The German officers stood aghast at her fury. They had had little to do with her, their welfare seen to by Frau Amelia. Frau Noyen had been polite when she met them but very distant; suddenly they saw another side to her as she faced them with stiff jaw and eyes blazing anger. They were impressed as most Germans were, Mary knew, by force and authority. They were under strict orders to maintain good relations with these occupied Britons and they *had* been in the wrong, teaching the Frau's son to play cards and sing *Horst Wessel* songs. They blanched nervously.

"Well?" Mary grated. It had been a terrible evening and now these Germans stood before her doing nothing, and William's face wore a look which infuriated her.

Raoul stood holding the battered cycle, astounded at Mary's temper. This was most unlike her and he wondered uneasily what had been the real reason for her delay in town. Never for one moment did he believe she had come off her cycle through the bad road surface. Mary knew every pothole between here and St Peter Port.

William took one step forward, quivering with rage and embarrassment. How dare his mother make such an exhibition of herself! This was nothing but a childish tantrum in front of his German friends. Who did she think she was?

"Mother!" he remonstrated coldly.

Mary forgot her bloody knees. She whipped around with speed which astonished all of them and let fly with the palm of her right hand. It hit William across the centre of his left cheek. William had no idea she was capable of such physical power. He rocked back on his heels, swayed precariously, tried to readjust his balance, failed and went flying backwards to land ignominiously on his bottom.

"Do not use that tone of voice to me!" Mary cried and turned back to the German officers who stood frozen and appalled. "As to you officers," she spat at them, "you disgust me! Look at my son! Defying his mother. This is your influence and I will certainly see about taking this matter farther. A lot farther!"

William scrambled sullenly to his feet, scarlet with humiliation and fuming with rage. All his carefully controlled emotions were shattered for once and now he regarded his mother with something not far short of hatred. That one blow, delivered before the audience that he had been trying so hard to impress, finished something which had inadvertently been started at his birth. Gritting his teeth, William glowered at her with clenched fists, vowing she would pay for his embarrassment.

The Germans were rattled. They sprang to attention, clicked their heels, and stammered their apologies; then the senior turned to the red-faced William.

"Obey your mother!" he ordered harshly.

Almost weeping now, William turned on his heels and bolted indoors, shaking with temper, vowing all sorts of revenges. She would pay. She would suffer. He would deal with her as he had that fool Edwin.

Raoul tactfully moved off quietly, half carrying the ruined cycle while Mary swept past the Germans and climbed to her room. She felt emotionally drained and all she wanted was her bed. Whether she would sleep she did not care to contemplate but sleep she did later. Only it was shattered when the nightmare came yet again in the same form with the menace larger and more horrendous. Once again she awoke with a violent start, heart-pounding terror, shoulders slumped. She shook her head, gritting her teeth. She would not let it get her down. Thank God she had Raoul and Amelia to turn to because there was no one else and even then, she could not confide everything to them.

NINETEEN

ONE EVENING MARY was sitting in the half-darkened shop which had officially closed but with the door unlocked in case of a caller. This was her practice two or three evenings a week when she would then walk home. The cycle was past redemption and another was impossible to obtain, even with rope tyres.

It was not that Mary minded walking. Under normal circumstances she would have thrived upon the exercise particularly as her island knowledge allowed her to take useful short cuts. The trouble was that she did not feel very strong. A walk was inclined to leave her far more tired than it should have but she knew what ailed her. Lack of proper food was affecting everyone similarly.

Amelia was a genius with what she managed to conjure up for their meals, which Mary now ate with the Ozannes at their cottage. The Germans themselves were not as well provided for as before but they did better than the islanders except for those engaged in black market profiteering. What William did or where he ate she neither knew nor cared. Since the day she had hit and humiliated him, something irrevocable had come between them. They saw each other rarely and when they did, passed each other in studied silence. Mary occasionally saw William with Raymond but she was far too tired to delve into their activities.

When the shop bell tinged she looked up hopefully but saw only a grizzled old man wearing a guernsey which, if it had been white, had long since forgotten that shade. He was a short, squat fellow with a black beret on his head from which peeped white strands of hair. His trousers were dark, tucked into rubber boots and from him came the unmistakeable odour of fish.

He stood for a moment, looking around owlishly then turned to her with grey eyes, narrow and sharp. Mary put him in his early sixties and his face was new to her.

"I'm really closed," she told him gently.

He gave her a long, hard scrutiny. "They say the fish will rise well tonight when it's high tide at Brecqhou!"

Mary caught her breath and slowly stood, going round to lock the shop door before facing him coolly.

"I expect they will get an even better catch around Burhou!" she replied.

They looked at each other. The old man spoke with a thick patois as if reluctant to use English and Mary had automatically switched to that tongue herself.

"Upstairs," she told him and went to check the back door was bolted before following him.

The old man's aroma of fish floated from him, making her nostrils twitch. This was the genuine article and he was no Guernsey man either, she reflected. His patois held an edge unknown to her and she wondered about him curiously, though had no intention of asking questions.

"I don't have much food but I'll give you what I can spare," she told him as he stood looking around, examining her flat carefully before lowering himself into a chair.

She gave him dry bread with the inevitable tomato jam and some tea made from her remaining precious leaves, which were carefully drained off and kept for reuse. The tea was wishy-washy but at least she had not sunk to an ersatz variety.

He pulled a much folded, badly creased and smelly letter from somewhere under the folds of his sweater and Mary's heart flipped over as she recognised Margaret's handwriting. Quickly, turning her back, she pulled up her man's shirt and slipped it between her breasts. Then she gave him her notes and watched as he carefully wrapped these in waterproofs and tucked them back next to his body.

He said not one word though as his keen old eyes studied her and the start of an approving smile touched his lips. He gave her a little nod then stood slowly, as if his knee joints were inclined to ache. Mary led him back down the stairs, opened the rear doors waving with one hand for him to wait. She walked silently down the track and looked carefully up and down the road, then hurried back and nodded to him.

Then he was gone and Mary took a deep breath. That was the most silent man she had ever met but she had a letter. She must get home and read it! Throbbing with excitement, she went through her checking routine, took the trouble to make sure both doors were secured then set off walking more briskly than she had for a long time. Again she was completely unaware anyone else was around and had no idea at all that this time she was under the observation of four eyes, two of which had no knowledge that another two were bent upon the same task.

Margaret's letter was brief, as if she had been given short notice again but Mary poured over the words with loving care, trying to read between the lines. Now Margaret was a transport sergeant and happy except for Michael's disappearance; then, at the bottom was a postscript, scribbled in haste. Splendid news had just arrived. Michael was alive and hopefully well in a German Stalag as a prisoner of war.

Now all she wanted was news of Victor but realised she was unlikely to get any. A man of his age could hardly be a front-line fighting soldier but with his skills he was no doubt a partisan somewhere, which would make any form of communication impossible.

Since that initial visit the old man had made three more visits to her, always picking closing time. Once he even brought her precious fish, which she had hurried home to Amelia who had cooked it that night. The three of them had sat down and slowly savoured each gorgeous mouthful, only wishing it had been larger but thankful to have it at all.

Guernsey bristled with guns. By careful observation Mary learned there were eighty-eight very heavy flak guns plus innumerable smaller calibre ones. One thing was for sure, she told herself, with all this fire power the Allies would be mad to invade Guernsey. The loss of life would be devastating, so did this mean they would be ignored? This awful question was one she kept to herself with growing apprehension as months slid into years.

In 1941, the Germans shot two islanders. One had sent a message to Britain by pigeon and another died for daring to favour Britain against Germany. There were a spate of V-signs chalked up on buildings which aroused the Germans' fury until they turned these into victory signs for themselves. Not to be outdone though, the natural Guernsey humorists pointed out that Sieg was the correct German word for victory and that the German version stood for Verloren or lost. After this the V-signs slowly faded away as Germans and islanders ran out of polite insults.

The next step of controlled defiance was the start of GUNS, the Guernsey Underground Newspaper dreamed up and run by very brave men. Raoul received a copy from a hidden source and when the three of them had read it, he then passed it on. Recipients of GUNS were carefully checked to avoid letting a copy falling into the hands of collaborators.

Sometimes Mary, Raoul and Amelia thought their little island must sink beneath the weight of German boots and slaves' rags. The TODT organisation had brought to the island thousands of wretches to work on the defensive fortifications. They were deliberately starved, dressed in threadbare rags, skeleton thin and often with lice on their bodies. The plight of these miserable men and boys was something the Germans tried to hide from the islanders' eyes without great success.

Rumours from Alderney reached them, which caused horror. Ill or sick slaves were thrown into liquid concrete as an easy way to dispose of their remains with barbaric ill treatment for those who had the misfortune to live. The males were a mixture of French, Spanish Republicans, Belgians, Dutchmen, Russians, Algerians and Moroccans.

Mary felt her gorge rise as she noted down this information. One day there would be the most terrible reckoning but what good would that do to those pitiful boys and men who laboured and died as slaves, treated worse than those owned by the Ancient Romans?

She had to admire German efficiency and forethought. Their fortifications were often built six feet thick, then sometimes disguised as artificial cottages with false flowers standing in open "windows". Her lovely Rocques was transformed with a garish concrete monster and she wondered what Victor would think about it all—if he were still alive.

Mary saw Amelia was cooking something that was a weird colour and texture. She and Raoul exchanged a look, but knew better than to say anything. Amelia did the best she could with what she could scrounge, steal or find. If the ingredients should be questionable, their job was to eat what she offered without comment or question.

Mary balanced on the edge of the kitchen table and started scanning the adverts in the paper.

"Dog basket for sugar or new gleaned flour."
"Gleaned oats for custard powder"
"1/2 ounce of onion seed for 50 British cigarettes."
"Salt for white beans or coffee beans"
 1 lb. candles and 1 lb. vermicelli for 6 lemons"
"Tin of fruit for a bar of soap"

"Nothing for us, Amelia," she murmured. Although bartering was officially forbidden, a blind eye was turned when the words "where permissive" were included. At least it was better than pandering to the black market whose prices were shocking. A quarter-pound packet of tea now cost over seven pounds and, on principle, all three of them refused to deal with racketeers.

"I hear an old cycle with rope tyres will now fetch fifty pounds," Raoul murmured, then looked at her. "I've had some enquiries about spares from your old cycle. Shall I see what I can get for them?"

Mary bit her lip. "Not for money. Try and get food or something we could barter for food. When this is all over I'm going to get myself the best car I can afford. I'll never cycle nor walk again."

"We have no eggs left, Mary!" Amelia told her.

Mary puffed her cheeks and shook her head. "Can't afford any," she said briskly. "They cost eight shillings each now, and I heard that a packet of cheap jelly crystals went for ten shillings last week."

"Good God!" Raoul exploded. "Even a top foreman only earns just over two pounds a week! How can poor people manage, let alone survive?"

Mary pulled out a chair and sat down. "It's going to get worse too," she said heavily.

Amelia was alarmed. "How can you say that?"

Mary faced her squarely. "Look!" she began. "When the invasion comes, as we—and the Germans—know it must, can you honestly see the Allies pouring troops in here against all those guns? They'll go straight to France and if the Germans here end up being cut off from Germany, who is going to feed them? It's quite likely we shall all go hungry, occupiers and occupied!"

Amelia and Raoul gazed at her with horrified looks, then turned to each other as her forecast slowly sank in.

Raoul nodded wearily. "You may be right, Mary," he agreed heavily.

"There is not a damned thing we can do to help ourselves that we are not doing already!" Mary cried with frustration.

Raoul walked a few paces in a little circle. "In that case," he said firmly, "it might be prudent to mount a night guard on the root crops we grow. Starving people won't hesitate to steal," he pointed out.

Mary went stiff. "I hadn't thought of that," she said biting her lip. It was a good idea but none of them were strong now. She flashed Raoul a look of worry and for once he was quick enough to understand. On the nights Mary sneaked back just before curfew, she would be in no fit state to stand a night guard on their growing produce.

"I'll work something out," he grunted, aware of his wife's presence. "There is another bit of news I heard and it seems fact, not rumour. The Germans are constructing a huge underground hospital at La Vassalerie in St Andrews Parish."

"Underground?"

"TODT slave workers are on the job. It's going to be just about invisible from the surface, except for the ventilation towers and there are even some islanders working on it. The pay is good."

Mary was thinking along other lines and she did not like her thoughts either. "That means," she began carefully, "the Germans have a good idea the invasion will be nothing to do with us. Their wounded will be safe here which all points to the Allies landing somewhere in Northern France. I know one thing; it only reinforces my opinion that when the invasion does come, we will be left alone—without food or medical supplies."

"Surely our Committee will have realised this and started trying to get stocks in?"

Mary knew there had been some frantic arrangements by the Committee in which some men had been allowed by the enemy to go to France with carefully saved money to buy precious foods and medicine. With an invasion, this would certainly halt.

"I don't like this at all," she told them both and her shoulders sagged for a moment before she straightened firmly. "But we mustn't let it beat us."

May's new contact now started to come on a regular basis, at least once every two months and she became used to his taciturnity. She worked it out that he must slip over from France and cringed at the risks he ran. The German sea patrols were fast boats with trained, armed men. This meant that several times she had arrived home only just before the curfew and Raoul became a bag of nerves.

He protested one evening when they were alone. "I don't like you walking in the dark so late at night, Mary. Remember I'm responsible to your daughter for your safety. I promised her."

Mary was touched. "I'm quite all right."

"What if a late patrol stumbled across you? They'd most likely shoot first and ask questions afterwards," he grumbled.

Mary threw him a wicked grin. "If there's any shooting to do, it will be me," she said and quietly pulled the derringer from her trouser pockets.

Raoul was shocked. Firearms were forbidden by the Germans and they could inflict ferocious penalties if an islander was caught with one. He opened his mouth to protest, took a look at Mary's grim face and snapped it shut again.

"Now, Raoul, don't fuss like a mother hen," Mary told him gently.

"Who else knows you have that?"

"Only Victor now, though Tante did—and approved!"

"Good God! Did she really!"

"Sam got it for me—long ago," Mary explained to him.

Raoul remembered. "It was you who shot Victor le Page!"

Mary threw him a lop-sided grin and nodded. "He asked for it and got it!"

359

The subject was dropped but then they had a fresh worry as deportations to the Continent began, brought about by a proclamation that those not born on Guernsey were to be deported forthwith. Mary was uncertain where she stood but kept the worry to herself. It was true she had been born on Mainland England and lived there for her first eighteen years, but that was so long ago. Sometimes it seemed impossible for her to realise she was not Guernsey born and bred. At least her main abode had been on the islands for over two decades and she wondered who really knew about her birthplace. Did William?

William was now a superb specimen of manhood, tall, broad and with flashing good looks. He was never sick or sorry and she had to admire his brilliant mind. Luckily, she rarely saw him now as he had lodgings in St Peter Port, arranged by his German employers. Mary knew he called to see Raymond occasionally, usually driving away in a small German car with produce to sell or exchange. Sometimes Mary thought he was more German than the Germans themselves and she wished he would to go to Germany and get out of her life forever.

She did not speak much to Raymond because everything seemed to be such an effort. She did note though that Raoul and his sister were growing apart and she wondered why. Had they rowed? Or was Gwen taking more after her husband? Tante's doubts about Raymond resurfaced yet she could find no fault with his work when she checked. In the end she put it down to the occupation. They were all under an unbearable strain from the German presence with no sign of hope for the future. They were also eating poorly which affected vitality and health. It was so easy to be tired when there was no meat to eat and, more than once, Mary found herself casting covetous eyes at the horses the officers rode.

As the war progressed the tide started to run against the Germans. The occupiers began to take repressive measures against the islanders. All radios had been seized and even the tiny wireless Mary had in the shop was confiscated. Mary had considered defying this outrageous order by hiding her set but decided against it. She remembered James' wise words about not drawing attention to herself. The last thing she wanted was the enemy searching her flat.

However, one or two bold islanders did defy the edict. It was from these brave people that Allied progress was able to infiltrate throughout the island. It was true renegade islanders would not hesitate to inform the Germans for a reward, so anyone with a radio was extremely careful as to whom he told the latest BBC news.

The old man came again after a long period without a visit and Mary had a thick wad of notes for him. He slipped into the darkened shop and stood at the doorway, poised, on edge, uneasy.

"People about!" he growled, holding out his hand. "I'm not stopping!"

Mary flew upstairs, collected the notes and ran back down to give them to him. Hastily they were shoved up the ancient sweater.

"Any letters for me?" Mary asked hopefully.

"No!" he grunted, still standing warily.

"Come out the back way," Mary said, pointing. "Don't go down the track. Go over the next fence, cross the back yard and leave that way."

The old man shut the shop door, slipping the bolt home. "I could have sworn I heard steps following me!"

Mary's blood chilled. "In that case go as quickly as possible," she breathed. If he were caught now with her notes they were both finished. It would be deportation and the Gestapo in France with a vengeance.

She opened the back door, listening carefully but the night was quiet.

"Are you sure you heard someone?" she whispered to him.

He glowered at her. "I may be old but I'm not deaf!" he retorted, then was gone and over the fence with a speed which astounded her. Mary stood with ears straining, heart thumping, but all was still. She glanced at her watch, over an hour to curfew time. She locked up and slipped on a short coat, now threadbare at the cuffs and collar. Her pre-war trousers were patched at the knees and baggy but new clothes were impossible to obtain. She wore men's shirts all the time as being more practical and she was on her last pair of lightweight walking shoes. She had no idea whether Raoul could repair them when the soles went. She always tried to walk on grass to save her precious shoes but she knew the day was soon coming when she would have to wear makeshift objects on her feet.

Outside there was a slight frost and her breath clouded a little. She shivered then, walking as briskly as her strength allowed, set off for home. She walked silently because Raoul had managed to obtain some rubber which he had carefully nailed to her shoes. Mary knew it was vital she was well into the countryside before the curfew began. If she arrived home after eleven, she could always stay the night with Raoul and Amelia. They accepted her without question, though Raoul's face was a constant mask of lined worry nowadays.

Mary had no idea that two sets of eyes watched her go. One set promptly began to follow her, walking with equal quiet and stealth and the first pursuer had no idea of the second, whose silence was even more practised.

Once clear of the houses, Mary climbed a five-barred gate and slipped into a field. She looked up. The night sky was relatively clear with only a few clouds but these were high. Where the clouds were missing, stars twinkled down prettily on her and the moon cast a silver beam over the wet grass and bare hedges.

She started to warm up as she walked, pacing herself carefully with head up and lungs enjoying the cold air. Somewhere she heard an owl hoot twice and she paused once to look around. She felt as if the island was hers in regal solitude. She slipped through well-known gaps in hedges, climbed gates and smugly congratulated herself on island knowledge. She checked her watch and saw she was making excellent time. She would be back well before the curfew hour started.

Her cheeks flushed pink from the exercise and cold air and she glowed warm. She was relieved the courier had called and taken her very large collection of notes and she wondered where the old man was now. It would be raw at sea tonight but the water would be calm.

Mary knew that before her was the lip of a long-abandoned quarry, shrouded with old, well established trees. As she neared she entered gloom and paused momentarily to catch her breath and listen. Somewhere behind her a twig gave a soft crack and she froze while her heart shot into her mouth. She thought rapidly. Had there been cattle in that field? No, and, even if there had been any, they would be lying down, chewing their cud,

She shrank back against an old oak tree, sliding slowly behind its ancient trunk. Overhead its bare branches and twigs made a lacy canopy against the sky when suddenly, the clouds moved across the moon's face and the field pooled into black.

She heard distinct footsteps. Someone *was* coming after her. Their steps made a soft whooshing sound through the wet grass. Mary's heart beat increased its tempo but she did not make the mistake of moving. With slitted eyes she waited, her face a cold mask. She was badly frightened, yet strangely, wildly exhilarated.

No islander would dare to be out on legitimate business here in the fields at night and it did flash through her mind that it had to be Raoul doing a mother-hen act, then changed her mind. It would have been impossible for him to have reached the shop in time to follow without her knowing.

The steps slowed a little as if the tracker peered ahead to locate whether she had turned left or right at the trees. She saw a shadow loom, tower over the gate then drop down smoothly on her side. A head bent to examine the damp grass and Mary realised her tracks must show in the wetness. A man's head came up, looked straight towards her and she guessed she had been located.

At that moment the clouds obliged and the moon shone down. Mary caught her breath then without further preamble stepped into his view.

"What the hell do you think you are doing following me?" she barked angrily.

William jumped with shock. He had not realised she was so near. She had been masked by the tree trunk and he had been very confident that his pursuit was silent. His heart lurched but only for a moment, then he stopped and looked down at her.

Mary stood before him, hands jammed casually into her slacks' pockets, Her eyes blazed with anger, yet she was at a loss for words as a hundred implications shot in and out of her head.

William felt cold triumph and frustrated anger. She was a woman and should have been terrified of him; instead, she stood cool, calm and collected, glowering at him. His temper began to rise.

For a few seconds mother and son glared at each other. Years of carefully controlled hatred from William were out in the open at last. Years of loathing and disgust from Mary glowed in her narrowed eyes.

"Well?" Mary hissed between clenched teeth.

"Traitor!" William shot back at her.

"Eh!" Mary gasped, taken aback for a few seconds until a chill entered her heart. "What do you mean?"

"You are a traitor to Germany," William announced pompously as his eyes gleamed triumph. He had her at last. Now she would pay with a vengeance for all his past humiliations. "You are a British agent. I've had my suspicions for a long time and I've watched your shop carefully but there was no pattern. Now though you meet that old fisherman fairly regularly, yet he never buys anything, does he? You know this island backwards and have been seen everywhere for no apparent reason at all. Why should someone of your age want to poke her nose about unless she wished to collect information?"

"It will look very interesting in a report, won't it?" William jeered. "Plus the fact you are not island-born either. You'll get your deportation papers and the Gestapo will be delighted to talk to you," he warned wickedly.

Mary could think of nothing sufficiently cutting to say so she kept silent but her resolve set rigidly.

"Now we know why you really wanted that shop and flat, don't we?" William continued. "So what about the girl there? I suppose she's in it up to her neck as well!"

Mary did not bother to reply. She simply studied William carefully. How was it that such a magnificent young man could be quite so rotten?

William would do well for himself, she mused. She would be a prime catch for him to parade before the Germans, then she felt a pang. How could her flesh and blood be prepared to drag in innocent people like Alice, Raoul and Amelia because catch them in his net he certainly would.

"Where is your proof?" she asked casually, wondering exactly why she felt it necessary to stall for time.

William hesitated and Mary noted this. That was the trouble, William told himself uneasily. He had not a shred of proof. Once again the old fisherman had simply disappeared into thin air and even when he took his mother in, he had a shrewd idea she would be a hard one to break.

"Have you gone deaf too?" Mary asked quietly. She had been straining all her senses as they stood facing each other. For a fleeting second, some instinct had indicated they were not alone but strain her nerves and senses as she might, she could pick up nothing to indicate a third party.

William had gone a dull red, Mary noted coolly. His hands were curled into enormous fists and his chest swelled before her eyes. Mary knew he was working himself up to attack her.

"You are the traitor," she grated at him. "My God! I did a bad day's work when I spawned you. You are rotten through and through and have been since birth. You are also a heinous murderer!"

William took a step nearer and a wicked glow showed in his eyes. After all these long years she was going to come out with it at last. She *had* known, all the time.

"You killed Edwin, didn't you?" Mary asked quietly now.

William laughed. "Of course I did! That fool kid thought he was better than me!"

"That's what is written down," Mary informed him softly.

William froze then. "What do you mean?" he blustered uneasily. His mother stood there just a little too sure of herself when she should be trembling.

"Take it from me, my deductions were notated years ago. I wonder what your wonderful German masters would think of you if they learned you were a child murderer."

William quivered from head to toe. "I'm going to kill you!" he announced and waited expectantly for her to panic.

Mary threw her head back and chuckled. "You'll find me more of a match than poor Edwin!"

Very slowly, almost casually, Mary withdrew the derringer from her pocket as William's eyes opened wide with astonishment. Mary knew he was well within range and she lifted the pistol as her finger took up the tiny bit of slack.

William pounced forward. The pistol discharged and the bullet entered his chest. He froze and looked down at gushing blood with complete disbelief. His aorta had been ruptured and the blood flow turned to a pouring dam of brilliant, sticky red.

Mary watched, feeling numb. It was her blood which had

brought him into the world. It was her sole right to rid the world of his evil.

"You've shot me!" William gasped. "I'm going to die. I'm your son!"

"Yes, on all three counts and may God have more mercy upon you than you had upon Edwin!"

Mary continued to stare with fascinated horror. She had never dreamed the human body held so much blood. As William's knees sagged, she held his eyes. They were starkly terrified. His mouth moved silently, then he fell down on the sodden grass, bled white. Mary took a deep breath. She had no regrets. Edwin was avenged—at long last.

"Frau!" grunted a voice from just behind her and Mary felt as if she leaped three feet into the air.

"Give me that pistol, Frau!"

Mary whipped around, trying to collect her shattered wits as the soldier lurched towards her, his right hand outstretched. His trousers were undone. He had obviously been out drinking and gone into the trees to relieve himself. He was not too drunk though to fail to take in what he had seen. He moved a pace nearer, his eyes focusing as the killing removed the beer fumes and military training took over.

Mary's brain slid into top gear. Without any hesitation she lifted the pistol, sighted high and fired the last bullet. It hit the soldier in the middle of his forehead and he collapsed in an untidy heap only a few paces from William.

Mary stood unmoving, senses alert, her mind appearing to work in two directions. The big shadow. The two red fires, the two bangs—*this* was the nightmare. She found she had been holding her breath and let it out slowly, acutely aware of her appalling peril. It was bad enough to kill a civilian but to murder a German soldier was enough to send the occupiers on a rampage of revenge.

She looked at the two bodies. Think, she berated herself furiously. An idea flashed into her mind which, at first, filled her with repugnance. She turned it over quickly and shook her head. She could come up with nothing else at such short notice and she guessed even German troops were not immune.

She took another deep breath and bent over the soldier. Grimacing with distaste, she pulled his trousers down and then his underpants. His penis lay limp. She straightened and studied how William lay. Thank God he had fallen within useful range of the soldier. She took the pistol and, with the rag she used as a handkerchief, carefully wiped her fingerprints away. Then she bent over William and forced the pistol into his right hand, clenching the fingers in what she prayed looked a natural position. She backed a pace and studied the faked homosexual scene. William had been importuned against his will. He had struggled. From somewhere the German had produced a small pistol and shot him. William had managed to grab this and kill the German in turn before he died.

It all looked so horribly flimsy and set up that Mary shook her head, but what else could she do? Then something else hit her. Their footprints which lay starkly clear on the wet grass. She looked at her watch, then studied the sky. With luck—and God knew she certainly needed some—the dawn would wipe them away. Even a tiny shower of rain would be a Godsend because there were no domestic animals near a quarry to obliterate three sets of tracks.

Mary looked once more at William. He had a strangely peaceful expression on his face that startled her. She waited for remorse to touch her heart but there was nothing. It was the end of something that had begun years ago.

She looked at her watch with a sinking heart. It was impossible to get home before curfew and she gritted her teeth, making herself think clearly. She must tell Raoul. If she failed to show up he would only set out looking for her, running impossible risks. Mary scanned the area yet again. Why did she feel an odd prickle at the nape of her neck? She shook herself, dismissed the sensation, then carefully stepped into the soldier's tracks.

She knew she was not far from home, which meant the German had to be one stationed at Cobo Bay. It crossed her mind to wonder where he had been drinking, then she pushed that puzzle away. She had enough problems without extra ones.

Mary reached the lane, stepping along it silently, looking around once more, then set off walking as quickly and quietly as she could. The observer never moved. The whole scene had shocked and astounded him, freezing his body into immobility.

It was with relief that Mary skirted her home and approached the Ozanne cottage from the rear. She stood and eyed the upstairs windows dubiously, then reached to pick up a light stone. She tossed it in an arc and, more by luck than judgement, it tinkled a glass pane with what seemed to be a sound of thunder.

She waited, biting her lip anxiously. Wake up, Raoul, she prayed and threw a small second stone. Finally his face appeared at the window, looking down at her with shock. Mary gesticulated wildly before stepping into a pool of deep shadow. Finally the back door bolts slid back, the door opened and Mary shot inside.

"What the—?"

"Ssh!" Mary hissed. "Amelia?"

"Sound asleep. What is it?"

Mary walked into the sitting room and fell into a chair. Raoul studied her, shocked and frightened. She was white-faced, her hands shook and he could see she was near to tears. Without a word he went to a cupboard, delved at the back behind humdrum objects and produced a precious half-bottle of brandy. He poured her a generous tot and handed it over.

"Get that down you before you talk, Mary!" he ordered firmly.

Mary was unused to spirit and she drank the lot in one gulp. The brandy bit into her throat as liquid fire, but she felt the trembles steady. Raoul looked at the time. It was midnight!

Mary sat a few moments, eyes closed, letting herself relive it all again but, most of all, she tried to check the fake scene. Would it pass muster?

"I've just shot William dead and a German soldier too," she said quietly.

"Bloody hell!" Raoul exclaimed then, reaching for a second glass, poured himself a drink. His mind spun with horror. This was the worst he had ever imagined.

"Tell me everything," he demanded with genuine fear.

Mary did as he asked while he listened speechless.

"If the bodies are not found until morning I have a good chance of getting away with it all. The tracks will have vanished naturally."

"What can I do?"

Mary shook her head. "Nothing!" She paused, then pulled a face. "I'll have to be on my way."

"What! Where?" he cried protestingly.

Mary turned to him. "Back to the flat, of course."

"What on earth for?"

"To make myself an alibi," Mary pointed out. "So that I can say I spent the night there. The Germans will know I've not been home. They'll come and ask if I was here. Amelia is a rotten liar so if I spend the night at the flat, there'll be no problem!"

Raoul saw the sense of this and he hastily stood. "You're not going back that long walk alone," he growled. "Give me five minutes!"

Mary lowered her head but was grateful. The very idea of trudging back the way she had come was almost too unbearable to contemplate and she would have to go a longer way around to avoid the bodies. She could easily make the excuse she'd been forced to stay at the flat because of the curfew hour; that she had been so involved doing her paperwork she had not noticed the time.

Raoul came back down the stairs fully dressed in shabby, dark clothes. "Amelia woke. I just told her I had to go out and not

370

to worry if I was late back," he grinned a little. "Fortunately she doesn't have a curious mind!"

Mary eyed the brandy bottle and decided against asking for another drink. She viewed the coming walk with gloom. Her legs were already weary and her mind was starting to numb.

"You know the way better than me," Raoul whispered as he opened the door. "So you lead."

"We'll go over the fields again but not near—them," Mary hissed back, mentally reviewing another route.

"Do you know the times of all the town patrols?" Raoul asked uneasily, as Mary unerringly led him from the back of the cottage, skirting her own home in a wide sweep.

"No," she confided. She had never been in town at night.

"Well," Raoul said slowly, "we'll just have to be extra careful. No talking. Be careful where we place our feet and, if we are spotted, run like hell in different directions. Divide and rule. If anyone should, by bad luck, spot me in the shop when I leave at six, we can say you've been stock taking and I stayed to help as you were not too well."

Mary nodded. It was an astounding improvisation from dour Raoul and she threw him a tired smile of approval. Then something occurred to her and she looked at him with concern.

"What about Amelia?" she asked with worry. She would never forgive herself if she was the cause of trouble between husband and wife.

Raoul gave a low chuckle as they strode over yet another soaking field. "My wife has the most innocent of minds and she thinks the world of you too so there's not a problem there," he assured her.

With that worry removed, Mary felt a tiny flame of hope. Perhaps she could get away with it? If not, the immediate future did not bear contemplation.

TWENTY

THEY ARRIVED AT the flat unscathed and Mary fell on her pull-down bed and went straight into a deep sleep. Raoul watched her as he slumped on the settee. He shook his head wearily. How much longer could she carry on like this in safety? She was living on a knife edge.

Mary woke with a start and found Raoul grinning down at her holding a hot cup of exceedingly weak tea. Mary knew the leaves had been used four times already and in reality it was nothing but coloured water but at least it was hot.

"It's just after six, "Raoul told her quietly. "You'd better let me out so I can get back home. Then I suggest you go back to bed so that your shop girl wakes you up. She can help make your alibi even better!"

"Good idea," Mary replied, getting up. She felt washed out though she had slept well for a few hours.

Raoul eyed her dubiously as they went downstairs so she could let him out.

"Mary," he said urgently, "you look like death warmed up. Try and do something with your eyes and cheeks. Don't come back home looking shattered. Remember the Germans have sharp eyes!"

She nodded, saw him out, relocked up then climbed the stairs. She was still dressed in her shabby trousers and decided it might be prudent to be in a nightdress for Alice's arrival. It would lend more colour to her story. Once the two bodies were discovered all hell would break loose and she gritted her teeth. At the same time, she examined her heart regarding her dead son but there was no feeling of remorse. She had only administered a belated justice even though she had been forced to act as both judge and jury. The knowledge William would trouble her no more was a great weight from her shoulders. No longer would she worry if he was peering over her shoulders but she wondered how long he had been watching her and whether he had confided in anyone. However, knowing William's devious mind and deep nature, she doubted he would have told anyone until he could produce a positive result. All she could do was pray the Germans believed her set scene. It did not bear thinking about if they should query it. The only flaw she could think of was what would a German soldier be doing with a derringer? Then she shook her head. The die was cast. She must wait and pray.

She lay in bed, waiting for Alice to arrive. When at last she heard fumbling with the lock and the bell's delicate warning ping, she quietly got up and flashed a glance in the mirror. Her eyes were ringed by a dark shadow but she had a tiny bit of cream left which hopefully could disguise these marks.

"Don't jump, Alice!" she called down the stairs. "I worked so late last night I forgot the time and had to stay the night because of the curfew!"

Alice did jump and peered up the stairs where she could see her employer in a nightgown with uncombed hair and a sleepy face.

"Oh Madam! You did give me a start!" but Alice accepted what she saw. It would have taken a far more astute mind than hers to question. "I'll make a cup of tea for you."

Mary grimaced but said nothing. The tea Alice would make would come from a dubious mixture of dried herbs and ground up plants. Then, she told herself, she'd better get used to it. Her precious real tea had gone and even their leaves would not brew up a fifth time.

By the time Mary was washed, dressed and ready to walk back

to Cobo, yet again she felt considerably better, even in a light frame of mind. She had disguised the shadows on her face and was prepared for anything. Well, almost anything, she told herself.

She set off and decided to stick to the roads. It would never do to cross the fields on this particular morning. Her legs were tired and she felt weak and a little light-headed but she plodded on grimly. Two German staff cars passed her but she stoically ignored them. Then from a side lane appeared a sight which made her heart drum with hope as the cart turned left.

"Hey!" she yelled frantically. "Are you going towards Cobo?"

The cart halted and a man whom she knew very slightly looked down at her. "A lift, missus?"

"Oh please!" Mary gasped, scrambling up beside him. "I worked late in town last night and had to stay there because of the confounded curfew and my cycle gave up the ghost long ago," she explained in a little rush of words.

He nodded, clucked to the horse and it broke into a shambling trot. Mary eyed him. He had lived only half a mile from them in a cottage on the front, which had been ruthlessly requisitioned by the enemy. He and his wife had been thrown out of their little home and were now forced to double up with other cottagers.

"It's all nice and quiet this morning," she said casually and waited with apprehension.

He grunted then turned to her. "Maybe 'tis here but when I came along earlier there seemed to be a bit of activity around your way," he offered.

"Oh!" Mary murmured as her heart rate increased. "I wonder why?"

He shrugged and gave another grunt. "Who's to say with the Boche?"

Mary turned and watched the scenery dawdle past while her mind worked rapidly. The soldier must have been reported missing. Now there would be a search for him because the Germans, always hypersensitive, would think of murder or revenge by an islander and very soon the balloon would go up. She wanted to be in the familiarity of her home when it did.

It was still raw-cold though the sun shone weakly. She looked at the fields and was relieved to see that though areas still held wet grass, in others it was going. With luck their multiple tracks should have vanished if only they did not find the bodies too soon.

The driver was incommunicative for which she was thankful as it allowed her to think and plot her lines. How she acted in the next few hours would determine whether she lived or died. The stakes were exceedingly high. He let her off not far from her home and with a cheery wave and false smile, Mary watched him go down another narrow lane.

Taking a deep breath, lifting her head high and ramming her spine straight, Mary walked briskly towards her home and up the drive. She felt exhausted but moved with false sprightliness.

Amelia saw her first. "You're back!" she said, beaming her usual, placid welcome.

"I worked late and had to stay the night because of the curfew," Mary said, knowing perfectly well some German would be bound to be listening somewhere near to hand.

"One of the officers came back from leave last night and he brought some real coffee!"

Mary's mouth watered. "Is there any for us, do you think?"

She had to admit that her billeted officers were not mean. To date they had always shared whatever they brought back off leave and, in her turn, Mary had allowed herself to be a little more friendly.

"It's brewing now and we can all share. Raoul has had his one cup, so have I. There is one left kept specially for you!"

"Marvellous!" Mary exclaimed. The very thought of a rare cup of real coffee brightened her spirits enormously.

She went up to her top-floor room and only then let her eyes close and shoulders sag a trifle before Amelia came up with a mug of coffee. Its tantalising fragrance drifted all over the top floor and Mary sat down, hands around the mug, just looking at the rich, dark drink. She sipped delicately and memories flooded back. It was just like old Tante had made it. It poured new life into her, thrusting down to her vitals. Oh now for some real food; white bread without sawdust in it, real cows' butter, fresh eggs with bacon, red meat and lovely greens, a proper pudding with Guernsey cream. Her mouth drooled. One day she promised. Yes! One day.

Later she changed into clean slacks and shirt, eyeing them with a sigh. She did not have any clothes left which were not patched, frayed or shiny. Even her shirts had collars and cuffs turned. Her wardrobe was a disgrace but they were all alike so no one looked too much like a tramp. Compared to the TODT slaves she was the height of fashion.

It was later that morning that Amelia tapped on her door, her face white and worried.

"There's a strange German officer downstairs to see you and Inspector le Norman's with him."

Mary started her act. She blinked, looked suitably surprised and nodded. "Five minutes."

Amelia trotted away and Mary took a huge breath to steady her nerves. This was it. She felt a sharp, desperate yearning to lay her head against Victor's broad chest and, closing her eyes for a second, she tried to visualise his presence with her.

She took her time going downstairs, walking with dignity and as much grace as she could muster in her shabby clothes.

"Gentlemen," she said softly, "can I help you?"

The Hauptmann was unknown, as Amelia had warned her, middle-aged with a stern face that was now set in a cold mask. Emil stood one pace behind him, his usual imperturbable self from which nothing could be read or deduced.

Mary led them into a room used as a general lounge by the billeted officers. One was present. He leaped to his feet, clicked his heels and tactfully made himself scarce.

"I'm afraid I've no refreshment to offer you," Mary told them politely.

Emil removed his police cap and studied the room, which he hadn't see before. Finally he stood, feet apart and let the Hauptmann talk. Mary gave him her full attention. Her heart was beating far too quickly but she was sure they could not know this.

The German fidgeted for a few seconds as if reluctant to speak, then he cleared his throat and drew himself to attention. "Frau Noyen, we have bad news for you."

Mary's eyebrows rose but she still waited, looking mildly curious. "Yes?"

"Frau—your son is dead!"

Mary put on the best performance of her life. Her eyes opened wide with alarm, one hand flew to her throat and her jaw opened a little. She fixed a blank look in her eyes, letting them move to each man in turn.

"Dead?" she asked tremulously.

The German nodded, his embarrassment growing. He wished the inspector would help him out but all these islanders were awkward.

"He was shot!"

"Good God!" Mary cried, swaying just one inch on her feet. "Shot—dead? How? Why? Who?" she croaked with a wild sob of distress.

The German stepped forward to catch her arm in support. "Sit, Frau!" he said gently, sweating more than a little. Emil stood like an unhelpful statue and the German cursed him under his breath. He reached in his tunic pocket and extracted a minute flask. Unscrewing it he carefully poured a small measure of Schnapps. "Drink this," he said kindly.

Mary hated the stuff but obeyed him, letting her eyes close while a look of horror etched her features. Then she opened them and looked up at him through her tears.

"Frau, when did you last see your son?"

Mary frowned, waiting before she replied. "Not this week, nor the one before. He works for you so we've not met much because he had lodgings in St Peter Port somewhere."

"Your son was murdered!"

Mary closed her eyes, licked her lips, which were very dry indeed, and gazed back at the German, horrified and frozen. "I don't understand!"

There was a pregnant silence for a few moments during which Mary made herself act as if struggling for self-control but when she spoke, her words quavered a little.

"I have a feeling you've not told me all," she whispered. "What else is there for a mother to know?"

This was the bit the Hauptmann had been afraid of. He flashed a look at le Norman for help but he was carefully studying his polished shoes. The German licked his lips, then plucked up courage.

"It is not nice, Frau," he began hesitantly. "Your son did excellent translation work for us. We thought highly of him, he was a clever young man. For some reason he was out late last night. Why we don't know or," he paused trying to frame the next sentence delicately, "we may know. Your son was obviously shot trying to defend himself. There was a violent struggle in which your son managed to wrestle a pistol off his attacker and shoot him in turn."

"Good God!" Mary gasped, eyes wide with disbelief. "Who was his attacker and why, for heaven's sake? William was a quiet boy!"

"The attacker was, I regret to say this, one of our soldiers and it seems, from the evidence and position of the bodies, that our man was—homosexual!"

"Oh no!"

"Yes!" the Hauptmann growled, humiliated. "We think he fancied your son, an advance was made and a small pistol produced though where a soldier obtained this is something we yet have to clear up. Anyhow that's how your son was shot. He did not die right away. There would only have been seconds in it but long enough for him to grapple the pistol from our soldier and shoot him between the eyes in revenge!"

Mary leaned back, eyes shut then lowered her head as tears flowed again; this time there was no faking. As the German had told the tale Mary had suddenly relived the horror again. She cried with genuine distress not for herself but for the unfortunate German soldier who would, she hoped, save her bacon.

She lifted weary eyes to the officer. "But soldiers have pistols, don't they?" she asked knowing perfectly well only officers did.

"No, Frau, only our officers have them and certainly not Derringers."

Mary frowned. "Derringer? What's that?"

He hastened to explain. This was going better than he had thought possible. The mother was distressed and sickened as he had expected but she was displaying remarkable fortitude under these harrowing circumstances.

"It's a very small American pistol, extremely rare nowadays. It only has two shots with a very limited range but effective when close to. In the last century it was highly popular in America with women and gamblers."

"But—?"

"Don't worry, Frau. We will investigate," the Hauptmann promised, though he doubted he would learn much. The rest of the man's troop would automatically close ranks and the soldier had stunk of drink even when they found his body. He intended to recommend that this group of men be transferred instantly to another field of operations. If a German soldier was to blame, as he feared, once the news was known God only knew what these stubborn islanders would do.

"Where is my son?" Mary asked, with a catch in her voice.

"His body has been taken to a civilian mortuary," he told her, glad the worst was over in one way but not liking what he would have to report to his senior officer. He threw a glance at the policeman, tried to catch his eye for help but Emil remained blank of expression and silent of words. The German's lips tightened. He could imagine the inspector's thoughts which, though these would not be aired, would do little to help German/Islander relations.

"There is a car outside for you, Frau. We will take you there now," the German told her, anxious to do anything to help.

Mary slowly stood. The Schnapps had gone to her head. "I will see my housekeeper first. If you will wait—?"

Mary found Amelia talking with Raoul who stood at the back door of the kitchen with muddy boots, not daring to enter while wearing them.

"I'm going out for a bit," Mary said generally. "I've had bad news. William is dead and I'm going to the mortuary."

"Mary!" Amelia cried with horror.

Mary nodded, lowered her head but managed to flash a reassuring glance at Raoul who went rigid.

"What happened?" Amelia wanted to know, leaning back against the table in shock.

"I'll tell you later," Mary said gently and turned.

She saw the Hauptmann waiting uneasily by the open front door and it was Emil who held out his arm to escort her. Mary did not know him very well but any friend of Victor and James had to be all right even if he did wear a police uniform.

As Emil walked slowly with her to the car, letting the German stride ahead, the fingers of his right hand rested on Mary's upper arm. They moved in little jerks. Mary was disconcerted. What was the matter with Emil. Anyone would think he had a twitch. Then—her brain snapped into action. Looking ahead, struggling to keep a sad look in her eyes, she understood all in a flash of lightning. Three quick squeezes and one long one; repeated again and again as the walked very slowly, Emil hindering her progress. The Morse code for V for victory. The sign famous in Britain, known to the whole world and hated by the Germans. Mary dared not look at him but she felt hope soar wild and free. Emil *knew*. She remembered back to those seconds last night when she had felt a queer instinctive urge she was not alone. It had been so outrageous she had dismissed it as tension but she had been right. It was Emil who had watched it all, and approved. Exultation filled her like a fresh, strong tide of power as his fingers continued to give three quick squeezes and a long one.

Emil must have known for some time! She was amazed at her rapid thinking as she entered the rear of the car with Emil sitting mute by her side; the Hauptmann in front with his driver. William must have been watching the shop and flat for goodness knows how long; thus her son had come to Emil's attention and *he*, in his turn, had watched William! What else did Emil know? Had James confided in him? She remembered James had left the keys and safekeeping of his house with Emil so did this mean the police inspector was privy to everything? It was possible, she mused, thinking more slowly now, oblivious to where the car was driven. It was vital she sort all this out in her mind. That meant Emil had always known she had an illegal firearm going back to when? The answer hit her like a hammer blow! Back to the time she had shot Victor! So why hadn't he challenged her for it? With tight lips she gradually worked it all out. Because he knew about James. He was a secret, albeit passive, ally because of his position and work. He was a true islander, British to the core, fiercely loyal to the crown but, because he *was* a policeman he was forced to co-operate with the hated enemy. She was *not* alone after all, and never had been! Her heart swelled with relief though she knew no words could pass between them. Emil had to continue working with the occupiers and she must carry on her secret work.

"Here we are, Frau," the German said as he leapt from the car to open the door for her. "Would you like me to—?"

"No, thank you," Mary said firmly. "The inspector can take me in."

The German was heartily glad to see the islander do some work and it neatly let him off any emotional scene.

"Afterwards, we would like to ask you a few questions."

"Of course," Mary told him evenly. "Anything I can help in this awful matter and—" She let a few more tears trickle from her screwed-up eyes.

Emil, still holding her arm, led her into the mortuary, nodded briefly to a German attendant, then more doors were opened and they stepped into a sterile, white-tiled room. There were high tables and on one of these a body decently covered. Mary wondered where the soldier was.

She stepped forward slowly, suddenly feeling panic. How would she react this morning when she saw her son? Emil tactfully pulled down the sheet then stood by her side. Mary looked at William. He seemed to be asleep. He had been washed. His face was clean and fresh looking, though from somewhere around came the sharp odour of formalin which made her nostrils crinkle.

Mary looked at William and waited. There was nothing. No pain, no remorse, no regrets; simply a void.

She took a deep breath, nodded to Emil who pulled the sheet up again. At the door, Mary stopped, turned and held his eyes. Very slowly, she gave a tiny nod and, resting her right hand on the wall, she let her fingers tap a silent, delicate, dot, dot, dot, dash in reply. Emil's expressionless face cracked, his lips twitching into a short grin. His eyes shone with the fire of respect and admiration. Then, he pulled himself to brisk attention and solemnly bowed his head to her in salute.

He opened the door and the Hauptmann was waiting. Mary fixed a look of misery on her features before turning to the German.

"It is indeed my son," she said heavily, shaking her head, puckering her face to suggest more tears hovered.

Emil solicitously held her arm in support while the German, hating his job at that moment, opened a large notebook.

"Where were you last night, Frau? he asked with quiet firmness.

"In St Peter Port," Mary replied truthfully, sniffing hard to keep the tears back and Emil's admiration moved to an even higher peak.

"Where?"

"I had to stay the night at my shop," Mary explained, using the rehearsed excuse. "I have a tiny flat above it and I worked on my accounts and part of a stock check. I simply never realised the time, then when I looked at my watch, I knew I could not get home before the curfew hour. I have a small bed so I slept the night there. I'm afraid I gave my shop girl a dreadful shock when she opened up this morning."

Mary knew perfectly well the story would be checked but she could find no flaw in it. She hoped he would not either.

"Do you do that often, Frau?" was the next question.

"Not often," she replied smoothly.

The German nodded and checked the known facts. They tallied. Already enquiries had been made but the Hauptmann decided this distressed mother had little to contribute to the investigation. She was the sufferer and really had behaved with commendable dignity throughout.

"Thank you, Frau," he said then, closing his notebook with a flourish. "If we discover anything you will be the first to know!" he promised.

Mary decided it would be an opportune moment to display another type of emotion. She stepped forward and offered her right hand.

"Thank you, Hauptmann. You have done an unpleasant task with tact and delicacy. If I am asked, I shall say so," she purred softly.

The German's expression changed to one of great relief. He clicked his heels meticulously, bowed his head, then bawled at the driver.

"Take Frau Noyen home with the inspector, then bring the inspector back to my office. You can do your report, inspector and it can go up with mine. I want to get this matter finalised as quickly as possible."

Emil nodded his agreement and the German, waiting for a salute than realising he would not get one without making a scene before the bereaved Frau, turned on his heels and strode back to the mortuary.

Emil flashed a look of triumph at Mary as his lips tightened. He would not salute a German if he could help it. It was such little flea bites of resistance that the Germans loathed but which were the islanders' only form of retaliation.

"Come, Madam," he said almost mellifluently at having bested the hated occupier, "I'll take you home!"

They drove in total silence, neither daring to say a word to the other with the German driver only two feet from them. They sat carefully apart, lost in engrossed thoughts. Emil hugged the episode to himself. How he would love to trumpet it all from the rooftops but he knew not one word must pass his lips.

Mary almost sagged with relief. Her instinct told her she had managed to get away with it. The most dangerous gamble of her whole life.

The car stopped outside her home, taking her by surprise, so deeply engrossed had she been in her thoughts. She turned to Emil.

"Thank you for everything, Inspector," she said heavily, aware of the driver's ears flapping with interest. "I shall arrange a very quiet, strictly private funeral which I think is best, don't you? Nothing in the paper but a notice of the day of the funeral and time of the committal. Would it be possible for you to see the editor for me? You see, I don't think I am up to getting in touch with him on the telephone, let alone going back into the town again. I also feel I would like to be alone."

"Of course, madam!" Emil promised quickly. Oh how he wanted

to give *her* a salute! He yearned to hug her for her bravery, but all he could do was throw her the most casual nod he could muster, see her to her front door and, slipping back in the car, order the driver away with a brief wave of his right hand.

Mary walked through to the kitchen where Amelia hovered over the stove, not doing anything in particular but seeming to bang saucepans unnecessarily loudly. Tears were in evidence.

"I'll tell you in a moment," Mary said. "Where's Raoul?"

"Out the back," Amelia said with a heavy sniff.

Mary stepped outside and Raoul straightened from where he was digging a small patch of ground. She walked quickly over to him.

"It's all OK," Mary told him rapidly, "but come in so I can explain to Amelia what she must know!"

"Right!" he grunted as relief made his legs turn to jelly. He was getting far too old for this constant tension and he had felt sick with fear as Mary had been driven away.

Amelia gave them a hot concoction of something with an odd taste but they drank it without question as they waited for her to sit down around the table with them.

"Yes, it was William," Mary started. "I identified his body!"

Very carefully, selecting each word with precision for Amelia's benefit, Mary told her story. Neither of them interrupted. Raoul was on edge, holding his breath but Amelia listened goggle-eyed. She gasped twice as Mary related the more unpleasant details while her cheeks turned bright red with embarrassment. Raoul watched his wife out of the corner of his eyes. It had shot into his head that his dear, innocent Amelia might not even know what a homosexual was. Obviously she did and he was slightly amused to wonder from whom she had acquired this titbit of information.

Mary knew all this. She had weighed up Amelia long ago, sometimes wondering how she managed to exist in such a state of blissful ignorance and she was as astonished as Raoul when she realised Amelia did know what homosexuality meant! It flitted across Mary's mind that perhaps the occupation had changed Amelia too. Did she hold unsuspected hidden depths and, if she did, how would these break out?

"Well!" Raoul managed, appearing genuinely shocked but inwardly writhing to know all that which had been withheld for the moment. "And now?" he asked tentatively.

"Life goes on," Mary replied stiffly, flashing him a look.

He got her meaning. "While you're here, Mary, there's some soil I'd like you to look at. It's land been lying fallow and it doesn't look all that good to me."

"Right!" she said forcing a brisk tone that she did not feel. If she wanted anything at all, it was a long, unbroken sleep in her own bed.

They walked out together, leaving Amelia going over the dreadful story, too disturbed at the two deaths to query such an abrupt departure.

"Thank God," Raoul told her. "I died a thousand deaths when I saw you drive off in that car!"

Mary wickedly related what had happened, then gave Raoul a queer look. "Emil is on our side."

Raoul was startled. A copper? "How do you know that?"

Mary explained Emil's secret aside. "I think," she said carefully, "when I stay late in town again I shall not have to worry," she told him meaningfully.

"Hah!" he breathed, feeling better. "That's good!"

"I'll go over to the glass houses and tell Raymond," Mary said thoughtfully.

Raoul nodded. "I'll be over later to get another spade."

With a nod Mary turned to walk to where the glass shimmered in the weak sun. Though she knew they were quite unheated, she thought there might be something growing there. She knew she had neglected this aspect of her income for far too long. Indeed it was weeks since she had paid any close attention to

Raymond's work, she had seemed so busy going to and from the shop. Mary had a dim idea dawning that perhaps the town days might be numbered. Once the Allies invaded France and the island was cut off, no one would be able to get in or out and work from her would have reached its useful end.

She turned up the short lane to the glasshouses. She saw Raymond bending down in one of them and, peeping through the glass, she saw him carefully weeding some root crops. Outside they had others growing but they lacked manure and their seeds were of very poor quality now.

Raymond was surprised to see her. He had been expecting William now for over two weeks and he'd not been near the place, which annoyed him. There were days now when he regretted getting involved with young Noyen, who had an arrogant, dictatorial side to him that no longer impressed Raymond. It was he, Gwen and Raoul who did the heavy, back-breaking work so why should William have an automatic share?

Mary entered the glasshouse, eyes everywhere. "Hello, Raymond," she said, thinking how well he looked. He was certainly fitter and moved more easily than she did and was that her imagination or had Raymond started a line of fat around his waist? How odd under their circumstances!

The glasshouse had been prepared for the spring sewing of the tomato seed on one side. On the other were parsnip and carrots growing, though Mary saw how stunted these were. Crops quite unsuitable for growing indoors but at least they could be eaten.

"Madam?" Raymond said warily, seeing Gwen move across his line of vision carrying rubbish away. Raymond had thought long ago that he did not really care for her. She could be abrasive but one had to hand it to her, when she worked here, she placed herself under his orders and obeyed them. For a woman of her age she worked well too, but there was always something about Madam Noyen that alarmed him. When he thought of the miserable life William had told him about, he could almost hate the woman as a mother.

Mary stood a moment then spun on her heel and headed towards the small shed where she knew Raymond did his paperwork. She halted, astonished to see it was padlocked.

"What's this for?" she snapped as Raymond hurried up.

"It's my private workroom, Madam!"

"On *my* private property! Open it up!" Mary ordered coldly.

"Well," Raymond stalled, patting his pockets nervously. "I think I may have left the key at home in my other trousers."

Mary's eyes narrowed. He was lucky to have two pairs of trousers in these days when nearly all the islanders had to dress in disreputable clothing. Certainly those which he wore now were almost too fine for his type of work. The cloth was of good quality, neither patched nor shiny anywhere. His blue shirt had collar and cuffs which had not been turned either. A dull suspicion, which she afterwards knew had been growing for a while, roused its head sharply high.

She turned around, saw a shovel on one side, picked it up and before Raymond could protest she smashed it down on the padlock's hasp. Her blow was accurate and it shattered. Mary dropped the spade, forced the door open and stepped inside.

It was nothing but an old-fashioned garden shed with a crate as a seat while another doubled as work table. A variety of plant pots lay higgledy-piggledy with various tools strewn around. On the wooden floor there was dried pellets of mud and much dust.

"This is my office!" Raymond protested flying into a panic as he saw his notebook there. It was large and thick, more of a ledger, which in reality it was.

"*Your* office?" Mary asked, with a dangerous edge in her voice. She walked over, picked up the book and opened a page at random. As her eyes read her lips were tight. She turned another page, her cheeks going pink with anger, then she went back to the beginning. "I'll read this in detail later," she said coldly, tucking the ledger under her arm.

"You can't do that!" Raoul cried. "That's my private property!"

"In which case it should not be here then, should it?" Mary said with sweet acidity.

"William won't like you coming in here interfering!" Raymond shouted, frightened now.

Mary threw him a long look. "William is dead. He's been shot by a German soldier. William managed to shoot him back though so that cancels that out. From now on I shall be here every day, running my business which I regret I have neglected. Rest assured though, I shan't any more!"

Raymond was thunderstruck. "William—dead?"

"Very dead." Mary confirmed. "I've not long come back from the mortuary and I don't weep crocodile tears either. I'm sure William told you long stories about me because we did not like each other and neither did we get on. However, I expect you only heard one side of matters which, when it comes down to it, don't concern you anyhow."

"Dead!" Raymond had to repeat, sinking down on his crate seat. "I can't take it in!" he groaned.

Mary's lips were tight and her nostrils pinched. She had a good idea now what she was going to find in this ledger. Raymond and William, no doubt with Gwen aiding and abetting, appeared not only to have been collaborating with the Germans but also dabbling in the black market. No wonder Raymond was showing fat when nearly all of them were getting thin. Thank God she had decided to pry. She berated herself for not doing this before. Had Raoul suspected anything but been too embarrassed to say as Gwen was his sister? It was more than likely, she told herself.

Raymond sat stunned, looking at his boots, good ones too, Mary noted again. She tapped the ledger significantly.

"If I find more of what I've already seen on two pages you are through!" she said coldly. "You'll be out on your neck first thing in the morning and I'm prepared to let the Committee know about your activities!" she threatened. "When the Allies win it will be God help you and the rest of your profiteers! Think about it all!"

Raymond did and quailed. William's death was bad enough but for Madam to have his ledger—his heart missed a beat and he stood slowly. Turning he stepped towards Mary, then he grasped her shoulder, in one strong hand spun her unexpectedly and grabbed the ledger. Mary was surprised but reacted with quick reflexes. She kicked out and hit him in the middle of his calf but it was an ineffectual blow and Raymond was a strong man.

"That's my book." Raymond growled. "You'll not have it!"

Mary snatched it free and stumbled outside with Raymond hot on her heels.

"Give me that," Raymond snarled, temper getting the better of common sense, "or else!"

Raoul appeared suddenly, followed by Gwen: "Or else what?" he roared and sprang forward, shouldering his sister aside.

Mary gasped. "Raoul! He's profiteering!"

"You bastard!" Raoul snarled, then flung out one fist. Ordinarily, Raymond should have been able to beat him easily because Raoul too was losing his strength on their meagre diet but Raoul had the edge of surprise. Also Raymond's mind had still not assimilated the news of William's death. He was in a state of shock, simply moving automatically.

Raoul caught him flush on the jaw. Knowing he must finish this fast, he let drive a hard left to Raymond's middle that doubled him forward. He felt surging pleasure. It was good to use his fists and lash out but if only this was a German. However if Raymond had gone bad, then he was the next best target. Again Raoul's right cracked out with every ounce of strength behind the shoulder. The blow caught Raymond on the exact point of the jaw and he went down, pole axed.

"Raoul!" Gwen screamed. "You've hurt him!"

"I'll hurt the bastard more before I've finished with him," Raoul shouted back at her.

Mary stood bemused, quite scared by this violence and wondering why this should be so after what she had been through only hours ago.

Raymond lay still, unconscious, oblivious to it all, so Raoul turned to Mary.

"Get on home quick," he snapped at her. "I'll handle this!"

Mary fled as Gwen fell to her knees, sobbing wildly.

"You've really hurt him. I hate you!" she screeched up at Raoul, tears flowing down her cheeks.

"If you've been in it too then I'm finished with you as well," Raoul told her in a low growl.

"Oh you stupid fool!" Gwen shouted back at him as Raymond opened his eyes, moved his jaw experimentally and looked around owlishly. "He's only been getting food to help."

"Help who?" Raoul barked. "We've seen none of it! You've both been black-marketeering for profit while there are women with children going without! You make me sick to the bottom of my guts. Well, I'd not like to be in your shoes in the morning *and*—" he paused for effect, "—the Germans don't take kindly to that kind of behaviour either. With William gone you've no protector against them and that's been it, hasn't it? William has been taking a handsome rake-off from you. Answer me, girl!" he roared down at her.

Gwen had never seen Raoul in such a white, blinding rage. All her life she had considered him an amiable, harmless brother, without a truly serious thought in his head. This bellowing maniac was terrifying. Even as a child, Raoul had been quiet and serious; it had been she who had led. Only marriage to the dynamic, more go-ahead Raymond had shown Gwen what a bumbling fool her brother was. Certainly this fiery-eyed man with snarling teeth and bunched fists frightened the life out of her. How he had thrashed Raymond too! Who would have thought he had that in him? Respect showed in her eyes, tinged with heavy regret.

"As we are brother and sister, why can't we—?" she started carefully.

Raoul swore. "Don't try and bribe me!" he spat back at her. "Good God! You're as bad as him! You *disgust* me. The pair of you!"

Raoul turned on his heel and stormed off. He knew if he stayed and Raymond staggered to his feet to try another blow, he would end up thrashing him with genuine violence.

"Mary!" he gasped catching up with her. "Are you all right? Did he hurt you?"

She shook her head. "No—but it's just as well you appeared when you did!"

"I've just had a flaming row with my sister. I think you are going to find those two were in it up to their necks, paying William some kind of commission. My God! My own flesh and blood crawling to the Germans. It's enough to make a man puke! Anyhow, she's through. Finished! Done!" he grated, still trembling with temper. "From this moment on, I have no sister!"

Mary halted and looked at him, biting her lip. "Raoul—are you sure?" she asked in a soft voice. "She is family. You don't have any others!"

Raoul's eyes flashed. "I have you," he explained simply, "and there'll be the boys coming back from war and—others!"

"I don't want to be the cause of family trouble," Mary told him.

Raoul shook his head. "It would have happened anyhow once I learned what the pair of them had been up to. Do you know Gwen even gave me a hint to join up with them? My own sister!"

"They are both out then," Mary told him, "but what do we do for labour to work the place?"

"There's me and you if you think you won't be going to the shop so much," Raoul suggested.

"We are not strong though," Mary remarked slowly.

Raoul thought about this as they stood on the drive. "I wonder if we could get a couple of TODT slaves? It would help them too. Although our food is rotten, it would be luxury compared to what those poor devils receive."

Mary nodded. It was an idea. "I expect the Germans would want a rake-off."

Raoul snorted. "It seems to me they've been getting this anyhow through William and those two back there!"

"I'll approach that Hauptmann who told me about William," she murmured. "He might be sympathetic. He can but say no!"

"Make it clear that we are on food production," Raoul added hastily.

Mary touched the ledger. "If I let the Hauptmann see this— Raymond and Gwen will be arrested. I'd not feel good about that. God knows where they could end up."

Raoul was inclined not to give a damn at the moment but he could see Mary would have a guilty conscience if they were deported.

"Just give the Committee the facts and ask them to arrange what they can," he suggested cunningly. "Why not let them see that book too!"

Mary brightened. It was one way out of the impasse and she put the ledger in his hands. "Here! You deal with it. I have a feeling if I read that and find what I expect to find I'll be after those two with the carving knife. Anyhow, I honestly don't feel like coping with any more worries. Tonight I want to sleep and sleep and sleep." she said, suddenly sad and washed out.

Raoul patted her arm. "Why don't you go in now and go to bed? Damn me, no one can blame you after what you've been through. Leave all this to me," he said kindly, pushing her towards the front door. "Go and sleep the clock round and let me handle what I can."

Mary turned, smiling gently. "Thank you, Raoul. You know,

393

my life these last few years would have been dreadful without you and Amelia. I sometimes doubt I could have carried on all alone."

Raoul went scarlet with embarrassment and pleasure. "Get in," he growled to hide his feelings, "and just do as you are told for once!"

TWENTY-ONE

RAYMOND AND GWEN were ostracised and left the parish and their home. The Committee had them both up for questioning and it was made very clear to them that they would be lucky to find any sympathy on the island, such was the disgust with which profiteers were held by the majority of islanders.

"Where did Gwen and her husband go, do you know?" Mary asked Raoul one morning.

"To the other side of the island, though fat lot of good it will do them. When the war finally ends, there'll be no place for them on Guernsey. They are relatively safe at the moment, living with others of their kind but God help them, a day of reckoning will come."

Mary wondered how they were managing to live. Without William's help they would have little money for food but she felt no pity for them. Their crime had been unforgivable when so many of the islanders were sliding into genteel starvation.

True to his word, Raoul found two TODT slaves to work in the glasshouses but the two skeletally thin youths who appeared had the gaunt faces of men three decades older. They were useless until they had been given food. Even the islanders' limited rations must have appeared as a banquet because it was wolfed down.

Somehow Raoul managed to browbeat the Germans into providing some extra rations and, for a while, they fattened up a little and were able to help. Then out of the blue, the TODT slaves were all removed from Guernsey and vanished as if they had never been.

In March of that year an Irish informer leaked to the Germans the names of the brave men who turned out the *GUNS* newspaper. They were arrested, interrogated with severity and sent to hard prisons on the Continent. Without the *GUNS* newspaper, information became hard to receive.

Owning a wireless was now as dangerous as having a firearm though a few defiant, heroic people still did. What they learned was passed only by quiet word of mouth to selected, trustworthy recipients because gradually, after so many years of occupation, a dull rot had begun to set in. Many girls were open Jerrybags and Mary was often scared about her work.

The fisherman's visits were erratic and how he slipped in and out of Guernsey was a mystery to Mary. He brought no letters though and it seemed ages since she had heard from Margaret or Victor. Even the Red Cross mail that did arrive was sparse.

Mary worried incessantly about her daughter and Victor, who now seemed a dream. Sometimes she had a job picturing his face and it was out of the question to think of him coming into her shop. This was another problem. The shop's shelves had so little to sell. What food they did manage to grow was handed to Amelia who stored it in the cottage loft for safety but she always set aside a portion to be taken to those worse off than themselves. They were gradually being reduced to eating anything which was not poisonous. Seaweed, tea from bramble leaves, boiling their precious root vegetables in sea water and eating bread which had so much brick dust in it that their teeth began to wear down. Fuel was more valuable than gold and there was only enough for cooking. In the cold weather people wore all their clothes and often went to bed in the afternoons to conserve energy and keep warm.

It was worst for the mothers with children. Mary heard of one poor woman who, at Christmas time, had searched her home.

All she had been able to give them for a present was one sugar lump each tinted with a little colour. For the children who had gone to Britain life would be better but, at the same time, they were growing up away from their island and estranged from their parents. Misery affected them all.

In March of 1944, Hitler designated all the Channel Islands his official land fortresses, which made the islanders feel even more cut off. There were eleven very heavy gun batteries with thirty-eight guns. The garrisons of Jersey and Guernsey now comprised 35,000 German soldiers when totalled with all their ancillaries. All had to be fed and looked after because although the Germans did bring food over, it was nowhere near enough.

The horses were turned out in the fields where hungry eyes often viewed them speculatively. In early June, a ripple of hysteria ran through the island at the Normandy invasion. Amelia wept for relief and Raoul brightened but Mary was not so sure.

"They'll not come here," she foretold as she had in the past. "They'll pass us by to get into Germany itself!"

Mary sat in the shop one evening as usual. She did not think the old man would turn up and was astonished when he did. Quickly she followed her usual routine. Now the old man knew how hungry they were, he accepted a cup of plain boiled water without comment. From under the same sweater he passed a little parcel. He was as taciturn as ever but Mary did not mind.

"What is it?" she asked hopefully.

"Some swedes, two parsnips and two onions," he said and beamed, pleased with himself.

"Oh!" Mary cried, hugging it to her. What Amelia could do with these roots! The struggle to give them all meals was a strain stretching even Amelia's inventive cooking with a corresponding effect on her temper. "Here are my notes," she said, handing them over.

"I doubt I'll be coming much more," the fisherman said. "Not with the invasion."

Mary's heart sank but she saw the sense of this. Why risk his neck when the Allies were in France? It was the beginning of the end for Hitler. She nodded. She would miss him. Even though little conversation had passed between them, the old man had become a cherished link.

"Take care then, old friend," she whispered, touching one gnarled, strong hand. "Don't run any risks at this late stage of the game."

"I'll not," he grunted, then, as silently as he came, he went. Mary waited until he had to be clear then opened her shop door and jumped as a shadow loomed.

"It's only me, Madam, 'le Norman'!"

Mary closed her eyes. She was getting to be a bundle of nerves from constant tension.

"Is there anything wrong, Emil?" she asked fearfully. It was the first time he had ever called upon her. Indeed she had not seen him since the day he had accompanied her to the mortuary.

Emil peered around in the subdued light, shaking his head at her shelves. The few goods offered for sale were stretched out in a thin line to cover blank spaces. He shook his head sorrowfully and nodded.

"As bad as that?" he asked quietly.

Mary nodded. "I should, if I had any sense, shut the shop down until the Allies come but it would mean putting Alice out of a job and she is walking out with a young man. She's such a nice girl, I cannot do it," she told him heavily. She'd like to shut the shop too so that she could stop coming into town. With the Normandy invasion she was, she knew, redundant. The old fisherman would certainly not come again. He had no need. Her usefulness was ended and she was not sorry. All she wanted to do was stay at Cobo and survive until they were freed.

Emil nodded to himself, having worked everything out in his sharp, methodical mind.

"If you think the girl can handle the few supplies you get coming in and you don't want to come to town any more, I'll keep an eye on the place," he offered.

He was concerned about the looks of Madam Noyen. She was horribly thin and not a good colour. She moved with an effort and he recognised slow starvation. Victor would never forgive him if anything happened to her at this late stage of the war. Since the shooting he had kept a discreet watching brief on her and always checked that the old man had managed to get away safely. It was the very least he could do though there had been many times when he itched to take a gun and kill Germans.

Mary looked at him hopefully. "Alice could do that," she agreed. "She knows my ways now and she could take her money from the takings. She is honest through and through."

"Well, consider that settled then," he told her. "You'll not be needed of an evening any more—now," he added significantly.

Mary gave him a sharp look and could not help a grin touching her lips. What a cunning fox he was!

"We'll have a lot to tell them when they come back, won't we?"

He nodded vigorously. "Indeed, yes."

Names did not have to be said. They understood each other and grinned conspiratorially. Mary thought Emil had aged but working all these years with the Germans must have put him under intolerable strain. We are all heart attack material, she mused to herself but I'll survive. I will, she vowed.

"The Germans are going to get hungry too," he predicted, acutely aware that once the whole French coast was in enemy hands, the Germans might as well surrender. Mary read his mind. "Will they?" she asked quickly.

He pursed his lips. "I don't know. I hope to God they do because if not—" He let the sentence fall.

"Surely they are not *that* stupid?" Mary objected.

Le Norman shrugged. "The German mentality takes some

understanding. A lot depends upon the man at the top and how much he happens to value his own skin!"

Mary gritted her teeth. "We are all so impotent!"

The inspector turned. The shop door was just ajar and there were only a handful of people on the street now. He moved a bit nearer to her.

"All the TODT slaves have been removed from Alderney," he said in a low voice.

Mary stiffened. "Have they?" she murmured thoughtfully. "That means the Germans expect the Allies to do something—or they want to hide the evidence of their cruelty from the world!"

Her expression changed as the thought of Alderney brought back horrible memories. She shivered suddenly, her expression turning grave, which Emil didn't fail to miss. He had often wondered and suddenly sensed now was the time to ask.

"Madam, off the record of course, what did happen on Alderney those years ago?" he asked softly.

Mary slowly lifted bleak eyes to hold his. "You must indeed have been puzzled but it was all quite simple and quite horrible. William killed his brother Edwin but there was never any proof and though William was only twelve years, there was no way anyone would have beaten a confession out of him. Even though so young, William always had a deep streak in him. I just had to live with it all."

Emil closed his eyes and shook his head before speaking again. "So *that* was it!" he paused thinking deeply, going over more recent events in his mind. "In which case, Madam, it was, shall we say, a late judicial execution. Your conscience is quite clear," he ended firmly.

Mary broke eye contact. The nightmares had stopped but the memories remained and one day she would have to tell Margaret and Victor—if he were still alive.

"Do you ever hear anything about James and Victor?" she asked hopefully.

He studied her questioning eyes and slowly shook his head. "I'm afraid not. Once I was privy to odd titbits of information but since the invasion little news reaches my ears. I'm afraid all we can do is wait until we are released."

With a heavy heart Mary shook her head, then reached into her pocket and produced the keys. She handed them to him wistfully.

"Perhaps you could explain to Alice?" she asked. "If there should be a desperate problem I'd walk over from Cobo but—" She paused. "I'll be glad to rest now."

"Just you leave everything with me and Madam, go home now," he told her kindly, sensing a wild desperation in her as her morale slumped. "Just hang on for a little while longer. It's all coming to a slow end."

Mary could say nothing, only throw him a grateful smile. Even the thought of walking back home now was daunting, yet the knowledge it might be for the last time gave her relief.

She thought it was the most miserable Christmas she had known. Their own food stocks were reduced to whatever they could obtain by bartering or what they had managed to grow and preserve. With the island completely cut off as the Allies fought their way towards Germany, conditions deteriorated badly.

"The Germans have started to kill some of their horses to eat," Raoul told them one evening as they sat around the kitchen table after a meal comprising a thin, tasteless soup Amelia had managed to make from some old root crops and a handful of poor potatoes.

"I wish we could get hold of some horsemeat," Mary sighed, knowing it was impossible.

The Germans too were hungry. Soldiers had been seen going through the islanders' dustbins searching for anything edible yet, she had to admit, their discipline held. The middle-aged officers at her house had lost weight like the rest of them. Their once snug uniforms bagged on thin bodies and their faces were gaunt though they were nowhere near the desperate state of the islanders.

"Churchill should not have stopped a food ship coming to us," Amelia said angrily. "It's all very well for him. He's not starving because that is what is happening to us."

Mary sighed. "The reason is because he doesn't want food going to the Germans to strengthen their hold here," she explained with a patience she did not feel. Nowadays Amelia was getting very argumentative, her natural reaction to a shrunken stomach.

"The Committee should do something!" Raoul said hotly. "Haven't they heard of the Swiss Red Cross?"

Unknown to all of them until it came out later, the Committee had indeed taken drastic steps. Victor Carey, a very much thinner Bailiff, did send a wild cry for help to the Swiss. In November he warned them there would be no bread left by the middle of December. Sugar stocks would run out in the first week of January while soaps and other cleansers were already exhausted. There would be no fuel, gas or electricity by the end of the year and medical stocks were already virtually exhausted. Disease stared the islanders in the face, both occupied and occupiers. Without fuel, water could not be pumped and sanitation would break down. They also heard rumours there was dire trouble between Count von Schmettow and Admiral Kranke in overall charge of Guernsey. While the Germans rowed between themselves, the islanders became thinner and hungrier, with many of the few remaining pets mysteriously disappearing.

"We are so weak. I don't feel as if I have the strength of a kitten," Mary said to no one in particular. "If only we could go and fish," she groaned one evening as she sat at the table, head in hands. By common consensus, the Ozanne kitchen had become their meeting ground. They spent much of their free time in the little room which was slightly warmer than anywhere else. All three of them wore all the clothes possible to keep warm, apparel which would have been thrown into the dustbin in pre-war days.

It was only the next day though that Raoul came up the road, walking faster than he should have in his weakened state. He had been down to see if there was a wild chance of finding any shellfish to eat on the beach where it was not mined but already others with the same hungry idea had gleaned it empty.

He entered the cottage, slumped in a chair, fighting to catch his breath while his eyes gleamed. Mary had just come in from hopefully turning over the cottage garden in case they had missed a potato or turnip in the autumn. She stood the dirty spade by the door. None of them bothered about mud or dirt now. They seemed trivial matters when the belly was empty.

"News!" Raoul managed to get out at last. "Wonderful news! The Red Cross are sending a rescue ship with food for us. It's supposed to be on its way right now from Lisbon."

Mary gaped at him and slumped against a wall. "Oh my God! Is that really true? Not a hoax?"

"Real—food?" Amelia asked, with a catch in her voice.

Raoul nodded and Mary turned to him. "Come on! Up to the house, I'll ring a town contact."

The ragged trio left the cottage and walked slowly up the lane. Mary led the way to her telephone and rang the number of a man with whom she'd done business long ago.

"Pierre!" she cried, ignoring the equally hungry Germans who lounged around apathetically listening curiously. "We have just heard a rumour there is a food ship on its way to us. Is it true?"

Pierre Lamond grated back at her, the line crackling. "You are out of date for once, Mary! It's not only true but the ship is coming into harbour right now. She's the *Vega* and is loaded with enough food to give each and every islander a personal parcel." Mary held the receiver so Raoul and Amelia could hear. "There will also be stocks for the Committee to apportion. The parcels have come from New Zealand and Canada. You'd better get yourselves here as soon as you can."

Mary dropped the phone, as tears streamed down her cheeks. Then she hugged Amelia and flung herself at Raoul. Finally the three of them became aware of eight German eyes watching wistfully. It flashed through Mary's mind that starvation would affect the Germans far worse than the islanders. The occupiers had been used to eating normally then suddenly their rations had vanished whereas the islanders' stomachs had shrunk gradually over the years and their tolerance was consequently stronger. Even the officers had been out early that morning hopefully combing the hedges for any edible berries.

"Today we rest," Mary said firmly. "Tomorrow we walk to town to get our parcels and news!"

Raoul and Amelia nodded. It would drain them of the little strength they had left but all of them knew they would march to Berlin to get real food.

"Food!" Raoul drooled, as they went outside away from gaunt German eyes.

"I wonder what will be in a parcel?" Amelia murmured wistfully. "Do you think there might be some real tea?"

Mary looked at her thoughtfully. Amelia, as their chosen quartermaster, gave the orders regarding what they ate and when. Months ago though they had decided that if a dispute should arise they would be democratic and vote on the matter. Mary hesitated. Amelia's temper was volatile these days but she had to speak her mind.

"If we should each have a little tea in our parcels, what do you say we give some to the Germans?"

Amelia went up in a sheet of flame. "Never!" she shouted, her cheeks going bright red with anger. "How can you even think of such a thing? You should be ashamed of yourself. They came here and occupied us without as much as a by-your-leave and we have been living under these conditions for nearly five years.

My boys are away fighting them and now you suggest we share a precious food parcel with them? NO!" she thundered.

"Amelia!" Raoul started gently.

She promptly turned on him, her breasts heaving her wrath. "And don't you start either!" she warned.

Mary took a deep breath. "I don't agree with you," she replied evenly as Amelia turned to glower at her. "They were good enough to share with us the rations they brought back from their leaves. Remember that fantastic coffee that day? I think it saved my life!"

Amelia had forgotten but she was wound up like a tight spring. The years of the occupation had changed her too.

"We'll put it to the vote later, shall we?" Raoul suggested delicately.

Amelia flew at him. "I shall vote No!" she said as if that decided the matter once and for all.

Raoul flashed a warning look at Mary. They were such good friends with secrets between them unknown to Amelia. She interpreted his meaning. He would work on Amelia in bed that night but now Mary must keep her mouth tightly shut.

They were all up early the next morning when breakfast was a cup of boiled water with a few dried herbs brewed in the communal tea pot and one slice each of stale, dry ersatz bread with nothing on it.

They set out walking gently, conscious of their weakened state but luck was with them, after only half a mile a cart appeared pulled by a bony horse.

"Going to town for the food ship," the driver bellowed with excitement. "Jump in!"

The three of them now filled the cart to overflowing. Each eyed the horse dubiously.

"We must all get out for the hills," the driver warned them. "I don't want the horse dropping dead in the shafts out here. If there's not enough food, my family and I will eat him."

They did not speak but each one of them quivered with barely suppressed excitement. Mary's mouth watered with anticipation and a sneak glance at Amelia showed a stiff, cool face. Anxiously she peeped at Raoul who pulled a face, then pursed his lips in a silent message. It was obvious Amelia was still in a mood but not as volatile as the day before. She was slowly coming round but it would be imprudent to mention a touchy subject at this moment. Far better to wait until they were back home with their precious parcels.

They left the cart on the harbour fringes because of the giant crowd of excited islanders all craning to peer at the rescue ship on which many men bustled about purposefully. Mary saw the Bailiff and members of the Controlling Committee with Germans co-operating in pushing people into an orderly queue. The line was long, winding backwards and forwards, but the islanders were patient. They had waited so very, very long, a little longer would make it all worthwhile.

Raoul turned to Mary. "It's going to take ages for our turn to come. Let's take it in turns to queue," he said sensibly. You go and sit down somewhere with Amelia. Amelia can give me a rest."

Mary saw through his game. "I can take my turn too!" she told him forcefully.

Raoul sighed. Now she was going to argue when he knew perfectly well she was the weakest of the three. He and Amelia had not been walking to town and back for years.

He took Mary aside firmly. "You, for once, will do as you are told. We have not been burning up energy like you. When your turn comes then you can come to the queue. Until then, get yourself sat down somewhere within sight of me and don't damned well argue. I'm not in the mood to cope with tantrums from you as well as my wife."

Mary blinked. She had never heard Raoul use such an exasperated tone of voice and a faint, hysterical hunger-giggle rose. Suddenly she did not wish to press the point because she realised how right he was. It was a simple relief to have everything taken from her hands; to let someone else deal with responsibility, marvellous to feel cherished and taken care of after battling by herself for so many years.

"All right," she agreed quickly. "I'll go and sit down there," she pointed. "On that bollard where those crewmen are working!"

Moving gently to conserve strength, Mary sauntered down the slope and propped herself on a cast iron bollard very near to the *Vega*'s bows. She was aware she was eyed by two German soldiers but they obviously decided one person so near to the ship could not make a riot.

Mary shivered. She felt so cold despite the layers of dirty clothing she was wearing. Her thoughts drifted from food to a hot bath. Nowadays she never felt clean. They had only cold water with which to wash and could not get their clothes properly clean. Her skin sometimes itched with ingrained dirt and dried sweat so she fantasised about steaming bath water with perfume in it and herself wallowing and luxuriating.

Idly she watched the *Vega*'s crew. How well fed they looked, how easily and quickly they moved about their tasks. Their clothes were clean, they wore good shoes on their feet and their eyes were bright within healthy faces. The giggle lifted again; what a lot of dirty ragamuffins the islanders must appear to them.

She became aware of one man halting now and again to scan the watching German soldiers, then examine the islanders' queue. He was not doing much real work, she thought curiously. He was more intent on studying starving, dishevelled people. How rude, she told herself indignantly. It's not our fault we are like this.

Then his eyes alighted upon her and his forehead creased in a frown. Mary looked back at him unblinkingly, noticing his dark grey hair with a thick beard to match. Fancy staring like that at me, she thought, and drew herself a little more upright to glare back at this impertinence.

The crewman jumped on the quay, spoke briefly to a German soldier then was striding vigorously up to her. He wore a thick rolled neck sweater of dark blue with trousers the same colour. Mary eyed the clothing. How wonderfully warm it must be and so clean and fresh! She could not help but feel a pang of envy. Averting her eyes, she threw a glance at the queue and Raoul waved back. Amelia was near him talking animatedly to someone. Mary gave a gentle wave to acknowledge Raoul, turned to look at the *Vega* again when the crewman appeared to stand before her only two feet away.

Mary looked up and her heart stopped dead. She would know those violet eyes anywhere. With a thud her heart started beating again as her mouth opened, lips moving in soundless wonder while a lump rose to lodge in the middle of her throat.

He knelt down so his eyes were level with hers. "Catherine! My sweet wonderful Catherine," he crooned. "I've been praying you'd be here. I've been scanning the queue for hours in a panic I'd miss you. We are not allowed to come any further on to the island than this. How are you?"

Victor was horrified. He had not at first recognised this bedraggled, starving, woman until she sat up stiffly with her old mannerism of lifting her jaw a fraction against whatever life was getting ready to throw at her. Her face was gaunt; the bones standing out in sharp relief. Her cheeks were white and unhealthy. Her hands trembled a little and he saw ingrained dirt. He wanted to take her in his arms, crush her against his chest, then jump on a magic carpet and fly her away to somewhere warm and sunny with food and clean beauty.

Mary began to tremble from the shock. She could not help it as the tears welled up unbidden to trickle down her cheeks as her lips quivered. It was him. As strong, virile and masculine as ever and he was safe, alive, here, looking at her, his eyes gentle, sad and appalled at her condition.

"Victor?" was all she could manage.

He took her hands gently, feeling how frail they were and his heart nearly broke. He shook his head, words hard to find for a few seconds.

"I had to fight like hell to get this berth to come here and see you," he told her softly.

"It—*is* you?" Mary asked, her voice breaking.

He realised he must lighten the situation. She looked as if she would faint.

"Well, how many other Heathcliffs do you know?" he jested. His hand touched his face. "It's the beard but it makes a lovely disguise!"

"Victor! Oh Victor! I am so hungry! We all are. Do you really have lovely food on that ship?" she nodded at the *Vega*. "Is it really true that we are all going to get a parcel? Please tell me," she cried.

He caught his breath. "Dear God! What the hell has been happening here?" he asked roughly.

Mary started sobbing gently, unable to control herself any longer. "I'm so hungry, Victor!" she whimpered, like a little child.

He was horrified, stunned into inaction for a few moments as the situation slowly dawned upon him. He threw a glance at the pathetic people collecting a parcel each. He saw how everyone's face lit up as a parcel was placed in two waiting hands. He saw how some stood, frozen, as if unable to believe their fortune while others wept unashamedly. Slowly each recipient walked away, holding the parcel, guarding it more preciously than gold. A lump shot into his throat while his face darkened with fury, then his eyes came back to her. She was looking hopefully at him from huge eyes. They were appealing but terrified as if it was but a dream that would change into a nightmare at any second.

He dived one hand into pocket. "Here!" he said. "Take this chocolate bar but eat it slowly!"

Mary looked down at it as if it were a grenade. She licked her lips, admired the wrapper's colours, stroked it then gently but carefully put it into one pocket of the greasy jacket she wore.

"I can't," she told him simply. "It's not allowed. You see, we pool our food and share everything. Amelia decides what we can eat and when. I take all my meals down at their cottage now. I only sleep at home."

"God almighty!" he roared and plunged a hand into another pocket. There was a second chocolate bar. With a murderous look in his eyes he stripped away the wrapper, snapped off a section and lifted it to her lips. "Eat or I'll make you!"

She opened her lips, he popped the chocolate in and slowly Mary started to chew. Chocolate! She had quite forgotten the taste. Wonder filled her eyes as he watched with a sick feeling in his guts and a grim scowl on his face.

"Slowly!" he cautioned, giving her another piece. He removed a clean handkerchief from another pocket and tenderly wiped her tears away. He had never been so appalled in all his life. They had all heard things were bad on the island but he had not envisaged this. Sarnia Cherie, he told himself, more like Sarnia hell.

Mary swallowed and looked at him with her big eyes. "That was lovely. Do you think I could have another piece without being greedy?"

His pockets were large and he'd had the forethought to fill them. Four more chocolate bars went into her hands as Mary looked at them in blind wonder. Very carefully though she opened one wrapper after putting three bars away to share. She ate slowly and was sure she could feel fresh strength going into her system from the rich food. When she had finished she licked her fingers thoroughly, then tucked them into her coat. It was joy to feel the bars of food nestling there. They were extra to the food parcels. Amelia would be delighted and should, hopefully, be in a more reasonable state of mind.

"There is more than enough food for everyone with some in reserve but I promise you, the *Vega* will be making regular runs to you now. It'll take a little while to build up stocks but you'll not be like this again. I promise you and Churchill agrees because the Germans have guaranteed not to take one crumb from one parcel."

"If the Germans have said that, then they won't" Mary told him. "They are terribly well disciplined though they are now hungry as we are."

He wasn't interested in hearing about the enemies' plight. "Tell me about you. It's been such a long time!"

Mary was reawakening. "Margaret and Michael. I want to hear about them first. I must! I've heard nothing in—years it seems," she told him, her voice rising a little with hysteria.

"Ssh!" he whispered, stroking her bony hands, wanting to hold her tight but acutely aware of the nearby soldiers. He was very much the enemy to them. A military man on active service, not in uniform, who had wangled a passage on a neutral ship. He could imagine the uproar if these soldiers realised he was a British soldier out of uniform. He dared do nothing untoward.

"Margaret is well and in the pink of health and condition. She cannot wait to get back to the island but as soon as Michael is released, they are going to have a quick, quiet wedding before coming back here to settle down."

"Without me?" Mary asked feeling sharp hurt.

He heard this in the two questioning words. "They don't want any frills or fuss. They just want to be together. You can't blame them when you think how they have been separated and even now Margaret has no idea how long it will take for Mike to get home when the war is won. Don't be upset about it all, just welcome them back as man and wife when they do come," he told her very gently.

Mary considered his words and gradually understood. "At least they are alive, which I should be thankful for," she agreed heavily. Her eyes studied him carefully now. "You do look fit and well. What have you been doing or shouldn't I ask?"

"It's no secret now," he told her. "I was dropped to a guerrilla group into France and I have been serving with them as liaison officer. That's why I was unable to let you know anything."

"The old fisherman came for a long time but then he stopped. He had warned me he'd probably not come again with the invasion. I wasn't sorry. It was such hard work walking from Cobo to town and back regularly."

His face became grim. "He's dead, I'm afraid."

"Oh no!" Mary cried. "How? What happened?"

"He made one trip too many on the wrong night," he explained slowly. "The Germans must have been getting suspicious of his activities. Anyhow, he was coming into harbour one evening when a fast sea boat challenged him. We'll never know exactly what happened nor what was in his mind. He had a revolver, pulled it out and let rip, killing a German. They opened up with a light machine gun and that was the end, I'm afraid."

Mary felt sad. "He died fighting though. He was wonderful and brave and kind, bringing us a little food when he could!" She turned her attention to him scrutinising carefully. His hair was iron grey but otherwise he looked exceptionally well and so weather beaten.

"You've not been wounded?" she asked softly.

He gave a brisk shake to his head. "I've been lucky!" he told her, not bothering to elaborate. So lucky that at one stage he had only just been a street ahead of pursuing troops, after his cell had been destroyed by a quisling traitor and he'd been forced to escape over the mountains to Spain.

"What about James—have you any news of him?"

"He's all right now but minus one foot and part of the leg. He stepped on a mine and don't ask me any more. He'll not fight again and probably he'll be back here before me but you should see him getting around now. He has an artificial foot and leg and he can just about keep up with me," he said, trying to make light of it all.

Mary's eyes closed with pain. At least *he* was alive. "Do you know anything of the Ozanne boys. Raoul and Amelia are my close friends, without them—"

"The last I heard of them they were living the lives of the devil wenching with the free French maidens, having themselves a real ball and I guess by now they'll be on their way to Germany and Berlin. They are a rough, tough pair, the salt of our Guernsey earth!"

"Thank goodness!" she breathed with relief. "I'll tell them when we get back." She nodded towards the slowly moving queue. "You can't sneak back to Cobo?"

He gave a heavy sigh. "I'd love to but I can't. We sail again today back to Portugal," he explained heavily. There was so much to learn about her; so much to relate but it would have to wait.

"Your family?" Mary asked him.

"James is at school, doing very well but infuriated the war's going to end before he can do his bit."

"Nicole?" Mary prodded.

He did stop to collect his thoughts. It was true Nicole no longer ranted and raved; instead there were days when she did not seem to be in the same world. It seemed he was doomed to be tied to Nicole and the only straw to which he dared cling was the idea she might get tired of him.

Mary sensed there was a problem but suddenly did not wish to know. One day perhaps, when it was all over and she might be able to help.

"When will you come home, as soon as Berlin falls?"

"I honestly don't know," he admitted sadly. "There's nothing I'd like more than to put my roots down here again but he who wins the war also has to win the peace. Don't forget there is still Japan. I hope to wangle a leave as soon as possible when the island is freed. Any problems with William?"

Mary was startled. "William is dead. He died quite a while ago," she said in a low voice.

He was staggered, quite unprepared for this turn of events. "What happened?"

It was her turn to touch one of his hands. "I don't want to talk about it," she told him firmly. "Not now."

He knew when he had been excluded deliberately just as he also knew when not to pry. When he did return, there would be ways and means to find out. He looked at her lowered head. What was she hiding? Dear God, what had happened to her after his last visit? There was such yearning inside him to kiss her but one of the soldiers cleared his throat and moved a pace nearer, eyeing them with the greatest interest.

"Mary!" Raoul bellowed down at her. "Come on now. It's nearly our turn!" he cried with excitement.

Mary looked up at Victor, eyes wide. "I'll have to go. I cannot bear not to have my parcel now."

He pulled her to her feet. "Go and get it and enjoy it. There will be plenty more coming. You'll never be hungry again, any of you."

"We'll all come back here!" she said quickly. She could not part from him so abruptly.

He shook his head slowly. "That might not be wise," he said flicking his eyes towards the soldiers, "and anyhow, I have to get back aboard. See, it looks as if the hold is empty which means sailing very quickly to catch the tide. Take care of yourself, heart of my heart. I will come back, but when I know not. As soon as you are liberated, Margaret will be here and James." He paused. "Ever see Emil?"

Mary nodded eagerly. "Often. He's tired and hungry too but well and has been good to me. He helped when I needed it desperately. Look, I must go!"

"Go then," he said softly and, damning the Germans, leaned forward to give her a quick kiss. He spun on his heels, glowered at the Germans, then vaulted up on deck again. Once more he was on Portuguese territory and no one could stop him watching her. He saw her join the Ozannes and realised he would never have recognised them either if Mary had not told him. It was a good job their boys were not here. They'd just as likely turn their guns on every German in sight. He stored up pictures and memories as he watched his personal group of three take a precious parcel each from the authorities. He saw them step aside and show each other. He saw them turn and three hands waved to him then, with Raoul in the middle, they slowly set off on the long haul back to Cobo. He strained with his eyes, not wanting to lose even one last peep but their heads were gradually lost among the crowd still winding their patient way down to the ship. Where was his spirited, fiery Catherine?

TWENTY-TWO

THEY SAT AROUND the Ozanne kitchen and listened to Mary's gentle words and tears streamed down Amelia's face while Raoul coughed, clearing his throat unnecessarily. They had had no idea with whom Mary had been talking. Victor's grey beard and hair had changed him completely and Mary had waited until they were back at the cottage before enlightening them.

"My boys!" Amelia sang softly.

Raoul was too choked for words but he sniffed, bit his bottom lip then unfastened his parcel. He dare not speak; he knew he would break down too which would never do.

"Look!" Raoul gasped and they all gazed with awe, hardly daring to do more than rest light fingers on their food. Real tea and coffee, biscuits, chocolate, marmalade, jam, cheeses, tinned meats—the parcel seemed never-ending, down to cigarettes.

"Oh!" Mary gasped. "And it's real too! Look at the wrappings! Feel! Real tea and coffee—" Then she stopped and threw Amelia a look.

Amelia's eyes held hers then dropped first. "Oh very well," she grumbled trying to be sour, but failing. Raoul's homily had gone home but the final breakdown of her resistance had been the wonderful news of her precious sons.

"Raoul?" Mary asked, holding up one packet of tea.

"Give it to them. I guess two wrongs don't make one right and they did share that coffee with us," he said with good nature then he turned back to the food, which Amelia was placing on the table with the loving care with which she would handle fine, delicate porcelain. "I wonder when we'll get some flour for real bread? Bread, butter and cheese," he anticipated, mouth slavering for in his parcel there was some tinned butter.

Amelia grinned at him, her heart lighter. What a wonderful start to 1945.

Mary picked up the packet of tea. "I'm going up to the house," she told them. "I know they are all now worried sick about the huge raids on Germany and their families. They are all frightened of what's going to happen to them too."

Amelia lifted her head and a reserve of tartness flashed. "In that case, they shouldn't invade people's islands!"

Raoul flashed a look at Mary and she took the hint, slipping out of the door before Amelia could change her mind about the small packet of tea. The last thing she could bear was a row between the three of them.

Mary went into her home, entering the lounge that the officers used. The four of them sprang to their feet at her arrival.

"We've just collected our food parcels," she began quietly. "You shared your coffee with us when we had none. Here is a packet of tea for you."

She thrust the packet into the hands of the oldest man, who must have been of her own age. He took the packet with wonder, his face creasing into great pleasure while the other officers looked from the tea, to the Frau and back to the tea again. One licked his lips with anticipation.

"Vielen dank, meine frau!"

They then stood, all slightly embarrassed, uncertain what to do or say next. Mary knew it was up to her to break this awkward impasse.

"Don't forget to warm the pot properly first and make sure the water is really boiling!" she told them, then turned, trotted up the stairs and locked herself in her room to burst into wild tears of longing, sadness and sheer exhilarating hope.

Relief charged her batteries. Margaret was safe and well and would be coming home later this year. The war was ending slowly but what would she now be like? She had been away five whole years and had left as a young girl. Now she would be a mature woman, one who had been through a different kind of war with the pain and anguish of being separated from her love.

Her thoughts switched to Victor and she smiled tenderly to herself. He had survived so far. Unlike poor James, he had shown himself to her sound of wind and limb. Pray God he continued with such luck. It occurred to her that he too might have stories he would never relate; bringing them out into the open would only cause pain. There were going to be many like her who would only wish to forget, to put it all behind them and start again.

She examined her true feelings. He still had that magic charisma for her which she knew no other man would ever produce. He was still married though, so where did that leave both of them? Mary had a shrewd idea that the long war would have changed standards.

She would live each day as it came and play it all by ear but, after being alone for so long, the thought of lying in his arms at night was touchingly painful. They were both in their forties and with good health, they could live for many years yet. She took a deep breath, her smile crinkling her lips, throwing light on her thin face as she pictured life with him.

The island throbbed with expectation as the Allies crossed onto German soil and it was a harrowing time for the occupiers. With the food parcels and the rations brought by the Red Cross ships, the islanders began to flesh out again.

The Jerrybags trembled, knowing full well how their fellow islanders might turn upon them once German protection vanished. The informers were petrified. They wanted to go but were trapped like everyone else. Many talked of selling up and migrating to make a fresh life. Once the liberation came, there would be scores to settle and fear filled the air to intermingle with hope.

For the Germans it was now their bad time. They suffered. They had no food parcels and it was they who became gaunt shadows but their discipline held firm. Not one German soldier stole an islander's food parcel. What crime there was over the parcels, including two terrible murders of an old couple, were the work of islanders. The Germans were apprehensive about their fate under the Allies but, most of all, they were worried to distraction at what was happening in Germany. As the weeks passed, the Allied Armies advanced and many of the islanders found compassion in themselves for the German troops especially the young raw recruits who had come to the island and been trapped. It was pointless to carry out a vendetta against these losers.

Through the early months of 1945 the tension rose with each month, then week. Rumour and gossip sped hot-foot all over the island and, in May, it peaked when it was known that HMS *Bulldog*, escorted by the destroyer *Beagle* had liaised with a German ship.

Now that she was stronger, Mary went into the shop once a week. There were some goods they could sell but mostly she went to get the current news, to chat to Alice, to talk with Emil and to prepare for the Great Day.

On one morning as she walked the last few yards she grinned to see Union and Guernsey flags already sprouting patriotically despite the fact they were still occupied. The few Germans she saw discreetly looked the other way so Mary marched into her shop briskly.

"Alice!" she cried. "We have a Union flag somewhere! Get it out and fly it high!"

The girl blinked at Mary's stern tone of voice. "The Germans?" she questioned nervously.

"Damn them!" Mary snorted. "We're not going to be the one place without a welcome to the Tommies!"

Alice hurried to the back room and found the flag, which had been folded, wrapped up and hidden from alien eyes. She emerged, red-faced but triumphant, holding it in her hand. Mary grabbed it, then ran up to her flat. It was a long time now since she had spent time in it and there was a coating of dust everywhere. This she ignored, flung open a window with a bang then, leaning out, fixed her flag to a short pole that had once been part of the wireless aerial. The flag hung limp for a moment, almost as if shocked from its sleep, then came a puff of wind and the Union flag stirred and waved. A few passers-by below caught the flash of moving red, white and blue and stopped to cheer approval. Mary heard the doorbell ting but ignored it as she leaned out, grinning wildly, feeling as mad and crazy as a young girl. *This* was what victory and liberation felt like! It was—wonderful!

"Madam!" Alice called up to her. "There's a woman wants to see you!"

Mary grunted, not really wanting to leave this delightful perch of triumph but she withdrew, shut the window and trudged downstairs. She looked over at the woman and scowled.

"Yes?" she snapped harshly.

Alice was startled, looking from one to the other she sensed something hostile. It was a long time since she had seen Madam wearing that cold mask and she hastily left the shop, tactfully retreating to the back room with a long handled brush.

"Oh Mary! Please don't you turn against me now!" Gwen Falla pleaded, wringing her hands, her face frightened and harrowed.

"What do you want?" Mary snapped not making any attempt to help her though she was taken aback at Gwen's appearance. There was an ugly bruise on her face and the woman was haggard, thin and unkept. She should not look like this. They should have received food parcels like the rest of them.

"It's Ray. He's hurt. He's been beaten up!" Gwen told her breaking into gasping sobs. "Please help him!"

Mary's lips set tight as mind and heart wrestled with each other. Sight of Gwen automatically brought back a vision of William as he lay dying; a memory she was trying to stamp to the dark recesses of her mind. She thought of Raoul—what would he do? He was not a vindictive man, but the Fallas had behaved deplorably and, Mary argued with her usual innate honesty, wasn't she just a little to blame? She had neglected the glasshouses at a crucial period. If she had supervised more efficiently, perhaps the Fallas would not have yielded to temptation or William's obvious blandishments and it was *she* who had produced William.

"Where is he?" she asked in a low voice.

"Round the back," Gwen whispered. "I managed to get him up the track without being seen."

Mary spun on her heel and shot through the back room making Alice halt with astonishment. She threw open the door and stopped dead with shock. Raymond Falla leaned against the jamb, blood streaming down his face. His lips were puffed, some front teeth were missing and he had a rapidly swelling left eye. He was pitifully thin and looked like an old man.

"In!" Mary barked unceremoniously. "Alice! Get some hot water if you can. Gwen, get him sat down on that crate while I try and find some gauze."

Mary rummaged around and found two clean rags and handed one to Gwen. Together they started to staunch the blood, dabbing, patting and wiping. Alice returned with some warmed water, which, luckily, she had been able to heat as there had been some electricity on. Just then the bell tinged again, making Mary mutter under her breath. Alice disappeared then came back eyes alight.

"It's Inspector le Norman," she whispered to Mary. Gwen caught the words and went even whiter.

"Carry on cleaning him up so we can see the real damage," Mary told Gwen, then went into the shop, carefully shutting the storeroom door behind her. "Emil!" she said smiling. She was always so pleased to see him. It had been wonderful to bring him up to date with the news of his friends and a rapport of genuine friendship now existed between the two of them.

"Someone in there?" Emil asked. Mary's firm closing of the door had been a little too obvious.

"The Fallas," Mary explained briskly. "He's been badly beaten up and Gwen has been manhandled too. He needs a doctor."

Emil sniffed, a malicious gleam showing in his eyes. "What did they expect?" he asked in a low voice. "They've been living with a roughish crowd who run with the hare and hunt with the hounds. Of course he's been done over. He was a profiteer and it flashed around the place his family had turned him out. You know what people are like!"

Mary knew what he said was only too true. "I have a feeling they might just have paid for what they did," she said slowly, frowning a little. "And anyhow, they are family and I can't stand by and see murder done. Can you help me get them to Cobo? Their old cottage is still vacant. The Germans never took it and I think I might be able to smooth Raoul over. I don't know about Amelia though," she added thoughtfully, "but it would be a refuge for them until they get off the island. They can't stay here, that's for sure. They'll be damned for all time because people have long memories."

Emil agreed with this sentiment. "I'll get them driven over in something. I'm in a position to lean heavily on the Germans now and they still have a tiny drop of petrol left. It's time it was used for an islander!" He grinned at her. "I had a feeling you'd be around, then when I saw the flag—" He grinned, flashing his teeth, his eyes sparkling. "I thought you'd like to lock up shop and the pair of you go down to the harbour. Within the next hour the German flag comes down and the Union and Guernsey flags go up officially. We will be—free!"

"Oh Emil!" Mary gasped, clasping her hands before her breasts in an instinctive emotional gesture.

"Shut up. You and Alice go there. Leave the Fallas to me. I'll join in the celebration later because, as you say, there'll be no murder on my patch!"

Mary shouted for Alice, gabbled the news and, clutching the girl's hand, dragged her outside. She saw they were just a small part of an ever-growing throng of excited people. She grinned at Alice. It still never ceased to amaze Mary exactly how news managed to fly around the island.

"Come on!" she cried. "We mustn't miss anything!"

Down at the harbour was a throbbing crowd of wildly excited people. Mary wished Raoul and Amelia were here too, then, turning, she saw them. She was astounded. How had they known? More to the point, how had they managed to get here so quickly? Then she chuckled. Someone would have told them and brought them on a cart pulled by a surviving, uneaten horse. She screamed at them and, even above the din, Raoul heard her and waved violently, grinning from ear to ear. Goodness, Mary thought, I hope we don't have any real thieves left here. Every home on Guernsey must have been left vacant to witness this historic occasion.

They watched as a German soldier hauled down the hated flag then slowly hauled up the two flags. Spontaneously the crowd broke into a roar of mad approval as people jostled each other, slapped shoulders, hugged, kissed and went wild as the first Tommies landed on Guernsey.

"We are free!" Mary screamed to Alice, almost beside herself with joy as tears streamed down her face. Five long, awful years could now become history.

"Free!" Alice choked and sobbed desperately with happiness.

"God save the Duke of Normandy!" someone bellowed.

Voices broke into the national anthem as the German soldiers gloomily stood back, eyeing their officers apprehensively. Would these islanders now turn on them? But they were safe. The people were too madly happy, all they wanted to do was mob the Tommies, hoist them high, parade them around, talk, shout and bellow their delirium of wonderful happiness.

How long they were part of the crowd Mary never afterwards knew. Finally she edged herself and Alice free, shaken and exhausted by it all but beaming at each other. Some words floated into Mary's mind. Who was it who had said that a person could not appreciate true happiness until he had tasted the depths of despair? For the first time, she understood the meaning.

"Go on home," she told the girl. "Go and celebrate with your young man!"

"The shop?" Alice asked conscientiously.

"Le Norman will lock up. No one is going to be interested in anything so mundane as shopping today. We will all start afresh later on this week. Let's just enjoy our freedom. Because by God, we've more than earned it."

She pushed Alice away, then standing on tiptoes strained to spot Raoul. Finally, she began to push towards where he had been when suddenly she bumped into him, he towed Amelia by one large hand. He slapped her back then kissed her lustily and she flung herself into his arms, hugging Amelia next. She turned back to Raoul and whispered in his ear.

"We have trouble," she hissed knowing Amelia's sharp ears. "The Fallas are in the shop in a bad way. Emil le Norman is getting them back to that old cottage of theirs. They need a doctor. Raymond has been thoroughly beaten and Gwen has been knocked about.

Raoul scowled. Much as he hated what the couple had done, Gwen was his sister and no man should ever hit a woman. But which way would Amelia jump? The tough side to her character which had displayed since the episode over tea made him wary.

"Let's go back to Cobo," he said to Mary.

"What are you two whispering about?" Amelia shouted, struggling to make herself heard over the boisterous hubbub. Mary led them aside, waiting a little impatiently for Amelia to catch up then she told her.

"Well?"

Amelia looked at her then Raoul and finally gave a little shrug. "Look after them if you like," she agreed slowly, "but don't expect me to like it!"

Mary let out her breath and smiled. That was another little hurdle successfully jumped. She flashed a look at Raoul who beamed at his wife, Gwen wasn't bad, she had perhaps been weak, unable to stand up to Raymond and, Mary reminded herself, she had been glad of Raymond's help on that day when Duret had tried to kill her.

They returned home, walking quite easily now but taking their time, chatting gently, almost at peace with the world. To accomplish this they wanted their families to be completed.

The Ozanne boys came home first. Luck had been on their side because although they had both received minor wounds, they were not in any way incapacitated. Their leave was a delirious time for everyone during which Mary and Amelia started upon the task of turning the house back into a home once more. The officers were now prisoners of war and Mary realised she had been fortunate. Damage was minimal though the furnishings and curtains were shabby. In due course they would all have to be replaced and suddenly Mary realised she had money gaining interest on the mainland. Exactly how much she was worth she simply had no idea but it would be needed. Once Europe could return to normality people would start to think of holidays again and her cottages would be in a deplorable condition after five years of occupation by troops and TODT slaves.

Her heart ached for Margaret to return and, to stop herself brooding, she and Raoul began to make plans for the inspection of each and every property. Mary wondered how Victor's hotels had fared. They had, so she gathered, had officers in them but would no doubt have been stripped bare of anything of value.

One afternoon, when it was hot and she had taken herself outside with a sheaf of pencilled notes, she tried to concentrate but could not. She felt almost relaxed, clean after a warm bath and she had managed to buy some fresh clothes, when some had appeared in the shops. They were not good ones but they were new and different.

She sat on a cane chair, face up to the sun, eyes closed, half thinking and half day-dreaming so she never heard the footsteps on the grass. Her eyes felt weary as the sun drew out the years of fatigue and Mary was in that delicious half-awake, half-asleep state of quiet euphoria.

Margaret stood looking down at her, shocked to the core. Although Victor had been to see her and warned her, she had not expected this. Her mother's hair was heavily shot with silver. Her face had crinkles around the eyes which, although she was putting on weight, would not disappear until she had gained at least another stone in weight. Her skin was dull and Margaret remembered how it had always glowed with health and vitality. She swallowed, trying to shift the lump in her throat and, with a finger at her lips, sent a silent message to the person behind her.

"Mother," she whispered, squatting on her heels.

Mary's eyes opened suddenly and fell on the face of a young, not quite beautiful woman but one who was strong, fine and lovely to look at. Her lips parted, her face crinkled and tears sprang to her eyes as she held out her arms.

They hugged each other, kissed and hugged again, then Mary pushed her daughter away to examine every tiny feature. Suddenly she began to utter a low throaty laugh of joy as she saw similar tears trickle down Margaret's cheeks.

"I thought you were never coming," Mary told her in soft wonder at having her daughter with her after five years.

"I thought we were never going to get here but oh! When we came down the Russel again, it was like being reborn!"

There was a discreet cough and Mary turned. "Michael—?" she asked a little unsure. For one second her imagination had told her it was a young Victor there and she had been whisked back to her early days on the island; the same stance with his feet apart, a similar cheeky grin.

"I wondered when anyone would remember me," he joked gently, touched by their reunion.

Mary turned and held Margaret's left hand. The wedding band gleamed freshly gold.

"Michael! Son!" Mary breathed and opened her arms to him again. Once more she had a son and this time, she knew, she had a splendid one. The ghosts and bad memories began to slide away into the distant dimness of history.

"Father will be coming to see you as soon as he can," Michael told her, amused at the way mother and daughter could hardly bear to break physical contact. He was more touched than he had thought possible but he too was remembering and his heart was aching. How Mary Noyen had altered! Later he would hear all.

Mary took them into the house, so happy that she felt as if her feet had been placed upon a frothy cloud of delight.

"The house is awful. It's shabby but clean. Oh! There is so much to say, so much to ask, I hardly know where to begin!" she cried, taking Margaret's hands and doing a hastily improvised waltz down the tiled hall that had once held a thick carpet. Their shoes clacked and Michael started to beat time clapping his hands.

Margaret eyed her mother. Her cheeks had become too flushed and she stopped slightly alarmed. How strong was her mother now?

"Have you come home for good?" Mary wanted to know urgently.

"We have ten days," Michael explained, bending to kiss his mother-in-law for the first time. "We have to go back to be discharged officially. We can't all leave at once. It would play hell with the labour market so we take it in turns. We should both be out if not by the end of this year then certainly by next Spring."

"Your father too?" Mary asked delicately.

Michael nodded. "He's due two weeks' leave and I know he plans to spend half of it here. He wants to see you and the Ozannes, to catch up on general news as well as to see to his hotels and his old pals."

Mary wondered if Michael knew anything. Certainly he appeared to be innocent but she had learned that people were often not what them seemed.

For three days they lived quiet lives, catching up on news but skirting difficult topics. One evening though Margaret came right out with it.

"Where's William?" she asked bluntly.

Mary did not answer straightaway but went still and paled a little. Finally she met Margaret's eyes frankly.

"He died a while ago and I don't want to talk about it. Not yet at least," she said heavily.

Margaret immediately sensed something was being withheld but she had enough sense not to push. She knew her mother. One day the story would come tumbling from her lips and she had a cold feeling she would not like it. Knowing his Germanic tendencies, she had presumed William would have fled with the retreating armies. It had never entered her head he was long dead.

"Good riddance," she said casually. "I never liked him indeed, to be honest, I loathed him!"

"I second that!" Michael concurred.

"In that case, let's talk of something more pleasant. Have you two any ideas what you want to do when you finally return?" Mary asked gently, waiting with a quickly beating heart. She had thought long and hard about the future and there were obvious moves to make but would the young couple have the taste for them? Perhaps they had their own plans? She just prayed they did not want to migrate like so many others, including the Fallas, who had already hastily departed Guernsey for good.

Michael spoke for both of them. "This is our island, our home. It's here we want to put down fresh roots and raise our children."

Mary decided. "Well, there's a job waiting for you which I don't think I want to do any more. I can manage to get the glasshouses going again but not the holiday lets. I have a feeling in my bones this could turn out to be big business in the next few years. How about you taking over for me? You would have this house and I would go and live in old Tante's cottage. It would be perfect for me while this large house is made for a family?" Mary waited for their views. She knew she would be bitterly disappointed if they refused.

"That's marvellous!" Margaret exclaimed getting in first.

"There's nothing I'd like to do more!" Michael confirmed.

Mary sighed with relief, aware she had been sitting as if on a prickly burr.

Margaret eyed her with amusement. "And then there's the shop?" she reminded her mother.

Again a veil seemed to fall over her mother's eyes and Margaret was puzzled. Surely there was nothing mysterious or sinister about the shop? How could there be, yet her mother had withdrawn into herself again and was holding something back.

She knew she would have to be exceedingly patient. Sometimes Margaret had caught an expression upon her mother's face that made her pause and reflect. Although the love between mother and daughter was now stronger than ever before, Margaret sensed it was still possible for a shutter to fall rapidly where she was left outside, excluded from some knowledge. She mentioned this to Michael but he had kissed her.

"Patience! Giver her time," he told her. "Five years of misery cannot all be told at once and, for all we both know, she may have undergone events which she does not consciously wish to remember.

From such wisdom, Margaret had learned to adapt herself to these strange retreats of Mary's.

"Change the company name," Mary said suddenly, breaking into her thoughts. "How about Noyen and le Page?" she beamed at them.

"Sounds good to me!" Michael confirmed grinning happily, sitting with one leg slung loosely over the other.

"I think tourists will come. I just hope they are not Germans," Margaret said thoughtfully. "All those hideous concrete fortifications everywhere. There was some character in the old Martello towers but the Germans' work is almost obscene!"

Mary gave her a long look. "I think it will be a long time indeed before Germans feel they are welcome here," she prophesied.

He came at last. He walked into the kitchen as if he had been doing it every day of his life. "Hello, Catherine!" he said as he took her into his arms. "I've waited a long time for this day."

They kissed, hugged and kissed again, words unnecessary as he stopped to let her take breath. Gently he guided her into the sitting room when he pulled her down on a battered but still serviceable settee. He slid his arm around her shoulders, taking firm possession and she leaned against him, finally at peace with the world.

They did not speak for a while. It was enough they felt each other's bodies and savoured each other's scents. Mary allowed herself two drops of daily perfume from her last, carefully hoarded bottle. He was freshly shaved and from his cheeks came an astringent aroma reminding her of new grass and fresh leaves.

"What happens now, Victor?" Mary murmured.

He pushed her away a little. "Thank God you don't look like a half-starved waif any more," he told her slowly. "Have you any idea what the sight of you did to me that day on the quay? I almost did not recognise you. Even so, you could do with a few more pounds of flesh on your bones because I like to have something to fondle." He grinned, "I've never cared for skinny women!"

He paused, studying her minutely. "I have to get myself demobbed, first of all."

Mary licked her lip. "Then?"

"Then I intend to instigate divorce proceedings. I gather there are ways and means even if it means committing false adultery on the mainland with a paid woman. I'll stop at nothing now to be free," he stated flatly.

Mary took a deep breath. "What will Michael think?" she asked hesitantly.

"I don't give a damn what he or anyone may think," he growled. "We are going to live our lives to suit ourselves now and devil take the hindermost!"

Mary felt troubled. The look on his face was implacable. "What will happen to Nicole?"

He grunted. "I'll see she never wants for money. Anyhow I don't think she'll ever want to come back to the islands. She'll make a home for young James and probably meet someone else, if she hasn't done so already."

Mary's eyebrows shot up. Tante's words came back to her in a rush and she turned them over in her mind. A jealous female was a dangerous one but if Nicole had met someone else, how could she object to being given her freedom? She wondered why unease touched her heart but she skilfully disguised this from him.

"I want to see James and Emil as soon as I can. I think James is heading back to the island with his family any day now. With all the upset of war, I bet he'll have plenty of matrimonial cases to deal with and his practice will grow. He can represent us too," he told her. "Then there are my hotels. I must inspect them while I'm here. With your cottages and my properties we can build up a business together."

"Michael is going to handle the cottages. I'll be content with the glasshouses," Mary told him. "I'm going to move down to Tante's cottage and let the youngsters have this house."

He nodded approvingly. Her cottage would be ideal for the two of them. Quite suddenly, the future beckoned promisingly.

"I have a feeling you have a lot to tell me," he asked gently.

Mary nodded and he did not miss the expression in her eyes. "One day," she promised.

He flashed a look at his watch and grinned. "I want to go and see Emil today. I shall be here for a few days staying in my hotel," he told her standing, reluctantly. "I'll be back in the morning so have some coffee ready." Diving into a pocket he pulled out some beans. "Get this ground ready for me!"

Mary did not want him to go but understood. They had the rest of their lives together. She waved with a light heart as he marched back down the path to where he had left a small army vehicle.

He hadn't been gone more than ten minutes when Margaret came back in, grinning a little sheepishly.

"That was a put-up job," Mary laughed, "but thank you."

Margaret put her arm around her mother. "You love each other very much, don't you?"

Mary nodded. "Since long before you were even thought of but I didn't have the sense to know it." She paused a little uncertainly. "Victor is going to divorce Nicole."

Margaret gave an approving nod. "Good. I shan't be sorry for one and I don't think Michael or James will either. Nicole's become—strange. Whether it was Jenny's death or what, I don't know, but I sometimes think she's not all there except, now and again, I have the vaguest feeling she's met another man, an airman.

I think you and Victor have earned your happiness," she replied and eyed her mother shrewdly. "Now what went on here, Mother? How did William die? I'd like to know."

Mary took a deep breath, then the words were blurted out. "I executed him."

"Good God!"

Never in her wildest dreams had Margaret imagined this. She was staggered and, sitting on the settee, put her arms around Mary's shoulders.

"Why don't you start at the beginning?" she managed to get out at last.

Mary did. She took a deep breath and slowly started. As the tale unfolded, Margaret's amazement grew.

"Mother!" she exclaimed with admiration. "I think you've been marvellous. Not many women could have done what you did," she hesitated. "Does anyone else know?"

Mary nodded. "I suppose I had become a little complacent. I never knew William watched me leave the shop just as he never knew someone spied on him. Thank God they did!"

"Who was it?" Margaret breathed with awe.

Mary would not be hurried now. Telling the story again was like a catharsis. "After I had shot William and the German and faked that homosexual scene, I began to have a queer feeling I was not alone. Yet I could neither see nor hear anything. I was on edge and I suppose it was a latent instinct."

"*Who* was there?"

Mary laughed. "Someone you'd never guess who would stand by, watch a killing and do not a thing about it. Emil le Norman."

"The policeman!" Margaret cried sitting up straight. She was receiving shock after shock.

With a great calmness Mary finished her story. "Emil and I exchanged silent, secret messages but, many months later, I told him the truth. I also explained about Edwin," Mary said harshly. "It was he who called it a judicial execution."

Margaret let out her breath, shaking her head at this incredible tale. "He was right," she said slowly. "Dear little Edwin, he would have made a lovely man but, at long last, he has been avenged. May his soul rest in peace."

"So now you know it all. I've yet to hear about your adventures."

Margaret shook her head. "Tame by your standards though I think Michael has some stories to tell and probably his father as well. Even so, I bet they can't match your tale."

"Incidentally, where is Michael?"

Margaret gave a chuckle. "He bumped into an old schoolfriend down the road and I left them yarning. You know how men talk. I'll go and round him up while you put the kettle on for tea."

Mary agreed and saw her daughter out but left the door ajar for their return. She boiled the water, warmed the pot, put the tea in and left the filled teapot to infuse. She heard a sound at the door and guessed they were back. They had timed it nicely.

"In the kitchen," she called merrily.

A figure appeared and blocked the doorway so Mary turned, her eyes opening wide with shock.

Mary's lips set tight. "Who are you? What's the idea of walking into my home uninvited?"

Nicole le Page eyed her while the erratic thoughts in her mind started to crystallise. There were so many days when she had headaches that only dear Henry could soothe when he stroked her head but now he was away getting his discharge. The urge to return to the islands had swept through her like a flood. She had simply followed her instinct. It was only when on the island that reason returned temporarily. She knew then what had to be done.

"I'm Nicole le Page," she replied to the question.

Mary's heart missed a beat. She did not like the look in the other's eyes. For a fleeting second, it was as if she were back facing Duret again. She would never have recognised this white-haired woman who had turned dumpy with a misshapen body. Then when the other moved nearer, Mary did see old similarities.

"You're my husband's mistress," Nicole hurled at her.

"Rubbish! We've been separated by a war!" Mary hurled back while her mind raced.

"You always fancied him before though, didn't you?" Nicole retaliated. "Oh I know! I'm not quite as stupid as Victor thinks. That kid of yours, the one that drowned. He was Victor's, wasn't he? Don't deny it. I could see a likeness!"

Mary snorted as she recovered from the initial shock. "You're the only one who could then. You must have an overworked imagination."

"Don't try and avoid the issue. Look how Victor was always around here—"

"Visiting his grandmère!"

"And you, you tart!"

Mary started to boil. "Get out of my home," she barked, in the tone of voice she had kept for William.

Nicole pulled a short coat aside and pulled out a long knife. "This is for you. You deserve to die so you don't steal other women's men!" she chuckled, a maniacal grate in her voice.

Mary swallowed and thought rapidly. If only Margaret and Michael would return! She eyed the knife and was disconcerted to see how steady it was in Nicole's hand. What also worried her was that Nicole held the knife in the correct manner for an upward swing, always more lethal and more difficult to block. It crossed her mind to wonder how she knew that or was it simply Nicole's luck?

She estimated how many steps to the door but Nicole blocked the way. There was only one thing she could do because in Nicole's eyes was lethal intent.

"I'm going to kill you," Nicole said in a slow, c— —ce and advanced a step.

Mary did not hesitate. She picked up t— —eapot, swept

the lid off onto the floor where it broke then, holding the pot with both handle and the spout, she hurled the hot contents in Nicole's face. The hot liquid splashed onto Nicole's face and she screamed with agony. Mary darted aside, knocked the knife from her hand as Nicole, screeching like a banshee, danced up and down in pain.

At the same moment, Mary heard a vehicle approaching then voices: Margaret calling, Michael shouting, then that which she most wanted to hear.

"Mary!" was Victor's bellow.

The pain and cacophony of unexpected sound tipped Nicole's mind off balance. Screeching still, she staggered back to the open door, her steps wavering as the hot liquid continued to scald ferociously.

In blind panic from pain and human noise, Nicole shot from the door. Her left foot only rose on inch from the ground and met the old iron boot scraper. She tripped, her body flying through the air with speed.

Margaret and Michael watched in stunned disbelief. Mary stood at the door, eyes opened very wide. Victor and Emil slithered to a halt. It became like a tableau of stone. Only one person moved.

Nicole's body twisted instinctively but her hands could not leave her scalded face. She spun a second time then hit the hard ground with her head in the wrong direction to the length of her body. Her neck snapped with an ugly crack they all heard.

"Nicole!" Victor bellowed. "Mary!"

"Mother!" Michael roared and they all sprang forward together, colliding in each other's way.

"Stand back!" Emil bellowed and they stilled as he bent down. He knew what he was going to find. One swift movement with his hand and Nicole's head rolled loosely. "She's dead," he said unnecessarily. "She's broken her neck!"

For forward heartbeats, Victor stood frozen, then he bounded grabbed Mary.

"Are you all right?" he shouted.

Mary nodded but shivered. "She had a knife. She came to kill me," she told them all, looking at Michael with fear.

Emil stood and strode into the house then came out after a few seconds. "Correct!" he grunted. "It's on the floor. No one's to touch it, for fingerprints," he warned them firmly.

"Michael?" Mary asked in a whisper, her brows creased with apprehension.

The younger man stood only a few seconds then gave a tiny shake to his shoulders.

"It's all right," he reassured her. "I have been expecting something like this for a while. Mother wasn't—I guess she wasn't right in the head. Not since Jenny died in the war," he ended with a heavy sigh. He crossed over to her and elbowed his father aside.

"Ssh!" Michael crooned as tears started to flood down Mary's cheeks. "If it hadn't been you, it might well have been Margaret. You see, Mother resented her because she was your daughter," he explained gravely.

Mary's tears stilled. This had not occurred to her. She looked at Margaret who nodded in sad confirmation.

Victor pushed Michael back with a proprietary gesture and turned to Emil.

"You all saw," he said pointedly. "You heard what my son said. In there is the knife and I expect there'll only be Nicole's fingerprints on it."

"When she threatened me, I didn't know what to do. I'd just made the tea. I threw it at her," Mary gabbled, hysteria rising.

"Ssh!" Victor crooned, taking her into his arms, ignoring the rest of them. "It's all over now. It's just me and you. I know. Let's leave Emil to do what he has to do." He looked across to Margaret and Michael. "You youngsters go in and make a meal. I'm taking Mary for a walk up the road. We want to be alone," he told them firmly.

With one arm around her shoulders, he guided her, shielding her from the sight of Nicole's body and they strolled down the lane then he turned right on the coast road. Way ahead were the Rocques, now almost disfigured with a huge concrete fortification, a landmark left by the Germans.

Mary looked up at him then smiled. He would want to take her there but she was puzzled.

"How did you know Nicole was here?"

"I was chatting to Emil when information came in that a strange woman had hitched a lift to Cobo. From the description I knew it had to be Nicole. It was a bit of luck I was with Emil. We raced outside, grabbed a police car and drove like madmen to get here. I've never seen Emil move so quickly in all my life."

He looked down at her, his smile gently warm. "But it's all over with now. We are free at last. See! The Rocques. It's been a long time since it all started there but we've made it in the end, haven't we, my wild sea witch!"

—o000o—

THE END